AWARD-WINNING BESTSELLING AUTHOR

ASHLEY FONTAINNE

EMPTY SHELL

*When hidden
secrets resurface,
how many lives will
be destroyed?*

This is a work of fiction. Names, characters, places, and incidents are products of the author's imagination or are used fictitiously and are not to be construed as real. Any resemblance to actual events, locations, organizations, or persons, living or dead, is entirely coincidental.

Publisher: RMSW Press, LLC
ISBN: 978-0692291368
Also available in electronic format

Cover and interior design: Ashley Fontainne
Photo credits: Nicolas Raymond   http://www.freestock.ca
Courtney Simonds http://www.csimondsphoto.com
Editor: BHC Editor Bailey Karfelt

Visit the author at:
Website *www.asheyfontainne.com*
Blog:
www.ramblingsofamadsouthernwoman.blogspot.com
Facebook: *www.facebook.com/ashleyfontainne*
Twitter: *@AshleyFontainne*

ALSO BY ASHLEY FONTAINNE

EVISCERATING THE SNAKE TRILOGY:
Accountable to None
Zero Balance
Adjusting Journal Entries

The Lie

Novella
Number Seventy-Five
(www.number75themovie.com)

For Janelle Taylor
Your support and belief in me brings tears to my eyes...
and a smile to my heart.
I am honored to call you my friend.

The eyes may deceive the mind but the heart never lies to the soul.

—ASHLEY FONTAINNE

CHAPTER 1 – SATURDAY MORNING

THE MORNING SUN WAS BRIGHT AND THE humidity staggering. Both bore down on him, making the sweat run faster down his neck and back as he walked. His heart thundered in his chest, and he fought to keep his breathing normal and his gait natural. The rush of adrenaline made his hands shake as he adjusted his ball cap.

He forced his facial muscles to respond to his commands, determined to keep his expression neutral so he would blend in. His mind was racing, unaccustomed to the violent behavior it had just experienced upstairs. His shaky limbs wanted to run the remaining distance to the safety of his vehicle and away from the nightmare of what he'd just done.

A small sigh of relief left his lips when he made it to his vehicle and slid inside, removing his gloves and shoving them deep into his pants pocket. It took him three attempts to insert the key into the ignition. He took a deep breath, held it, and then released it in slow, controlled bursts. He had to get it together or he would have an accident on the way home. He gripped the key tighter in his sweaty fingers and tried again. To his relief, the engine turned over. Fighting the urge to look behind him to see if he was being followed, he eased out of the parking spot and merged into the mid-morning traffic, careful to keep his eyes on the road.

Anything to keep from looking at her sticky red blood on his clothes.

Oh God, what have I done?

CHAPTER 2 – MONDAY, EARLY MORNING

"TURN THAT DAMNED THING OFF!"

"I'm trying, but it's stuck or something."

The door flew open and Jack stormed into the bedroom. In three quick strides he crossed the floor, his face and chest beet red from his interrupted hot shower. With a sheepish grin, I held out the noisy thing to him. He didn't even try to hide his irritation as he yanked the screeching clock from my fumbling hands. His body language made clear his thoughts about my inability to perform such a simple task.

His angry hands used to touch me with gentle caresses. *God, how I miss them.*

I shrugged at his nasty attitude, walked back over to my side of the bed and searched under the pillow for my glasses. Without them, I couldn't see anything that wasn't within eight inches of my face. No wonder I couldn't find the off switch on the alarm.

With my back to my annoyed husband, a small grin of triumph niggled at the corners of my mouth. Listening to him struggle to silence the little plastic piece of hell was rather entertaining. At least I wasn't the only one finding it difficult to shut off.

The noisy clock was another irritating purchase Jack had made online while watching one of those brain-numbing reality shows he loved so much. It served him right that he now held a worthless pile of junk. What a waste of forty bucks. The alarm clock that was supposed to wake us up to sounds of nature sounded more like a screaming, rabid howler monkey. One with its tail caught in a trap—and it seemed to be stuck in the permanent *on* position.

My grin became a full smile when I found my glasses; now I could fully appreciate watching him attempt to find the off switch. The anticipated fun disappeared in a flash when I turned around to ask Jack if he was ready for a cup of coffee and realized what he was about to do. With one final grunt, Jack launched the clock against the wall in frustration. It disintegrated into a pile of broken plastic, leaving a fist-sized dent in the newly painted sheetrock.

The one good thing resulting from my husband's tirade was that it killed the incessant buzzing. Jack's damp, dark brown hair flopped forward, releasing thinning bangs. The way his hair tumbled almost looked like it was taking a bow for saving our ears.

"Guess you just answered my question about coffee. Obviously, you haven't had any yet."

Jack shot daggers of rage at me with his hooded, deep-set brown eyes. He didn't speak as he moved past me and slammed the bathroom door behind him.

I let my own irritation out with a small sigh. For a second, I stared at the two-inch thick wood separating us. I wished the door was the only barrier that life had erected between husband and wife. At least the door was a block-ade I could see—and knock down if I wanted to.

Problem was, did I?

I looked over at the mess Jack had left on the floor. I started to bend down and gather the broken remnants, but stopped short, my fingers hovering over the rubble. *No. Not today. Not again.* I decided to leave the twisted wreckage right where it was. Let Jack pick up after himself for a change—a small test to see how long it would take for him to do so.

And maybe to let him know how fed up I am with his mood swings. Whoever said that men don't suffer from hormonal influxes was obviously in a serious state of denial. Maybe I should start spiking Jack's coffee with my hormone pills. He needs something to take the edge off and make him less bitchy. They always work for me...

The smile I sported earlier came back in the form of a sly grin. My knees popped as I straightened and made my way down the quiet hallway toward the kitchen. Bright, early morning rays of vibrant yellow danced across the remodeled countertops and floors. The sparkle from the sun reflected off the polished steel of the new appliances. A delayed flash of anger hit me as I thought about the hole in the bedroom wall. After months of dealing with hordes of crack-showing, tobacco-spitting and stinky construction workers, they had finished and left us in peace two weeks ago. Now I would have to call the owner and make arrangements to have him send a worker back to patch and repaint the bedroom wall.

No, not me. Jack. His temper tantrum—his dilemma to solve. Not mine.

I pushed aside the thought and followed my nose to the source of the smell of freshly brewed coffee. I had enough on my to-do list and I wouldn't allow any more to weigh me down. I was barely able to breathe as it was. So much for my relaxing getaway with Regina this past weekend, which I had taken with the hopes of easing some of my stress.

Ah, another fun morning in the Dickinson household...thank goodness for an automatic coffee maker...Monday, Monday...da da la de da...

Coffee fixed and eyes focused, I decided to offer a flag of truce to my temperamental spouse. No sense in starting the week out on a sour note. He was stressed too with all the finals he had to grade, so I decided to cut him some slack. I carried two steaming mugs back down the hall toward the bedroom, Jack's with two sugars and mine black as coal.

Thoughts of my mother's wedding day advice on marriage years ago made a quick lump form in my throat. While pretending to be having trouble with the clasp on my dress, she had spoken about the various duties of a wife and how a couple could weather numerous ups and downs over the years.

"The key to a long lasting marriage, darling Melody, is communication. You can never stop the sharing of your innermost thoughts and dreams with each other. Communication is the water that nourishes the seed of love. Without it, your marriage will wither and die."

I had responded with some gushy, naïve comeback about how there was no *way* Jack and I would *ever* stop talking and sharing with each other. After all, we were in love.

Our tastes for life were very similar. We both adored classic rock, Italian food, fast cars, dogs, and hours spent watching reruns of *Star Trek* and *Monty Python.* But our biggest two connectors, which were what brought us together in the first place, was a strong affinity for history and deep Christian faith. That first *World Civilizations* course in college threw us together as study partners and led to our first date. The moment Jack held my hand in his during a walk across campus, I was hooked. The connection that travelled between the two of us was more than electric—it was cosmic.

Back then—*oh my God it was almost twenty-one years ago*—I couldn't breathe without Jack. My existence hung upon his every movement, every touch and every caress. His deep voice would lull me into a state of bliss at night while we lay awake, planning our life after college. What career paths we would take. How we both wanted two children—a boy and a girl—named Jacqueline and Jordan. The type of house we would live in, the vehicles we would drive. The various places we would visit and make love in before parenthood arrived.

Jack's eyes had mesmerized me with their liquid stare. Those beautiful sable orbs pulled me inside his soul, leaving me breathless. I had looked at him and become lost in a sea of blissful tranquility. His muscular arms had embraced me in a cocoon of warmth and provided quiet shelter from the world. Back then, we couldn't get enough of each other.

My, how times have changed.

Somewhere, as we walked down the path of marriage together, we got separated, our loving grip on each other yanked apart by unseen forces. The fork in the road appeared when, after more than ten years of trying and thousands of dollars spent on fertility treatments, we realized that I would never be able to carry a child. We dealt with our grief alone, each trying to hide the pain from the other instead of working together to overcome our mutual sadness.

Big mistake. Huge. Gargantuan.

I went flying off in one direction and Jack ran in the other. Our late night cuddling and cooing sessions began to stretch out to twice a week, then once a month, then maybe every six weeks. Now, I couldn't even remember the last time we had held each other close and let the world around us disappear. Two, three months? We were like that old raunchy joke about how elderly couples engaged in sex by passing each other in the hall and yelling "Screw you!"

I approached the bedroom door and snorted at my mother's words still resounding in my head. *Hmmm, communication may be the key to a happy marriage, but what does one do when the signals are hopelessly crossed? When nothing remains but dead air? The magical sparks are long gone. Quick, someone get the paddles out and crank us back to life! Clear!*

Jack was still in the bathroom, so I set his mug by the door and walked back into the kitchen. I didn't have time to coddle him. I had to get ready for work and stop mulling over things I couldn't change—at least not with a simple cup of coffee. It was the end of the month, which meant I would be swamped while preparing the billing for over six hundred clients. Oh, and experiencing the joy of fixing tons of data entry mistakes, just as I had been forced to do numerous times the last nine months. I knew they would be there, input by the newest assistant at my office.

Serena Rowland. A young blonde with racehorse legs who wore skirts so short that the color of her underwear was damn near discernible to anyone within twenty feet of her. It made my stomach churn to see the way the male attorneys at the office ogled her—like she was the last meal before the executioner's noose or something. It was like watching a room full of Pavlov's dogs. The minute her heels clacked down the hall, they all began to salivate. Since the girl was the daughter of one of the firm's biggest clients and a personal friend of my boss, none of the drooling males had the balls to chase Serena around her desk, but oh the mental gyrations they threw her direction! Not to mention, Serena's ridiculous attachment to the color pink made me want to scream. Her desk space looked like the bedroom of a teenage girl, complete with pink note-cards, spotted pink pens, and even two photo frames with frilly pink lace. I tried, but couldn't recall a day since she'd started working at the office that she hadn't worn something pink.

The entire female population at work hated Serena the minute her long, curvaceous limbs walked through the front door. Nothing like having cellulite on your butt, arms that jiggle and a not-so-flat stomach to change your perception of youth. No woman, including me, wanted to be confronted on a daily basis with the fact that—*gasp*—her youthful tight rear and smooth abs had mysteriously been replaced by gelatinous goo. It irritated me even more because I couldn't blame motherhood for the changes to my body.

It was simply due to age, stress, and countless hours spent glued to my chair at work, which made it even worse because it was *my* fault. If I really wanted to change my appearance, no magic pill or secret diet plan would do the trick. It would require hard work, tons of sweat and hours of reshaping my body. At my age, the thought of becoming a slave to my body again didn't interest me. It wasn't like it mattered anyway. Jack wasn't interested in me anymore, so what was my motivation?

Alas, watching Serena prance around like a prized show horse in her not-on-any-planet-would-this-ever-be-

appropriate office attire every day was like having someone screeching in my ears: Hey, you're *old*!

Lost in thought about how I could cajole my boss Roger to fire Serena for her mountainous mistakes, I padded
over on autopilot to the cabinet to grab a cupful of kibble
to feed Simba, my surrogate child. My adorable six-year-
old mongrel had been dumped in our backyard five years
ago. Poor thing was so starved she couldn't even whimper.
Patches of her fur had been missing, almost like it had
been torn out in chunks. Jack had chastised me for trying
to rescue her, saying that she didn't stand a chance and the
most humane thing I could do was have her put down.

Like hell. The look I gave him that sunny morning outside had silenced his mutterings as I scooped the dying
pile of flesh and sporadic fur up off the soft grass. It took
three weeks of constant nursing and two very expensive
trips to the veterinarian before Simba roared back to life.
Simba's loving spirit, clumsy nature and enormous tail that
never stopped wagging filled some of the longing for a
child that churned inside of me. The bond between dog
and master was set in stone. I saved her, she saved me. We
were even.

I noticed a slight tremble in my hands when I scooped
up Simba's breakfast. Guess my nerves were more fraz-
zled than I thought. I wasn't doing myself any favors by
getting all riled up about Ms. Serena Short-Skirt this early
in the morning. I had other things to tend to.

*Yeah, that's it Melody. Unleash all your inner angst
from your crumbling marriage and sagging rear out in the
form of the green-eyed monster, rather than confronting
the problems with Jack head-on. Serena isn't the issue.
Your relationship with Jack, or rather, the lack of one, is
the problem.*

I shook my head and willed myself to not think about
my disintegrating marriage until after work. Maybe I
would leave early and come home and fix Jack's favorite
dinner, light a few candles and serve the food in front of
the fireplace. The finishing touches would be relaxing music, fine wine and chocolate covered strawberries for dessert. Set the mood and maybe open up the channels to start

talking again, once our minds were plied with food and alcohol.

Wow, how cliché Melody. Yep, life's troubles can be solved over a fancy dinner and some booze. Right. When did your life become a commercial? You already know what the problem is. You two need to get your butts back in church. And you need to open up to Jack. Tell him the secret. It's eating you alive and now, it seems, it is munching away on your marriage. We need a good, heart-to-heart talk. Maybe an overnight stay at Lake Catherine, like we used to do. God, how long had it been since we've camped out? I could get him to dig in the garage and find our camping equipment…

Simba's breakfast retrieved, I was in full stress mode about the upcoming hectic day and what salve I could use to soothe my irritated husband and repair our relationship. At first I didn't notice Simba wasn't in the kitchen. Normally she performed a morning ritual of circles and jumps in eager anticipation for her breakfast.

"Simba…here girl. Come eat."

A twinge of worry hit my gut when no response came.

I started down the stairs to the lower level of the house, thinking maybe she had closed herself in the laundry room again. Silly girl had done it twice before and what a mess it had been to clean after a night with a bursting bladder! My foot made contact with the second to last step and Simba's hairy body bolted around the corner, colliding with mine. Somehow I was able to stay on my feet, but Simba's bowl of food tumbled down the remaining stairs. The small round bites shot out in every direction.

"Well, good morning to you too! Looks like you will get a bit of exercise while you eat, chasing all your food around."

Simba's black tail thumped the hardwood in response as she dropped something from her mouth and began to chomp on the kibble.

"Whatcha got there, girl?"

I bent down to pick up a pair of underwear. Simba had developed a taste for underwear, socks and t-shirts in her youth. I groaned, thinking I must have left the clothes hamper on the floor of the laundry room again, which meant I was about to stumble upon a shredded mess of clothing.

I walked over to the laundry room door and eased my hand inside, grazing the wall until I felt the light switch. I was surprised to be greeted by a clean and tidy room, which is how I remembered leaving it. The clothes basket sat on top of the dryer, full of only the clean blue jeans I had folded last night.

Huh, wonder where Simba found my underwear? It's not like I dropped them for Jack during a heated session of lovemaking.

I flicked off the light and shut the door. I would figure out when I got home later where Simba confiscated my undies from before she ingested more. That would end up costing—

Wait...these are silk...

Upon closer inspection, my heart skipped a beat. I caught a whiff of a familiar scent of perfume but couldn't quite place it. Chanel? Obsession? I walked over and held the underwear in front of the window, examining them under the morning light. They weren't even *close* to what I would consider wearing. Perhaps they weren't even panties, because the miniscule swatch of sheer material was barely enough to cover three inches of skin and maybe four pubic hairs at best.

Confused, I stared at Simba while she happily crunched on the remaining nuggets of her breakfast. She'd been inside all night, so where did she get them from?

"Hey girl. Good girl. Here, you want these back?" I cooed, squatting down to her level and dangling the chewed up panties in front of her. "Come on, come here. Show Mommy where you found these, huh?"

Simba ignored me and continued to scurry after the bits of food. I stood up and glanced around the room Jack and I called the media room, which was nothing more than a couch and big screen television. The downstairs only consisted of the laundry room with an attached bathroom, media room and the small room next to the stairs Jack used as his office. My heart pounded faster as I scanned the open area for any signs of clothing and found none. A knot formed in my stomach as the sensation of something wrong took control. Hard, tight and pounding, the pressure pushed a wicked thought up to my brain: *I will find the answer in Jack's office.*

I spun around and darted down the hallway, then stopped. Jack was a stickler about keeping his door shut. He didn't want Simba, or me, messing up his workspace, or nosing around the neatly stacked piles of papers that he graded or the lesson plans he worked on for his honors history class.

I winced when I noticed the door was slightly ajar. I peeked in and saw the mess inside, and blood whooshed in my ears at the thought of Jack's reaction. He was going to flip when he saw the after-effects of Simba's night of fun. *Oh well, he should have made sure the door was locked before he went to bed last night.*

I pushed the door all the way open and scanned the room. My eyes settled on the briefcase and Jack's travel bag amongst the shredded papers, useless pillows and one computer chair leg Simba must have chewed off. The black leather bag sat open in the middle of the floor, the edges gnawed and Jack's work papers covered in dried slobber and teeth marks. I almost laughed—and then I spotted another pair of panties on the floor next to it.

I bent down and picked up the silken material, unearthing a small scrap of paper embedded inside them. It looked like a receipt from a hotel. My hands shook when I brought it closer to my face. The five-hundred-dollar receipt for a one night stay in room 510 was from *The Duchess*, an overpriced hotel downtown that I had never stayed in, nor had Jack, at least to my knowledge.

The receipt was dated for last Friday night, when he was supposedly attending a two-day conference for work. But the thing that really caught my attention was the faint smell of a familiar, feminine perfume.

I recognize that scent. Chanel. That's the fragrance Serena wears. Wait a minute. On Friday, Serena called my cell and told me she was sick and wouldn't be in, and I had to call that temp to cover her absence...could it be? No way...

A small vibration caused me to nearly jump out of my skin. It was the buzz of a cell phone on vibrate. That made no sense because Jack's was upstairs on the charger, right next to mine. He had another one? I groped around in the zippered pocket and sure enough, there it was. One of those cheap, disposable phones you pay cash for each month. I flipped it open and read the first, unviewed text that had a picture attached from *"SR"*:

Do me again baby I want you now Fri & Sat rocked! Meet me @ lunch Mon? Ur wife will be busy...got some new panties since u ripped my others

The crotch shot of a woman popped up. A woman with long, tan legs, wearing hot pink underwear that looked exactly like the ones in Jack's briefcase and Simba's mouth. I pushed the back button and my stomach churned. I recognized the number the text was from. I had seen it numerous times because she called at least twice a week with some inane excuse for being late.

I pushed my glasses up and brought the receipt closer. I almost fainted when I saw the name.

Serena Rowland.

It took a full minute for me to regain control of my faculties. Sorrow and anger fought for control of my mind. A wave of dizziness threatened to knock me off my feet, so I braced myself against the doorframe for support. After all these years, all the love we shared, how could Jack betray me like this? Worse yet—the betrayal sealed with a boney-assed dingy blonde who worked at my office!

A flashback to last year's Christmas party clouded my vision. I recalled the look on Jack's face as he tried to keep his jaw from dropping when a tipsy Serena sauntered over and introduced herself in her skintight, hot pink dress. I remembered the pang of jealousy that poked in my gut, but had dismissed it as nothing. Hell, all men looked at her like at, so why would my all-American, red-blooded husband be any different?

Because he was *my* husband.

Memories of our nights together, holding tightly on to each other for comfort at yet another disappointing attempt to conceive almost made me cry. My heart was shattered—visions of Jack in the arms of another woman made me clutch my chest in physical pain. Was Serena the first? Oh God, what if she wasn't? I glanced back down at the phone in my hands. Her text seemed to magically remove the blinders I didn't realize I had been wearing from my eyes. The last six months of Jack's moodiness and complete and utter lack of interest in me sexually made sense.

Guess he doesn't need hormone pills after all.

No, I wouldn't succumb to the tears that threatened to burst out of me. Not today. Later, I knew they would come, and the deluge would drown me. I stuffed them deep inside and let my anger take full control of my mind.

Decision made as to which emotion would win at the moment, I found my voice. I stepped out of Jack's office and walked to the bottom of the stairs. Simba had just finished her last morsel and waited patiently by the back door to go outside and do her business.

I ignored her. Hopefully if the urge to relieve her bowels hit, she would do so on the briefcase. Maybe throw up her kibble, too. That would be a nice touch since it was what I wanted to do.

"Oh honey, could you come down here? Seems Simba made a bit of a mess in your office last night. Looks like you'll need a new travel bag and briefcase, too, unless you want to keep ones covered in teeth marks."

I heard Jack grumble, his footsteps heavy above my head as he moved down the hall. An evil grin pulled my lips tight as I wondered if he felt even the briefest sense of panic, knowing I was in his office. Was his mind trying to recall if he had locked his briefcase and emptied his bag? Were the wheels spinning off their tracks, wondering if his little secret was exposed?

The doorframe was strong, the wood smooth against my skin. I leaned against it and waited for the war of words.

Communication was about to commence. Oh yes, *lots* of communication. One-sided communication. I didn't plan on giving Jack a chance to say much.

My fingers were wound so tightly around the little piece of black plastic that my knuckles were bone white. The minute I showed the undeniable, incriminating evidence to Jack, I planned on doing the exact same thing to it as he did to the alarm clock this morning.

Well, with one minor difference.

I didn't plan on throwing it at the wall.

CHAPTER 3 – MONDAY, MID-MORNING

MY USUAL THIRTY-FIVE MINUTE DRIVE TO work on I-30 took me less than fifteen. It helped I was running late and missed the morning traffic that turned the three lane freeway into a congestion of vehicles. Although it wasn't even nine yet, the heat already shimmered across the blacktop, an indicator it was going to be another sweltering summer day. Just what I needed—a hot, humid Arkansas afternoon to help fuel my fury.

With my foot planted against the pedal, I zoomed in and out of traffic, greeted by honking horns and the extension of several middle fingers from irritated drivers I blew past. I pushed my Camaro past ninety a few times. How I didn't get pulled over for speeding was beyond me.

I shoved my car into park and exited it in an annoyed huff. My heels clattered on the concrete in the parking deck as I stomped toward the elevators. Still on an emotionally-charged high from my confrontation with Jack, I planned on using the boiling anger to rid myself of another huge thorn in my side.

Serena.

Before I left the house, Jack had been forewarned not to attempt to contact the little blonde hussy and inform her that I knew about their unholy trysts. I told him that if he did, he *would* regret it. He'd already betrayed me enough. He *owed* me the chance to confront her face-to-face, catch her off guard and speak my peace. I had solidified my threat to him with a well-placed throw of the cell phone, smacking it against his cheek. I was confident the neighbors had heard me scream that if he warned her, the next body part that would feel pain would be his crotch.

The expression on the face of our elderly, and extremely nosy neighbor, Ms. Preston, had been photo worthy. She had been standing in her front yard watering her gardenias and heard my last harsh words flung at Jack. I doubted thoughts of providing water to her plants were on her mind after the early morning show she witnessed.

Disturbing thoughts muddled my brain as I walked through the quiet parking deck. While driving, I had waffled back and forth about whether or not I would end our twenty year marriage. Could I forgive him? Should I forgive him? If this would have happened earlier in my marriage, when my faith was stronger, I would have turned to God for strength, support and wisdom. But that line had long been disconnected after years of my tearful pleadings for a child went unanswered. I hadn't stepped foot inside a church in two years and quit sending up prayers over a year and a half ago. Why bother? God had more important issues to work on and had left me to navigate the tumultuous seas of life alone. So, as with all the other sorrows life had thrown my way, I would deal with this one by myself.

Would I be able to ever look at Jack the same way? I certainly wouldn't be able to trust him, but was our love strong enough that he would be willing to try and regain it? Had he used a condom? What if he hadn't and he contracted some venereal disease and passed it along to me? I made a mental note to make an appointment with my doctor for a full checkup. Jack had sworn that the affair only started three months ago and that the mess with Serena was the only time he ever strayed, but was that the truth?

I solidified my decision to end our marriage when I thought back to the last time we made love. It had been a few months ago, after a long day of meetings with the designer and contractor whom we had just hired to renovate our house. I had been standing in the room that was set aside for a nursery, tears running down my face, knowing I would never step foot inside the dainty space as a mother. Jack's way of offering comfort was to lead me to our bedroom. If he was telling me the truth about the time frame of the affair, then it began right around that time. How could he have been so loving, so comforting, so concerned about me, then rush right into Serena's bed? Fresh pain ripped at my chest as dueling images of our sweet lovemaking fought for control over the concocted one in my head of the Jack and Serena going at it.

No, I couldn't do it. Couldn't rest beside Jack at night knowing he opted to find his own solace with another woman when we needed each other the most. When *I* needed him the most. How could I ever wipe the thoughts away? They would haunt my every waking moment. Maybe invade my dreams.

Over the years, I had watched too many of my friends go through this nightmare. Held them while they wept, hearts ripped apart. So many strong women turned into empty shells, nothing but former husks of themselves. Some went crazy and spent every penny they could scrape together on invasive surgeries, expensive cosmetics or extreme weight loss methods. All sad, vain attempts to regain their youth through modern technological advances. The thought process seemed to be that if they could somehow turn back the clock, love would find them once again. Others found comfort in the arms of a younger lover, which just made them look like fools.

Who knows? I might end up following the trend and doing the same, silly things to bandage my wounded heart. I wasn't able to think that far ahead at the moment.

I punched the third floor button with enough gusto that my nail snapped down to the quick. My foul-mouthed response reverberated off the metal walls of the elevator, thankfully heard only by my own ears. I always tried to refrain from swearing. My mother thought it wasn't very ladylike, but there were days when the f-bomb seemed, well, appropriate.

Today was one of them.

While I fumbled around in my purse with my other hand to retrieve a napkin and stop the blood from dripping all over my pants, the shoulder strap on my bag snapped. The contents made a huge racket as they skittered across the tile floor. A lump of hot tears lodged in my throat, my stress level in the stratosphere. Jaw clenched, I shoved the pain down deeper.

Can't lose it now. Maintain, Melody. Just get through the day.

I scrambled to pick up all the pieces, wincing when I heard the ding of the elevator as the doors slid open.

"Good morning, Melody. Oh, it looks like you could use some help."

I glanced up in mid-swipe, no smile on my face as I looked at the concerned countenance of my boss, Roger Stanek.

Dandy. Now he knows that I'm late. This Monday is one for the record book. Worst. Day. Ever.

I grabbed the last few items and stuffed them inside my bag before he had a chance to help. The heat of anger and embarrassment crept into my cheeks. "No, but thank you Mr. Stanek. Sorry I'm late. Busy morning and, as you can see, it's a Monday. Complete with a bleeding finger, traffic and a ruined purse." I stepped out of the elevator and into the main lobby of Stanek, Overton & Smith, my home away from home for the last ten years. Something felt odd, out of place. The air was thick with tension.

Oh, my God. Does the office know? Has Jack already called and warned Serena? Lord, she probably has been bragging to others behind my back!

"Don't worry about the time, Melody. It's understandable, considering things. Oh, you *are* bleeding. Sarah," Mr. Stanek called to the receptionist, "do you have any tissues or a bandage?"

"I think I have some in here somewhere," Sarah replied, her voice thick and distant as she rifled through her desk.

I didn't want to stand there and be the subject of pity. Mr. Stanek and Sarah both looked more distressed than a bleeding finger called for. "I'm fine, sir. Really. I'll just freshen up a bit and then get right to work. I'll make up the time at lunch, if that is acceptable."

Mr. Stanek cleared his throat, his dark brown eyes not missing a thing. I knew he saw right through my façade, but he didn't verbalize his perceptions. He nodded in silent agreement and turned on his heels.

Sarah stood up and handed me a bandage, her hand shaking. "Here, Ms. Dickinson. Sorry, it's old. There might be some more in the kitchen. Want me to go look?"

"No, I'm fine. This will do. Thank you, Sarah."

"Oh, Melody?" my boss called. "Once you bandage your finger, please stop by my office. There are some pressing issues this morning that need tending to, as I'm sure you are aware."

Though I tried to fight to keep control, my body began to tremble. My plan to storm in to work, demand with righteous indignation the ultimatum of *it's either Serena or me* took a nosedive. Obviously, Mr. Stanek already knew that my husband was banging her and wanted to diffuse what he rightfully assumed would be a volatile situation once she arrived at work.

Controlling my breath, I summoned my voice. "Yes sir, I'll be there shortly."

Mr. Stanek turned the corner and disappeared down the long corridor toward his office. I let out my breath and offered a feeble grin to Sarah as I moved in the opposite direction toward the restroom.

"Mrs. Dickinson? I...I just wanted to say how sorry I am about this. I can't imagine how you must be feeling, working so closely with Serena and all."

The shame and embarrassment I'd felt a mere second before vanished with Sarah's words, replaced with anger and indignation. My heart thumped faster, pounding my blood through my veins. If I didn't walk away, *right now*, I feared I would have a heart attack or stroke. Or worse, unleash my sharp tongue on poor Sarah. She was a sweet, quiet girl who didn't deserve to bear the brunt of my anger. I decided not to respond with anything other than a nod of agreement and practically ran down the hall to the bathroom.

Inside I slammed the stall door and plopped down on the cool seat. It took all my intestinal strength to keep the sobs of sorrow in check. I couldn't very well have a full crying jag, then go talk to Mr. Stanek. Or worse yet, let the other employees see me falling apart. Most importantly, I wouldn't give Serena the satisfaction of seeing how much pain she had caused me.

Nope, no way. Histrionics would be reserved for later. Maybe over several bottles of wine at Regina's house tonight. Although she didn't know about what happened yet, or my intention of staying with her for a few days until Jack could move his stuff out of the house, it didn't matter. Once I told her, I knew she would be there for me, just as I was for her three years ago when her marriage ended. For the very same reason. The sympathy I had for her when she walked that valley now morphed over to empathy.

I dabbed my bleeding finger with toilet paper, then opened the door and went to the sink. The cold water felt so good that I grabbed a few towels and wet them, pressing them around my burning neck.

Buck up, Melody. You can't walk in and start demanding your way while blubbering about this like some silly teenager. It happened, now you need to take care of yourself. You need this job if you end up going through with a divorce. Be firm but calm. Breathe.

Finger bandaged and composure back, I grabbed my purse and held my head high as I walked out into the hallway. I nodded my head to several coworkers as I passed by and sensed their stares bearing into my back. The hallway seemed to be two miles long. My heart skipped three beats when I knocked on Roger's door.

"Come."

This is it, Melody. Stay strong. Focus.

My mind may have been ready for this, but my body wasn't. My hand shook as I opened the door and walked in, my palms wet with sweat. "Good morning again, sir. May I?" I said, nodding my head at the chair in front of his desk.

"Of course. Coffee?" He rose from behind his oak desk and walked over to his credenza. One of his favorite material possessions was his single-cup coffee maker. He drank enough coffee throughout the day to keep a dozen people awake for days. When he bought the machine two years ago I had been thrilled, since it kept me from making numerous trips to and from the kitchen to bring him refills.

I eased into the leather chair, grateful for the coolness against my damp shirt. Once settled, I answered, "No, thank you. My nerves are already on edge today, sir."

"Yes, the entire office is suffering from that malady today, I believe."

Heat spread up my neck. *This isn't going to be easy. God, where do I begin?* I waited until he walked back to his desk and sat down. "Mr. Stanek, I know this is, well, an extremely difficult topic to broach…" I stuttered.

He interrupted, his voice firm yet quiet. "Melody, there is no need for stuffy office protocol, especially not today. You've been here over what, ten years?"

"Yes sir. August fifteenth will be eleven," I agreed, unsure what he meant. Was he going to fire me for this? That really would send this day to the top of the Worst Day Ever pile.

"Eleven years and countless requests to call me Roger, and yet you still hold on to old southern traditions long since passed. Though appreciated, I believe that it's time to move on to just Roger."

My nerves settled a bit and my hackles recessed. Roger Stanek may have been one of the best damn criminal defense attorneys in all of Central Arkansas, a proverbial shark in the courtroom, but it was all a carefully acted persona. I knew within the first year of working for him that underneath all the bravado and pompous attitude beat the heart of a kind man.

"Thank you, sir...um, Roger. Okay, well since you brought it up, I believe that in the almost eleven years I have been employed here, I don't think I would be overstepping my bounds by saying that you have considered me a valuable employee, correct?"

Roger's dark brown eyes didn't flinch but I saw a fleeting, questioning look behind them. "Invaluable. You aren't just an employee, Melody. You're the firm's right hand. *My* right hand. You know how much I rely upon you to keep the ship sailing straight, so to speak."

Confidence growing, I let a small smile appear. "Thank you. I hope you keep that perception of me at the forefront of your mind when I tell you why I am late this morning— and then ask you for a really big favor. Huge, in fact, but one duly justified, I believe."

It took all my strength to keep my eyes focused on his. The quizzical look on his face surprised me. Surely he knew what I was about to ask? He leaned back in his seat and began chewing on the inside of his cheek, a habit I didn't think he was aware he had when his internal wheels were rolling a dilemma around.

"What exactly is on your mind, Melody?"

Here goes nothing.

I cleared my throat and forced my hands to remain in my lap. Gaze steady, I began, "There is no delicate way to broach the subject, so I'll just be blunt and try not to delve too deeply into the sordid details. Bottom line is that I need to request three things from you."

Roger nodded for me to continue, the gnawing of his cheek increasing in intensity.

"One was to know that I am a valuable, long term employee, which you graciously already confirmed. Two, since we don't handle domestic relation cases here, your recommendation for the best divorce attorney around, and three, that you fire Serena Rowland."

There, I said it. It may have been ugly, but it was short, sweet and oh so to the point.

I was expecting all sorts of responses, but not the one that Roger gave. His face paled, the look of astonishment almost comical if we had been discussing any subject besides the demise of my marriage. He struggled to formulate a reply. His poor cheek was probably bleeding at this point. I'd never seen him like this before. Had I overstepped the bounds of employee-employer relationships with this request?

Oh God, please don't let him fire me!

Roger rose from the chair and walked around the desk, then leaned against it. The look, his demeanor, the air about him—it was all wrong. He didn't seem angry, upset or irritated by my requests. Although it made no sense at all, the feeling I sensed from him was deep sadness.

"Melody, before I ask you anything else, kindly expound on your reasons as to why you want me to fire Serena."

Flat. No emotion. Just a plain and simple question delivered in a quiet monotone.

Something isn't right here. I thought he already knew! Why is he acting like I just told him I'm really a man or something? And if he already knows, why in the Hell does he want the details?

Heart pounding, I swallowed my fear and let my anger loose. "Well, to be quite honest, Roger, I don't think I can work alongside the woman who has been having an affair with my husband. And I don't understand this. I assumed from our earlier conversation you already knew? That the entire office knew? Isn't that why everyone is acting so, well, odd?"

I didn't think it was possible for Roger's face to become any paler. I was wrong. He looked like he'd just seen a ghost. He let out a heavy sigh, moved to the chair next to me and sat down.

"Melody, when and how did you find out?" he asked, his voice low, his worried eyes never leaving my own. My heart began pounding faster, my mind racing to sort this out. Why did he care about the particulars? I mean, he would either fire Serena or not. My anger was reaching a boiling point. If he wasn't going to stand by me, he needed to just say so.

"I don't see where that has any relevance, but this morning, as we were getting ready for work."

"Did he tell you about the affair?"

"What man tells his wife he's been cheating on her without prompting? Of course not," I said, aggravated. I stood and began pacing around Roger's office. My frustration couldn't be contained in a seat any longer. "Actually, my dog found the evidence that I confronted him with. He couldn't deny the truth when I shoved this in his face, along with revealing texts and pictures." I pulled the waded receipt out of my pocket and handed it to Roger. His eyes widened.

"Melody, you need to sit down. Now, please."

Anger dangerously close to spewing out, I stood firm and growled, "I can't, Roger. I am about to blow my top. The only thing that will calm me down at the moment is to hear from you that I have your support in this. I can't, no *I won't*, work with her. I realize I am asking a lot, since her father—"

"Please, Melody. I understand you are upset but take my advice and sit down," Roger insisted, his tone that of someone speaking to a small child. "Please?"

"Fine," I shot back.

"Oh God...you don't know, do you?"

"Know what?"

"You obviously haven't listened or read any news coverage in the last two days, have you?"

What difference could that possibly make?

"No. I was at the lake all weekend at a spa with a girl-friend. Got back home late last night. Then, I was occupied with other, more pressing issues than watching the news. Why?"

Roger swallowed hard a few times and cleared his throat. His eyes were full of pain when he said, "Melody, I can't fire Serena because, well, she's dead."

****

I understood now why Roger had insisted I sit down. Had I been standing up, my legs would have buckled and I would have collapsed in the middle of his floor. I felt dizzy, lightheaded. A wave of nausea caused my mouth to fill with hot saliva, and I forced myself to swallow without gagging. *Good, she deserved it,* I thought, but then was overcome with shame and guilt for thinking such a thing. Yes, I was hurt, angry and furious. I'd had visions on my way to work of slapping the fire out of Serena, which, of course, I would never in fact do. But death? No way. I couldn't even stand to squish a bug under my shoe, much less think about hurting someone. I would never wish death on anyone, not even my husband's mistress.

Truth be told, it wasn't really Serena I was angry at, well, at least not all of my rage was directed her way. After all, it wasn't like we were friends or anything. We were just co-workers—strangers thrown together eight hours a day with no bonds of friendship attached. I was just another over the hill officemate to her. My connection to her was that of a supervisor who often pointed out her mistakes. We didn't hang out together after work. We didn't share any common ground—well, except for Jack. We had never gone to lunch together or shared personal stories with each other in the break room. There was no commonality between the two of us. Hell, she was almost young enough to be my daughter.

It dawned on me then that her death was the reason the office was acting funny. Heat raced up my chest to my cheeks again. How could I have been so stupid as to conclude that the entire firm knew about Jack and Serena's affair? No wonder Sarah had been on the verge of tears earlier. And poor Roger! He had probably wanted to discuss what implications Serena's death would have on the firm. Her father, Philip Rowland, was our only client on retainer and one of the wealthiest men in Arkansas. Roger's bread and butter, so to speak. Roger probably called me in to his office to talk about making arrangements for flowers, maybe sending some food to the Rowland residence. Maybe he was worried Serena's death would cause Mr. Rowland to seek legal counsel elsewhere, since visiting our office would just be another reminder that his daughter was gone. No wonder he looked so shocked and perplexed when I demanded he fire her. He was thinking I was the world's most callous person!

Serena had driven her brand new, sleek black Corvette like she was an Indy car driver. Just last week, she had been ticketed for going eighty-five in a sixty miles-per-hour zone. I only knew that because I had overheard her whining to Roger, begging him to *make it go away* so she didn't lose her license again. The jealous monster reared its ugly head as a fleeting thought of Jack riding shotgun with her made me cringe. If she died in an accident, I thanked God that Jack hadn't been with her in the car. Dealing with his infidelity was difficult enough. The thought of burying him made my head spin.

"Roger...I don't know what to say. I'm...oh God, I'm so sorry. Honestly, I didn't know she'd passed. And here I was, blabbering like a fool about her and Jack. What happened to her? Car accident?"

Roger wasn't looking at me. His focus was on the receipt from *The Duchess* still clutched in his hand. His throat muscles clenched, his jaw set in stone. Worry furrowed his brow; I'd seen it numerous times before over the years when he was working on a rather difficult case. The room was silent except for the distant sounds of the phones ringing on the other side of his closed door and the pounding of my heart. I waited for his response, the tension in the room rising exponentially. The hairs on the back of my neck and arms stood up, driven by some strange instinct. The fear instinct, brought on by a heavy rush of adrenaline.

Why won't he look at me?

"No, Melody. It wasn't a car accident. Serena was...murdered."

"What? When, how...oh my *God*!"

My body went limp in the chair, as if all my bones had disappeared. Roger's eyes pulled away from the receipt and looked at me. I read behind them and the room began to spin.

"Someone beat her, then strangled her with a pair of underwear. Her body was discovered late Saturday night. I'm sorry to be the one telling you this. I just...well I assumed you heard already. But this...this changes everything."

My heart was beating so fast that I could barely breathe. Roger continued to talk, but his voice seemed muffled, his words distant and indiscernible to my ringing ears. My brain tried to comprehend all the information it had been overloaded with during the last three hours.

Jack and Serena. The hotel receipt. Pink silk underwear. The picture sent to Jack in a text. His tear-filled admission earlier to his transgressions, his voice cracking as he begged me to stay and talk things through. Crying as he spouted how much he loved me while whimpering for for-giveness, promising me he wouldn't see her again. The look on Roger's face while he stared at the flimsy piece of paper in his hand.

No. Please God. No. It can't be.

"Where?" I eked out.

"Are you asking me where Serena was found?" Roger clarified, his voice audible now. I nodded, the tears already spilling down my cheeks. My gut had given me the an-swer—one I surely didn't want to hear. I knew Roger's response would be no different.

Roger reached out and put his hand on my shoulder, his touch soft. "She was found in her hotel room at The Duch-ess, Melody. Room—"

His hand fell away as I jumped out of my seat, my bones back and legs on autopilot. "No! No! No! Don't say anything more! This can't...be...happening," I yelled, my voice breaking as I tried to control my tears. "Jack...wouldn't...he couldn't..."

Roger stood up to follow me but paused in mid-stride when his desk phone buzzed. He reached across the table and snatched it up. "Sarah, I told you to hold all calls...what? Already? Okay, just tell them to have a seat and I'll be out in a few. Is Overton in yet? Good, good. Yes, please tell him to keep them occupied until I come out. Thank you." He replaced the phone and walked over to where I stood by the window.

I heard him come up behind me but couldn't bear to turn around and face him. If I just closed my eyes and kept them shut, I would wake up from this nightmare. The liv-ing hell that I was trapped in—it would go away if I willed myself awake.

"Melody, the police are here to begin questioning the employees about Serena and gather evidence from her workspace. That's what I wanted to talk to you about ear-lier—the fact that they were coming and to ask for your help to coordinate the employee interviews. I had no idea about Jack. You do realize, now, that—"

He never had a chance to finish his thoughts. They were interrupted by my cell phone, which I had forgotten to silence. Jack's personal ringtone, *Always on My Mind* by Willie Nelson, blared from the confines of my bag.

I turned and stared at my purse like it was on fire. Dueling emotions kept me frozen in place, my nerves unsure which signal they should follow. Was Jack calling to apologize again? Doubtful. If that were the case, he would have done so already, blowing up my phone with calls and texts until I answered. But he hadn't. Not a peep since I left him at the front door, his last words "Mel, please?" barely heard over my angry shouts.

The only logical conclusion was that he had heard about Serena and lost his marbles, assuming that I would think he was involved. Or worse—he was calling to tell me he was. After all, he knew where and for whom I worked.

My body was numb. I didn't recall walking over to fetch my phone but I must have, since it was now in my hand. On autopilot, I answered and held it up to my ear. "Jack?"

"Oh God, Mel! Oh God! I didn't do it, I swear to the Lord Almighty above, I didn't. Please, please tell me you believe me! You know me, Mel," Jack's sobs of despair screeched across the airwaves.

Though I heard the words, they seemed foreign, like he was speaking in another language I didn't comprehend. I tried to focus, tried to respond, but found it difficult to remember how to talk.

"Mel, are you there? Mel, please, answer me! Are you at work?"

"Uh-huh," I heard myself mutter.

The room began to change colors, the vibrant hues morphed into dingy gray tones. The obnoxious Oriental rug under my feet, the power mahogany on the walls, my orange bag, all were now one mishmash of solid drabness.

Jack's voice grew fainter, like he was miles away, the sounds muffled by the loud thrumming in my head. The last thing I heard clearly was a heavy sigh and then a strange request.

"Mel, I need to talk to Roger. Right now. Hurry, they're coming up the front steps."

Like an obedient child, I held the phone out to Roger and watched as the grayness around me turned to black, welcoming the enveloping shroud of darkness.

CHAPTER 4 – MONDAY, MID-MORNING

Sinking to the bottom
Of a blessed abyss,
Save me? Oh, it's too late.
Sensation is all I know,
The crushing weight.
The water bears down.
Thus sealing my fate.

THE POEM FROM MY YOUTH PLAYED OVER AND over in my head, the morbid phrases accompanied by a strange gurgling sound. Where I had read it or who wrote it escaped me, but it didn't matter. The words brought a sense of comfort. Peace. They filled my thoughts, and I felt nothing but detachment. Nothing mattered. Everything was just dark, simple and pain free.

Sheltered in a cocoon of weightlessness, I floated. Time didn't exist nor did I have any sensation of the passage of it. The sound of organ music began to play haunting chords, stirring memories of my Meemaw's funeral.

My mother weeping at the open casket, her hair disheveled from her wracking grief. My stoic Papa holding her as she wept for her mother, while he kept his own tears locked inside his heart. Me, a terrified six-year-old with my head buried behind my dad's arm, unwilling and unable to watch my mother and Papa in such pain. The pastor's words that I didn't understand the meaning behind, though everyone else in the pews nodded their heads in agreement, punctuated with an occasional "Amen" or "Praise Jesus".

The dark casket, the shiny metal handles glistening in the sun as it was lowered into the ground by faceless men. No more organ music now, only the off-key voices of the graveside mourners as the final goodbyes to Ethel Mae House were sung under a green tent at the cemetery. The endless parade of people who walked past our plastic chairs lined up in front of the gaping hole in the ground. Their hushed murmurs of sympathy.

All gone now, silence. No music, no voices, no crying. I stood at the edge of the grave and stared down at the freshly packed dirt and the wilted flowers that rested atop of the mound, their scent no longer fresh. Meemaw was gone, buried under piles of filthy soil, locked away, unmoving, from my grasp. My heart ached for her to comb my hair one more time. Just one more pie baked together. One more laughter-filled day on her front porch shelling peas. My soul cried out for one more hug and gentle kiss from her sweet lips. I felt the hot tears cascade down my face and watch them form a puddle of mud at my feet. I hear myself cry, "Meemaw, I miss you. I need you."

"Then come to me, child. Come, come down here. You can rest with me. No one will bother you down here. All the pain will end," whispered Meemaw's voice, but it was all wrong. Brooding. Heavy. Gravelly.

Icy fear raced through me, but I was unable to move away from her final resting place. The ground quivered and my eyes watched in frozen horror as the dirt began to separate. Gnarled, bony fingers protruded, beckoning me. Light glinted off the wedding ring that I recognize as the one Meemaw wore.

"No! No! No!" I screamed.

"Ms. Dickinson, it's okay. Shhh. Breathe. In. Out. That's it. Now, sit still and give yourself a chance to fully wake up before you try to move."

A raging headache throbbed in my temples. The horrific visions from my dream still clung to me and I felt a shudder of fear amble down my back. God, I hadn't had a nightmare about my Meemaw in years. The last round of troubling sleep had been three years ago, when the genetic counselor told us that there was nothing more we could do and that it was time to consider other options to become parents.

Wait until I tell Jack about this dream! This one was the most frightening yet. I could smell the decay. Oh Jesus. Maybe Jack will be able help me figure out why...wait? Was that Sarah talking to me? How? I'm still at home in bed...

I blinked twice and shook the dream-spun cobwebs from my head. Sure enough, Sarah was leaning over me, her hand holding something wet and cold—a washcloth?—to my forehead. Everything looked out of place, skewed. I realized that was because of my viewpoint. I was looking up from the floor, the surroundings all wrong.

"Sarah, what...what happened? What are you doing at my house?"

"Ms. Dickinson, you fainted in Mr. Stanek's office a few minutes ago," Sarah said. She was trying to keep her voice lighthearted, but it wasn't working.

Full clarity hit me hard. I flicked Sarah's hand away and scrambled to my feet. On wobbly legs, I spun around, searching. My conversation with Roger slammed into my head, the enormity of the situation just beginning to take shape.

"Where's Roger? I need...I need to talk to him. And my phone. Sarah, please help me find my phone."

"Ms. Dickinson, please, sit back down. Here," Sarah said, reaching out her cool fingers. She grabbed my elbow and tried to guide me to the chair in front of Roger's desk. I jerked away from her, spotting my cell phone. I snatched it up and headed for the door.

"Where's Roger?" I asked again.

Sarah didn't have to answer. Roger burst through the door at that very moment and motioned for Sarah to exit. "Thanks Sarah. Please go to the kitchen. They are ready for your statement."

Sarah scurried away without another glance in my direction. Roger was in full legal mode, his words clipped and tone forceful. He slid the lock into place on the door and ambled over to his desk. "Melody, please sit. We have a lot to discuss in a very short time. I can't have you fainting again."

I was too overwhelmed to argue.

"Listen closely and do exactly as I say. Can you do that?"

A nod of my head was all I could muster.

"Good. First off, your husband has been arrested and will most likely be formally charged with Serena's murder. I told him not to say a word and wait until legal counsel arrives. He asked me to represent him but, as you and I both know, I cannot. Don't worry though, I've called Bertrand LaFont. He's on his way to the P.D. right now."

Bertrand LaFont was the only other criminal defense attorney in the state who could be considered an equal to Roger. He took on the cases Roger refused to touch for personal, moral reasons. Big, high profile cases of the worst of the worst, the dregs of society accused of committing horrible atrocities that were so vile, even a horror writer wouldn't touch them. If Roger had called Bertrand in, then things were bad. Really bad. Worst case scenario bad. Numbed from shock, I tried to concentrate on Roger's voice and not slip away into the dark recesses of my mind.

"Secondly, a CSI team is at your house right now. It will be hours, if not an entire day, that they are there, which means you can't go home."

Poor Simba. She hated strangers, especially men. She would be petrified of the intrusion of so many people inside her domain. She'd probably messed herself. Worry for her safety allowed me to find my voice. "My dog. I...I need to get Simba."

Roger's eyes softened, the creases along his brow easing. "Your dog is fine, Melody. Jack put her out back before he opened the door. And I spoke with the lead investigator. He agreed to let a family member or friend retrieve the dog. So you will need to call someone to do so."

"Why can't I?"

"Melody. You aren't thinking straight, which is understandable. If you show up there, you will be the next one to be interrogated. Detective Knowles is leading this investigation and you know how gruff he is. You think you could handle that right now?"

My throat clenched shut and I tightened my grip on my cell phone at the mention of Detective Knowles. To say he was intimidating was an understatement. Over the years we had dealt with him on numerous cases where he was the lead detective. Several times I had accompanied Roger to court and watched the two strong willed men butt heads. Roger was a beast when cross examining someone and could usually find a chink in the armor of the witness, but he never had any luck cracking Detective Knowles on the stand.

A shudder of fear at being on the other side of the investigative table from him hit me. On a good day he would intimidate me. Today, he would annihilate me.

"No," I croaked from my parched lips.

"This leads me up to the third point. You can't go home for a few days. The investigators who are out there searching through Serena's workstation aren't aware you're back here. I plan on keeping it that way. You need to lay low for a few days. Have a private breakdown, then gather your wits back. I can stall Knowles for three or four days, but eventually, you will be called in for questioning. I've already spoken with Kent Hall and he has agreed to represent you when, and if, the time comes."

The flip flops my stomach was doing caused me to let go of my cell phone and grip the arms of the chair for support. *This isn't happening. Please God, let me wake up.*

"The press is going to be relentless. No one, and I do mean no one, from crib mates at the day care center you attended to the guy who served you coffee last week at Yo Mama's Café, will be immune. Every person you and Jack had any contact with has the potential to be approached for a blurb. Do not answer your phone unless I call you. Same goes for your email. Don't even open it. I will only contact you by phone, so don't be tricked into responding to an email purportedly from me…"

Time passes like cold molasses on a winter's day. A phrase my Meemaw used to always say that often made me smile. It certainly wasn't going to elicit any happy thoughts today. It was doubtful a smile would cross my lips anytime soon, if ever again.

Roger's voice droned on and on, full of depressing instructions and strict advice. Unable to comprehend everything, I nodded at what I thought were appropriate times. Bits and pieces of his long list of do's and don'ts broke through my stupor. Don't watch or read any news. Don't stay with family or friends. Do not attempt to contact Jack in any way. Take a vacation and stay away from work for at least a week, if not more.

I had no idea how I was supposed to remember all of it. The paralegal in me was screaming, "Take notes, idiot!"

but I couldn't seem to get my fingers to let go of their death grip on the chair arms.

Roger or Sarah must have turned my phone over to silent while I was splayed out on the floor. I realized it had been vibrating in my lap for the past ten minutes. Already, the fracas had begun. Little Rock may be the capital city, but the reality was that it was a big, small town. News spread faster than a wildfire in the desert. I couldn't count the times we had worked on a case that had caught the eye of the media and marveled at how the rumor mill swept through like a plague. And this case would top them all. Philip Rowland's bank account was only matched in numbers by the amount of people who hated him. The news of the death of his only daughter would be the headliner on every news station for weeks.

Dear God...

The walls were closing in, the sensation of stifling pressure crushing down on my chest. Where was I supposed to go if Roger didn't want me to stay with my family or my friends? I *needed* them right now! How in the world could I even attempt to function without their support? Not to mention the fact that the joint bank account with Jack was running on fumes. I mailed the last check in for the remodel last Monday, which meant I couldn't afford to even stay at a cheap motel.

How was I going to tell my family? I thanked God silently that Jack's parents were no longer living and I didn't have the task of making *that* phone call. The news that their only son was an adulterer and murder suspect would have killed them. Especially his father. A fire-and-brimstone pastor if ever there was one.

The only who could ever reach me, was the son of a preacher man...

"Melody, did you hear me?"

"Um, yes?"

Roger let out a sigh as he walked over and sat down next to me. "I can only imagine what is running through your mind right now, Melody. But please, try to focus on what I'm saying. Listen, you haven't used all your vacation in a few years, so you have plenty built up. I am officially informing you that you are taking it, no objections. We need to get you out of here before they figure out you arrived at work. Do you…do you have somewhere to go? Can you drive?"

Though I tried to fight them, hot tears spilled out and flowed down my face, dripping onto Roger's hand as he gently clasped mine. I shook my head.

With a reassuring pat, Roger stood up, reached across his desk and grabbed his briefcase. "Pull yourself together. Here," he said, handing me a set of keys. "These are to my cabin. You remember how to get there, right? You and Jack…" Roger stopped himself before he continued his thought.

The tears fell faster as I reached out and took the keys. Yes, I remembered. The lovely little cabin that overlooked the Caddo River. Jack and I spent our last two wedding anniversaries there, compliments of my boss. My stubborn, never-show-your-emotions boss, who was now looking at me with overwhelming pity on his face. This was beyond bad. It was, in a word, catastrophic.

Roger reached down and picked up my phone from my lap. "One last thing. Whom shall I call to come pick you up?"

I thought about my Mom, but quashed the idea. She was not due back from her trip to Hot Springs until later today, and she was too old to handle this much drama, let alone be able to drive the fifty miles. Kendal, Jack's best friend, was an option, but I dismissed the idea. He was down south somewhere on a jobsite, at least that's what I seemed to remember Jack saying. The thought of telling either of them about not only Jack's infidelity but this latest bombshell made my chest hurt. Only one solid option came to my depleted mind.

"Regina," I squeaked.

Within seconds, Roger found her number and was on the phone, barking orders at my best friend for over twenty years. I sat in silence, near comatose, as everything I knew lay in broken pieces all around me. The shattered remnants of what had been a pretty idyllic life were piled high, close to burying me in the rubble. I had no idea where to start the cleanup process so I could breathe again.

"Good. Ten minutes? Fantastic. I'll inform the receptionist to bring you straight back. Don't tell her your name, just that you have an appointment with me. Uh huh, yes. Great idea. Melody will be pleased. See you shortly."

Roger disconnected the call and handed me back my phone. I glanced down and winced at the numerous missed calls and text messages. The majority were from my mother. I stood up and moved toward Roger's private bathroom.

"Excuse me, but I need to use the restroom and call my mother. I'm sure she is beside herself."

Roger nodded. "Understandable. Remember not to tell her where you are going, only that you will be someplace safe. Might want to warn her about the media, too. Perhaps encourage her to take an impromptu vacation."

I closed the bathroom door and stared at my phone. It took a good three minutes before I found the courage to dial her number. Once we spoke about this, it would solidify in my mind. Become real. Right now, I clung to the hope that I was dreaming. But I knew once I heard her sweet voice on the other end, everything would change.

Forever.

CHAPTER 5 – WEDNESDAY AFTERNOON

PHILIP ROWLAND SAT WITH HIS BACK ERECT against the hard pew, his meaty arm resting across the petite shoulders of his destroyed wife. Her unrelenting sobs of anguish filled the church sanctuary, drowning out the words of the priest as he tried to finish Serena's service. Philip winced inside, kicking himself for not insisting that Miriam take the Valium the doctor had prescribed for her. When he suggested it as they dressed for their daughter's funeral earlier, Miriam had flown into a rage, screaming that she refused to be drugged out of her gourd, unable to release her grief at the loss of her only child.

He ignored the vapid words of the priest, like he always did whenever Miriam or Serena cajoled him into attending services. All the ridiculous pomp and circumstance, the comical attire of the clergy, the incessant rehashing of the same old subjects, made Philip want to pull what little hair he had on his head out. The hollow words about a loving God and an afterlife of joy and peace were laughable at best, and something Philip didn't buy in to. Sins and morality did not mesh well with the way Philip conducted his life outside of his family. He didn't become a multi-millionaire before thirty-five by following some ancient rules about ethics.

But, his wife and daughter were his Kryptonite and saying no to either of them wasn't something he was adept at, so he attended at their insistence. After all, it helped his standing in the community to be seen as a churchgoer tossing large chunks of cash in the collection plate every now and then, plus it appeased his two favorite girls.

No longer listening to the priest, Philip's mind wandered over to the morning's confrontation with Miriam.

****

"You will *not* deny me my grief, Phil. My baby girl is *dead!* Beaten and murdered by some low-life professor *twice her age!* It's your fault. You should've put your foot down and insisted she continue to work for you. But *noooo*. *'Let her explore, Miriam. Let her learn about the real world. Let her taste life on the other side. I guarantee you she'll be running back in six months when she gets a good taste of it'*, you said! Now, less than a year later, our child is dead. *Dead!* Don't you realize what you've done?"

Philip stood in the middle of their bedroom and watched in silence as Miriam tore through her closet, flinging expensive clothes across the room. With each word ripped from her broken heart, her pitch rose, her intensity level peaked. Philip didn't attempt to stop her tirade. Part of the reason he didn't was that he hoped her fit would release some of the pressure inside her before the funeral. He also felt like he deserved to bear the brunt of her anger, and though he would never admit it to anyone, he agreed with what Miriam said. It was his fault for not corralling his headstrong daughter sooner.

But the biggest reason that Philip remained quiet and let his wife rip him to shreds was the plan. A plan that had begun to form the minute he received the phone call Sunday morning informing him Serena had been murdered. He kept his temper at bay by shoving the raging anger deep inside of him and focused his attention on Miriam. And the investigation. He fought every urge of applying the same tactics he used in the business world—ruthlessness and intimidation—and instead convincingly played the part of an overwrought parent. He didn't call upon any of the numerous favors that various higher ups on the police force owed him. He didn't bully his way inside the investigation to keep abreast of every piece of discovered evidence. When new information became available, those on the inside indebted to him were either too scared not to tell him or enjoyed being the bearer of such tragic news, for Philip was kept abreast of any new developments without asking.

No, Philip waited, occupying himself with keeping his beloved wife from sliding into insanity and handling each painful detail of the funeral for his darling daughter. When the arrest of Jack Dickinson happened Monday morning, Philip's plan was completed. He wouldn't dare rely on the corrupt legal system to dole out justice for his precious princess. Hell, he knew from personal experience how much it would cost to make sure a case went his way. He knew which official could be bought, how much cash or blackmail it would take to make evidence disappear. How memories could be blurred, stories changed, witnesses vanish to never take the stand. Bam, case closed and reputation intact.

The painful impact of a shoe against his head stirred Philip from his thoughts. Miriam was beyond angry. She was livid, her makeup no longer on the parts of her face it was supposed to be. Her eyes were rimmed with black and her hair a sweaty mess, the neat bun from earlier gone. His wife was screaming obscenities that rivaled Philip's own filthy mouth when he was at work. Hearing the composed, dainty southern belle he'd married over thirty years ago spout such vulgarities made his cheeks flame with embarrassment.

In five long strides, Philip was across the room and gathering his wife into his arms, her feeble attempts to pull away rendered moot. He held her close and stroked her hair, murmuring comforting words as he eased them both to the floor of the closet. His back steady against the wall, Philip pulled Miriam's small body against his chest as tears replaced Miriam's anger.

The gut wrenching wails of his wife washed away any doubts he had over implementing the plan. A plan that had been set in stone earlier when Philip took the call from the coroner's office with the news he had yet to share with Miriam. He couldn't find the words to tell her Serena's body wasn't the only one they were burying.

The fate of Jack Dickinson was sealed with the coroner's phone call and salty tears of Miriam.

And, to Philip's surprise, his own.

****

The long service ended, and Philip was glad he took a mental hiatus rather than listening to the prattling of the priest. He led his wife into the meeting hall, which was packed full of bodies and food. The tables were draped in pink silk, topped off with glittering crystal vases stuffed with pink lilies, hydrangeas and roses. Pink candies, pink napkins and pink punch topped the room off. Philip realized as soon as he walked into the room that he went overboard. The room looked like someone blew up a Pepto-Bismol factory inside of it. Miriam, who had stopped crying near the end of the service, burst into fresh tears when she walked in.

"My baby, oh my baby. She would love this! It's perfect."

Philip leaned down and kissed the top of Miriam's head in response and gave her hand a gentle squeeze. He didn't have time to speak as they were surrounded by hordes of people. Some faces he recognized, others he didn't. Each one seemed insistent upon offering a warm hug, handshake and words of encouragement to the distraught parents. It was as if they hoped the souls of the grieving parents would be soothed by their displays of sympathy.

For thirty minutes, Philip played the game. He shook the germy, sweaty hands of men he didn't know. His grip was more forceful on those he did, making them immediately pull their hand free and move over to converse with Miriam. He endured the hugs of women from all ages, the concoction of offensive perfumes threatening to make him puke. He played the stoic, silent father lost in grief to perfection while he nonchalantly searched the crowd every few minutes for the one face he was waiting for.

Frustrated and in fear the volcano inside of him was close to exploding, Philip's painful wait was rewarded.

"Mr. Rowland, my sincerest condolences sir. And to you, Mrs. Rowland."

The monster who towered three inches over Philip's own six foot two frame was Serena's high school sweetheart, Bill Witham. Philip shook the hand of the man whose life he destroyed, memories of the past flooding his vision.

****

Philip and Miriam tolerated Serena's infatuation with the boy during her senior year, even succumbing to her pleadings to attend the prom with him. Their hope was once graduation passed and the two lovebirds went their separate ways, the puppy love would be over. Countless sleepless nights were spent with Philip and Miriam lamenting their only child's choices in men. Bill Witham was a star athlete, a basketball player extraordinaire, but that was his only redeeming quality. His family consisted of an absent father and a drug-whore of a mother. Basic white trash—someone who might be able to skate through life on his athletic prowess but would never, ever fit in to the social arena the Rowland family dominated.

In short, Bill Witham wasn't good enough for their daughter.

Miriam came to Philip in a panic one night after she overheard a conversation on the back porch between the two of them. She insisted Philip just *had* to do something. Somehow, Serena had been swayed by the dark hair, brown eyes and physique that men would kill for, to move to Alabama with him while he played for the Crimson Tide.

Philip did what he had to do to ensure his baby girl wouldn't end up being the mother to Bill's children. He knew Serena was flighty by nature, her concentration easily broken and led astray when something new or shiny caught her eye. Her graduation present was a three month long trip through Europe with her mother. The shopping, dining and site-seeing would be enough to turn her attention away from Bill. The minute their flight left the tarmac, Philip put his next phase of the plan in motion: he made sure that Bill Witham never played another sport again.

The car accident happened on Highway 65 South near Lake Village. Bill was travelling to the sunny beaches on the Redneck Rivera, courtesy of Philip and Miriam. A graduation present and congratulatory gift from the Rowlands for signing with the Crimson Tide. All it took was one dinner date. The two "bachelors" shared dinner and cigars until almost midnight. Philip insisted Bill stay and rest before he started his ten hour drive to Pensacola. Once Bill was sawing logs on the couch, Philip opened his suitcase and replaced Bill's antihistamines with the Xanax bars from Miriam's stash.

The next morning, Philip watched Bill down two pills while he slurped his coffee and breakfast, then waved goodbye from his porch as Bill drove away. Less than four hours later, the news broke about the accident.

Philip's scheme almost backfired because Bill came close to dying. Idiot wasn't wearing his seat belt, so when his car left the road and wrapped around two trees, Bill's head went through the driver's side window. The jarring blow left him in a coma for two weeks. When it was determined Bill had fallen asleep behind the wheel due to the drugs in his system, his reputation took a nosedive. Though he vehemently protested his innocence, it didn't matter. The damage was done.

His left leg was ruined after the four fractures that required numerous surgeries to correct. Serena heard the news and begged her mother to cut the trip short and return to the states. Upon arriving at Bill's bedside, Serena tried to be strong, but she couldn't. It wasn't in Philip's daughter's nature to be nurturing. Serena couldn't stand to look at the cuts and bruises on Bill's face, or his shaved head that sported an eight inch gash and tons of staples.

When it broke about the Xanax, Serena was out. Serena may have been a lot of things, but she was against drug abuse. She left Bill's side the minute the reports hit the airwaves and never looked back.

****

"Good to see you, Bill. Thank you for coming," Philip said. The cool, firm handshake from Bill brought Philip out of the dark memories of how he had ruined the boy's life.

"Yes Mr. Witham, how very kind of you to pay your last respects to our darling Serena," Miriam Rowland said, her swollen eyes holding their gaze on Bill's myriad of scars.

"I'm so sorry for your loss. I...I can't believe she is..." Bill began, his words trailing off as he fought for control over his emotions.

Philip leaned in close to Bill and whispered, "I can't take another minute of this. I'm going outside for a smoke. Care to join me?"

Miriam glared at her husband but didn't speak, turning her attention to the next person in line. Bill nodded in agreement and lumbered toward the exit.

Philip bent down and placed a light kiss on Miriam's head. "Time to right the wrong."

Miriam Rowland never said a word to her husband. She didn't have to. Her blue eyes, full of grief and sorrow, also held understanding behind them. Philip squeezed her shoulder and turned to walk outside.

It was time to avenge his daughter's murder.

And the avenger, unknowingly, awaited him outside.

****

Bill Witham's frame dwarfed the iron chair sitting under the large magnolia tree behind the church. Philip produced a crooked grin, handing Bill a cigar. Once both men were puffing away, the fragrant smoke lingering above their heads in the heavy humidity, Philip broke the silence.

"Nice tie. I see you remembered her signature color."

Bill glanced down at the hot pink silk tie around his neck and tried to smile. "Serena loved that movie line. Quoted it almost every time she wore pink. I never could keep a straight face when she tried to mimic Julia Robert's accent. She adored that movie."

"Yes, she surely did. God, we watched it so many times I believe even *I* could quote the entire movie verbatim."

Bill took a huge drag off the cigar, his hands shaking while he stared at his feet. A sense of excitement and anticipation momentarily replaced Philip's crushing grief as he began to steer the conversation in the direction he wanted it to go.

"Thanks, Bill, for giving me an out. I couldn't breathe in there. It was like the walls were closing in. The next stranger who walked up to me and tried to express fake condolences was going to get a fist in their face."

"That certainly is understandable, sir. I admire your strength at holding back. I'm sure I would be straight jacket bound if she were my daughter. Hell, I'm barely keeping it together and I haven't seen her in years."

"Bill, it doesn't matter how long it's been. Serena was just one of those people. Once you met her, you never forgot her. She…she stayed with you."

A single tear slid down Bill's face. Philip watched the young man struggle for words.

"I never forgot her, Mr. Rowland. Never stopped loving her, even after what went down between the two of us. It took me four years to get back on me feet and clean up my life. Pulled my head out of the bottle and manned up, as they say. For Serena. Going on two years at my job now. I just got a promotion, too. I…oh God…I…"

"It's okay, son. I know. You did it for our Serena, didn't you? Wanted to show her the man you could be—how strong you are. What you would do to win back her affection. Isn't that right?"

The tears fell faster down Bill's face at the kind, understanding words. Philip had known they would do the trick. He knew how Bill felt about him. On more than one occasion, Bill had mentioned he hoped someday Philip would be his father-in-law.

"Yes, I did. You don't know how hard it was to be patient. To wait until I got my career going before I asked her out again. I've loved Serena since the first time I saw her at her locker in eighth grade. Now, it's too late…too late to tell her how much I loved her."

Philip leaned over and gave Bill a fatherly pat on the back. It was time to dig the hole and drop the seed of revenge into the fertile soil. "I know son, I know. It's all so overwhelming. It's hard enough to lose your only child. Miriam is close to a nervous breakdown. I'm not too far behind her. We could possibly learn to cope with her death had it been natural, normal. But it's damned near impossible to grapple with the manner in which she was taken from us. God, she was so young. So innocent. No one will remember Serena's sweet smile or her kind heart. All they'll remember is that she was murdered, her life stripped away by a vile monster. Her remains left sprawled naked across a bed, eyes frozen in terror. In a hotel I own. God, it just isn't fair."

"No, it ain't fair at all, sir. I...I shouldn't have waited. I should've been there for her. Oh God, why was I so stubborn? It's my fault...I let my pride get in the way. Felt like a failure, like I was less of a man after the accident. I mean, what did I have to offer her then, after losing my scholarship? I was nothing but a washed out high school hoopster who couldn't play ball anymore."

"Life is all about choices, Bill, and learning to live with the consequences from them. Good or bad, whatever they may be. Sometimes, we are afforded the opportunity to right a wrong. Sometimes we aren't. It's just the way of the world. You lost that chance through no fault of your own. The choice was yanked away from you by Jack Dickinson."

At the mention of Jack's name, Bill shot out of his chair. His entire body shook as he stared toward the cemetery where Serena's body would be laid to rest in less than an hour. "I...I...could just kill him. Almost did when they booked him Monday night," he whispered.

Philip's chest tightened at the words he'd been waiting to hear, spoken by the man who worked at the jail where his new nemesis, Jack Dickinson, was being held. He pretended to not hear Bill's comment and let some of his own pain free.

"Miriam can't handle a trial. Quite frankly, neither can I. Miriam's heart problems aren't going to withstand weeks of sitting inside a courtroom. That scaly bastard LaFont will trot out his dog and pony show for his client. His *guilty* client. Heaven forbid he finds some legal loophole and Jack walks free. And if somehow, by some miracle from above, the justice system actually works and he is found guilty, it still isn't fair. It isn't justice. That evil vermin will get to spend the rest of his life in prison. Three meals fed to him each day. Free medical care for the remainder of his life. Watch television. Talk on the phone. Have visitors. *Live*. Live while my daughter rots in the grave."

Philip stopped himself to catch his breath and fight for control of his tormented heart. "Where is the justice in that? He takes my baby's life but gets to keep his? Oh, if these old hands could only find their way around that bastard's neck, I'd make sure he'd pay for what he did to her. For what he did to my sweet Miriam. Eye for an eye, isn't that what the Good Book says? I failed you, Serena," Philip moaned, tears streaming down his face as the volcano of grief inside him was released through salty lava. "I wasn't there to protect you and now, I'm too old to avenge you! Oh Jesus, how are we ever going to get through this?" Philip broke down into a slobbering mess and let his tears soak into Bill's heart. He didn't have to wait long.

"It may be too late to tell Serena, but it certainly isn't too late to show her how much I loved her. And you and Mrs. Rowland. I'll right this wrong, I promise you Mr. Rowland. I'll right this wrong," Bill declared.

Philip's troubled heart grabbed onto the sprig of hope. His plan had been executed perfectly, the evil seed he'd planted had sprouted up and taken root inside Bill's soul. He did his best to fake confusion. "What…what are you saying, Bill?"

Philip watched as Bill's face flushed with anger, his hands clenched at his sides, knuckles white. His jaw flexed as he ground his teeth. Philip sensed the internal struggle and watched Bill grapple with the decision he had hoped he would make. Sure enough, Bill's jaw relaxed a bit and he took a deep breath.

"I'm saying there's a reason I work at the jail. And my choice is to—"

Philip held up his hand to stop another word from leaving Bill's mouth. Now that the poisonous plant had thoroughly taken hold of Bill, Philip dried his tears and allowed his own fury to fertilize the vine. "Don't say another word. Just promise me one thing."

Bill motioned with a slight nod of his head for Philip to continue.

"Don't let Miriam or me be forced to attend another hearing."

The pain behind the young man's eyes lessened as they filled with the spark of redeeming revenge. "Consider it done."

Bill stretched out his hand and Philip met him halfway. They solidified their pact with a hearty handshake under the cloudless sky. The only sound was the chirps of the birds perched in the magnolia tree above them. Not another word was exchanged as they made their way back inside the sanctuary. Philip knew their mutual festering wounds of grief at the loss of Serena had been coated with the salve of revenge.

As Philip walked through the door and over to his wife, he thought, *Let the healing begin.*

CHAPTER 6 – THURSDAY MORNING

"IT'S GOOD TO SEE YOU EAT SOMETHING. YOUR aversion to food was beginning to scare me. More coffee?"

I nodded yes, my mouth full of dry toast. Regina filled my mug and sat down across from me, waiting to see if I would continue the conversation. During the last three days, I had spoken about two full sentences, most of them incoherent blather. After seventy-two hours of constant crying, bouts of violent retching and no food, I'd fallen asleep around six the night before and slept all night.

Each moment of the last three days had been filled with intolerable anguish. I didn't just walk through the valley of the shadow of death, I crawled. Felt each sharp rock of fear rip through my skin, every thorn of betrayal puncture my flesh. Each breath sent fresh pain flooding through my soul, the realization that I was still alive cemented in the oxygen.

I prayed for death to end the misery. Cursed the day I met Jack and the day the firm hired Serena. Thanked God for keeping me barren so our children wouldn't be beside me, suffering the same torment.

Then I prayed for forgiveness for thinking such things. Curled up in the fetal position on the floor, I tried reaching out to God. To find solace in the scriptures I knew by heart. I even recited some of the Psalms over and over, chanting the ancient words so many times in my head I nearly screamed. The more I begged for understanding, peace, strength, or to feel His presence, the angrier I became at the mind-numbing silence.

When my body finally shut down from lack of sleep and food, so did my mind. I didn't dream, at least not that I could recall. I slipped into the darkness, blissfully free from the spinning images and thoughts of my ruined life. Waking earlier, I was still brokenhearted and terrified of the vast unknown that awaited me, but the rest had revived me—to a point. Enough that I knew I couldn't hide inside the dark caverns of my heart any longer. Couldn't cower from the situation like a frightened child.

When I crashed, my accompanying emotions were sadness and grief. When I awoke earlier, a new one had taken hold—anger. Deep, soul piercing anger. Most of it directed toward Jack and some at Serena. A dollop for the entire situation we faced. But mostly, what ate away at my insides was what this whole debacle was doing to my mother. She was in her mid-eighties, of fading health after my father's death four years ago, and the only family I had left. I cringed at my callousness for leaving her to alone to deal with this.

I clung to this new sensation like a lifesaver and held on tight, determined to wade through the burning fire and be there for my mom.

"Thank you," I managed after swallowing a gulp of hot coffee. My stomach lurched in protest at the reintroduction of food. Even the dried toast didn't want to stay down.

No, no more. I won't puke again. Not today.

Regina reached across the table and patted my arm. "If you are thanking me for making you bland toast, wait until you see what I'm making for lunch. A culinary treat, I assure you."

I wanted to smile at my closest friend's humor, but couldn't. The muscles of my mouth didn't recall on their own how to and my brain certainly didn't have the ability to force them to oblige. It was too preoccupied with other things. Things that were shredding me to pieces on the inside, tearing my soul into useless chunks. Things that, if I didn't let out, would eventually kill me.

"Bologna sandwiches?" I muttered.

"Huh?"

"Bologna sandwiches? Is that the culinary delight I have to look forward to?" I asked, my first real, cohesive sentence in days.

"Yep. And if you're lucky, I might just boil some water and put something in it tonight for a hot meal. Whoever said I was a bad cook lied like a dog. Lied, I tell you!"

Simba whined from under the table, her tail thumping on the floor. My furry best friend only left my side each day when Regina came to gather her off the bed and take her outside for a walk to do her business. She wouldn't even leave her spot next to me on the bed to eat. Regina had to bring her bowl to her and set it on the edge of the bed. She whined softly beside me whenever I cried, her warm tongue caressing my skin occasionally, like she was trying to heal my wounds. When I paced the floors, she matched each step with me. Poor thing, she was exhausted, just like her master.

I grabbed my coffee cup and stood up, then walked over to the counter and picked up Simba's leash. Three bites of toast were all my shrunken stomach was going to allow me to feed it. I knew if I stayed put, Regina would try to force me to eat more and I was determined not to be sick today. Three full days of projectile vomiting was enough.

"Come on, bring your coffee and let's sit outside. I...I'm ready to talk, if you want to listen."

"Well, I have been waiting since Monday morning to hear those words leave those cute little lips of yours, sweetie. I'm all ears!" Regina gushed. She wrapped her arm around mine, a smile stretched from ear to ear as we walked outside.

The minute we stepped out onto the deck, the peaceful sounds of the river, the happy tweets of the birds and a few distant moos from the cows in the pasture over the small rise greeted us. The air was thick with humidity, the morning fog still lingering over the meandering river as it wound its way through the valley below us. Roger sure knew how to pick a quiet retreat to escape from the world.

Miles from the main road, the four bedroom cabin wasn't an actual cabin, but a home—complete with a wrap-a-round porch, a three car garage and big screen television sets in every bedroom. The landscaping was impeccable. It was made to look like nature had taken over and created everything, but I knew from my own experience with flowers and shrubs that it took a lot of time, effort and money to achieve that look. Plus, I paid all of Roger's bills each month and I *knew* how much it cost to keep the place running.

It was a perfect hideaway and one that no one would ever find without a detailed map or guide. Nestled amongst the trees on the top of a small hill, with back windows facing the Caddo River. The closest neighbor was ten miles to the east. No sounds of the city to destroy the natural hum. I couldn't think of a better place to unload my baggage at Regina's feet.

Simba finished with her morning ritual, and Regina and I settled on the swing that hung from a gigantic oak limb facing the water. I reached down and unlatched the leash from Simba's neck.

Regina grabbed her collar "Won't she run? Chase the cows or something?"

I smiled and patted Simba's fluffy head. "She hasn't left my side for three days. What do you think?"

Sure enough, when Regina let go, Simba stretched and then curled up under my feet. "See. Told you. I may not know much, but I do know my dog."

Regina sipped her coffee and waited. She knew I was ready to talk, but she didn't pry or try to force the words out of me. Her unending patience was one of her many virtues, along with her sense of humor, and yet another reason I adored her so.

"I want to thank you for being here for me. And the clothes. And for getting Simba. I mean, you dropped everything for me. I don't think I will ever be able to say—"

"Stop right there. Friends don't thank friends for *being* friends. And the clothes? Hey, we've shared them for years. Why do you think I picked you for a best friend? We're the same size. Swapping clothes cuts down on expenses. But, this conversation isn't about me, it's about *you* and this…situation. So, leave me out of it, unless, of course, you have instructions that I need to carry out. Bidding to attend to. Wishes to grant."

Regina clasped her hands together in mock prayer and bowed. Nothing like a friend with a sense of humor that knew no bounds to help ease her troubled friend through the murky waters of uncertainty.

I took one last sip of coffee and began the line of questions I was petrified to ask. I forced the paralegal inside of me to emerge, though I had no idea how long she would remain in control. "I assume you have kept in touch with Roger? My Mom?"

"Yes," Regina's reply was hesitant. I heard the heaviness in her voice. She sensed the questions were forced. My clipped words were a sham that could end at any moment. Thankfully, her cadence mimicked my own.

"Have you watched or read any news?"

"No. I followed Roger's instructions to the letter. No news media. Only used my cell to converse with him and your Mom. I shut yours off once we arrived here. Thing was going crazy. You probably will need to change your number."

Keep it together Melody. Steady. For Mom.

"Is my mother okay?"

"Holding on. Best as can be expected. She's more concerned about you, though."

Thank God.

"Has he been, I mean, have they…formally charged him?"

"Yes. Tuesday night."

Oh God…no.

"With?"

"Capitol murder."

Breathe.

"Bond?"

"One point five million."

My vision blurred for a moment as the gray threatened to overtake me again. I forced the toast and coffee to remain in my stomach and pushed the impending darkness that I wished would swallow me whole out of my mind. There was no way I could ever come up with the bond money. All of our remaining assets were used up in the house renovations. I didn't own anything worth the one-hundred-fifty thousand dollars it would take to secure a bond, nor did I know anyone who did. The paralegal disappeared at this latest news. The horrified wife emerged.

"For the first time in my life, I don't know what to do next," I confessed. "I've *always* had a plan. A map of what direction my life would take. High school, college, a job. Marriage. A family. I'll admit, when reality hit that I would never be a mother, it threw me for a loop. No, it threw me and….*Jack*, for a loop." Saying the name of my husband out loud caused some of my bravado and anger to disappear. A lump of hot tears at the mention of his name formed in my throat, but I ignored them.

"I should have seen it coming. The signs were all there. His mood swings, lack of interest in me, the weight loss. I didn't help our situation any when I started spending more time at work, especially when the construction started. I was so wrapped up in my own pain, trying to deal with things, I ignored his. He wanted children too, you know."

"I know he did," Regina said, her eyes watching my every move, full of worry and pity. I closed my own to rid myself of her piercing stare.

Sighing heavily, I continued, "It wasn't my idea to renovate the house. He wanted to change it. I fought him hard for almost two years after he first broached the subject. God, how we argued! I couldn't stand the thought of covering over the stencils I had painted years ago. Getting rid of all the baby furniture he had refinished by hand. I wasn't ready to throw in the towel, so to speak. But the incessant arguing got to me so I finally gave in. He just wouldn't leave it alone. The first day the workers arrived, I felt…I felt something die inside me and I knew I couldn't bear to watch them destroy my last tie to motherhood."

Regina produced a tissue from her pocket and handed it to me. I dabbed my eyes, wondering how in the world there were any tears left to cry.

"I was so mad at God. I would have been a good mother and I didn't understand why He wasn't answering our prayers to bless us with children. The last visit with Dr. Moore broke my spirit. When he told us that there was nothing else he could try, no miracle medical treatments, and that we should consider other options, like adoption or surrogacy, my faith dried up. So did Jack's. We haven't been back to church since."

"Mel, are you telling me that you don't believe in God anymore?" Regina asked, shocked.

"No, of course not. I just doubt His interest in granting my feeble prayers. So, maybe this…this is punishment for my doubts."

"I don't believe that for one second, Mel. And you shouldn't either. You know as well as I do that the Lord doesn't work like that."

"Really? Well then please explain to me why my husband of twenty years decided to start playing around with a woman *half* our age and then...oh God...and then...Why? Oh dear Jesus, this isn't happening."

Regina's arms encircled me as I burst out in tears. For a few seconds, I melted into her embrace. Tried to feed off of the love she exuded to help calm me down. Unfortunately, it didn't work. I pulled myself from her arms and stood up, my frenzied pacing from the previous two nights back in full swing.

"What am I supposed to do now, Regina? Huh? How am I supposed to deal with all of this? I don't even know where to begin! My husband, charged with murder! It's not like the affair wasn't enough to overcome, but hey, I could've tried. I survived losing my dad. Came to grips with the fact that motherhood wasn't in the cards for me. Probably could have forgiven Jack once I stopped being so angry at him. But *murder?* I can't even wrap my head around it! How will I be able to pay for his defense? I mean, Roger *said* not to worry about it, but how can I not? We depleted all of our savings on that stupid house!"

My mouth was moving at the speed of light now, my frantic steps around the swing nearly as fast. I knew I was ranting, but I couldn't stop the flow.

"I don't want to be indebted to my boss forever! And really, who knows how long I will continue to work there? Talk about uncomfortable! Can I just waltz in there and sit at my desk, pecking away on my computer like nothing ever happened? Maybe. But I don't think the atmosphere at the office will *ever* be the same. I mean, come on. Serena's desk was *right outside my office*! A glaring beacon of my husband's betrayal and crimes will hit me, and everyone else, in the face each time we walk by it! Can you imagine the things that will be said behind my back? Oh, and what will I say to Mr. Rowland when he comes in to see Roger? I won't be able to face him."

"Honey, sit do—" Regina began, trying to slow my tirade. Like a tidal wave that ignores a seagull in its path, I kept talking without acknowledging her words.

"Oh, and let's not forget about the fact that I spent over twenty years of my life with a man suspected of beating a woman to a pulp and then strangling her to death. *Murder!* I mean, I can't even *fathom* those words ever being tied to Jack Dickinson. Can you? What am I supposed to believe? He already admitted to the affair, which I never thought he was capable of, so is it a real stretch to believe he committed murder? I'm forty-three years old, for goodness sake. It's too late to start all over again. My God, I feel like I've stepped into a horror movie or something. *This just isn't happening!*"

Fury raced through me, my nerves burnt to a crisp. I hurled my coffee mug across the lawn and watched with delight as it smashed into pieces. I wanted to hurt something, to transfer my anguish from my body before it destroyed me. Unable to control myself and not satiated from tossing my cup, I scooped up a handful of rocks at the edge of the hill and threw them as hard as I could at the giant tree trunk closest to me.

"You *bastard!* How could you have ruined our lives like this?" I screamed. I bent down and grabbed more, grunting as I chunked them down toward the river. "What am I supposed to do now, huh? Why Jack? *Why?*" Spent, I crumpled to the ground, incapable of stopping the deluge of tears. Regina and Simba were by my side in a flash.

"Breathe, Mel. Breathe. Shhhh…come on now. You've cried enough tears. Time to let the stubborn, never-accept-defeat Mel come back and take control. I don't know how to handle this mess of the woman I used to know."

"She's gone," I whimpered into Regina's sleeve.

"No, she isn't," Regina insisted, pulling my face up to hers. Her brooding eyes commanded my attention. "She's right here." She pointed to my chest, her boney index finger making brusque contact with my bare skin. "I'd like to speak with her now, please, because this blubbery mess stymies me."

Simba shoved her snout between us and licked my face with her rough tongue. Between the two of them, the heat of anger began to dissipate. Regina was right. I was a fighter. Always had been. My mother once called me a weeping willow because I could bend, yet not break when life's storms hit. Maybe she was right. This was a hurricane, tornado, tsunami and earthquake all rolled into one, yet I was standing. Leafless, but still anchored to the ground. My roots were deeply embedded in the soil of faith, and I had a strong sense of devotion to my remaining parent.

"You're right, as usual. Time to stop the pity party and fix this," I said, wiping my damp face on the sleeve of her shirt. "Guess I just needed to vent. Exorcise the demons, if you will. Can't have my mom seeing me like this. Come on, you've got some work to do."

"Well, first things first. I need a new shirt, *then* you can start ordering me around. Yeah, you needed an exorcism all right. I was afraid at any minute, green pea soup would start shooting out of your mouth."

I scrambled to my feet and held my hand out to Regina, surprised when I noticed I was smiling. Not a huge grin, but a smile nonetheless. Regina was doing her best to force back her own tears, presumably of happiness at seeing me come alive again.

As we walked back toward the house, Regina asked, "So, what's on the work agenda for today, boss lady?"

"I need your cosmetic skills. Can't go to visit my husband in jail looking like this, can I?"

Regina almost walked into the door frame. "Come again?"

"No more hiding under the covers, Regina. I need to talk to Jack. Face to face. I...I need to know. Need to look into his eyes when I ask the question."

Regina eyeballed me, seeming to come to grips with the fact that I wasn't kidding. That I was stone-cold serious and wouldn't be deterred. She knew me better than to argue or attempt to change my mind.

She let out a quiet rush of air, then pointed to the bathroom. "If you want me to make you presentable, please give me a clean slate first."

"Fine. But don't you dare use the time I'm in the shower to call or text Roger. Or my mother. I don't want anyone to know I'm going in to town before I'm *ready* for them to know."

"Mel, there are some things you should—"

"No. My plate is full enough. One more scoop and it will bust."

Regina looked dubious.

"Look, I promise to tell them both *after* the visit. I need to stop by the office and pick up my car anyway, so I'll talk to Roger after I see Jack. Make sure I still have a job and all. But, while I'm at the jail, will you please go pick up my mother and bring her back here? I need to see her."

In mock surrender, Regina held up her hands in submission. "Your wish is my command, oh Crazy One."

CHAPTER 7 – THURSDAY AFTERNOON

I WATCHED REGINA PULL OUT OF THE PARK-
ING lot with trepidation. Part of me wanted her by my side
as support to face what I knew would be one of the most
difficult moments in my life. But the other part couldn't
handle the shame that was surely going to accompany it.
That part won out.

*Do you really want to know? What are you going to do
when...just run away, idiot. Pack up and run away.*

The sun beat down on me as I walked down the long,
concrete walkway that led to the security checkpoint at the
Pulaski County Jail. I pushed the tormenting thoughts
away and concentrated on my surroundings, putting one
foot in front of the other. The red brick exterior of the never ending buildings loomed before me. Beads of sweat and
fear trickled down my back and forehead. High tempera-
tures and emotions threatened to undo the stellar makeup
and hairdo that Regina had created. I'd barely recognized
myself when I looked in the mirror back at the cabin.

I moved along with the others who had come to visit an inmate incarcerated inside the massive concrete structure. Although I'd spent the last ten plus years dealing with people who found themselves locked inside, I had never stepped foot in the place. Jack and I had never been in trouble with the law—not even a speeding ticket.

Until now.

I tried not to stare at some of the visitors while we moved like sheep to the slaughter van. My tan slacks, white shirt and low heels made me look like a librarian compared to some of the outfits that passed me by. I tried to blend in, keeping my head down and heart beating at an acceptable rate, but I stood out like a sore thumb.

Please, don't let anyone recognize me.

I let all the others pass me and stayed at the back of the line. My hope was that when each person ahead of me made it through the checkpoint, they would move far enough out of earshot not to hear my name or see my identification. When it was my turn, the guard behind the plexiglass asked me the same thing he had all the others, not looking up from his papers.

"Your name, inmate and ID."

"Melody Dickinson. Jack Dickinson," I whispered. I slid my driver's license through the small opening.

"Speak up."

I cleared my throat and tried to quell the panic in my gut. "Melody Dickinson. Here to see Jack Dickinson."

Fortunately the guard heard me and the remainder of the impatient group did not. He tried to look nonchalant but I saw something behind his brown eyes. Distaste? Irritation? I looked away before he stared a hole right through my glasses.

"Remove your sunglasses. Place your bag on the scanner."

His voice was no longer dull, monotone. It was gruff, to the point. Angry. My heart raced as he stood. He made my five foot ten frame look like an Oompa Loompa. He slid my license and visitor's badge through the opening with such force that they popped out, skittering across the cheap laminate and landing on the floor. I retrieved them and moved over to scanner to watch my bag get x-rayed, relieved to be away from the gargantuan.

Ten minutes later, we were called out by groups to follow the guard. I stood against the gray wall in the back, trying my best not to run out of there screaming. I hated enclosed areas and there wasn't a window in sight. The smell of the place didn't help, either. My nose burned with each breath. As each group of twenty left, I calmed down a little, the sensation of being a sardine packed in a hot can passing. My group was the last to be called.

It seemed like we were moving in circles as we were led down twisting hallways, my shoes clacking against the filthy tile. It took us eight full minutes to reach the door marked *Visitors – Cell Block D-7*. The guard unlocked the massive steel door and stepped aside as we all moved in.

The little cubicles looked exactly like a scene from a movie. Twenty or so orange chairs sat in front of their own small window, blocked from their neighbor by a four foot high piece of wood. Telephones that looked like throwbacks to the seventies hung on the right of each wall. They were so dirty it was hard to tell what their original color had been.

The stench from the waiting room was like summer rain compared to what this new area smelled like. Body odor, cheap perfume, cleaning solvent and other, more rancid odors that I feared trying to place assaulted my nose. The guards should have passed out masks with the badges.

The women in front of me fanned out and plopped down in chairs closest to them. I waited until everyone had a seat before I took mine, stifling the urge to spray it down with disinfectant. The inmates hadn't been led in yet. The other side of the thick plexiglass was empty.

A buzzer sounded, startling me. A green light blinked above the door and then the men arrived. Clad in traditional orange jumpsuits and flip flops, they walked in single file and found their loved ones in no time.

I froze when Jack walked in—last, just like me. Unshaven and haggard, he looked like he'd dropped twenty pounds and aged ten years. His beautiful, curly hair was clumped together in tight knots. His right eye was almost swollen shut, surrounded by nasty purple and green bruises, and he had a long gash above his eyebrow. He looked like a frightened animal searching for the nearest predator hiding in the shadows. I watched him, my throat in my chest, as he scanned the visitors with little interest until he saw my face.

Jack didn't move as his eyes locked with mine. The loud conversations around us seemed to disappear, locking us in our own private hell. He didn't smile, didn't cry. To the onlooker, he showed no outward emotion. But I saw his shoulders sag with relief as he forced his muscles to work and walk toward me. My hand shook when it latched onto the phone. Time stood still, at least for me. I knew that once the conversation started, the nightmare would cross into reality.

"Mel…I…I…wasn't sure if you'd come. I've been praying that you would at least come visit me. I know you aren't here to bail me out."

Jack looked broken. Like someone had reached inside him and scooped out his innards. Hollow. Empty. Exactly the way I felt. But there was something else—fear. It danced behind his bloodshot eyes despite his efforts to hide it.

I swallowed hard and forced myself to retain eye contact.

You must do this. Block the pain…remain neutral. Pretend you aren't talking to your husband behind the glass. He's just another inmate. You are here to gather information.

"You're right. You know we can't afford that, so I guess you're stuck for a bit. What happened to your eye?"

The damage to Jack's eye was far worse up close. The lid was grotesquely swollen and the large cut above his brow looked infected. The bruising was ugly and dark and the torn skin inflamed. It looked like he'd been hit with something, and not just someone's fist.

Jack gave a slight nod of dismissal. "Doesn't matter now."

"Are you eating? Did you tell them about—"

"Not much and yes. I stick to the bread and nibble on the few raw vegetables, just to be sure. They took my medic alert bracelet off when they...arrested me. I told the jailer on duty I was allergic to peanuts, but...well...his response wasn't too positive," Jack whispered, his index finger flinching up toward his black eye. "So, the rest of the food I don't touch."

Oh Jesus...this isn't happening.

"It's good to see you, Mel. I—"

I held up my hand. "Stop, Jack. I only came here because I need to know. I need to hear from your lips what happened. You owe me the truth."

"Oh Mel. I don't even know where to start. It's all such a mess."

"At the beginning would be the appropriate place."

I wasn't sure if the liquid that leaked from his eye was a tear or his body's response to the injury. The cause didn't matter, because it had the same effect on me—tears sprang into my own eyes. It took every fiber within me to keep them from running down my face.

"Yes, yes you're right. The beginning. Well, you remember the Christmas party?"

I nodded that I did. *How could I forget?*

"A few weeks later, Serena started emailing me."

"When did you give her your email address?"

"I didn't. She said she looked it up on the university's website."

"Interesting. Go on."

"First, it was just funny jokes, you know the ones that make the email rounds? Then she started making noises about going back to school, finishing up her degree. She wanted to make her parents proud of her. She wasn't happy working in the legal field. Wanted to get her marketing degree and go back to work for her father. She asked me about the process to enroll and if she took my history class, would I help her study. Friendly, mindless chit chat, you know?"

"Um hum," was all I could muster.

"Then, about four months ago, she showed up in my class. I didn't know until the end of the lecture that she was there. Said she wanted to discuss her career path and asked if I would grab a cup of coffee with her in the cafeteria to talk about it. I didn't see any harm, so I agreed. The conversation started out innocent, but then she mentioned that you seemed rather distant and preoccupied at work. Asked me how things were going at home. I...I started out telling her about the construction fiasco and that ended up spilling over to our struggles."

Anger welled up inside and burnt away my tears. Heat pulsed through me like a living entity. I let out a bit of steam with a tart response, "You decided to share our marital issues with a stranger? Perhaps that discussion would have served us both better had you had it with me."

"Of course it would have, Mel. And I'm sorry that I didn't. If I could go back and change things—"

"Don't try to go down that road, Jack. That train left the building ages ago. Continue."

"I can't explain what happened next, or where my head was at, Mel. All the pressure, the loneliness, the feelings of inadequacy as a man, they tumbled out. She was a surprisingly good listener and sympathetic to my pain. But when she reached across the table and tried to hold my hand, I realized I was crossing a line. When her hand touched mine...I felt my passion stir. God help me, I was hooked."

I had no doubt now that it was tears leaking from his eyes. And I had no internal control anymore to stop my own from following. "Oh Jack, how could you?" I choked.

"You have no idea how much I wish I wouldn't have succumbed to my desires. I should have relied upon God—to ask for strength to overcome my weaknesses. Deceiving you tore me up on the inside, but she was like a drug and I was fully addicted. After a few months, I couldn't stand to look in the mirror. The lies, the deception—I didn't recognize myself anymore. That's why I was so angry all the time. I knew I needed to stop but honestly didn't know how. I...I strayed so far away from God that I couldn't even pray anymore. Couldn't ask for forgiveness, couldn't beg for help. That is, until two weeks ago. I realized that I hit rock bottom when I bought a disposable cell phone from one of my students."

"*That* was the catalyst that made you realize you had a problem? Funny. I would think it should have been the first time you screwed her."

"When I heard the kid talking to another student how they can't be traced, I was excited. Thought that it would be a great way to keep you in the dark because, believe it or not, I didn't want you to get hurt."

"Oh, how kind of you, Jack."

"Mel, please."

"Was Friday night the first time you spent the night with her?" Somehow I wished it was.

"Yes. And it was only the fourth, um, *time* that we'd been...intimate. By the time Friday night rolled around, I'd made up my mind to end it. Planned on telling her it was wrong, over, that I couldn't do it anymore. I sat at the bar for two hours going over what I was going to say a million times. To her and to you. You see, once I ended it with her, I planned on coming clean to you. Since you were gone for the weekend with Regina, I figured I would have time to sort through the fallout before you came back on Sunday night. Serena had quite the temper and I was afraid things might not go too well when I told her I wanted to end the...relationship. So, I thought if I had a bit of liquid courage, it would steady my resolve. Problem was, I had too many."

"Did you? Tell her that, I mean."

"She was very, um, persuasive, when I first arrived. Between that, the booze, and then her greeting me at the door with…I…"

"Yeah, I get it, Jack. I really don't want to hear about your sexual exploits with Serena. Answer my question. Did you tell her?"

"Yes, early Saturday morning when I woke up. I was sick, and I don't mean from a hangover, although I did have one. I was angry at myself for being such hormone-driven idiot. I made Serena sit and listen to me. I pled for her to understand why it should never have happened and that we were done. She tried every trick in the book to change my mind, but I was adamant. She refused to speak to me, so I went and took a shower to wash the stench of our tryst away before I came home. When I walked out of the bathroom, she was sitting on the edge of the bed, the entire room in shambles. I mean, she had wrecked the place. I think that's when she put the receipt and under-wear in my bag, too. My guess would be that she wanted you to find them, or at least make me a nervous wreck when I opened it later. You know, like holding it over my head that she could out the relationship at any moment and what she was capable of."

"Sounds like she had feelings for you, Jack," I sneered.

"In her own way, I believe she did. Oh Mel, I can't imagine how much I've hurt you. I'm destroyed on the inside, paying for my sin. And look where I am? Charged with a crime I did *not* commit. I swear to Almighty God above that reigns on high that I did not kill her. I left a few minutes later, after she dropped the news on me. Actually, I ran. I ended up driving around in a fog for hours before I went back home. I may be guilty of a lot of things, like poor judgment, being a terrible husband, and a lowlife adulterer. But I am not a murderer, Mel. You *know* me. That's not who I am. Hate me. Never speak to me again. Divorce me and curse my name for what I've done to you with my betrayal. But please, please believe that one thing. I didn't do it."

"Oh God, I don't know what to think. My head is so scrambled right now I can't focus. I want to believe you," I admitted.

"Mel, I swear, I'm innocent. I left the hotel around ten that morning! Bertrand told me the coroner's report listed her time of death around eleven. Someone else killed her, not me. When the detectives interviewed me, they made me watch a surveillance video from the hotel. It made no sense! It clearly showed me leaving the room a few minutes after ten, but then someone else, who they claim is me, walked back in around ten-thirty. The guy looked like me, even had the same type clothes on that I did, *but it wasn't me.*"

Steady...ask the right questions no matter how much it hurts.

"What else happened during the interview?"

"They showed me pictures of her, accused me of beating the daylights out of her, then strangling her with underwear they say I bought her. But none of that is true! You know me; I don't have a violent streak. Hell, the only fight I ever had was in was back in the eighth grade! They showed me pictures, forced me to look at my *handiwork* to make me admit that I did it. Oh God, her face was ruined, Mel. I almost vomited when they made me look.

"Not only that, but you know I've never stepped foot inside a lingerie store in my life. They had the pictures she sent me in texts blown up and printouts of the text where she said I bought her the underwear. They said the underwear at the house was the same as the pair around her neck. It all just doesn't make sense. When I left, I didn't go back. I didn't buy her anything. I never laid a violent hand against her, never forced her to have sex with me. I...oh God, someone set me up but I have no idea who, or why."

"Where did you go when you left? Did anyone see you who could provide an alibi?"

"I drove down to Sheridan and wept on my parents' graves for hours. By the time I got back home Saturday, it was after nine. I was an emotional wreck and crashed downstairs in my office. But I have no alibi for that missing time. I didn't stop anywhere for gas, talk on the phone with anyone, nothing. Mel, please say that you believe me. I can't go through this without knowing you do. I know I have no right to ask you, but I need your support. I'll gladly pay for my mistakes with you, but not behind bars for something I didn't do."

"I don't want to think that you are capable of such a thing. I want to believe that I know the man I have spent nearly half my life with," I choked, my senses overloaded as I tried to process all of what he was throwing at me. "But the evidence is pretty damning. I assume the fact that you were having an affair, in their opinion, was your motive? Do they think that you killed her because you couldn't figure out any other way to end the relationship? Was she threatening to tell me?"

Jack struggled to maintain his composure as he wiped away the tears soaking his face on his dirty orange sleeve. The stress of the last few days, coupled with the injury to his face, made him look like a withered old man. The last time I'd seen him look so distraught was when he stayed at his father's bedside for three days as the man lay dying of cancer. The haunted look behind his eyes ripped me apart as I watched his features contort with pain.

Something he said earlier hit me, the words bursting back to the forefront of my mind while the acid in my stomach churned. "And what do you mean 'after she told me'? What did she tell you, Jack? What did she say that made you leave in such a hurry?"

Jack's expression fell, the shock real. "Oh Jesus. You don't know...okay, wait. Mel, where have you been the last four days?"

"What does that have to do with this conversation, Jack?"

"You haven't talked to my attorney, or been interviewed by the police yet, have you?"

My anger from earlier waned. Icy tendrils of fear clawed inside me. *What is he getting at?*

"No, I haven't. I've been hiding out from the fracas, trying to pull myself together and make sense out of this living nightmare that you've put us in. But that is beside the point, Jack. You want me to believe that you didn't kill Serena, yet the police arrested you and charged you with capital murder. Why? What was your motive? *What did she tell you?*"

Jack's hand shook as he wiped his face. I noticed the burn scar on his left hand was more prominent than ever from lack of sunlight. He'd earned that scar while pushing me out of harm's way when I tripped and stumbled towards a campfire our first year of marriage. Now we both wore scars inflicted by the other, except the one on my heart wasn't visible.

"Mel, before I answer that, I want to say this first. I love you. Always have, always will. I will never be able to take back the awful things I've done. Never be able to heal the damage I've caused you, our family or friends. I was a dope, a middle-aged fool who sought validation of my manhood from someone other than my wife. For that, I am truly sorry. You didn't deserve this. Nothing you did or didn't do caused me to stray. It was my own fault, my own lack of morality and loss of willpower. I...I never had feelings for her, Mel. She never got inside my heart and soul. Couldn't have. They're already occupied by you."

Tears were streaming down his face, and my own dripped on to the cheap Formica that separated us. His words hit me like an emotional freight train, my heart spinning from the heartfelt, genuine pleas. But the knowledge that he was about to drop another bomb on me, one that my gut seemed to know would ruin everything, gnawed inside me.

"Motive, Jack," I said, my voice so low I doubted he heard me.

"Serena told me…right before I left, that she was three months pregnant with our child. And the police think that's why I killed her."

My world crumpled as the acid in my stomach burned a hole through me.

"You *bastard!*" I hissed into the mouthpiece, slamming the phone down and standing up so fast I tripped over the chair. I couldn't think, couldn't breathe. Nor could I hear the sounds around me. Someone grabbed my arm and helped me up. I tried to free their grip but it was too tight. I looked up and realized it was the guard who signed me in.

"Bathroom, please," I mumbled through my hand that was clamped across my mouth.

"Hang on ma'am. It's this way."

The guard held on and managed to keep me upright as we stumbled out the door. My eyes were unable to focus on anything but the brightly lit hallway that would take me out of this hellhole and away from the lying, cheating mouth of my soon to be ex-husband.

****

"Honey, ya'll need some water or sumptin'?"

"No, thank you."

"Are ya sure? Kinda green around the gills still."

I leaned over the sink and turned the water on, rewet the paper towels in my hand, and applied them to the back of my neck. The woman who had been sitting next to me in the visitor's room stared at me with knowing eyes and smacked her gum.

"Really, I'm fine. What I would like though is some gum. Do you happen to have anymore?" My voice shook.

"Sure thing, darlin'. Here, this'll help set ya'll right," she said after fumbling around in her bag. "Lawd, I ain't seen nobody spew that hard since I was a teenager."

I took the gum, unwrapped it and popped it into my mouth. I hated peppermint, but it was better than the taste in there already. "Thank you."

"No thanks needed. First time in here, I did the same thing. Twice in the parking lot when I left."

"How did you...?"

"Honey, ya'll reek of newbie. The hair, the clothes, those shoes. And yer man in there? He better learn to hide that fear. Ain't no room for fear in jail. Show it, and he'll end up lookin' like he got hit by a truck—worse than he already does."

Though I appreciated the gum, I had no desire to stay in the filthy bathroom inside the bowels of the jail and continue this conversation. I had to get outside and clear my head. Problem was, I had no idea which direction I should turn when I left the bathroom.

"What happens to him, at this point, is his problem, not mine. Besides, I don't plan on returning to see if he has any more wounds. So, could you please point me in the direction of the front entrance? My visit is officially over."

"Yep, newbie. Listen sweetie, let me share some things with you. One, you can't just waltz around the halls like ya own the place. We walked in here as a group and we leave as a group. Them's the rules. Visitin' time is over now, but thanks to that little show ya'll put on in there, it's a bit longer today. Everyone is waitin' outside so we can leave together."

"Oh, that's just great," I muttered.

"Number two. Those dividers don't mask anythin.' I didn't hear all but enough to know that he was cheatin' on ya and that he's up for murder. Them's hard pills to swalla. Ya'll married?"

"Not for much longer."

"Welp, now's the time ya'll find out what takin' vows really means. Ya either stand by him or walk away. I'll tell ya, it's a choice that ain't easy to make."

I'd heard enough. I moved to the door and jerked it open. "Well, it isn't hard for me. I won't step foot inside this place ever again."

"Sass it up now missy, but that's just anger talkin.' Ya'll be back. I can see it in ya face."

I didn't respond or look her way again as we exited the bathroom and followed our group to the jail exit. I had to force myself not to scream at everyone to hurry the hell up. I wanted to run down the halls and never look back. I wanted to tell the brazen woman she didn't know me, had no idea what I would or would not do. How could she when I didn't even know? I wanted to walk up to the guard who kept giving me the evil eye and ask him what his problem was. He stared at me like I was his enemy and I didn't know him from Adam. I wanted the glass that had separated Jack from my fingers to have magically disappeared so I could have strangled him.

But mostly, I wanted this horrific dream to end.

Please God, let me wake up.

CHAPTER 8 – THURSDAY AFTERNOON

ANGER CONSUMED ME, BLINDING MY VI-
SION WITH a dark red haze. I stepped outside, wanting to
scream at the top of my lungs. Wanting to hit something.
My fingers clenched as fury ripped my sanity to shreds. I
was already beginning to sweat. I scrounged through my
purse for my sunglasses, only to catch my wedding ring on
the clasp. Freeing my hand, I stared at the shimmering
gemstone with disdain. The gold circle that held the ex-
quisite diamond shone in the sunlight, but instead of the
beauty of the colors, all I saw was red. The symbol of uni-
ty, of uniting two hearts as one under the eyes of God,
seemed laughable now.

To love, honor and cherish my ass!

I forced the tears that threatened to overtake me down,
the emotional urge squashed by my rising rage. In a huff,
not thinking about anything other than putting as much

distance between myself and the jail as possible, I began to walk.

My original plan with Regina was to call a cab when my visit with Jack was over, since she would be across town picking up my mom. That plan was now blown to smithereens. It was all I could do to remember how to walk. Operating a phone was impossible in my current state. Putting one foot in front of the other was all the skill I had left in me.

The walk under the relentless sun left me sweating and took me through some of the seedier areas of downtown Little Rock. I ignored my safety and wellbeing, almost hoping that someone would dare approach me. I would have welcomed the distraction and the chance to unleash my wrath on any unsuspecting passerby. Cars honked, and disgusting innuendoes were hurled, but no one tried to hassle me. I guessed my anger made me seem taller and more of an opposing figure. Maybe it was the way my feet stomped on the hot pavement as I strode down the cracked sidewalks.

How am I supposed to handle all of this? What the hell am I going to do now?

"Melody, what in the world are you doing?"

Through the pea soup haze of my mental meanderings, I heard the familiar voice calling. Roger's black BMW had pulled up alongside the curb and he leaned across the passenger seat. "Get in."

"No. I need to walk. Clear my head," I said and kept walking.

"This is not a good area of town to take an afternoon stroll through, Melody. Please, get in. Wouldn't want some rouge reporter who works the crime beat to see you, now would you? I don't think you are ready to face the press just yet. Or Detective Knowles, who has been hounding me for your statement."

Those things I hadn't considered when I started on the trek to my car. Oh, who was I kidding? My thoughts were consumed with images of my life sinking into a mud hole. My internal hysteria left little room for anything else. Without a word I turned around, walked back to his car and opened the door. After I was situated, Roger jerked the wheel hard and headed toward the office. Awkward silence enveloped us until he spoke.

"I really wish you would have told me your true plans for the day, Melody. I would have done my best to persuade you otherwise. This was not a good idea."

"I don't think I can handle a lecture right now."

"Cold, hard facts aren't a lecture. They are simply the truth. I assume your visit did not bode well with you?"

I snorted. "You assumed correctly. Say, how did you know that I—"

Roger's eyes cut over to me, his irritation clear. "I knew the danger was there when you sent the text saying you were coming to get your car. Besides, I have connections in the jail. I asked to be informed of any visitors who came to see Jack. I was afraid this might happen."

Small damned town.

I tried to hold the catty response that danced on the tip of my tongue in check. I couldn't afford to lose my job, since it looked like I would be the sole contributor to the household for…oh God, who knew how long. I knew Roger was perturbed at me for going to see Jack and didn't want to make things worse. "I needed to see him, Roger. I had to look him in the face when I talked to him about this…situation. I can tell when he's lying."

Roger pulled into the parking deck and tried to hide the doubt on his face by turning his head to fiddle with his window and insert his security key into the card reader. I caught a glimpse of his raised eyebrow before he looked away, which was a dead giveaway to his thoughts. "Can you? Lie detectors, even human ones, are not always reliable and can be easily fooled by a skilled liar."

The heat of embarrassment tinged with a smidgeon of anger crept up my neck. "That was low, Roger."

"It wasn't said in the form of a dig at you or your marriage, Melody. It's a mere statement of fact."

I didn't respond as we wound around through the parking deck to the top level where we both parked. Roger was right and I understood the point he was trying to make. For the last four months, my husband had been cheating on me and I had been oblivious.

But then it hit me. I never *asked* Jack because it didn't occur to me to do so. I'd been too wrapped up inside my own depression to really focus on what was going on with him. Had I asked him, would he have been able to lie to me convincingly? Would he have caved and told me the truth? I tried to think back over the span of our twenty-one years together to recall if he'd ever lied to me before. I couldn't readily recall any instance where he had. Hell, even when he tried to plan a surprise thirtieth birthday party for me and I called him out on it, he faltered. He had stuttered some inane excuse which I saw right through, though I pretended not to. I didn't want to ruin the surprise he'd worked so hard to achieve.

Had I confronted him about the affair, would I have been able to see through his lie? Were the eyes that stared through the glass at me earlier telling me the truth when he spouted his innocence? Or was he just a desperate man clinging to the last person who he hoped would believe him, despite the mound of evidence stacked against him?

There was only one way to find out.

"Roger, I need to go see Bertrand."

His hands hovered over the steering wheel while he formulated a response. I could tell that he wasn't sure if he should shut his car off or not. He leaned back in his seat and stared at me for a few seconds before asking, "Are you sure?"

"Yes. I need...no, I *want* to see the evidence against him. Jack told me some things today that I believe will require my own eyes to look at before I make my next move."

Roger let out a small sigh and rubbed his forehead while chewing on his cheek. "Did he tell you…everything?"

"If you mean about Serena being pregnant and the video purportedly showing him returning to the hotel after he claims he left, then yes."

"Melody, why don't you wait until tomorrow? Today has been traumatic enough."

"Roger, it's much easier to rip the bandage off in one fail swoop rather than peel it back slowly and feel the agony of every hair being ripped out. The pain may be intense, but it's over quicker when it happens all at once."

"That certainly is an interesting metaphor and one that I can't really argue with. You're one tough cookie, I'll give you that."

"It has nothing to do with toughness. It is more about necessity. Waffling back and forth about my husband's guilt or innocence is tearing me apart. I can't think with a clear head when talking to him. I'm too emotionally involved and easily swayed by his words. I need to see the evidence for myself, then make a decision. One way or another. I have to know."

Roger nodded in slow agreement, I think realizing that he couldn't argue with my logic or say anything that would dissuade me. "I'll call Bertrand's office and set it up. Do you want me to go with you?"

"No, I'll be fine. My heart's already broken so there's nothing left to break. But thank you for the offer. I'll head that way now. Please let him know I'm on my way and that I won't take no for an answer."

I exited Roger's car before he could respond and headed to the elevator. Bertrand's office was on the third floor of our building and, though I couldn't stand the obnoxious little jerk and loathed the idea of talking to him, I was glad his office was close to ours.

****

"Mrs. Dickinson. Please, have a seat."

"Thank you for seeing me on such short notice, Mr. LaFont. I'm sure I don't need to explain why."

"Well, if it weren't for your boss letting me know that you were still alive, I would have begun to worry about you. Generally, the loved ones of a client are knocking down my door to offer their assistance in helping in the defense of the wrongfully accused."

Oh God, this is going to be harder than I thought. He gives me the creeps.

I forced myself to sit down and watch his short frame waddle over to the other side of the enormous conference room table. His salt-and-pepper hair was slicked back, his dark brown eyes intense, and his pudgy body poured in-side an expensive suit. It made the stuff Roger wore look like something bought off the rack. If ever there was a man that looked the part of a shyster lawyer, Bertrand LaFont fit the bill. Inwardly I cringed at the thought of the low life criminals who had sat in the very same spot that I was now, waiting to hear their high-priced lawyer's plan to keep them out of jail.

Never a place I thought I'd be. Dear God, give me strength.

He busied himself with several files and then buzzed his assistant. "Liz, please bring in the CD that has the sur-veillance tape in the Dickinson case. I believe it is still in my disc drive. Oh, and some water and coffee. I'm afraid Mrs. Dickinson looks a bit parched."

"I'm fine, thank you. If we could just get started? It's been a very long day for me."

He swiveled his high back leather chair around to face me. No, to *study* me. His eyes didn't miss a thing. "Yes, I heard. Understand you went to visit your husband today. I'm sure he was relieved to see you."

"I did. His thoughts or feelings on the matter are not what I came here for, Mr. LaFont."

He leaned forward and placed his elbows on the glossy table, lacing his stubby fingers together. The smile on his face wasn't friendly or comforting. It was downright eerie. "Yes, I know why you are here. But, before we get started, I have some questions I need to ask you. Ones that, hopefully, will assist me in providing a top-notch defense for your husband."

Hold it together. You knew he would ask questions that would be difficult to hear. Tell the bare minimum.

I had a chance to mentally prepare myself when his assistant entered and set down the items he requested. She walked out, and I realized as I watched him pour a glass of water that I was thirsty. He must have sensed it too and poured a second glass, gathered up the files in front of him, then walked over to where I sat.

"Please, have a drink. This could take a while and I don't want you to lose your voice." He sat down right next to me. His overpriced cologne made me want to vomit. "Let's begin, shall we?"

"Okay." I took a hefty sip, hoping it would ease my queasy stomach.

"You've had several days to contemplate the situation, plus you met with your husband today. Do you believe your husband killed Serena Rowland?"

Wow, right off the bat. Way to shove the dagger deep!

"I'm not going to answer that, Mr. LaFont, unless you extend me the same courtesy. Do *you* believe Jack is responsible for Serena's death?"

Mr. LaFont squinted, the shock of my question requiring a few seconds for him to formulate an answer. It was a calculated risk asking him, but my hope was that he would whip out the typical attorney card and sidestep it.

"It is the job of the jury to decide Mr. Dickinson's guilt or innocence, not mine. My role is to provide him with the best defense possible and raise reasonable doubt in the minds of the jurors, nothing more, nothing less. My personal views regarding this case are not essential to my defending it."

Gamble taken, hand won.

"Nor are mine," I said, hoping my reply carried enough temerity for him to leave the question dead in the water. My eyes locked with his, stern and determined. He recognized the brick wall, backed up and came at me from another direction.

"Were you aware that your husband was seeing Ms. Rowland?"

"No, I was not."

"When did you find out?"

"Monday morning."

"Did he tell you?"

"No, I figured it out on my own."

"Mrs. Dickinson, please don't be trite. I'm trying to understand every single piece of this case to help your husband. You do realize that he's been charged with capital murder?"

I swallowed another sip of water, hoping it would cool the rising anger inside me. "Yes, Mr. LaFont, I do. Perhaps if you wish different answers, you should ask different questions."

Anger flashed behind his eyes and I offered him a wicked smirk.

"As you wish. What evidence led you to discover that your husband was sleeping with Serena Rowland?"

"I found two pair of pink, silk underwear Monday morning. One pair was in the mouth of our dog, Simba. The other pair was in his travel bag. Along with another cell phone in his briefcase that I was unaware he had. It buzzed with the alert that a message was waiting to be viewed and I looked to see what it was. It was a picture of a woman's torso wearing the same type of underwear. I also found a receipt for Friday night at The Duchess. Although it wasn't possible to make out the identity of the woman in the text, I recognized the incoming telephone number as that of a co-worker of mine, Serena Rowland. How's that?"

He was too busy taking notes to come back with a tart reply to my sarcasm. "What time was this?"

"About six forty-five a.m. We were getting ready for work."

"Did you confront Mr. Dickinson?"

"Yes. I yelled for him to come downstairs and then I showed him what I found."

"Did he deny the affair?"

"He did not. Caved like a kid caught red-handed stealing candy."

"Then what happened?"

"Well, there was a lot of yelling, mostly from me, and a lot of pleading and crying, mostly from him. I told him I wanted him out of the house before I got home from work. He begged me to stay home and talk things through, although I think he was more worried that I was going to go to work and kick Serena's ass. I believe, at one point, I mentioned something along those lines."

"So, you threatened to harm Ms. Rowland?" I saw the glint of interest behind his beady eyes.

"I was angry, Mr. LaFont. Hurt and in pain. I lashed out at my husband. Who wouldn't when they just found out that their spouse of twenty plus years was having an affair? I didn't threaten her life. I believe my exact words were, 'If you call that bitch and warn her I plan on having her fired today, I'll kick both of your asses.'"

Mr. LaFont leaned back in his chair and chewed on the tip of his pen, eyeing me. I could see the wheels spinning as he internally navigated what question would be next. He was trying to unnerve me by making me wait, but I'd seen Roger perform the same mental jousting with clients and kept my cool—and my silence.

It was two minutes before he spoke. "Before your little *tete-a-tete* with Mr. Dickinson Monday, when was the last time you spoke with him?"

"Friday morning before nine."

"And what was the extent of the conversation?"

"Mundane, household things, you know. We were both going out of town for the weekend, so making sure we each had everything we needed packed, household items unplugged. That sort of thing."

"Yes, you mentioned earlier that you were gone for the weekend with a friend. Can you prove that?"

He thinks I'm involved! Typical.

"My friend Regina paid for our hotel room, but I bought dinner and paid for our massages at the spa, so yes. Plus, we stopped at Fred's Stop-n-Go on Highway 70 to pick up dog food on our way back. I have that receipt as well."

"Your friend's last name, and the name of hotel, please?"

"Pearson. Regina Pearson. Mountain Top Retreat at Lake Ouachita."

"When did you leave for this trip and when did you arrive back home?"

"Regina picked me up around eight thirty Friday morning and dropped me off close to ten on Sunday night."

"Was Mr. Dickinson still at home when you left or had he already left?"

"He was still there."

"Was Mr. Dickinson home when you arrived back?"

"Yes, he was sleeping already though so we didn't talk. I finished some laundry and went to bed around midnight."

"Interesting. You didn't wake him up to let him know you were home?"

Steady. Don't show your frustration.

"No, I did not. I let him sleep. I *figured* the conference I assumed he'd attended was exhausting, as they usually are, so I let him rest."

"So, the next morning you found out about the affair and confronted him. Did you discuss at all the fact that Ms. Rowland was dead?"

"I didn't *know* she was until I arrived at work later, so no."

"Did Mr. Dickinson say or give any indication that you can recall that perhaps you missed at the time of the argument, which would lead you to believe he knew about her passing?"

"No."

"Did he admit to being with her at the hotel?"

"Yes. Although during our argument that morning, the particulars weren't mentioned. Once he admitted to the affair, things became quite heated and I left for work."

"So, you never noticed anything during the conversation, no mannerisms or facial expressions that would indicate he was hiding something else?"

"No, nothing."

"All right. Let me recap here. You both left town on Friday. You for a weekend vacation with a friend and Mr. Dickinson purportedly left for a conference, but was actually with Ms. Rowland at The Duchess. You arrived back home late Sunday night. On Monday morning, you find out he has been having an affair with Ms. Rowland and a heated conversation ensues. Nothing came up during the confrontation about the fact that Ms. Rowland was already dead and then you left for work. When did you find out about Ms. Rowland?"

"Good summation. Let's see, I left the house late, around eight forty-five. I think I made it to work close to nine. I went in to talk to Roger about the situation, to tell him what was going on. I requested that the firm let Serena go, considering the circumstances. That's when Roger told me."

"Your story is that you were unaware of Ms. Rowland's demise until that point, correct?"

"It's not a *story*, Mr. LaFont. It's the truth."

"One person's truth may be another's lie, Mrs. Dickinson."

That's enough.

"Look Mr. LaFont. I didn't come here to be grilled like I'm on trial. My *husband* is the one sitting in jail, not me. I came here for some answers to this whole nightmare. I could have gone to the police to find all this out, but I didn't. I came to you, the man who is supposed to be defending him. Let me make a few things very clear. I didn't know about the affair until four days ago. I did not kill that girl and don't appreciate your veiled insinuations that I did. I *want* to believe my husband didn't do it, but honestly, I don't know what to think anymore. I thought my visit with him today might help to clear things up for me, but it only made things worse. When I looked into the eyes of the man I have spent almost half my life with, heard his words, I wanted to believe him. But that is an emotional response. I'm here now because I want to know—I want to see—exactly what evidence is against him. Then I can make a decision based upon facts and not wants or wishes."

Raw and exposed, like I was naked in the middle of a room full of perverts, was how I felt. Mr. LaFont's gaze was piercing. Dirty. Like he had some sort of x-ray vision into my heart. I sensed him crawling under my skin, burrowing his way through my thoughts as he watched me intently. I knew his type well enough to realize that he wasn't going to offer anything up without prodding, so I took the reins.

"Jack told me Serena was pregnant. Did the autopsy report concur?"

He waited for what seemed like an eternity before he answered, "Yes."

Arrow one launched. Target hit.

"Do you have a copy of the autopsy report?"

"Yes."

"May I see it please?"

"Mrs. Dickinson, autopsy reports are technical and require—"

"Mr. LaFont, you seem to have forgotten where I work. I've read plenty during my employment with Mr. Stanek. I understand the technical jargon."

"As you wish," he said, then opened the thick file and flipped through the pages until he found it. He shoved the report over to me.

The report noted all the bruises and markings on Serena's upper body, arrows indicating specific places of damage. I scanned further down and my stomach knotted up as I read her injuries. A broken nose. Her right cheekbone shattered. Four teeth knocked out. Evidence of recent sexual activity, but rape not suspected. Pregnancy noted, the baby at close to twelve weeks. Time of death around eleven o'clock a.m. on Saturday morning. Cause of death was listed as asphyxiation due to strangulation.

This was a vicious attack by someone consumed by rage. Jack...no way. He just isn't the type.

I reached the last page of the report, felt the photos underneath and knew I couldn't handle looking at them. Reading about Serena's violent death was enough. I closed the file and pushed it back over to Mr. LaFont.

"Well...your thoughts?"

I took a deep breath and tried to keep my voice steady. "My husband is simply not capable of the violence inflicted on Serena. A monster did this, and that monster is not my Jack."

"So, you are saying that Mr. Dickinson has never displayed any violence toward you, or others?"

"No, never. Even during arguments over the years he never really yelled. The only time I ever saw him really angry was—" I stopped, wishing I'd just kept my mouth shut.

"When, Mrs. Dickinson?"

Too late now.

"Monday morning. I couldn't shut the alarm clock off. It was stuck and when Jack tried, he couldn't either. He...he flung it against the wall and it broke."

No longer looking at me, Mr. LaFont concentrated on scribbling notes on his pad. "Was this before or after you found out about the affair?"

"Before."

"And before then, your recollection is that he hadn't acted aggressively in the past?"

"That's right."

"But he was angry that morning *before* you spoke to him about the affair, correct?"

Damn! Should have kept your mouth shut.

"Yes."

"Why do you think he was so angry, Mrs. Dickinson?"

I let out an exasperated huff. "I don't know. You'd have to ask Jack."

Mr. LaFont looked up from the paper. "Mr. Dickinson already related this story to me. Complete with the details of the broken alarm clock. According to him, he was struggling with the fact that he had to tell you about the affair…and the pregnancy."

Ouch. Another direct hit. Time to shift gears again.

"You said you have surveillance video from the hotel. I would like to watch it, please."

Mr. LaFont gave a curt nod of his head and retrieved the CD. He inserted it, fired the big screen television up, and walked back over to his seat with the remote control before pressing play. My pulse quickened as the screen lit up.

The footage was fairly clear. The camera faced the elevator, and three rooms on each side of the hallway could be seen. According to the time stamp, Serena exited the elevator at eleven fifteen, right after check in. She went in to the first room on the left, alone. Then the images sped up as time whizzed by on the screen. Out of my peripheral vision I could see Mr. LaFont pushing the button to fast forward. At seven thirty that night, Jack exited the elevator and knocked on the same door. His gate was unsteady, his jeans and shirt disheveled, his travel bag on his shoulder and briefcase firmly in hand. A piece of my heart died when the door opened and a scantily clad Serena lunged out of the doorway and greeted him with a kiss he hungrily returned. They disappeared inside.

Arrow number two, dead center.

The tape sped up again to the next morning. Just as Jack said, the door opened at ten fifteen on Saturday morning and he sprinted out of the room to the elevator, Serena right behind him. It was clear that she was yelling at him and when Jack retreated to the elevator and the doors closed, she flipped him off, stormed back inside the room and slammed the door.

The tape kept rolling. When I realized Mr. LaFont wasn't going to stop it, I knew what was coming next would destroy my world.

At ten thirty, the elevator doors opened and out walked Jack, minus his bag and briefcase, plus his favorite Chicago Cubs ball cap. He was wearing black gloves. At least it *looked* like Jack. The hat was pulled down over his face and he almost seemed aware of the video camera's location because he kept his head low, the brim covering his features. In three long strides he was back at the door and knocking. Serena opened it, looking surprised to see him back. She didn't move to let him inside, so he landed a punch dead center on her nose. She crumpled and he shoved her inside, flinging the door shut behind him. Less than ten minutes later, he exited the room and took the stairs rather than the elevator.

Arrow number three—right in the heart.

With a quick flick of his hand, Mr. LaFont stopped the playback. Too numb to formulate even one word, I sat like a stone and stared at the blank screen, feeling shattered.

I was married to the monster. Dear God...

"There is one more piece of evidence we received just yesterday from the prosecuting attorney. Here," Mr. LaFont said, sliding over a glossy eight-by-ten picture. "The investigators went to the lingerie shop at Park Hill Plaza. One of the employees snapped the picture on her cell phone. Thought she could use it to convince her boyfriend that men really did come into the store to buy sexy gifts for their women."

I swallowed hard and looked down. The room began to darken as the walls of what sanity I had left closed in, crushing me like a bug under a heavy shoe. The Chicago Cubs hat. The dark, curly hair. A pair of pink, silk panties in one hand while the other reached for a bin that held countless others. I didn't need to see the face to know that I was staring at Jack while he purchased the underwear I found at the house. Underwear identical to the pair used to strangle poor Serena.

"Mrs. Dickinson…"

I knew what the little twerp was going to ask me. Holding up my hand to stop him, I nodded my head yes, then bolted out of my seat to the door, Mr. LaFont's words falling on deaf ears.

Arrow number four—I'm dead.

****

My car was still in its spot in the parking deck. Though it had sat under the cover of the concrete roof the last four days, the air inside was stifling. It took five minutes for the air conditioner to cool the black leather enough so I could breathe. After running through the building and out to the parking deck like a crazy woman, my chest was heaving.

My tires squalled as I rounded each level, and I zoomed up I-40 like a bat out of hell. The pace made my frantic drive to work on Monday look like a toddler had been behind the wheel. With no clue where I was going and not caring, I let my body take over and steer me in whatever direction it decided to go.

Somehow, about forty minutes later, I snapped out of my numbed state and realized I was pulling into the parking lot of Pinnacle Mountain State Park. It was quite odd, since I had been travelling in the opposite direction earlier and didn't remember turning around. Thankfully, the parking lot was almost empty, which meant the climb to the top of the peak wouldn't be crowded with people.

I shut the engine off and stared at the sign that said *East Summit Trail*. God, how many times in my youth had I trekked the two mile trail up to the summit? I hadn't been here in years. The last time I hiked the rugged trail was on my thirty-fifth birthday, then two weeks later, I'd torn my ACL while playing tennis. After two surgeries, I had feared reinjuring my knee and given up hiking.

I glanced down at my phone, seeing all the missed calls, text messages, and voicemail alerts. It was just a piece of plastic with metal guts, but it sure could bring a lot of heartache and pain. As I exited the car, I threw it on the passenger seat next to my purse and locked the door.

I attacked the trail like a woman possessed, the rocks digging into my feet through the thin soles of Regina's shoes. Overgrown tree limbs yanked and pulled at my hair and skin. The afternoon gnats and mosquitoes buzzed around me. Sweat dripped from my hairline into my eyes.

I ignored it all. The pain in my feet I welcomed. The insect stings to my body and the burning in my lungs as I gulped in the humid air with each footfall, I relished. The stitch in my side, the shooting daggers behind my knee—I used it all as a mental blanket. I embraced anything that would blot out the agony inside my heart and stifle the gut-wrenching truth that my life would never be the same.

Run, Mel. To the top. It all can end at the top. Don't stop, just run.

Twice I lost my footing and nearly fell down the steep cliff. I stopped at the second near miss when I heard strange laughter in front of me. If other hikers were headed my way, I needed to shift direction before they saw me and decided to be friendly and offer idle banter to a fellow hiker. I was in no mood to talk to anyone in a civil tone, much less a complete stranger.

Then, to my surprise, I realized the maniacal laughter came from *me*.

Oh God, I am losing it.

I picked up the pace and raced to the peak. The sun was starting its slow decent in the west and casting vibrant shades of orange and red across the jagged slopes. The clouds above me looked like carnival cotton candy. It was beautiful. Somehow being on top of the summit and staring down at the world made me feel closer to God.

So, I let Him have it as I collapsed in a drenched pile on a boulder, my words screaming inside my head.

I know You told Job not to question You because Your ways are not ours. You see everything, know everything: past, present and future. Our little human brains can't fathom the realm You reside in nor how You think. I get that. But I'm human, Lord. I don't understand why You put me on this earth. To experience this? All this sorrow, heartache, pain. What doesn't kill me is supposed to make me stronger, right?

Well, wrong. I'm not strong. I'm weak. Tormented. Broken beyond repair. If I had the strength right at the moment, I'd go ahead and continue this conversation face to face. Jump right off the edge and be done with it.

Why? You placed Jack in my life as my partner, my husband. I knew that the moment we met. I've been a devoted wife my entire marriage and for what? This is what I had to look forward to? Spending the rest of my days here alone as the wife of a man behind bars for killing his lover?

I don't understand. You denied me the ability to conceive, yet Jack fathered a child with another. It's all too much to comprehend. I can't deal with this. Can't live with all this agony. Please, God, if You ever loved me, make the pain stop.

"*Make it stop!*" I screamed, yanking the symbol of my marriage off my finger and flinging it across the open expanse.

My words and the loud sobs that followed were heard only by the silent trees and hidden animals of the forest overlooking the raging Arkansas River.

CHAPTER 9 – THURSDAY EVENING

——————————————————————————————

"WITHAM, DID YOU SEE THIS?" SHIFT SER-
GEANT Tommy Collins boomed across the pod.

Bill Witham looked up from his desk and the paperwork he'd just finished and watched his supervisor waddle
over to him. The dark blue uniform of the sergeant
stretched and bulged, the seams pushed to their limit by his
enormous weight. Bill forced his face to remain neutral
and not give away the disgusted thoughts he had toward
the rotund jerk.

"See what, sir?"

"This. The note on Dickinson. He was supposed to go
to the infirmary today and have that eye looked at. Why
didn't you take him?"

Trying to cover up your work, huh Sarge? Bill thought
to himself.

Sgt. Collins breath was so rank that Bill could smell it and he was still ten feet away. He couldn't stand being so close to the overweight, out of shape blob. Any other day, he would have had to bite his tongue and save his nasty comments for the locker room at shift change, but not this evening.

This evening, Bill *needed* the interaction. Craved it. It was crucial to his plan. Because the night would end the way he'd meticulously planned it during the past thirty-six hours. "I'm sorry, sir. Today was visiting day and things were busier than normal. I forgot. I'll take him tomorrow."

Sgt. Collins slammed the file from Inmate Jack Dickinson down on the desk next to Bill. "No, you will not. That cut is infected for sure. Could tell last night when I came on duty, that's why I wrote this," he squawked, pointing to the note on the front jacket. "Because he ain't gettin' all sick and pukin' on *my* watch. No way. Besides, he could have some disease or gungacocti gunk that ain't no antibiotic could touch. What if he spreads it around? I don't want none of that crap. You take him *now*. Ain't got no distractions as an excuse at damn near midnight, boy."

Bill hid the raging storm inside him well. Years of playing through sports injuries had taught him how to mask his feelings. He wanted to grab the cop wannabe by his chunky throat and squeeze until he never made another sound. Bill knew he could take him, easy. Six foot six against five foot nine was a cake walk. Bill had a permanent limp from his accident, but the rest of his body, especially his hands, were lightning fast and strong.

No time to live out that fantasy at the moment. I have other dreams to fulfill, Bill thought, a faint hint of a smile on his lips. "Yes sir. Sorry sir. I'll take him right now."

"Damn right you will. Lazy, no good jock," Sgt. Collins snorted, walking away.

Bill called the infirmary and forced his smile to remain hidden when he heard the bored male voice on the other end.

"Firm."

"Bringing down Inmate Dickinson for a look-see. Potential infection. Be there in fifteen."

"Oh joy, bandaging a booboo. I'm too excited for words," drawled the on-staff RN, Frank Jefferson.

Out of all the medical staff that could have been on duty, Frank was the one that Bill had hoped for. The guy was a lowlife and not much better than the inmates. He'd lost his nursing license twice in less than two years for testing positive for marijuana and prescription drugs—once while on the job. The reasons the State of Arkansas let him have his license back still eluded Bill, but tonight, it was like winning the lottery.

Easy-peasy.

Bill hung up the phone and heard Sgt. Collins across the pod barking orders at the incoming and outgoing staff for the night. Bill glanced around the area to check if the coast was clear, opened up his drawer and grabbed the small plastic casing he'd brought from home. The slender, inch-long piece meant for pencil refills slid with ease under the band of his watch, unnoticeable to anyone but Bill. Satisfied it was securely in place, Bill stood up and made his way toward cell block D-7, concentrating on keeping his smile contained.

He made one pit stop. Inside the stall, Bill reached into his shirt pocket and pulled out the three remaining Oreos from his dinner. Like he used to as a child, he twisted the cookie until the creamy center was exposed. With delicate moves of his meaty hand, Bill dribbled several drops of peanut oil onto the white filling, then replaced the hard cookie cover. Not enough to leak out or give a hint as to the alterations, but enough to be deadly to someone with a severe allergy to peanuts.

Satisfied with his work, Bill replaced the cookies in their original plastic wrap and headed toward his target.

Justice is coming, my love. Justice is coming.

****

"Dickinson, wake up. Sarge says you gotta have that eye checked out."

Jack Dickinson's head jerked at the sound of Bill's voice.

"You know the drill. Hands through here."

Jack moved slowly, his mind still fuzzy from sleep. He eyed the jailer from his bunk and blinked several times before standing on wobbly legs. "Now?"

"Yes, now. Not my orders but Sarge's. Kind of took a butt chewin' for not takin' you sooner. Won't take but a few minutes."

Bill knew Jack didn't trust any of the staff since Sarge had been the one who cracked his head to begin with. He would have to work at his sweet talk game to gain Jack's trust during the short walk to the infirmary. Bill sensed Jack's reluctance to come closer to the bars.

"Look, I just want to go home. Sarge says I can't leave until we get you looked at. So let's just get it over with, okay?"

Jack nodded and moved over to the bars, then turned around and put his hands through the small opening. Bill secured the cuffs with a loud click.

"Stand back. Openin' the door," Bill instructed and leaned toward the microphone on his shoulder. "Badge 647 to station. Unlock D-7-4."

"Copy that." The metal creaked and groaned as the heavy door slid open.

Bill watched Jack lumber out of the cell into the hallway. "Let's go. Sooner we get there, sooner you can get back to bed."

They moved through the maze of locked doors and cell blocks, and Bill decided it was time to start the idle chit chat, before they made it to the side of the jail that housed the infirmary. "So, you had a visitor today, huh? Who was she? Your attorney?"

"No, my wife," Jack said, his voice cautious.

"Well, I'll be. Yeah, guess that makes more sense, since she seemed a little too upset when she left to just be your lawyer," Bill remarked and paused, enjoying watching the pain cross Jack's face. "So, she finally came to see you, huh? That's a good sign. Usually, if they come to visit during the first week, they'll stick by you. Least that's what I've seen durin' my time here."

"I sure hope so. I don't care what the world thinks about me. Only my wife."

"Understandable. We all want the support of the ones we love, right? Whether we're guilty or innocent."

Jack looked up for the first time since they started their walk. "I *am* innocent."

"Oh, if I had a dollar for every time I've heard that! I'd be rich, living in a cabin on the lake without a care in the world, except for when I was gonna go fishin' again and if I had enough bait."

They rounded the last corner. Bill knew he had to hurry. "Hey, who am I to judge? I'm just the gatekeeper, so to speak. Decidin' guilt or innocence is way above my pay grade. But I'll tell you, in all the years I've been here, I ain't never seen a man so emphatic about it. You got a good lawyer?"

Bill saw the ice break behind Jack's haunted eyes. "Yes. The best. But no matter what happens, *I* know I'm innocent. God knows I'm innocent. The only person I worry about convincing is my wife."

Bill and Jack stopped at the double doors leading to the infirmary. Bill watched Jack out of the corner of his eye while he fumbled with the key card to unlock the doors. He sensed Jack was warming up to him. He'd counted on it. Since Jack was older and injured, he'd been in a cell alone for the past two days. The lack of human contact and conversation drove some inmates nuts and made them willing to seek out any sort of connection when offered the chance.

Inside the first set of doors, where Bill knew from experience the cameras of the jail didn't reach, he would only have a few moments to unleash his plan.

"Hey, look, I just want to apologize for what Sarge did," he said as he pointed at Jack's swollen eye. "You caught him on a bad day, but that ain't no excuse for what he did. Thing is, he'd just lost a loved one and he probably wasn't thinkin' straight. But that still ain't fair to you. And it's my fault for not doin' right by you and bringin' you down here to get patched up earlier. Can't break the blue code and snitch on him for what he did. Gotta keep my job, ya know?"

Bill was convincing and he knew it. He watched Jack's feeble grin and nod of understanding and enjoyed the rush of excitement as his plan flowed smoothly. Bill swiped his card over the reader and ushered Jack into the quiet infirmary. The door closed behind them, and Bill unlocked the cuffs and let Jack move his hands to the front before recuffing him. Jack produced a faint smile at the kind gesture, and Bill returned it with his own grin.

****

Bill watched with minor disgust as Frank Jefferson lanced the cut above Jack's eyebrow and drained the greenish pus from the wound. To Jack's credit, he didn't wince when the scalpel slid through his flesh and Frank pinched the folds of the skin together to release the fluid.

"There. All finished. Last thing is some antibiotics. I'm gonna give you a shot to speed things up, then get you on a full round in pill form. Make sure you take them until they're gone."

Jack looked perplexed and Bill almost laughed. "Don't worry, Mr. Dickinson. Inmates on medication are brought their pills with breakfast by the nurse on duty. We won't let you forget. Any medication you are allergic to?"

Jack turned around and fumbled to lower his pants with his cuffed hands. "No. Only peanuts."

Bill forced himself to remain quiet. He watched Frank load the syringe up and swipe the alcohol-soaked cotton across Jack's rump. When Frank slid the needle into his flesh, Bill wished it was cyanide.

"You might feel a bit off once this hits your blood stream. Maybe a bit sick to your stomach or a rush of heat. Penicillin tends to do that, but it will pass quickly."

"Fine job there, Frank. Okay, now to end this shift and get home. Come on, Mr. Dickinson. Let's get you back to your cell."

Frank ignored them both and started cleaning up the mess left from Jack's wound. Bill rolled his eyes at Jack and gestured for him to walk toward the exit. Back in the small alcove, Bill stood in front of Jack and motioned for him to raise his shackled hands.

"Okay, gotta get these cuffs back on behind you. Ol' Sarge woulda had him a rip roarin' fit at me if he knew I moved them. Proper procedure and all, you know? But hey, it's not like you coulda sat down right proper while ol' Frank fixed you up in there, now could you?"

Jack held up his wrists. "Again, I thank you for your kindness. And for bringing me here. I feel better already. The pressure around my eye was beginning to get to me. I was having a hard time sleeping."

"Well, we got that infection on the run now. Feel for you though, having to take that medicine. Yuck, the last time I had me a round, I puked my guts out like there weren't no tomorrow when I took them on an empty stomach. That no good, idiot nurse in there ain't got the sense God gave a dust mite. I sorta figured he wouldn't make sure you had a full stomach before he loaded you up. So, here," Bill said, handing the cookies from his pocket over to Jack, "eat these before you start pukin.'"

Doubt and distrust passed across Jack's face, followed by hunger and relief. Bill knew from the mostly uneaten food trays that Jack was almost starving and had counted on hunger to win him over.

And it did.

"Thank you. Much appreciated," Jack said, taking two cookies from Bill's hand. In two huge bites, they were gone.

Bill ate the third and final one. "You're welcome. Don't want you thinkin' that all us jailers is like ol' Sarge. He can be a real snake in the grass as you well know. One or two bad apples mar the whole bushel. Ain't all of us cruel like him."

Cuffs securely in place, Bill led Jack back through the maze to his cell. As they waited for the last set of doors to open in block D-7, Bill noticed that Jack's breathing had become labored.

"Thank you again, um, Mr…?"

"Witham. Corporal Bill Witham."

"Corporal Witham. Thank you again. I won't forget your kindnessth…"

Bill and Jack were only steps away from Jack's cell, and the door was still open. Bill noticed his own hands shook from the rush of excitement he felt at hearing Jack slur his words. The peanut oil worked fast.

Bill watched Jack take a wobbling step through the doorway. He knew the cameras were on so he reached out and grabbed Jack by the elbow, ushering him inside.

"I don't….feel well…mouth ith swollen…" Jack whispered.

He led Jack to his bunk and uncuffed him, unable to stop the smile as he watched Jack struggle to breathe. Even in the low-lit confines of the cell, Bill could see Jack's face was beginning to swell and his lips were twice their previous size. His pulse was elevated too, judging by the throbbing vein in his neck. Jack's hands flew to his neck, clutching and clawing.

Bill leaned down and spoke quietly near Jack's ear, his voice low enough that the sound wouldn't trigger the audio to begin recording from the camera in the hall. "What's wrong, Mr. Dickinson? Looks like you are having trouble breathing. Hmmm, maybe you are allergic to penicillin. Lots of people are."

Jack looked up at Bill with his one good eye, the pleas for help behind it unmistakable. Bill didn't move, didn't say a word, didn't offer any aide. It took about thirty seconds but Jack's eye told Bill when his brain processed what was going on.

"You...the cookiesth..." Jack mumbled as the tears of ultimate fear fled down his swollen cheeks.

"Oh wait, I know what it is! You're allergic to peanuts. Of course I remember now, which means you're goin' into shock," Bill hissed, then brought his lips to Jack's left ear. "Was Serena as terrified as you right now when you choked the life out of her? Did you enjoy watchin' her suffer as much as I am enjoyin' watchin' you? Hope you liked your last meal, you murderin' bastard. That was for Serena."

Jack couldn't respond. Bill pulled away and watched for another thirty seconds as Jack's airway constricted tight and rendered him speechless. Jack lost consciousness, his body collapsing on the dirty bunk in a small ball, like he had just curled up and gone to sleep. Bill marveled at the speed in which the peanut oil worked at taking the life of the man who killed the only woman Bill had ever loved.

Justice is now served, Bill thought as he exited the cell door, locked it, and ended his shift with a smile. A quick glance at his watch told him that the next bed check was a full ten minutes away, and Jack's life expectancy was about three. Bill smirked with satisfaction as he imagined ol' Sarge's surprise when the discovery of Jack's dead body on his shift was found.

CHAPTER 10 – FRIDAY, EARLY MORNING

I WOKE UP ON THE COUCH AT THE CABIN TO THE sounds of my mother and Regina whispering in the kitchen. I glanced at my watch, shocked to realize it was after two in the morning and I was still in my soiled clothes. I'd arrived near eight thirty, hugged my mom, told her and Regina that I needed a shower to help ease my migraine, and then crashed on the couch before I ever made it to the bathroom.

Neither of them had pressed me for any details of my long absence and let me be. I'm sure the fact that I looked like something out of a horror movie helped. My makeup, hair and clothes didn't fare too well during my breakdown on Pinnacle Mountain. I stunk from the tears, sweat and dirt on me. My contacts burned from crying and not washing my filthy face. I needed to hit the shower and recharge.

I stayed under the soothing water long past the point of getting clean. The hot vapors, the feeling of the water cascading down my back, sent me into a state of nothingness. The warm liquid on my skin was my form of mental yoga.

I ran out of hot water, and with a sigh of reluctance I stepped out and toweled off. Every inch of me throbbed. My calves and thighs, not to mention my feet, weren't used to the activity I now forced them to participate in. I'd worn my contacts entirely too long and there was no way I could attempt to reinsert them for at least twenty-four hours. But all the scrapes, aches and pains didn't come close to the devastation inside my heart. At least the minor body issues would repair themselves in a day or two. My heart? Oh, it was like a cracked walnut shell—in useless pieces. All the meat scooped out and the hard carcass tossed aside to the junk pile.

The strength to dress and go talk to my mom and Regina eluded me. How in the world could I face them and tell them what I'd discovered? Mom was already frail. Would the news that her son-in-law was truly a murderer be too much for her heart? How would I be able to relate what I experienced without losing my own control again? It's not like *I* was a spring chicken. People in their forties and even thirties died from heart attacks or strokes. Had I come close to reaching my body's limit? The heaviness in my chest told me I had.

I stared at the dark ceiling, unwilling to look at my reflection in the mirror and fretting over my next move. So many images swirled by that concentrating was impossible. All the memories of our life together, the happy times and the difficult ones, sped by. Trips, adventures, laughter. Those thoughts didn't last long, because they were followed by the newest ones now forever ingrained in my memory. Jack sitting on the other side of the dirty glass, staring at me, imploring me to believe him. The nasty wound on his head. The look on his face when I stormed out. The video of him at the hotel with Serena. The picture at the mall. The autopsy report confirming the pregnancy.

Although I was emotionally drained, I couldn't stand another second inside my own painful thoughts. If I stayed in here alone, I would go stark raving mad. Before I had time to consider what I was doing, I jerked on my pajamas, slid on my glasses and was out the door, heading into the kitchen.

"Oh honey, I'm sorry. I hope we didn't wake you. We were trying to be quiet."

I watched from the doorway as my mother rose from the small kitchen table and went to the coffee pot. Her thin body didn't need to lose any more weight, but she looked like she'd lost about ten pounds since the last time I saw her two weeks ago. Her hair, once a vibrant red that started turning gray when I was in high school, seemed whiter than before. I wanted to kill Jack for what this whole mess had done to her. Mom was only a few months away from her eighty-fifth birthday and I worried every day about her declining health. This little nightmare sure wasn't going to help.

She poured a fresh cup of steaming coffee and motioned for me to sit. I moved across the tile floor like a zombie and sat down. She brought the mug back, set it in front of me and then leaned over to kiss the top of my head before she sat back down.

"Thanks, Mom. No, you didn't wake me. I just couldn't sleep anymore. Tired of nightmares, I guess. Plus, a shower was in order. I smelled like a sewer."

Regina piped up, "Mel, have you eaten? If not, you need to. I saved you a plate."

I shook my head no. "I doubt it would stay down. But thanks anyway."

"Melody, eat. Starving yourself isn't going to help this situation one bit. I'm going to fix us both some oatmeal and you *will* eat it. It's just plain rude to watch someone else eat a meal alone. Even if it's just a few bites," my mother said as she rose again and went over to the stove. "Everyone thinks better when their gas tank is filled up."

I knew better than to argue with my mother when she took on that tone. "Okay. I'll try."

"Do not try, do," Regina said in her best Yoda voice.

I forced a weak smile for my best friend, who looked just as rough as I knew I did. "Comic relief is why I keep you around."

"And here I always thought you kept me around for my skills in the kitchen. Glad to know I serve other purposes in your life."

The mindless chit chat continued while we all ate. Somehow I managed to keep down several healthy bites of the bland mush. Simba had found me and curled up asleep under the table on my feet. The presence of the two most important women in my life and the love from my furry companion kept me from running over to the kitchen drawers and pulling a knife across my neck.

But even through the light banter, the ginormous elephant remained seated next to all of us, waiting to have its presence acknowledged. My mother, the quintessential southern-belle and my sweet best friend, waited for me to open Pandora's Box. I held my tongue until all the dishes were cleared, then unlatched the lock I wished I never had to open.

"I'm sorry that I was gone and out of touch for so long yesterday. Things didn't go exactly the way I'd hoped they would."

"We're here, honey. It's okay. Take your time and say what's on your heart."

"Mom…it's not good. Are you sure?"

"Child, I survived burying my parents, my sister and my husband. Made it through three wars, two bouts of pneumonia, childbirth and heart surgery, so I figure I'm a pretty tough ol' bird. Don't you worry none about me."

A lump of heavy tears pressed down on my vocal chords, so I took another sip of coffee. I would never make it past the first sentence if I didn't rein in my emotions. "My visit with Jack did not end well. He tried to convince me of his innocence, which I almost bought. Until he told me…um…that…the reason the police think he killed Serena was that she was…"

I couldn't say it. The word *pregnant* just wouldn't leave my mouth without being followed by my oatmeal.

"It's okay, honey. We know. Roger called and told us yesterday."

Stunned, I shouted, "He did *what?*"

"Now don't be upset with him, honey. He was afraid that we might hear about her pregnancy on the news before you had a chance to come back and tell us. He thought it would be better if we heard it from him rather than some stranger on the television. Plus, I think he was worried about how *you* would handle the news."

"When did he call?"

Regina leaned across the table and grabbed my hand. "Right after you went to Mr. LaFont's office. He thought that once you met with him, you might need some time alone."

"Well, he was right on that part, I'll give him that. The meeting just made things…worse."

"Any contact with Bertrand LaFont always causes discomfort. The guy's so slimy he makes wet gummy worms look dry."

"Regina, honey, you do have a way with words, I'll give you that," my mother said after we all stopped laughing. The old saying about laughter being insanity's closest relative never rang truer.

"Thank goodness I don't plan on stepping foot inside his office ever again. I will always envision him as a pink, round and wet gummy worm now. Thanks, Regina," I said, wiping the coffee from my mouth.

"Melody, what did you find out that makes you unwilling to go back and talk to him?"

Here it comes, Mom. Lord, brace her heart.

"After I left the jail, I was a mess. Confused. Unsure what to believe. I mean, I wanted to believe Jack. *Needed* to believe that my husband wasn't capable of such vile things the police say he did. But, when he told me about…the motive, I sort of flipped out. All I could think about was seeing the evidence against him with my own eyes. So, that's why I went to Bertrand's office. He basically interrogated me for about fifteen minutes, which I expected to happen. Then, when he tried to nonchalantly question me about my whereabouts and intimated that I might have had something to do with this, I took over. Shut him down and insisted he show me what evidence the police had on Jack."

"See, slimeball. Just like I said. To think he had the nerve to question *you.*"

"Standard line of questioning, Regina. He wouldn't be a very good lawyer if he didn't ask. Anyway, he showed me security footage from The Duchess and a picture from that lingerie shop at Park Hill Plaza…" I choked on the last sentence, unable to hold back the tears any longer, "It…was…Jack. Oh God, it was *Jack!"*

Regina and Mom both stood up and came over to me. I melted into their warm embraces and wept like a newborn kitten for what seemed an eternity. At last, between their loving strokes and softly spoken words of comfort, the tears dried up.

My mother cupped my chin in her gnarled hands and spoke quietly, her watery blue eyes soft yet determined. "Honey, are you one hundred percent certain it was Jack? I mean, did you really feel it in here?" she asked as she moved one hand over my heart.

"Mom, I know my husband."

"Baby, eyesight isn't always reliable. Things can get distorted, especially when you are upset. Images can be altered. The soul, on the other hand, always knows the truth. The soul is our connection to God, and He never lies to us, we just fail to listen. Now, answer my question. Did you feel it in your soul?"

"I…I…I don't know."

"Then, until you do, Jack needs your support."

Aghast, I pulled my head away in shock. "Mother! You didn't...you weren't...you haven't *seen* nor heard...what he said, what he did..."

"Melody Marie, don't you sass me. I may be old, but I'm no fool. I've known that boy just as long as you have. I've seen the way he looks at you. The way he doted on you. How destroyed he was when the doctors told you there was no more hope for children. No man, except your father, has loved a woman like he loves you. Now, I realize that he committed the sin of straying outside his marriage bed, but that don't make him a killer. I'm shocked that you have already condemned him as guilty. I didn't raise you like that."

"How can you stick up for him, Mom? He *cheated* on me! He admitted to it. To my face! He knocked up Serena and panicked when she threatened to tell me. I saw the video of him going into her hotel room, Mom. I watched him slam his fist into her face when she opened the door. Saw the picture of him buying the underwear. The same kind she was killed with. I'm not condemning him. He did that to himself already."

Mom rose from her spot at the table, walked over to the sink, and dumped her remaining coffee while I sat shaking, my anger on full boil. Mixed emotions spun through me. I loved my mother but didn't understand why she was being so blind. I was her daughter. She should be standing next to me holding the rope while I verbally strung Jack up by his lying words. *Why is she supporting him when I need it?*

"Melody, I'm going to bed. I suggest you do the same. Your emotions are on high alert right now, and ain't nobody in the world ever solved a dilemma when their thoughts are hotter than a firecracker. Put aside your anger and listen to what God is saying to your heart. I have been, and at no time have I heard Him condemn Jack for killing that girl. Only for adultery. I suggest you don't throw that first stone before you get your answer. I love you," she whispered as she walked out of the kitchen. "Goodnight."

My mouth hung open as I watched her pad off to bed, her back erect with almost righteous indignation.

"She sure can give quite a speech, can't she?" Regina remarked.

I swung my gaze over to Regina, my heart pounding with anger. She looked as confused as I felt. Her enormous green eyes were like saucers. No wonder. What a show she just witnessed.

I respected my mother enough not to unleash what I was really thinking within earshot, so I stood up, grabbed my mug, and headed out the back door. Simba followed me like a shadow, her soft fur rubbing against my bare legs. I walked through the damp grass to the swing and sat down.

I knew my best friend wouldn't leave me hanging and sure enough, I heard the flick of her lighter behind me.

"Got another?"

"Mel, you quit ten years ago. Don't."

"Regina. No lectures, please?"

Regina's bare feet were silent as she walked around and sat down next to me in the swing. Reluctantly she reached into her pocket and handed me the pack and the lighter. My hands were trembling so much that I couldn't control my fingers enough to light the cigarette.

Regina lit it for me with obvious reluctance. "When you die of lung cancer at the ripe old age of a hundred, please don't blame me."

The large plume of white smoke left my lungs with practiced ease. Ten years away from the toxic chemicals and yet it seemed like just yesterday I'd had one. "I will place blame exactly where it belongs: Jack."

"Don't you think Jack's got enough on his blame card, Mel?"

"Oh, please don't tell me you have decided to jump the *SS Melody* too? Because trust me, the *SS Jack* is like the *Titanic*. It's going down, fast. Iceberg, dead ahead."

Regina took a heavy drag of her smoke. A twinge of guilt for putting her in the midst of this whole mess stabbed at my chest.

"I'm not taking any sides here. I'm like Switzerland at the moment. It wouldn't be fair for me to cast my vote in either direction based solely off of our friendship without seeing the evidence for myself, now would it? The Melody I know, you know, the one who works for a defense attorney, would suggest that all the evidence and a heavy dose of common sense and gut feelings be taken into account before a verdict is reached. Am I wrong?"

I glared at her and blew out the last drag. "It's a little different when it's *your* life that's been turned upside down. I mean, yes, in theory, you're correct. All circumstances surrounding a crime need to be taken into consideration. What you and my mother seem to forget is that I have done all that. I went and talked to Jack. I listened to what he had to say. I looked at the evidence against him. There isn't a crack, not one sliver. He admitted to the affair. He told me about the pregnancy. Those things are motive, Regina. And yes, he may have told me the truth about some things, but he lied about others."

"Such as?" Regina prompted.

"First of all, he told me he left the hotel around ten Saturday morning. That part was true and verified by the timestamp on the security footage. But, he also told me that after he left, he drove around in a daze, went to Sheridan to visit his parents' graves, drove aimlessly for hours and then came home late Saturday night. That part was a lie. Less than twenty minutes after he left Serena's hotel room, he came back. Saw it with my own disbelieving eyes."

"What else did he lie about?"

"Said he didn't buy the underwear for her. Swore that he'd never been inside a lingerie store in his life. But the picture of him holding the panties told a different story. So you tell me, what am I supposed to think? I mean, the cold, hard truth slapped me in the face yesterday. There is no ignoring it. I would be a fool if I did."

"I just can't believe—"

"That he did it? How the hell do you think I feel? I mean, I'm numb," I said, motioning for another cigarette before I continued.

"When I saw him walk in to the visiting room, my heart broke. My first thought was *my poor baby.* He looked awful. His face was gaunt from lack of food and sleep. He had a large cut over his eye that looked infected. Someone clocked him, a jailer I think. The wife in me mourned for her husband. But it wasn't long before the scorned woman in me took over. Especially after he told me…about…"

"I can't imagine how you must feel. And honestly, all joking aside, I don't know what to do. Or say. I just know that I love you and I'm here for you, whatever you decide to do, whatever direction you move. Because, I'll tell you, if I were in your shoes, I wouldn't know what to do."

"You were, once. If I recall circumstances correctly, you pulled a gun on A.J."

"True. But I caught him in bed with the little trollop. Temporary insanity. Once that passed, I just divorced him and am now enjoying half of all his money."

"You were a basket case, Regina. I know you remember. One minute you wanted to kill him, the next, you wanted to bring him back to the marital bed and show him what he was missing. You loved him and hated him with equal intensity and sometimes, at the same time."

"You're right, I did. So again, as I said a minute ago, I can't image what I'd do if I were in your shoes. No matter what you do, you'll always be my hero."

I didn't respond, inhaling the cigarette like there was no tomorrow. The babbling river below us, the endless chirps of the katydids, the faint moos of the cows—they did nothing to help calm me. They were a stark reminder that life goes on for others even when your own life has come to an abrupt halt.

After about five minutes of silence, Regina asked, "Mel, if all the other mess wasn't a part of this, and the only thing you were dealing with at the moment was Jack's infidelity, would you have forgiven him? I mean, would you have wanted to save your marriage?"

I flicked the spent butt across the yard, watching the faint red glow from the end sail across the expanse. It landed without a sound in the damp grass and went out, the light from the fire extinguished forever.

Sort of like my life.

"I don't know, Regina. I don't know anything anymore."

****

Mom and Regina were asleep in separate rooms of the cabin. I listened to their faint snoring and felt a stirring of jealousy inside, wishing I could just shut my mind down and do the same. For the past four hours I'd paced the floors so much that my feet were numb. Unable to take another step, I collapsed on the couch and Simba joined me, snuggling close. I couldn't help but wonder how Roger would react to having a hairy dog on his fine leather.

Turning the television on wasn't a risk I was willing to take. The way things had been going, it would be tuned to the channel that just happened to be running a rehash of local news and my worst nightmare would be blazing across the screen. Roger wouldn't be too happy if I told him that I broke his television set in a fit of anger.

The thought of trying to read a book almost made me laugh out loud. Like I could even concentrate on one sentence, much less a paragraph or chapter. Struggling to fight the nervous energy, I went to the kitchen and found Regina's smokes on the counter. I grabbed them and my cell phone, opened the back door and slipped into the early morning air, Simba right on my heels.

Situated in the swing with a cigarette lit, I decided to clear out all the unwanted garbage on my phone. Three hundred emails. Seventy-eight missed phones calls and thirty-seven voicemails. Sixty-two text messages.

Good thing I can't sleep. This is going to take hours.

I ignored the emails and pushed the button to clear all my notifications. Then I dialed my voicemail, sat back in awe and listened, almost grateful for the mundane to take my mind off the impossible.

My mother. Regina. Roger. My dentist office confirming my appointment on Tuesday. Jack's boss, Everett. Every major news anchor from all three stations wanting a comment. The mortgage company wanting to know where this month's mortgage payment was at and to please call them. Bertrand, asking me to come in and speak with him.

To erase this message, press 7. Delete. Delete. Delete.

The last three messages were from Kendal, Jack's best friend. My throat tightened when I heard his choked up voice.

"Mel. It's Kendal. I...I just got back in town and heard about what happened. I don't...oh God, are you okay? Please, call me back and let me know if there is anything you need. I'm here for you. And for Jack."

"Mel, it's Kendal again. I'm really worried about you. Went by the house today to check on you and didn't see your car. Called your office and they said you were out. I can't imagine that you feel like talking, but please, send me a text or something and let me know you're okay. Please?"

"Mel, it's Kendal. I saw you today...walking outside the jail. I...I was going to go visit Jack, too, if they'd let me. But, when I saw you, I left. At least I know you're okay. If you feel like talking, call me."

I couldn't believe I'd forgotten about Kendal. Guilt at my selfishness punched me in the chest. Jack and Kendal were closer than flesh and blood brothers. They looked enough alike in the face to pass as kin. Their friendship had started in the sixth grade and never faltered. Kendal was the best man at our wedding, and a permanent fixture almost every weekend at our house, especially during football and basketball season. They were as close as Regina and I were, if not closer.

My guilt morphed over to irritation the more I thought along those lines. They were close. Did Jack tell Kendal about the affair? Did he confide his transgressions to his best friend, maybe seeking guidance, redemption or spiritual support? Even, maybe, to brag about his new squeeze?

I deleted the last voicemail and clicked over to my text messages. The most recent one was from Kendal, sent about three hours ago.

Mel, praying for you both

Kendal was right—I didn't feel like talking. But suspicion niggled away at me until I couldn't stand it anymore, so I decided to send him a text.

I'm okay. Laying low for a bit. Things are not good. Not in mood to talk on phone, but wanted to say I'm sorry I haven't responded until now.

Regina's pack of smokes was half gone and my mouth tasted like a dirty ashtray, but I didn't care. I lit another one and waited as the sun began to rise over the hill to see if Kendal was up and would respond. I didn't have to wait long.

Oh Mel! Good to hear from you. This is just awful. A nightmare. Are you somewhere safe? What can I do to help?

I decided not to tippy-toe around and just flat out ask him.

Nightmare is putting it mildly. Need to know something. Kendal, did you know about the affair?

Less than fifteen seconds later, my phone buzzed in my hand.

No, Mel. I didn't. I would have said something to you or convinced Jack to tell you. You know how I feel about that subject

Indeed I did. Kendal had been married for six years to a woman who cheated on him so many times we all lost count. When he decided to end the marriage, she beat him to the punch and drained his bank account before splitting town with one of her lovers. Poor Kendal came close to a nervous breakdown. Hit the bottle heavy for two years until Jack convinced him to get help. We watched him go from a destroyed man to a new one when he gave his life over to the Lord. He'd been standing on the solid rock of his faith ever since. My guilt came back for even suspecting he knew.

Mel, please, call me? I hate this form of communication. It's worse than social media

Jack's parents were dead and like me he had no siblings, so the only person who knew him better than I did in the world was Kendal. The urge to hear his voice hit me hard, so before I could stop myself, I pushed the button and called him. He answered on the first ring.

"Thank goodness. My fingers were getting tired."

"Hey Kendal. I'm…I'm sorry I waited so long."

"Mel, please don't be. I'm surprised you're even coherent. I'd be a drooling fool. Almost am as it is."

"Oh, I've already had several breakdowns. One of them was on top of Pinnacle yesterday. Another was inside the jail. Fell face down in front of a crowded room of visitors and inmates. Fainted dead away in Roger's office on Monday when I…found out about Serena. Blew up at my mother, my boss, my best friend. It's been fun."

"Girl, I always knew you were strong but this is like Greek lore. You're a regular Hercules."

"Well, like Hercules, fire can kill him. This firestorm has burnt me. To a crisp."

"But, you're still standing. So, are you back at home?"

I sighed and lit another cigarette. "No, but I'm going back tomorrow. Roger said the police finally cleared me to go back. Can't wait to see the mess they left. My house is probably in shambles. At least I'll have the weekend to work on cleaning up. Besides, I'm tired of not sleeping in my own house. Roger's place is nice, but it isn't home."

"That was really nice of him, letting you get away from not only work but the prying eyes of the media. Isn't his place in Mount Pine, deep in the woods?"

"No, Caddo Valley. But as much as I appreciate him letting me hide here, I have to go back to reality and start trying to pick up the pieces. I have to function as the sole bread-winner, which means I have to keep my job. There's no telling how long all of this will last or how much it will cost. And whether I end up spending the rest of my life alone while Jack is behind bars."

Kendal sighed. "So, you went to see him. Do you want to talk about it?"

I knew that wasn't the only reason Kendal asked. He wanted to know if the man he had loved for longer than I did admitted to taking the life of another. "Look, Kendal. I know you want to talk about this and really, I understand the need to. You love Jack. He's your best friend. I love Jack. But our love for him doesn't change what's happened."

"Oh Mel, there's just no way. Jack wouldn't...he couldn't...the news reports are just filthy lies."

"Kendal. I read the autopsy report. Viewed the mountain of evidence against him and watched some of it with my own eyes. The case against him isn't just circumstantial. It's a slam dunk."

"Did you meet with the police today?"

"No, I went to see his lawyer, Bertrand LaFont, after I left the jail. When Jack dropped the bomb on me, I went straight to Bertrand's office. Roger said the police still want to talk to me, but I knew I couldn't handle that meeting without losing my marbles. Turns out, my meeting with Bertrand wasn't any better. Guess the venue really doesn't matter when you get blindsided with what I saw today."

Uncomfortable silence ensued. I couldn't bring myself to rehash the events of yesterday and I sensed Kendal didn't want to know the gory details that would seal the coffin on his friendship with Jack. Fatigue bore down on me and I found it difficult to keep my eyes open. I decided the insects had fed enough on my blood and that I should go inside and attempt to get some rest. My eyes were getting heavy and my head was pounding from all the squinting the last several hours. I cursed my weak eyes.

"Kendal, listen, I'm exhausted and I need—"

"Please, don't apologize, Mel. Go, get some sleep. Thanks for calling me back. I've…I've really been worried about you. If you need any help cleaning up this weekend, call me, okay?"

"Sure thing. Listen, one favor?"

"Anything. Shoot."

"Pray. For all of us. Because I can't seem to do that right now."

"Always, Mel. Always."

I disconnected the call without another word. I could hear the pain in Kendal's voice and knew our conversation would be relived later through his tears, and my own.

Simba followed me back inside and curled up next to me on the couch. Thankfully, sleep came quickly for us both.

****

The water was cold but not freezing. The brilliant azure liquid shimmered all around me as I floated effortlessly under the waves. The tranquil silence enveloped me in a state of bliss and I watched colorful sea creatures swim by, oblivious to my intrusion into their world. I looked up and watched the sun sparkle through the depths and felt myself smile.

Basking in the comforting water, my eyes soaked in the beautiful surroundings. Free and unchained, my body moved without my prodding, bringing me closer to a school of candy-colored fish. The montage of color turned the blue sea into a living rainbow as the fish swam in practiced unison.

Drifting inside their midst, I realized the colors weren't from the fish. The fish weren't fish at all—they were floating pictures of my life with Jack. The water seemed warmer as it embraced me, my heart swelling with love at the memories in front of me.

Jack and I on our first date, the first tender kiss received in full view of the sparkling stars on the park bench under a magnolia tree. Jack and I at the zoo the day he arranged for a private tour of the newborn tigers, the smallest one with a bow around its neck, my engagement ring daintily swaying from the end of the ribbon. Jack in his tuxedo as he stood at the altar while I walked down the aisle, his grin brighter than the candles surrounding him. The day we signed the papers and bought our first house, and celebrated with a passionate evening of lovemaking in front of the fireplace. Yet another of the evening he saved me from falling into the fire pit and ended up burning his hand.

Even though I was underwater, I could feel the tears fall from my eyes. My husband, my lover, my best friend and soul mate. The man God sent to me and my reason for getting out of bed each day. His smiling face, his lovely rugged features, and his dark curly hair—my heart pined for it all.

"Yet you doubt him," whispered the voice of my mother, her words like a dagger thrust inside my heart.

The water turned cold and blood red, and the happy images vanished. I realized I was sinking, unable to move my limbs to swim to the surface.

"But I saw…" I shouted in my head.

"You didn't look with your heart. Look again."

The image of the hallway appeared, and I watched Jack exit the elevator and approach the room, almost in slow motion. This time, I noticed something.

His gait was wrong. His shoulders were too narrow, the thighs too thin. The curls that peeked out from under the ball cap were too loose to be Jack's. His hair was much curlier. Thicker. Coarser. The image changed; now it showed the man approaching a hotel room door, moving past a large vase of flowers on the small table in the hallway. I could see the tips of the flowers above his head. My mind conjured up the image of Jack leaving the same hotel room and watched him pass the same flowers. I couldn't see the tips.

Because the man who walked by was shorter by at least one full inch.

The video image disappeared, replaced by the enlarged picture from the lingerie store. My eyes were immediately drawn to the hand holding the underwear.

There was no scar. The hand that held the silky panties didn't belong to Jack.

"Now do you see?"

Yes, yes! Oh my God—it's not Jack! Praise Jesus, it's not my Jack!

A surge of adrenaline kicked me into gear and I found I could control my limbs. I swam toward the intense light on the surface, my heart bursting with renewed vigor.

And love.

****

I jerked up from the couch like a bolt of lightning had just shot through me. Simba started barking as she followed me through the living room and into my mom's room. Mom was sitting on the edge of the bed tying her shoes.

"Mom, oh my God! You were right—Jack didn't kill her!"

"Child, calm down. I can't understand you when you talk so fast."

My noisy entrance to the real world seemed to have woken Regina, and she stumbled into the room, her hair sticking every which way from a rough night's sleep. "What's going on?"

"I missed it, I totally missed it!"

My mother grabbed my hand and pulled me down to sit on the bed. Her voice was calm, quiet. "Missed what, honey?"

"His scar! You know the one on his hand from when he got burned so badly? In my dream, the things I saw yesterday appeared. The picture at the lingerie store—it wasn't Jack. The guy in the photo doesn't have a scar. Plus, the hair isn't curly enough. Too stringy. And the body type—it's smaller than Jack's and the killer is at least an inch shorter. Oh Mom, you were so on target. I feel it, right here," I said, pointing to my chest, "someone else killed Serena. Not my Jack."

"Glory be to the Heavens, girl. Prayers have been answered," my mother said, and hugged my neck with ferocious intensity. "See what happens when you rely on Him to guide you? You were blind, but now you see."

"Amen, Mom. Amen."

Tears streaked down Regina's face as she moved in for a group hug. Her voice was muffled when she asked, "So, what now, Mel?"

Through my tears of joy, I answered, "I'm going to do everything in my power to help free my husband from jail for a crime that I know he didn't commit."

****

Regina shut her trunk when the last bit of luggage was loaded, and I hugged her neck. "Thank you. For everything. You are coming over tonight, right?"

She smiled, her face covered in sweat. The heat was unbearable already and it was only ten o'clock in the morning. "Well duh. Like I'm going to let you tackle the house by yourself. I'm the obsessive-compulsive one, remember? There's no way I'm going to let you tackle that mess alone."

I pressed my sweaty forehead up against hers and smiled. "In case I haven't told you today, I love you."

"Love, is a many splendored thing...la la la don't know the rest of the words," Regina quipped. I shook my head at her purposefully poor rendition of the classic song. Regina never had been able to handle deep emotions without becoming a blubbering fool, and tended to hide behind sarcasm. She pulled away from me, trying to hide the tears in her eyes. I smiled and watched as she hopped into her car and sped off. My focus shifted over to my mother, who was trying to lug her heavy suitcase out the door.

"Mom, please. Let me."

"I'm not an invalid, Melody Marie. I'll get this and take a quick gander inside to make sure we didn't leave anything. You go take that dog of yours for a walk. It's too hot outside to be stopping along the way."

"Yes ma'am," I said as a smile crossed my face. Mom surely was the tough old bird she claimed to be. And stubborn as a mule and feisty to boot. She was also the person I admired the most on this earth because of her strong faith. Though I doubted I would ever admit it out loud, I knew that God had spoken through her yesterday to reach me. He planted the seed in me, using my mother as the vessel to deliver the message. Ever since my dream earlier, I realized I hadn't felt this strong and close to God in years. No longer was the dark, never-ending hole inside me, the one that had been filled with fear, anxiety, worry, pain and anger. It almost was like the water from my dream somehow cleansed me, washing all the darkness away and filling me with hope.

Thank you, God, for allowing her to be my mother.

I opened the back door and Simba lunged out, nearly knocking me over. "Come on girl, get busy. We're going home."

Simba sniffed and snorted around the yard until she found the perfect spot to do her business. I walked over to the swing and stared across the Caddo River valley, watching the swift moving water race through the twists and turns cut into the mountainside. The humidity was near eighty percent and sweat plastered my shirt against my chest and back like a second suit. The birds flitted about their merry morning rituals, matched only in dedication by the squirrels that jumped from tree to tree. I saw the hint of pink out of the corner of my eye and smiled, recognizing that it was a resurrection lily. They were one of my favorite flowering bulbs not only for their beauty, but the legend behind them. The poem from my youth popped into my head.

This delicate flower
Is nature's way
Of reminding us what is to come
On that sweet, blessed day.

We are like the spring greenery
That shoots forth to the sky,
Before full beauty is reached,
We all must die.

To achieve our glory
We need the Master's touch.
He cares for us in His garden
Because He loves us so much.

Unwilling to cry anymore, I shook the poem from my thoughts and opted to not pick the delicate flower from its spot against the house. Roger obviously enjoyed them too, since the entire flowerbed was bursting with pink. I couldn't help but feel that their presence was another sign from God. A sign of a new life, new hope, and new direction. Plucking one wouldn't hurt, but I'd already invaded every other spot of Roger's house. I wanted to leave some things untouched. Normal.

"Come on Simba, let's go home."

Furry tail wagging like a flag, Simba danced around me like a puppy, like she knew we were leaving. Once I got her situated in the back seat and the air conditioner on full blast, I took one last look at my hideaway and backed out of the driveway.

"Honey, your phone has been going crazy. Keeps beepin' and buzzin. You—"

I reached out and grabbed my mother's delicate hand, brought it to my lips and kissed it gently.

"Not now, mom. I want to tell you all about my dream. There will be plenty of time to play catch up once I get home. So," I began, releasing her cool hand to mute my cell phone and the radio, then focusing my attention back to my rock, "I was underneath the ocean, or in a lake or something, not a care in the world, full of peace and tranquility. The water was warm, comforting…"

****

"Mom, are you sure you want to come stay? There's no telling what mess awaits me at the house. Wouldn't you like to wait until at least tomorrow, give me and Regina a chance to at least create a path to walk through?"

"Melody, you're acting like a tornado ripped through your house or something! I'm sure it will be messy, but manageable. I doubt walls have been torn down or holes punched in the floor. So yes, I am sure. Let me just run inside and get another change of clothes and my other shoes. I'll be right back."

Before I could protest, my stubborn mother was out of the car. I watched as she walked through the carport and unlocked the side door, then disappeared inside. I hoped she would hurry. Simba was drooling all over the back seat and my shoulder, her hot breath making the car smell like dog chow.

Mom was back in a flash and I backed out of the driveway, grateful she only lived three miles from my house. I was afraid that Simba's bladder was as close to bursting as my own. I turned onto my street, jabbering away with Mom about my plans for the day.

"Let me get you situated and then make a few phone calls. I need to go by and give my statement to the police and then go and see Roger. Gotta make sure I still have a job. Hey, look, Regina beat us here. And Kendal and Roger are here too! Looks like the cleaning brigade decided to arrive early! Goodness, what a great boss Roger is—after all he's done for me—for us—I won't be able to ask for a raise for years."

"That's my girl—acknowledging her blessings. God takes care of his children, even the ones who've wandered from the fold. Our Heavenly Father doesn't stop loving us even when we walk away from Him. Parents are like that, you know."

I smiled at my mother's gentle urging to go back to church and start my relationship with the Lord again. She was right, though I didn't like admitting it. Jack and I both lost our footing when we started walking our own paths, away from the solid ground of faith. Once he was home, that would change.

I pulled into the driveway with a smile on my face, grateful that Regina decided to come early and that Kendal and Roger were here as well. Regina didn't have a job to call in sick to since she was divorcee-wealthy, but Kendal did. And Roger had a large law firm to run, and was doing so without his paralegal. I tried to mentally review his calendar, wondering if he had court today. I came up blank.

God, I'll be glad when all this is over and I can actually concentrate on things again. Jack will be home soon and we can work on restoring our marriage. It'll be a tough climb, but we can do it.

It was sweet of Kendal to blow off work on a sunny Friday afternoon to come help me, rather than smacking around a few golf balls like he often did when he played hooky. It was above and beyond the call of duty for Roger to show up. I couldn't imagine my wealthy boss helping clean my police-ransacked house. Since I paid his monthly bills, I knew he didn't clean his own place in town, or the cabin. He paid a service to come and perform the boring, mundane household chores that he did not have time for. I almost laughed out loud trying to envision him scrubbing a toilet. Maybe he'd just come to supervise our clean-up efforts, ready to record any permanent damage that the CSI team might have done to my house. All of them must have known that I would be devastated when I walked inside my house for the first time.

Thank you, Lord, for surrounding me with such good friends and a wonderful boss.

The heat hit me like a wrecking ball when I opened the car door and stepped outside. Thunder rumbled in the distance as dark, ominous storm clouds loomed overhead. Mom was terrified of storms ever since she'd experienced two tornadoes in her youth. One destroyed the farmhouse she grew up in while she cowered in the storm shelter with her parents. The other was almost thirty years ago when she and Dad were on vacation in Missouri. That monster twister roared through the town and leveled it. I needed to hurry up and get her, and our luggage, inside before the inevitable torrent of rainfall hit.

"Hey guys! Thanks for…wait, what's wrong?" I asked, stopping short when I saw the looks on all their faces. My stomach rolled as a wave of fear overtook my body. Gut instincts told me something was wrong.

And the thunder rolls, the lightning strikes…

Tears were streaming down Regina's face and she wasn't trying to hide them. Other than the last few days, I'd only seen her cry twice—when A.J. broke her heart and when her father died eight years ago. Her eyes were swollen, the rims beet red, like she'd been crying for quite a while. The tissues in her hand shook as she hurried to wipe the wetness off her face before I saw her tears. I glanced over at Kendal, who wouldn't look at me, his hands shoved deep inside his pockets, his head staring down at his feet. I saw tears drip off his face and land on his shoes and started shaking as I backed away from them.

I looked at Roger and time seemed to stop. He was pale, his eyes unreadable covered with sunglasses, his jaw clenched shut like a steel trap. He stood in the middle of Regina and Kendal, a supportive arm draped over each of their shoulders. With a pat on both their backs he moved away, unwilling to look my direction as he headed for the passenger side of my car.

"Mel, honey, let's go inside," Regina choked out as she nodded toward the door, "come on, Roger can help your Mom and Kendal can get Simba."

Ice filled my veins as fear travelled through me at a sickening pace. Kendal raised his head and looked at me, and I saw the devastation in his eyes.

He looks like...a man who just lost his best friend. Oh God, no...

My face crumpled as I shifted my gaze between the two of them, my own tears springing forth and clouding my vision with a wet haze. My body sagged against the doorframe while I shook my head violently back and forth. "No, no, no, no! Please, go away! Don't say another word. I can't hear this...oh God..."

"Melody, honey, what's wrong?"

I heard my mother ask the question and it registered somewhere inside me that Roger had helped her out of the car. Roger's deep baritone voice was whispering to her, but I couldn't make out a word he said. I was lost inside my own world, trying desperately to escape the real one barreling down on me with more intensity than the storm that surrounded us. I clung to the doorframe of my car and closed my eyes, willing this to all be a dream. The horror hit me that I was truly awake when I heard my mother's weak voice say, "Oh no. Oh Jack. Dear Jesus."

I sensed Kendal's body near me, his pain a living entity that seeped over and wrapped itself around my heart, cloaking my soul with the dark news. I opened my eyes and whispered, "No, please. Jack's okay, right?"

"Oh Mel, he's gone. I'm so sorry," he whispered back and pulled me close, his sobs of grief indecipherable from my own.

CHAPTER 11 – TUESDAY AFTERNOON

When I die don't cry for me
In my father's arms I'll be
The wounds this world left on my soul
Will all be healed and I'll be whole
It don't matter where you bury me
I'll be home and I'll be free

OUR SMALL GATHERING OF CLOSE FAMILY AND friends listened to the soothing voice of the pastor sing the haunting lyrics of Jack's favorite hymn, *All My Tears*. Regina sat on my left, my mother on my right, each one holding my hand in gentle clasps as the pastor began the service. My husband's funeral service—a place no woman ever wants to be sitting in the front row as the last goodbyes are said.

Ever.

I couldn't get the words to register right in my head. I understood the meaning, but not the application to my life. *Widow.* My new life, alone as a widow at forty-three. It made no sense. My eyes settled on the small slab of concrete, where some unknown hand had carved the name *Jackson Tyler "Jack" Dickinson* followed by his birth date and the day he'd died in the gray stone. The intricate lettering was no different than the other headstones that stood alone, erect pillars aged by the weather and time, a last monument to the once living bodies now forever entombed underground.

Jack's headstone lay on the ground, waiting for the service to finish so the gravediggers could set it up and end their day. Once we left and the final touches were completed, Jack's final resting place under the watchful eye of the weeping willow trees would be quiet. And alone.

Just like the grave.

The drone of the preacher sounded like a bee buzzing around my ear. I heard it but didn't pay attention. My mind wandered over to the events of the last four days after the news broke that I was now a widow.

I'd cried out all the tears my eyes could possibly produce, mourning the sudden loss of my soul mate. The first few days, my thoughts ran amok, my mind close to snapping. One minute I blamed God for Jack's allergies, and the next, I blamed the jail for allowing him to be injured, then waiting too long to provide adequate treatment, until the wound had festered and required antibiotics. Then I shifted and blamed Jack for not knowing he was allergic to penicillin and for starting this whole sordid mess in motion by stepping out of our marriage bed. I blamed the detectives for arresting an innocent man. I even blamed the medical examiner, who told me in his most solemn, practiced voice when I questioned what happened that "anyone, anytime, can become allergic to any given item".

While bouncing from one end of the blame spectrum to the other, I discovered my tears wouldn't stop. Mom, Regina and Kendal tried to comfort me, but their attempts were hopelessly lost on me. That first day was a blur. I had collapsed into the arms of Kendal, practically catatonic, my heart frozen as Regina and Kendal drove me to the coroner's office to identify Jack's cold, lifeless body. When the coroner pulled the sheet back and I stared at the swollen, almost unrecognizable face of the man I loved, a huge part of me died. The last image I would take with me, the most recent, fresh one, was his dead body. I acknowledged that it was Jack with a solemn nod of my head and a cavalcade of tears shed on Kendal's strong shoulder. On the drive home, none of us spoke a single word, each lost inside our grief.

For the next two days, I stayed locked inside Jack's office and went through the little remaining pieces of paper, shreds of clothing and files left behind by the police, just to smell him before his scent dwindled away with time. I threw back glass after glass of wine on an empty stomach while I looked at photographs of our life together until I couldn't focus my eyes another moment and passed out. The next morning, I woke up and repeated the process.

On Monday morning the tears stopped. They dried up like the last remaining rain drop in the Sahara desert. Poof—gone. The blame game had its final contestant and the winner was chosen.

Me.

I'd let my own pride, my own pain, my own wants and needs come before Jack's. Worse, I let my anger push me away from God. My heart had been embroiled in turmoil. I longed for a child and it consumed everything inside of me once the reality hit home that it wasn't to be. Six months ago, I started experiencing the first symptoms of menopause, which sealed the coffin on the little hope I'd kept alive in the back of my mind.

Jack, noticing my moments of internal spontaneous combustion, tried to convince me to consider adoption. We had just started tackling the mounds of paperwork and background checks less than five months ago, after I gave in to his endless pleadings. It would satisfy his longing for a child and, in a way, mine too, but it wasn't the same for me. I felt less than a woman—not whole, broken—for not being able to do what my body was created to do.

I lost myself in the agony of knowing I would never feel the excitement of watching the stick turn blue, find some creative way to tell Jack we were pregnant, or feel a part of us move inside my belly. Never would I experience the strange food cravings, watch my belly swell with our growing child. We would never get to lie in bed at night and whisper our hopes and dreams, worries and fears for our baby. No first step. No first words. No kissing boo-boos or wiping tears away. No first day of school, date, driving lesson, prom, graduation, marriage or grandchildren.

Nothing.

I was lost inside the empty shell of my womb, unable to find my way out of the darkness.

I'd watched Jack suffer but turned a blind eye, some-how convincing myself my pain was worse than his. I hadn't just lost interest in sex, but intimacy. When Jack would come near me, even just to be close, I brushed him away. Not because I didn't love him, but because I feared the sadness that, in recent years, followed intimate contact between the two of us. It was a reminder of my inability to conceive a child, and it was easier to deal with Jack's an-noyance than face my own pain.

Plus, being in Jack's arms was a painful reminder that, after all, it was my fault that we couldn't have children. It was a shameful, dirty little secret why my womb was a barren wasteland and one no one else knew about. For twenty-two years, I'd kept the secret, burying it deeper than what I was watching happen to Jack's body.

But yesterday morning, in the midst of Jack's papers and clothes, his scent already fading, I sat on the floor and felt the shame of my selfishness burn my tears away. Shame, for not standing by him when he needed me the most and for not believing him when I watched him beg for my forgiveness and vehemently bemoan his innocence. Devastating humiliation, for so callously turning my back on him when I should have granted him the same forgiveness for his mistakes as God granted to His children for their sins. The last words I ever said to the man who loved me were *you bastard.*

That realization filled me with renewed fervor amidst the pain. God had taken my husband home and left me here for a reason. And that day, on the messy floor of Jack's office, I knew why God left me here. I knew it would be an incredibly difficult journey, fraught with stumbling blocks and self-doubt, but I made the commitment to stand strong.

As Pastor Trent spoke about Jack and his new home above, my mother and Regina gripped my hands tighter, trying to convey comfort, love and support through their squeezes.

But I felt none of it. It was like I was dead inside, no different than the corpse of my husband less than ten feet from me.

Jack was gone, only his hollow shell resting inside the sleek, black coffin. A tube covered with a huge spray of pink lilies—Jack's favorite flower. His essence, his soul, were free of the bonds of the sinful flesh. For a split second, I envied him. I watched the beams of the late afternoon sun sparkle across the rounded top, mesmerized by the intensity of the light and heat waves that rolled off of it. Like a moth drawn to the flame, my eyes were transfixed on the casket that housed the earthly remains of Jack. It sat on top of the metal apparatus that would lower it into the ground, next to the grave of his parents. Forever entombed in the rocky ground of Ten Mile Cemetery in Sheridan.

"Join him, Melody. Join me. Join us. It's easy. Just climb inside and close the lid. The darkness will give you comfort," the voice of my grandmother beckoned, piercing through my mind. Her sweet, southern drawl flowed like

warm sugar, coaxing my body to heed her words. *"Come, unto me. I will give you the rest...the rest of the punishment you deserve. The eternal damnation we all deserve. Ha ha ha ha ha..."*

A shudder of fear shot through me as the voice I recalled from my youth changed into a guttural hiss, mocking me. I closed my eyes and fought for strength and control of my own thoughts. *Get thee behind me, Satan. You ruled my thoughts once—I won't let you again. Jesus, give me strength.*

"Don't go gettin' all righteous on me, girl. I didn't abandon him in jail—you did. Called him a bastard and walked out. Broke his heart, yes ma'am, you surely did. I heard him cryin' in his cell for you, beggin' God for forgiveness for his sins and another chance with you. I tried to reason with him, whispered in his ear that it was your fault for not bein' a good enough wife. Not providin' him an heir to his name, not carin' for his manly needs. But he's here, now, with me. So come on, join the party, honey. We have room...we're waitin'..."

"Oh Jesus, help me," I whispered. Only my mother and Regina heard my desperate plea, and they answered by hugging me close for the duration of the service.

Less than twenty people had attended, which was by design. I refused to let the media feed off the grief of those who loved Jack. They'd already hounded me and my family and friends enough. The frenzied school of blood-thirsty sharks attacked without mercy when the news broke about Jack's death.

My mother balked at the idea of a quiet graveside service at first; her southern traditions of viewings, services, and burials followed by food receptions were ingrained deeply in her psyche. I told her that very few people would be attending the service of a man accused of such a brutal crime, friends included.

She didn't have a valid argument in response to that.

The temperature was near one hundred, which was normal for July, so the service was set to last less than twenty minutes. Under the thin green canopy erected by the funeral home, the thirty chairs situated in neat rows were all empty now, the service concluded, the words meant to comfort the living, spoken. I shook sweaty hands, received damp hugs and tried to listen to the murmured words of encouragement mumbled in hushed tones. I nodded my head at the empty condolences and prayers from Jack's boss, a few of his co-workers, one college friend and a distant cousin on his mother's side. A handful of people from my office came, including Roger, as well as a spattering of old high school friends I hadn't seen in years.

But my core of strength didn't let me weather the storm alone. Mom, Regina and Kendal surrounded me like a brick fortress, shielding me from the sensation of utter helplessness. They deflected nosy questions, scooting the spectators down the receiving line with kind words and smiles. In less than five minutes, the gravel parking lot was empty of the vehicles of the guests. The only cars left were the hearse, the family limousine that would take us back to the funeral home to retrieve our vehicles, and the beat up truck of the gravediggers. The two silent men waited next to the open hole for their cue to lower Jack's casket.

I couldn't move from my chair. I paid no attention to the sweat that ran down my face or the mosquitoes that swarmed. My focus was on the red and white roses that the guests left on top of Jack's coffin. They were already starting to wilt under the hot sun, along with the funeral spray of the pink lilies.

"They are rotting, just like dear old Jack and I are, sweetie. All living things die, then rot away. The worms crawl in, the worms crawl out...Come now, dearie, I know you want to rot away too..."

Everyone was startled when I shot out of my chair. Right away Kendal's protective hand braced my back, probably assuming I would faint or fall over. I shook him off and moved from under the cover of the canopy toward the gravediggers. "I need a few minutes. Alone. Kendal, will you please help my mother to the limo? I need to say goodbye."

My mother stepped over and kissed my cheek, then led the small processional to the cool confines of the limo. The two gravediggers waddled across the grass, eager to sit inside their truck with the air conditioner on as the rain began falling, the droplets tinkling on the top of the casket. Alone at last, I bowed my head and said my peace as the cool water peppered my back.

Jack. My Jack. I'm so sorry for doubting you. I let my hurt and anger blind me to what my heart was trying to say to me. Since you are there now, you probably already know this, but God showed me in a dream the truth. The truth that my heart knew but my angry mind overrode.

You didn't kill Serena. I know that with every fiber of my being. And I'm sorry for not being a better wife, for not seeing and responding to your needs. I was too wrapped up in my own to see your pain. I have forgiven you, and I hope you forgive me. Forgive me for not standing by you, for running away and leaving in a fit of anger. For my last words to you. For not fighting for your freedom sooner. Had I come to my senses earlier, you wouldn't be gone.

I won't let this go, Jack. I won't let the world label you as a killer. I won't let them laugh at your expense, mocking you for dying in jail. I will hunt, search and seek, until my last breath is taken, and find out who did this. I will clear your name. As God almighty is my witness, I will clear your name.

Now that you are with our Savior, I ask just one thing. Please ask Him to give me strength, to run this race and not give up. Not for me. For you. Because I love you so much, Jackson Tyler Dickinson. I love you so much. I promise, I'll make this right, no matter how many roadblocks and tricks the Devil throws at me.

I will, so help me God.

****

The street was quiet, the reporters gone. I breathed a sigh of relief as Kendal maneuvered his SUV into my driveway. My poor neighbors. Prior to all this, our little neighborhood was peaceful. The kind of place where you could walk down the sidewalk without worry, wave hello to your neighbor and see children playing outside until dark. In the last week and a half, the entire block had been subjected to cops, news crews and more cops, causing most of the residents to hide behind locked doors and closed drapes until the onslaught passed.

It was just the five of us now: me, Mom, Regina, Kendal and Roger. Regina had kindly but firmly informed the few mourners at the service that there would be no visitation at the house afterwards. Considering the circumstances around Jack's departure, no one batted an eye.

We walked inside in silence and headed straight to the living room. Simba was still curled up on the same spot in the corner. She hadn't moved from Jack's chair for three days except when I forced her to go outside and pee. She hadn't eaten, either, or come down to check on me. Normally she was a bother under my feet, my little furry shadow that followed me from room to room, eager to be a part of whatever I was doing. But she knew. She sensed that something was wrong, that Jack wasn't coming back. Her animal instincts kicked in and she mourned in her own way the loss of her other master.

Her coat was dull, the vibrant sheen gone. It looked almost dingy gray now rather than ebony. She wound herself into a tight ball and whined every now and then, sometimes licking the arms of the chair or rubbing her face on the backrest. *She wants to remember Jack's scent, too.*

"Come on girl, let's go outside before it starts raining," I said, opening the back door. Her brown eyes looked at me, the sadness unmistakable. I saw her eyes move from Regina to Kendal, then to Roger. A low rumble left her throat, followed by a slow whine. He was an unfamiliar presence in the house and she didn't like it. Simba gingery clambered off the chair onto the floor. She walked through the living room into the kitchen, stopping in front of Kendal to give him a good sniff.

Poor thing, he looks so much like Jack she has to smell him to make sure it isn't. Oh Lord, she's taking this really hard.

Regina opened the fridge door and pulled out the pre-made tray of food she'd prepared earlier. She plucked out a fat shrimp and tossed it to me. "Here, see if Simba will eat this."

"Come on girl. Look, yummy shrimp," I said, wagging the cold carcass in front of her. Despite her yearnings for Jack, she followed her nose, and me, out the door.

I tossed the shrimp across the yard and Simba bounded after it, gobbled it down, and started sniffing around to find her favorite spot. Lightning crackled a few miles away, followed by a loud clap of thunder. The summer had been unseasonably wet in Central Arkansas. All the rain and high humidity made for misery when one dared step outside. I counted the seconds between the bolt of lightning and the roar of the thunder. The storm was about fifteen minutes away, which meant I had enough time to smoke a few cigarettes before the rain came. I sat down in the wicker chair on the deck and reached under the seat for my hidden stash of smokes.

Seriously, who are you hiding them from? Jack's not here to scold you for picking up this nasty habit again. Oh Jack, I wish you were here…

"I thought you quit."

Roger's voice startled me; I hadn't heard him walk up behind me. Before I could light my cigarette, a lighter appeared in front of my face.

"Desperate times call for desperate measures," I replied, leaning toward the flame my boss offered.

"May I?" Roger asked, holding up a slim cigar.

"Of course."

The sweet aroma of black cherry hung in the damp air as Roger puffed away on the stogie. He walked over to the railing at the edge of the deck and tried to pretend he was watching the incoming storm, but I could see he was eye-balling me. It was still a bit unnerving having him here, wallowing in the pit of my troubles right alongside me. Seems once we crossed the unseen line of boss and employee relationship, there was no going back to it.

"Roger, thank you for all you've done during the last week and a half. I couldn't have asked for a more support-ive or understanding employer. Really. I don't know how I can ever repay you."

"Melody, do you remember when Corinne died?"

Indeed I did. I'd only been his assistant for six months when Corinne fell ill. Roger had died a little each day, watching his wife dwindle away as cancer destroyed her body. We had been forced to transfer all his cases to other associates during the last two months of her life so Roger could be by her side and care for her. He'd refused to hire a stranger to come to his house and take care of her, and threw a rip-snorting fit when the doctors suggested she be moved to Hospice care. He declined help from any family members or friends. I suspected he didn't want them to see the deteriorated state of his once beautiful bride. After he told me about her diagnosis, I did a bit of research on the last stages of someone with a brain tumor and was shocked at the symptoms they could suffer from. Corinne had been a vibrant, lovely woman, full of intelligence and grace, not a charity she wouldn't support or help raise money for. Her outward beauty couldn't even hold a candle to her lu-minous soul. I'd surmised that Roger wished to keep those legacies alive rather than the final ones of her slow and agonizing death.

When Corinne succumbed to the tumor inside her brain, Roger took a three month hiatus from work and travelled to the Greek Isles to spread Corinne's ashes over the azure waters of the Mediterranean. He'd told me he was leaving the States for a while to "take Corinne where she always wanted to go", and I realized then what kind of man I worked for. I saw behind the façade of hardened lawyer he put on for the public into the heart of a man who dearly loved his wife and mourned her loss with great sadness. I'd never seen a man so broken.

"Yes, Roger. And I'm sure all of this brings back some horrible memories for you."

"I won't lie—it does. I…I know what you're going through—the pain, the sorrow. Wondering what you could have done different, said different. Did you say 'I love you' enough and did they really know the depth of your feelings? The thought of going to bed terrifies you because you don't want to sleep next to the empty spot alone. The painful memories of what used to be, staring you in the face with each step you take and haunting your dreams. And all that I experienced over a natural, normal death. Your situation has…complications. You're going to need time to get through this, Melody. You need time to sort through the jumbled thoughts in your head, to mourn fully and deeply, and then time to recover. So, what I'm saying is, I want you to take all the time you need to grieve properly all that has befallen you before you come back to work. You have plenty of vacation built up and we'll just get a temp in until you come back. Take whatever time you need." He turned and looked at me, his eyes full of sympathy and moisture. I was taken aback by his candor and it took me a few seconds to regain my faculties.

"You are too kind, Roger. And though I appreciate the offer, I respectfully decline. You know me—I hate being idle. I've always zoomed from one project to another while juggling numerous others on the backburner. My mom always says that *idle hands are the devil's playground* and I never forgot that. Jack told me on several occasions that I thrived on the adrenaline rush of overextending myself," I explained, forcing the lump of hot tears back down after saying Jack's name.

"The thought of sitting here at the house alone, crying myself to sleep while I trudge around in my pajamas doesn't interest me. I *need* work to do to occupy my mind. I *need* this job, Roger. Things will be really tight for me, financially. In fact, this weekend, I will need to come to a decision about several things, including whether or not I will put the house up for sale. Besides, I'm going to need your legal expertise to help me. I made a promise to Jack today. Promised I wouldn't give up until I solved this puzzle and cleared his name. I *will* find out who killed Serena. For Jack's sake, for my family and for Serena's. Her parents deserve to have the man who murdered their daughter brought to justice. I…I can't rest, won't be able to stop, until I do."

Roger flicked the ashes off the end of his cigar into the ashtray and eyed me. "Melody, are you sure? I mean, you've been through an inordinate amount of stress during the past two—"

I held up my hand as I stubbed out my smoke. "Roger, there are three things in this world that I have never been more positive about. One, my salvation and relationship with God. Two, someone framed my husband for murder and three, my very last breath will be spent discovering who that someone is. I won't rest until Jack's name is cleared. Period. So, will you help me?"

Roger studied me for a full minute. I could tell he was assessing my sincerity. His face softened and he remarked, "You know I always stick up for the wrongfully accused. It's why I became a lawyer, so how could I say no?"

I stood up and whistled for Simba as the thunder grew louder and the sky darkened. Any second now, the bottom was going to fall out and drench us both. "Thank you, Roger. I'll be at work tomorrow. The first thing I would like to do is go to Little Rock P.D. and talk to Detective Knowles. You know, show him the evidence and try to get him to reopen it. My guess is that the prosecutor's office won't even think about touching it without him on our side."

"Good guess. The head prosecuting attorney, Alex Renfro was handling the case himself. No way was he going to pass it along to a deputy p.a. Considering the victim is the daughter of one of his biggest supporters and that it's an election year, it would take an act of God to change his mind."

"I figured as much. If we can't convince the Detective Knowles to help us, I would like to set up a meeting with Mr. Rowland. Perhaps he would be interested in finding out that his daughter's killer is still out there, and Mr. Renfro would certainly listen to him."

Roger nodded his head in agreement as he put out his cigar. "I'll only agree to this if you wait to come in till Monday. Seriously, take the rest of the week and the weekend off and finish getting things sorted out here. I will make some preliminary phone calls. I suggest we start with Detective Knowles first—and on our turf. Philip Rowland is going to be a tough sell and if we can get the police department behind us, approaching him may be easier."

I knew arguing with the lawyer in Roger would be useless. I also knew he was right—I had plenty of things here around the house to keep my hands, and mind, from becoming the devil's playground. Life insurance forms needed to be submitted, paperwork from Jack's pension plan through the college needed to be filled out, and bills needed to be paid.

"Agreed. Monday it is," I replied, holding the door open to the kitchen. Simba bounded inside the door and went looking for more shrimp, her dirty feet leaving paw prints all over the tile floor. Thankfully, the food distracted her from Jack's chair. I sat down on the barstool and prepared to eat a few bites of food myself. A lot needed to be done in the next couple of days and it would require every ounce of energy and strength to accomplish.

Regina poured us all a glass of Jack's favorite Cabernet Sauvignon and we toasted to the memory of Jack Tyler Dickinson.

Thank you God, for blessing me with their presence. Please, watch over us and pour out Your strength and love on us all. And guide my hand in getting justice for Jack. Amen.

CHAPTER 12 – WEDNESDAY MORNING

My EYES OPENED TO FIND SIMBA STARING AT me, her hot breath caressing my cheeks, tail wagging against my blanket. I moved my head away from the smell of her rank morning breath and realized I was on the couch. Rubbing my eyes to remove the heavily caked sleep trying to seal my lids together, I heard a soft moan from across the room. I didn't need to see the face to recognize the voice. It was the low rumble of Regina after a long night of too much red wine, too many smokes and way too many tears.

I felt around for my glasses and found them resting in the knotted mass of my hair. My head thumped when I stood and my mouth tasted like an entire ashtray sat inside it. Simba leapt off the couch, her mood much peppier than it had been the last few days. I maneuvered around the kitchen at a snail's pace to prepare some much needed espresso, feeling like a fool. I was a forty-three year-old woman, a widow, who'd acted like a teenager that just discovered the keys to her parents' liquor cabinet. The first few glasses last night went down in salutations to Jack, but the remaining bottles we drank were medicinal, numbing the pain in our hearts.

While the machine spewed out the mahogany hangover cure, I slipped over to the back door and let Simba out. I peeked around the corner at Regina, who was splayed out in Jack's old recliner, snoring away from her night of inebriation with me. One look around the kitchen told the story of our evening. Six empty bottles of wine and an empty fifth of Jack Daniel's littered my new countertops. I hadn't seen this much alcohol in one place since Jack and I were in college.

Coffee in hand, I walked down the hallway toward the master bedroom. I needed to wash my face and put my contacts in. I heard Kendal snoring from the guest bedroom, and tried to remember if Mom and Roger stayed and drank the night away as well. God, I hoped not. The thought of my mother or my boss seeing me in such a state made me want to crawl under the nearest rock. Thankfully, a fuzzy memory materialized of Roger taking my mom by her frail arm and leading her out to his car at dusk. By then, Regina, Kendal and I had been on our way to being quite hammered.

I washed my face with the refreshing cold water and recalled Roger left when Kendal began regaling us with quirky tales of his childhood adventures with Jack. Blood staining my cheeks, I remembered why Roger took my mother home—Kendal had discussed the first time he and Jack had a crush on the same girl and Jack ended up winning her affections after a fumbling excursion in the backseat of Jack's car.

I shook my head in amazement at the crazy conversations that'd taken place. Death of a loved one brings out the strangest memories and thought patterns of those left behind. Well, death and alcohol. The same thing happened after my father's wake. People drank, ate and told stories from the past, some cute and whimsical, others more embarrassing and downright raunchy like what Kendal had shared. A twinge of guilt hit me when I tried to remember how many years of sobriety Kendal had under his belt before falling off the wagon last night.

Contacts in and fully awake, I forced my gaze to remain locked ahead. Although Regina had cleaned up the master bedroom, I had yet to sleep in the bed or go inside except to use the bathroom and grab clothes. I knew if I stayed too long, I would get lost inside the memories that permeated every inch of the space, and I couldn't handle that right now.

I headed back to the kitchen to try and straighten up the mess. I had to get organized today; there were a ton of things that needed tending to, bills to pay and death certificates to mail in.

Death certificates to be sent in by the Widow Dickinson. Oh Jesus, give me strength.

Lost in thought, I turned the corner and ran into Regina. "Oh wow, that was close. You were almost wearing my coffee."

"Hey, I've worn worse. Felt worse, for that matter. Good morning, sunshine. How's the head?"

I ambled over to the counter and plopped down on the barstool. "Pounding. Yours?"

"Same. Haven't drank that much since…oh, I don't know when."

"Me either. Let's see, in the space of two weeks, I've taken up smoking and binge drinking. Sounds more like I'm experiencing a mid-life crisis rather than in mourning. Guess it is a good thing I don't have any children. What kind of example would I be to them?"

Regina filled her mug with hot coffee and sat down next to me. Her arm was comforting as she draped it over my shoulder. "The best one—ever. Considering everything you are dealing with, I say you couldn't be handling it better. Of course, Kendal and I aren't really much help. Seems all we have done is aide you in picking up bad habits again."

"I don't know what I would do without the two of you," I said with sincerity. "Seriously. You've been my rock and Kendal has been amazing. You stayed by my side while I had my meltdown at the cabin, helped with all the funeral arrangements, and cleaned up the mess the cops left while I locked myself away, mentally and physically. And Kendal! He's kept the yard up, taken my car in for service, shooed the press away and gone grocery shopping, plus fixed the leak under the sink. I'd still be in a ball downstairs, lamenting my lot in life if I didn't have you all here to keep me going."

Regina smiled and took a hefty sip of coffee. "Okay, enough of this kind of talk. I believe all this mushy mumbo-jumbo is what got us all into trouble last night. And I'm way too old to try to repeat it again tonight. So, let's say we shelve the ruminations of the past away and deal with the now. What's on the agenda for today and how can I help?"

"We, how can *we* help," Kendal said.

Regina and I jumped. "Jesus, Kendal. It's just not proper to sneak up on people like that! Didn't your momma teach you any manners?"

"Yes, Regina, as a matter of fact, she did. She taught me it was rude to interrupt a conversation and to wait until the parties finished yappin' before you spoke your peace."

Regina pointed at the coffee pot. "Looks like someone else woke up with a hangover. Get you some coffee, son, and have a seat. Mel is about to tell us what our jobs are today."

"Okay you two, enough. And quit talking so loud. My head is already thumping enough. Gosh, there is so much to do I don't know where to start."

"Let's eat this elephant one bite at a time, small nibbles first. I'll clean up the kitchen and start breakfast—which you *will* eat some of missy—and Kendal, what—"

"I'm sorry, you two, but I've got to head into work today. I've been putting off a big bid that's due tomorrow. I should have it finished around three or so and then I need to make a quick trip by my house. If I don't do a bit of cleanup the city might condemn it as not fit to live in. Then I'll be back. Want me to pick up anything on my way back over here after work?"

"Oh gosh, Kendal. I'm so sorry. Sometimes I forget that not everyone is jobless like me," Regina said, pink staining her cheeks.

"I thought you hired a cleaning lady to come in once a week?" I asked.

"I did Mel, and she was great. Kept the place clean as a whistle. But she hasn't shown up the last two Sundays and I haven't had time to call the service and request someone else."

"Listen, Kendal. You just take care of what you need to and I'll take care of Mel," Regina reassured him. "And if you want to give me the number of the service, I would be more than happy to—"

"Guys, look," I interrupted. "I appreciate every single thing that you both have done for me. I was just telling Regina earlier that I could never had made it through the last two weeks without you both. But really, I'm okay. Sad, but okay. I know life without Jack will be hard, but I'm not the first person in this world to lose a spouse. I'll get through it, day by day, perhaps only minute by minute, but I will make it. It took me losing my love to get my faith back and I'm not about to veer away again. There will be days I cry and days I laugh, maybe both at the same time, but I will survive this. And not just because I have you all, but because I have Him. So Kendal, go—get back to your daily routine, just like I will eventually do." I blinked back the tears in my eyes and saw droplets brimming in their eyes also.

Regina broke the teary silence. "Wonder Woman has spoken and we, your humble servants, shall stare in awe at your wondrousness and heed your instructions. The shower awaits Kendal to rid him of the stench of booze before he spends a long afternoon crunching numbers, and I shall retire to the kitchen to prepare a feast. My lady, go do what wondrous things Wonder Woman does. Now, off we go!"

A few quick hugs ensued and then we all went our separate ways, nibbling on the metaphorical elephant.

****

I'd been crammed inside Jack's office for four hours straight, digging through the mess left from the police. It took me one full hour just to find the file that contained his life insurance policy and another hour to find the folder with his employee benefits package from the college. Once I found the correct mailing addresses to send his death certificates to, I wrote out a few cover letters and prepared the envelopes.

A few times I had to stop and catch my breath to fight back the tears that threatened to overwhelm me. The first letter I had to scrap because my tears stained the paper as grief overcame me.

Nibble by nibble, Mel. Nibble by nibble.

Once that huge task was accomplished, I made phone calls to all our creditors, informing them of Jack's death and promising to send payments for the bills that were behind. Satisfied that I'd kept the collectors from knocking down my door, I stood up and stretched. My shoulders, back, and fingers ached from being perched in the same position for so long. I decided I needed to get out of the house and get some fresh air to help clear the pangs of sorrow that seemed to continuously stab at my heart.

Upstairs, Regina was folding laundry in the living room. "Decided to leave the dungeon while it's still daylight outside?"

"Needed to stretch my legs," I said, walking over to my purse on the end table and depositing the envelopes. "Don't let me forget to mail these today, okay?"

"But of course. Say, I think Simba wants to stretch her legs, too. She's been holding that for the last twenty minutes, giving me the 'please take me outside' look." She nodded towards Simba sitting by the back door with her leash in her mouth.

"Poor girl. She misses her walks. She doesn't understand why I haven't taken her," I said, peeking out the window. "Now that the press is gone, I should be safe. I'll take her around the block a few times, then be back."

"Take your cell phone just in case one sly reporter is hiding in the bushes waiting for you or something. I'll gladly come to the rescue. Maybe accidently run them over with my car."

I smiled at Regina, my crazy best friend who I had no doubts would do that in a heartbeat and claim she thought she'd run over a snake. She hated the media almost as much as I did. They had been relentless hounds when she was going through her divorce with A.J. It had been local tabloid gossip because of their wealth and the dirty little secrets exposed when A.J. was caught on film in a rather compromising position. The rags splashed their private lives all over the front page, not caring for the feelings of the individuals involved.

I shook my head at her and excused myself to slip my tennis shoes on, feeling thankful for her wicked sense of humor. I needed her witty banter to keep me from going bananas.

****

Ten minutes later, Simba and I were on our second loop around the neighborhood. Even though it pained me to watch my former friends turn their heads and shoo their kids inside as I walked by, like I had some contagious disease or something, the exercise felt good. Refreshing. Normalcy. Until I cleared Jack's name, stares and whispers would be a daily part of my life and something I would have to get used to. The neighborhood shunning and awkwardness was just a precursor to the fun that work would be on Monday.

Joy.

The skies were overcast again, a hint that rain would hit us by late afternoon. The air was thick and heavy and the clouds a dull gray, just like my mood. My skin was coated in a light sheen of sweat from being outside. The humidity had to be close to ninety-five percent.

A miserable summer for a variety of reasons. Hey, but this is Arkansas. Tomorrow, it could snow.

Passing Mrs. Preston's house, I noticed she was out in her garden. As usual, she was wearing her standard gardening frock, the kind that dated back to the fifties. Her frocks always made me laugh. They reminded me of what my Meemaw used to wear around the house. Mrs. Preston had them in just about every conceivable color and wore them even during the dead of winter. I sometimes wondered where in the world she bought them, because I hadn't seen any for sale in decades.

I waited for her to turn tail and run for the hills like the others the minute she spotted me.

"Oh, Ms. Melody! So glad to see you."

Well, I'll be—the last person on the block I expected to talk to me turns out to be the only one.

"Afternoon, Mrs. Preston. Your plants are looking lovely."

"Of course they are, dear. With all this rain we've been gettin', they don't need me to coddle them. Sure has cut down on my water bill," she exclaimed, setting her gloves and snipers down in the dirt by her roses. She walked across her lush green lawn to the sidewalk where Simba and I stood.

"Honey, I'm so sorry about…what happened. I was goin' to come over tonight and express my condolences once the pie I'm makin' you finished bakin' and cooled off. Ain't right to pay your respects to the grievin' without somethin' sweet to help ease their sorra."

"Oh, Mrs. Preston, that isn't necessary—"

She waved me off with a swift flick of her slim wrist. "I won't hear no more now. I feel just awful not knowin' about this sooner and comin' to help with whatever you needed. It just ain't right! That's what neighbors is for, to be there in times of need and joy. But, my lack of payin' you a visit weren't 'cause I didn't want to go. I simply didn't know. Been out of state you know. When I read the papers that were stacked in my mailbox, my heart nearly gave out, especially when I realized I missed the services."

I found myself stunned by the first person who was being supportive and nice to me in the neighborhood. "It's okay, Mrs. Preston. We just had a simple graveside service. And no, I didn't realize you'd been out of town. When did you get back?" *No wonder she is being so nice—the cops probably haven't grilled her yet and the media didn't pick her bones clean since she wasn't home.*

"Late last night. Been down at my sister Imogene's in Louisiana ever since last Monday. Won me almost five thousand dollars at the casino in Shreveport. But, that's enough of me yammerin' on about my borin' life," she said and paused, her light blue eyes clouding as she gave me a good once-over. "I'm so sorry that you are now a member of my club."

Confused, I wondered if she was experiencing a momentary lapse in her neurons firing on all cylinders. Perhaps they had wandered back into her numerous attempts to get me to join bridge club. I cocked my head to one side and asked, "Club?"

"The Widows Club. It's a lonely and sad group to be a member of, believe me, I know. Been a member ever since I lost my Stan. Don't matter what the reasons are behind the loss. Still hurts like hell."

The ever-present lump of hot tears popped up again in my throat. "Yes, it is difficult. Taking things day by day, sometimes second by second," I managed to eke out.

Mrs. Preston scooted closer and tried to put her arm around my shoulder. Our height difference made it difficult, so her frail limb ended up around my waist. She smelled like White Shoulders, which had been my Meemaw's favorite perfume, and apples. The familiar scents of my beloved grandmother released a few salty tears from my eyes.

"Honey, it may not feel like it now, but things will get easier over time. One day, you'll be able to say his name and look at his picture without cryin' like a lost kitten. Took me three full years, but it did happen. The livin' eventually come to terms with dyin.'"

"I sure hope so," I sniffled.

"You will, child. Trust me. God comforts those who ask, even when the tidal waves of life are tryin' to drown them."

I had to get out of there before I drowned myself with my own tears. "Thank you, Mrs. Preston. I look forward to you stopping by later with the pie."

Mrs. Preston released me from her warm embrace and bent down to rub Simba's soft fur. "Let the tears come, honey. Not only do they cleanse the soul, it's why us womenfolk live longer. Bottlin' those feelings inside is what causes the men to have a heart attack or stroke so early in life and make us widows."

"I certainly don't seem to have any problem letting them go," I smiled through my tears.

Simba licked Mrs. Preston's fingers, her tail wagging so fast it looked like a boat propeller.

"Well, you just keep this lil' treasure close for comfort. I know my kitty Fluffball has been my warm rock. Yes, she's a good girl," she cooed, running her fingers over Simba's head. She stood back up and chuckled. "Please excuse my laughter. I just…well, it was so funny…oh, I'm all a flustered now. Tell you that story later. You best get across that street and back inside. Looks like an unwelcomed visitor is lookin' for you."

I followed her gaze across the street and sure enough, a slow moving black car was approaching us. My gut told me it was a reporter, so without a word, I tugged on Simba's leash and jogged across the road to my yard. The sleek vehicle stopped in front of my driveway and the morning news anchor for Channel Eight opened the door and tried to flag me down.

"Mrs. Dickinson! Erin Corpian from Channel Eight. I'd like a word—"

Simba and I burst through the front door before the nosy wench made it up the walk in her high heels. I yelled, "Get off my property and don't come back!" and slammed the door shut.

Safely inside with the door locked, I leaned against the wall to catch my breath.

Regina bounded down the stairs. "What's wrong? Are you okay?"

"Seems I was wrong about the reporters being gone," I explained. "That chick from Channel Eight almost caught me."

Regina fumed and reached for the door handle. "Let me take care of this."

I grabbed her arm and pulled her away. "No, let her be. She'll leave when she realizes her trip here was a waste of time. They can't stand being ignored."

Sure enough, the knocking stopped and a few seconds later we heard an engine start up and drive off. Upstairs, we peeked out the window and saw the car was now in front of Mrs. Preston's house. Although I couldn't hear what she said, Mrs. Preston was obviously giving the reporter what-for, based on her body language and expression. Within twenty seconds Erin Corpian was back in her vehicle, disappearing around the corner. Probably to go find another neighbor who wasn't so feisty.

I flopped down on the couch and let out a huge huff. "God, when will they leave me alone? Don't they have any compassion? I just buried my husband!"

Regina sat down next to me and put her arm around my shoulder. "Nope. They never do. Vultures, I tell you. Circling the skies looking for a body that's down for the count to feast on. Makes me sick. But," she said, offering a reassuring hug, "don't you worry. If that scrawny bitch comes back, or anyone else for that matter, I'll make sure they leave with an earful of comments not suited for television." She disappeared into the kitchen and returned a minute later with two tall glasses of iced tea. "Now, put that out of your head. We'll need to be a bit more vigilant before we let you step outside. You just relax a bit. Lunch is almost ready."

I tried to smile but it didn't work very well. The thought of eating food made my stomach roll. Regina had outdone herself at breakfast with a full southern meal, complete with biscuits, gravy, eggs and sausage. I had only managed to eat a few bites, barely making it to the bathroom before those few nibbles ejected from my stomach.

"Actually, will you just keep a plate warm for me? I'm feeling a bit tired and think I will go downstairs and take a nap on the couch. Will you make sure I'm up before three? I have some phone calls I need to make before five."

Regina eyed me with suspicion but didn't say a word. I stood up, took my glass of tea, and headed downstairs, Simba padding behind me.

I sat on the couch and Simba joined me. I took the comforter that Jack's mom made us and wrapped it around me. I had always hated the ugly thing with its mish-mash of colors and rough texture. But it smelled like Jack, so I buried myself underneath the scratchy material and inhaled the faint scent of my husband. My tears ran free until sleep overtook me.

****

"Mel? Honey, wake up. It's three o'clock."

Regina stood over me, her warm hand on my shoulder. I blinked and tried to get some moisture back in my eyes. I should have taken out my contacts before I crashed; my eyes felt like sandpaper. "Okay. I'm up. Need more coffee."

"I think you need food, but what do I know? I'm just your best friend, watching *her* best friend wither away to nothing. Pretty soon, you'll be a figment of my imagination."

"When food decides to stay down, I'll resume eating. Until then, it's just a waste," I said, standing up to stretch. "Any calls?"

"Only a few today. One of them was from your office, the other from Mr. LaFont. No random numbers."

"Well, that's a good thing." Regina and Simba followed me upstairs. I felt like I had an entourage.

"Oh, your neighbor, Mrs. Preston, dropped by about an hour ago. I told her you were sleeping and to come back around four. She said she would. I hope she does because the pie she had with her smelled heavenly."

"She is a great cook. Last year at the July Fourth block party, her pies lasted about as long as an ice cube on the hot pavement. Jack always loved…" My voice hitched and I stopped for a moment to gather my thoughts and steer the conversation in another direction. "Anyway, I've got to return those calls and then take a quick shower before Mrs. Preston and Kendal arrive. Come on, Simba. Let's go outside."

I grabbed my cell off the counter and opened the back door. Simba bounded past me and I resumed my new favorite spot on the wicker chair and snatched a smoke from underneath the seat.

Thirty minutes later, I disconnected the call with Mr. LaFont and smiled. Not a fake one, but a real smile. The conversation with both him and Roger had gone well and *Project – Justice for Jack* was in full swing. Though I had a hard road ahead of me, I could see the proverbial light at the end, and it gave me renewed strength and hope.

Regina popped her head out the door. "Hey sweetie. Mrs. Preston will be here any minute. Better hurry and get in that shower. I'm salivating already and can't promise you I won't eat the entire pie if you aren't there to stop me."

I squashed my smoke out in the ashtray and headed inside. "Goodness! Lost track of time again. Good thing I have you here to keep me in line."

"Oh, a new title to add to my bag of tricks. Timekeeper. I like it."

I chuckled softly and headed to the shower. *Timekeeper? Nope, Mindsaver is more like it. Thank you, God, for Regina.*

****

Sure enough, the doorbell rang at four o'clock on the dot. Regina and I were sitting at the kitchen table as I told her about my conversations with Roger and Bertrand, filling her in about our plans for next week.

"Oh, one homemade pie coming up!" she said, bounding out of the chair and down the stairs like a little kid. The woman certainly loved her sweets.

I heard her exchange pleasantries about the new interior with Mrs. Preston as they made their way up the stairs and into the kitchen. I couldn't recall the last time my neighbor had been inside. Maybe three years?

Mrs. Preston took the seat next to me. She was all dressed up with pearls, earrings, a pretty sundress and cute little sandals. She looked like she was going to church. I felt a tad embarrassed at my grungy attire of shorts and a white t-shirt, no makeup, and my hair in a messy bun. Instinctively my hands flew to my hair and I sat up straighter.

"Oh sugar, don't you fret none about that," she purred, motioning with her hand to my hair. "When my Stan passed, I don't think I even took a shower for the first two weeks. It's called *mourning* and ain't nobody expected to put on airs. I just gussied up because I don't get much chance to anymore and besides, can't change tradition in an eighty-year-old woman. My momma, God rest her soul, woulda skint me alive if she knew I didn't put on my best when payin' my respects."

"Well, you look lovely and quite proper. Thank you for stopping by."

"And for this pie. Okay, I'm sure I'm breaking ten social protocols here, but I can't wait. Time to share some!" Regina said, moving over to the cupboard and grabbing three dessert plates.

"You just dive right in, sweetie. And you too, missy. Looks like you've missed a few meals," Mrs. Preston said, her grin wide and proud at Regina's excitement.

Within the space of a minute, Regina had dished out three huge slices and passed them around the table. She dug in with gusto and swallowed two big bites before commenting, "This is the best thing I have ever eaten! Before you leave, would you please share your recipe with me?"

"Well thank you, sweetie. Of course I will. That's what we women do best—share. And speaking of sharing, I have some things I would like to share with you, Ms. Melody."

Regina was right—the pie was incredible. The bite I tasted was like a piece of sweet heaven. I was hesitant to take another nibble, preferring to wait and see if my stomach agreed with my tongue. Besides, if what Mrs. Preston was about to say centered round the subject matter of Jack's death, I was afraid I might start tearing up again and didn't want to choke.

"Yes, this is wonderful. As all of your dishes I've ever tasted have been," I said, hoping she'd veer back to the subject of her culinary skills.

"Sweetie, let me tell you some things. First of all, I don't believe what I read or hear in the news. Ain't no story ever been reported that was the honest to God's truth. My Stan always said that the news was a smidgeon of truth mixed with a whole lotta dirty, unsupported opinions and I agree. I don't know, maybe seein' their words in print or the lights of the camera blind them. Make only dollar signs appear. Maybe one of the classes they take in school stripes them of their morality. Who knows? All I know is that I go by what my own eyes see, what my ears hear and what my heart tells me. Now, I know from what I witnessed last Monday that you and your husband had quite the tiff about his philanderin'. Gotta say, I did smile when I saw you stand up for yourself and give him what for. Reminded me of me."

Regina stopped in mid-chew and I dropped my fork with a loud *clang* on the table.

"Oh, don't look so surprised, ladies. If you don't know by now, then I'll let you in on a little secret my Nana told me when I was approachin' my courtin' age. She said, 'Jerlene, men all suffer from the same affliction. They's born with it. It hides inside them 'til their manly hair starts growin' under their arms. When that happens, they get TR Syndrome and it lasts until they die.'"

"TR Syndrome?" I repeated, reaching for a glass of tea to help my bite of pie finish going down.

"What's 'TR Syndrome?'" Regina asked.

"Testicular Retardation. All men are afflicted by it. Once those little swimmer guys start flowin' through them, they all lose their minds."

Regina and I looked at each other and burst out laughing. Tears of hysteria ran down our faces and Regina turned blue from not being able to catch her breath. I wrapped my arms around my stomach as great gales of laughter burst out of me.

"Ya'll go ahead and laugh, but I'm tellin' you the truth! No man is immune! Even my Stan had it."

Regina still couldn't catch her breath. I wasn't doing much better, but through my laughter, I said, "Testicular retardation—it does make sense! Men do go nuts when they hit puberty."

Mrs. Preston took a sip of tea and a bite of pie, then continued, "That hormone starts pulsatin' through 'em and they can't shut it off. Oh, some men try to ignore the guttural callin', but most can't. Now, I tell you this because the fact of the matter is, men cheat. The right little filly sashays by and that ol' TR Syndrome kicks up and they become slaves to their pants. Even my Stan, after twenty-seven years of marriage, fell ill with the bug. When I found out, I cured him sure enough. Just the way my Nana told me to."

Regina found her voice. "That is the funniest thing I have ever heard—bar none. Oh, and I don't mean about Stan, I mean, oh God, can I borrow that from you? TR Syndrome. Priceless."

"Well of course you can, sugar. I told you we women-folk are best at sharin'. So, back to my story. I cured my ol' Stan from his ailment by sneakin' in the bedroom the night I found out what he'd done and cuttin' all his hair off. Felt right like ol' Delilah, I'll tell ya. Men don't like to admit it, but they's just as vain as women, especially when it comes to their hair. Ol' Stan, he had a head full of the thickest, blackest curls that women would kill for. The next mornin' when he came to the kitchen for coffee and started whinin' about what I'd done, I told him he should be thankin' me that I cut off something that would grow back, because the next thing I cut off wouldn't.'"

Her story brought another round of raucous laughter from Regina and me. My sides were hurting from laughing so hard. *God, it feels good to laugh.*

"Now, I didn't tell you that just to bring a smile to your face, though I'm glad it did. Laughter is just as powerful of medicine as tears. I opened with that story because I reckoned from the argument I heard and saw last Monday that your Jack had him a bout with the disease. I left a few minutes after you did to head to Shreveport, so I didn't have a chance to tell you about the cure. But, from what I witnessed, you seemed to have a good grip on things, so to speak, so I went on my merry way.

"Of course, then I returned and heard all the hubbub about him bein' arrested in all. I knew it was a load of cow manure from the minute I found out. Bein' a cheater don't make you a killer. If that were the case, the human population would cease to exist because adultery has been a dark stain on humanity since the dawn of time. And *that* is the reason I'm here now. To tell you why I believe one hundred percent that your Jack didn't hurt that girl."

Our collective laughter stopped with Mrs. Preston's last comment. Both Regina and I stared at her, waiting. Her warm brown eyes moistened and she held out her bony hand and clasped mine.

"I know I'm just the nosy ol' lady from across the street, but I've been around long enough to be a great judge of character. Your Jack may have stepped out on you, but I watched him cry like a baby when you drove off. Only a man who really loves his woman sheds those kinda tears. And a man who has those kinda emotions don't kill. Period. Somethin' stuck in my craw the second I heard what happened. I knew in my heart that Jack didn't murder that girl, but it wasn't until I saw you walkin' this precious one," she said, looking over at Simba, "that I remembered why."

My heart skipped two beats, my grip tightening on her frail hand. Regina was uncharacteristically silent.

"What did you remember, Mrs. Preston?" I whispered through my tears.

"My memory doesn't always work, but if prompted, I am able to recall things. And after seein' you with your dog earlier today, it reminded me of the Friday 'fore last. Your friend here had already picked you up. Your Jack was walkin' out the front door when your lil' pooch here popped out and took off down the street. I had me a good laugh watchin' him chase her down. She kept him hoppin' for nearly twenty minutes before she finally let him catch her. He was sweatin' bullets by the time he wrestled her back inside. He didn't come back out for another twenty minutes and, when he did, he was wearin' new clothes and his hair was wet. My guess is that's because he took him a shower after all that runnin' around."

Chill bumps appeared on my arms as my adrenaline kicked into high gear. I was about to pose a question when I realized she was speaking again.

"When that memory came back, the gnawin' inside me got worse. I went back inside and flipped through all the newspapers I kept from last week. I'm an ol' lady and don't throw nothin' away. Planned on usin' them this winter for my fireplace. Anyway, I searched through the pages and found the picture taken at that fancy pants store. It had a date and time on it, and when I looked at it after puttin' my glasses on, I knew it wasn't Jack. He was here, in the street, chasin' that cute critter down. He pulled out of the driveway at eleven fifteen. I know the time is exact, too, because that's when my watch beeps, remindin' me to take my pills. Sure enough, when he drove by my yard, my watch beeped."

Regina gasped. I let go of Mrs. Preston's hand and slumped back in my chair. A wave of dizziness overcame me as the enormity of her words sunk in. *Dear God, thank you! More answered prayers.*

The dizziness passed and my mind shifted into legal mode. I had to focus and take the proper steps to make sure that this little nugget of gold didn't slip away.

"Sugar, are you okay? You look kinda green 'round the gills. Here, have a sip," Mrs. Preston said, handing me my glass of tea. "I hope I didn't upset you too much. Just tryin' to help ease your mind about your Jack. It's one thing for a man to cheat, but havin' to live the rest of your life thinkin' he might have been a killer is another."

Fighting back the tears of happiness that threatened to explode, I took the glass of tea and set it back down. I leaned across the table and hugged the neck of the woman I used to consider nothing more than the neighborhood gossip monger. She'd just handed me, and Jack, a wonderful gift.

"Oh no, Mrs. Preston. You just gave me the gift of a lifetime!" I gushed, my words stumbling out faster than I anticipated. I squeezed her frail shoulders. "I...I don't know how I could ever thank you for what you just told me. May I ask you a favor?"

Mrs. Preston smiled, the thin skin around her eyes crinkling, satisfied with her work for the day. "Of course, sugar. What is it?"

I wiped my eyes and cleared my throat. "Would you be willing to share your recollection with my, I mean, Jack's attorney? I'm afraid I have a hard road ahead of me next week with trying to convince them they arrested the wrong man. Anything and everything will help. Your words will give solid credence to mine."

"Honey, I'll stand out in the street and shout it out while wearin' a sign that says 'Justice for Jack!' on my back if it will help."

I clapped my hands with excitement and my dear old neighbor jumped. Regina was already out of her seat, heading straight toward my cell phone lying on the counter.

"Let me make a phone call and get someone here to take your statement, if you don't mind waiting a bit?" I said, taking my cell from Regina's shaking hand in my own.

"Sugar, I'll stay all afternoon if you don't mind keepin' company with an old woman."

I patted her hand reassuringly as I stood. "You are a Godsend. You are always welcome in my home and can stay for as long as your heart desires! Excuse me for just a moment and let me get the ball rolling. I'll be right back."

Rushing out the back door to the deck, I dialed Bertrand's number. My fingers were shaking so much I gave up on trying to smoke; I couldn't hold the lighter long enough to get a spark. *Come on, come on, come on! It's not even four thirty yet! Please Lord, let Bertrand pick up.*

"Bertrand LaFont."

"Mr. LaFont, it's Melody Dickinson again. Listen, you said to call if any new evidence popped up, and boy, did it ever."

"Another dream, Ms. Dickinson?"

If I wasn't jumping out of my skin with joy, his little dig would have annoyed me. But I was on cloud nine and the snide remarks of a snarky lawyer wouldn't bring me down. "No, not this time. Jack was seen at home by a witness during the time the picture at the store was taken. Not only that, the witness is here at my house, right now, ready to give a sworn statement. I—"

"Say no more. My assistant and I will be there in twenty. Has this witness told the police this juicy bit of news yet?"

"No. She just told me."

"Wonderful! I love being able to beat them to crucial evidence and then throwing it back in their faces! Hang tight. We are walking out the door now."

I hung up and let out the breath I didn't realize I was holding during the conversation with Bertrand. I felt silly thinking of him as Mr. LaFont now, even though it was proper social etiquette. No one other than my family knew so many intimate, shameful details about my personal life as he now did. With all he knew, I contemplated calling him "Buddy".

I peeked through the glass door and saw Regina and Mrs. Preston gabbing it up like two old friends from way back. Somehow I didn't imagine that my best friend was picking the brain of my neighbor for recipes. Regina was probably asking for in-depth details of the day that Mrs. Preston threatened to castrate her wayward husband. A brief smile appeared at the thought; a new bond formed between the three of us, held together by the sticky mess of betrayal. One woman let her mate walk away, unable to forgive the act. The other took control, forgave, and stayed together until *death do us part*.

Under the scorching heat of the afternoon sun, as I sat watching the two women chatter, I knew what my ultimate decision would have been had Jack lived. Grief and sadness smothered me, knowing I would never have the chance to tell Jack I forgave him or fight for my marriage.

Jack---can you hear me? I forgive you. I love you. And justice is coming—handed to me by the Lord. I won't fail either of you again—so long as you both give me strength.

I won't.

CHAPTER 13 – MONDAY

Arriving for my first day back at WORK A little after eight, I was greeted by a strained atmosphere. No one really knew what to say to me other than good morning. It was awkward walking through the central area where the secretaries and interns worked. Eyes were averted and voices hushed as I moved through the desks toward my office. My chest tightened when I passed the empty spot where Serena used to sit. Her desk had been cleaned off, not one picture, file, pencil or computer screen left. Had I been a new employee, I would have never known someone recently occupied the space.

I took solace inside my closed office and tackled the stack of work on my desk. None of the other employees were proficient enough to run the monthly bills, at least not in the eyes of the attorneys. Even the secretaries of the four other lawyers didn't run their boss's bills. I was two weeks behind on not only billing, but all the other work I did during the course of a workday. Those things would have to wait. Invoicing for our services was top priority in the eyes of the partners. Once I opened the billing program, I shut my mind off and dove in, grateful for the temporary distraction.

Hours later, I glanced up from my files and checked the clock. It was after four. Burying my head in my work seemed to help the time fly by. Of course, I hadn't left my office except to use the restroom during the last seven hours. I stretched my back, cracked my sore knuckles and buzzed Roger. "Billing is finished. I just sent out the files via email to everyone. I'm going to run to the restroom, then I'll meet you in the conference room, okay?"

"Sure thing. Detective Knowles should be here any minute. Bertrand is in there already and Philip just arrived, so we'll meet you there," Roger said, then lowered his voice and added, "Melody, are you sure you're ready for this? I mean, it's only your first day back after…Jack's service."

Sorrow pricked my heart, but I buried it deep inside. The time to grieve had already passed for me; I had replaced my sadness with a redemptive mission of love. I swallowed the grief and forced my words to not betray my pain. "Yes, Roger. I'm sure. I won't let my husband down again. I owe him that. I'll see you in a minute," I said, and disconnected the call before I said anymore.

A surge of nervousness swam inside my stomach. I'd called Detective Knowles late last week, and he hemmed and hawed, then brushed me off. Even when Roger contacted him he balked at attending a meeting to discuss new evidence in a case he considered closed. But when Bertrand LaFont called him and spouted key words like "police cover-up", "miscarriage of justice" and the biggest kicker, "media frenzy" if the news happened to find out that new evidence in a high profile murder case had been overlooked, he reluctantly agreed to meet with us.

Although my first encounter with Mr. LaFont had not gone well, I was still amazed at the amount of support he'd given to me during the last week. When I contacted him last Monday to discuss Jack's case, he'd been more than eager to help. I doubted his willingness to assist me stemmed from any sort of altruism, though. I suspected Mr. LaFont's support likely sprang from the fact that he would enjoy the sound of his own voice as he proclaimed his client's innocence and lambasted the shoddy investigative techniques in front of the local police and media. Whatever the reason Mr. LaFont had didn't really matter to me because in the end, clearing Jack's name was my sole focus. I was simply grateful for his help and the items he'd prepared for today's meeting, since it was taking all my energy to keep a cohesive train of thought on the tracks.

I slipped out of my office and took the back hallway to the restroom. Oddly, I wasn't nervous about talking to any of them, except Mr. Rowland. The man was in the middle of grieving for his daughter and probably felt a great weight had been lifted off his shoulders when he heard Jack was dead, believing my husband was the one who killed her. I understood the feeling. Even though Jack's death was accidental, due to a previously unknown allergy to penicillin, I still wanted answers. Finding out exactly what happened to him was next on my agenda, after today's conference.

Washing my hands, I made the mistake of looking at my unrecognizable reflection in the mirror. Gaunt, pale, black circles the size of saucers under my eyes. Dull, gray hairs seemed to have sprouted up everywhere overnight. I looked twenty years older. Mom and Regina were right—I was starving myself to death as grief ate away at me. I made a mental note to fix a healthy meal tonight— something with a lot of protein—and force myself to eat it. I should have listened to them sooner. I was about to walk into a meeting and try to convince two people who were adamant of his guilt that Jack was innocent, and I looked like a walking corpse.

I walked back to my office and dug through my bag, clutching my evidence to my chest. I said a silent prayer and headed to the conference room, steadying myself for the battle I was about to wage, cloaked only in the shield of faith and love.

****

Roger, Mr. Rowland and Mr. LaFont were already seated around the oval conference table. The air of the room shifted when I walked in. The quiet mumbling between the three powerful men stopped, and intense anger bubbled under the surface of Mr. Rowland. The old saying *If looks could kill* never rang more true. The electrical charge of his anger was so strong, the small hairs on my arms and neck stood erect. *Breathe. You can do this. For Jack.*

"Good afternoon, gentlemen. Thank you for coming," I said, my voice sounding much more confident than I felt. I moved to the open seat next to Roger, unsure as to whether I should pass my condolences along to Mr. Rowland or not.

Thankfully, I didn't have to make that decision because Detective Knowles sauntered in right behind me and barked, "All right, everyone is here. No time for beating around the bush. Why did you call us all down here, Mr. LaFont?"

Bertrand smiled, his Chicklit teeth gleaming across the room. "Why, Detective Knowles, I thought I made that *very* clear on the phone. A miscarriage of justice has been done, and we brought you here to help us rectify it. To help us not only clear an innocent man's name, but find a killer who is still at large."

Before the detective could sit down, Philip Rowland interjected, "I'm only here because Roger insisted I come. I don't appreciate this little game, whatever the reason. I'm in the middle of dealing with the loss of my daughter, brutally slain by *your* husband, Mrs. Dickinson," he growled, his enormous sausage-like finger pointed at me. "My wife and I are still trying to come to terms with her death, and now you want to rip open the wound that's still in its first stages of scabbing over and pour a bucket of salt on it? It's simply deplorable. Downright deplorable."

"Philip, please," Roger soothed. "I've been your lawyer *and* your friend for over twenty years. You don't really think I would put you through this if we were just running on hunches here, do you?"

"I'm not sure what to think anymore, Roger. For God sakes, I just buried my only child less than two weeks ago," Philip said, slamming his fist on the table. "Less than two weeks!"

Please Lord, give me the words. Open their eyes and hearts to the truth. "Gentlemen, please. This situation is difficult for all of us. Mr. Rowland, my heart aches for your loss because, believe me, I understand the crushing grief of losing someone you love. Serena's life was cut short by the hands of a brutal killer, but it wasn't my husband."

The room went deathly silent as Philip Rowland locked eyes with me. Intense hatred shot from them, the grief and anger consuming him. For a moment I thought he might come across the table and attack me. Had I been a man, he probably would have. I held his gaze, unwilling to let his anger dissuade me.

Detective Knowles sat down at last. "So, Mrs. Dickinson, instead of wasting any more of our time and causing more pain to a grieving father, show us your purported evidence."

Roger piped up, "There is no need for adding fuel to an already volatile situation, Detective. Please, all that we are asking is five minutes. Let Melody and Mr. LaFont speak and show you what they've found."

"You've got two minutes and then I'm gone," Philip Rowland hissed. A large vein that meandered from his left eyebrow and disappeared into his hairline throbbed with fury. His fingers were interwoven so tightly together that they had turned white from the pressure. I read the look behind his eyes; he wished they were around my neck.

My fingers shook as I placed the photographs I brought from home on the table. I slid one set over to Mr. Rowland, the other to the detective. Mr. LaFont produced still copies of the surveillance video, one set labeled *A* of Jack when he arrived at the hotel, a *B* set when the perpetrator exited the elevator, and a close-up picture taken at the lingerie store, labeled *C*.

"If you'll look closely at the body shape, style, girth, and height of the man in picture *A*, you'll see he is bigger than the one in picture *B* by at least one full inch and probably twenty pounds. Note the height difference in comparison to the flowers on the table. Jack stood six foot one barefooted. You'll notice that between the two images, in the *B* image the man is a little over one inch shorter. The flower stalks are visible above his head, whereas in the first picture, they are not."

Detective Rowland at least feigned interest in looking at the photos, but Philip Rowland's eyes never left my own. His ruddy face was now glowing red, like he had been in the sun all day. It looked like he was going to explode at any second. If I didn't hurry up and get to the other image and the affidavit of Mrs. Preston, I was afraid he would storm out, so I continued.

"Now, if you notice the picture labeled *C* was taken at the lingerie store. Mr. LaFont was kind enough to have it enlarged. I ask you all to look carefully at the skin on the hand holding the underwear. Jack had a scar from a burn that covered nearly all the skin on the back of the same hand. The pictures I placed here in the middle of the table are recent photographs of Jack, clearly showing the scar. Now, if you'll—"

"Enough!" bellowed Mr. Rowland. The power and timbre of his deep voice made me jump. He stood up so fast his chair flew out behind him and fell over with a loud thump. "I've heard enough. Roger, I can't believe you thought this drivel would be worth my time. You brought me here to look at altered photos and listen to the wife of the man who killed Serena ramble on about her pathetic fantasies? I'm done."

"Philip, listen, just sit down—"

"There's other evidence as well, Mr. Rowland, if you'll just—"

Mr. Rowland cut both lawyers off by addressing Detective Knowles. "If you so much as think about reopening this case and try to drag me and my wife through this sideshow song and dance, I'll have your badge and you won't be able to find a job guarding a portable toilet. Screw this, I'm done. Oh, and Roger," he added, turning his attention away from the detective, "our friendship just ended. If you wish to keep me as a client, then get rid of her. Because the next time I come in here and see her, I may forget she's a female."

Mr. Rowland stormed out, the sound of the door almost being ripped off its hinges resonating throughout the room. Three sets of eyes moved from the door over to me. Roger looked like he was going to be ill as he stood up, excused himself and went after his friend. Mr. LaFont looked a bit stunned, while skepticism and disgust graced the face of the detective.

"Well, that could have gone a bit better. He didn't even give us a chance to show him the—" my lawyer began, and Detective Knowles interrupted.

"What did you expect, Mr. LaFont? For him to stand up and shake your hand for telling him he can't put this nightmare behind him yet? Please. He's right. These pictures aren't near enough to dispute the solid evidence we have against Mr. Dickinson."

"You have his DNA from a *consensual* sexual act, Detective Knowles. Recall during your interrogation with my client, Mr. Dickinson readily admitted to being in the room and having sex with Ms. Rowland. You have the emails and text messages exchanged between the two of them from the last several months where it is very clear that they were engaged in an affair. He also admitted he fled the room in a panic soon after he was told about the pregnancy. His recollection of events is supported by the video evidence. And yet I recall two more pieces of information *you* seem to have forgotten. One is that he had no defensive wounds anywhere on his person, nor marks on his hands. Judging by the injuries Ms. Rowland sustained to her face, the perpetrator would have at least had a few scraps or cuts on their hands, especially after the blow to her mouth. Even while wearing gloves."

"Are you suggesting—" Detective Knowles seethed, but Mr. LaFont ignored him.

"And two, correct me if I'm wrong, but the articles of clothing you obtained from Mr. Dickinson's residence—I bet you dollars to donuts when the tests results are in, there will be no blood found. The photos taken from the Dickinson household show no immediate evidence of blood."

Detective Knowles rose from his chair, his anger rising with him. I decided I needed to intervene before a full out brawl ensued.

"Please, Detective. No one here is trying to undermine your investigation of the case. I'm his wife for Heaven's sake and even I had initially believed he was guilty based off what I saw in those photos and all the other evidence. But after I calmed down and looked through the pictures with less emotional eyes, that's when minor inconsistencies began to pop up. To be honest, in the back of my mind, I thought it just might be wishful thinking on my part, you know, to force myself to believe Jack was innocent. Swallow the story so I could live the rest of my life without going insane thinking I'd been married to such a monster.

"But, when my neighbor across the street came over and told me this," I said, sliding a copy of the sworn affidavit of Mrs. Preston in front of him, "I realized I'm not some rambling mad widow who refuses to believe she lived with a dormant killer. I'm the widow of a man wrongfully accused and incarcerated for a murder he did not commit. I am asking, no, I'm *begging* you, to look at what we have brought to you with an open mind. If you do, I guarantee you will come to the same conclusions we have, and realize Jack was innocent."

I could see the conflict battling behind the detective's eyes. He was both drawn and repulsed to the piece of paper in front of him. The law enforcement side wanted to view the new evidence, damning to his credibility or not, but the human side of him wanted to walk away with his ego still intact. The room was silent while the war raged on inside him until a winner emerged. Out of the corner of my eye, I could see Bertrand was frozen in his seat, eager to speak but savvy enough to know better. I was damn near chewing a hole through my bottom lip to keep my own voice silent and my gaze steady with the detective's.

The cop side won and Detective Knowles averted his angry green eyes away from me and down to the paper. I watched his eyes scan the page, his face betraying his doubt, his brow furrowing with concern as he flipped the pages and continued reading. He reached the end, and I couldn't read his face.

Please, please let him see. Soften his heart, Lord.

He looked deliberately at me. "The *memories* of an eighty-year-old woman, plus these pictures, aren't enough. They don't negate the solid evidence and I'm certainly not going to approach the prosecutor with this so-called new evidence. As I said earlier, the case is closed. Mrs. Dickinson, I'm sorry for your loss, but it's time you moved on. Forget about this fairy tale and get on with your life. Good day."

I tried to hold the tears at bay, at least until the detective exited the room. It didn't work. They burst from my eyes like a levee had just broken, splashing down on the conference table in silent drops. I hated myself for being weak, for letting my emotions get the best of me. Bertrand noticed and followed the annoyed detective out the door and into the lobby.

The room blurred as my tears continued to fall. I slumped down in the seat and let them come. This had been our one chance to get everyone on board, to present them with what we'd found, and it just blew up in our faces. Not only would none of them ever listen to any of us again, but from the sound of things, I might be out of a job. If Mr. Rowland was serious about wanting me fired, I couldn't imagine Roger would stand up for me. I was, after all, just a paralegal. I didn't bring any revenue to the office—Mr. Rowland did. Huge money. Money talked and people listened, and if Roger listened, I would be living with Regina quicker than I thought.

I closed my leaking eyes and prayed, *God, why? You showed me all these things, yet no one will listen to me— or any of us! If this isn't the road you want me to travel, I understand. But I believe it is, and it seems divine intervention is going to be necessary to make them see.*

A surge of peace washed over me, enveloping me like a warm blanket fresh from the dryer. It might have been my mind's way of keeping me from sinking into a nervous breakdown, or it may have been the voice of an angel or even God himself, but I clearly heard in my mind, *"Oh ye of little faith."*

I clung with all my might to the words, beseeching the Lord to keep me strong.

****

"You're still here? Goodness Melody, you need to go home. It's been a very long day."

I hadn't been working for the last two hours while I sat at my desk. A stack of untouched paperwork sat on my desk, and I couldn't get my brain cells in line to concentrate on them. I had been staring out the window in a comatose-like haze as my mind spun through scenarios of what I needed to do next. Overwhelmed with too many choices and unsure which direction to take, my body took over and forced me to remain motionless until my brain slowed down.

I glanced at the clock and saw it was after eight in the evening. I rubbed my tired eyes and apologized to my worried boss, "I'm sorry, Roger. I sort of zoned out. I didn't notice the time. You're right, I need to go. Can't seem to get the work juices flowing. I'll be back early in the morning to finish up the filings and work on dictation."

"No, you won't," Roger said, lowering himself into the chair in front of my desk. He looked just as tired as I'm sure I did. My pulse quickened, terrified his next words would be to say I was fired.

"You will go home, get some rest, and do exactly as I told you before: take some time off from work. I'm not trying to be rude, but Melody, you look like at any moment you are going to collapse. You have pushed yourself too hard, too fast. We will manage without you for a while. You need to concentrate on taking care of yourself."

"Is this your polite way of firing me?"

Roger gave a small smile, his bloodshot eyes never leaving my own. "Melody, of course not! If I didn't want you in my employ any longer, I think you know me well enough to realize that I would just flat out tell you. As I have said before, you are an invaluable asset to this firm and I can't imagine trying to train someone new to handle all the things you do. You will have a job here for as long as you wish."

I couldn't stop the heavy sigh of relief. "Oh, thank God. I think that's why, subconsciously, I didn't go home. I was waiting for the bombshell of losing my job to hit. You know, after what Mr. Rowland said..."

Roger sat forward and leaned against the edge of my desk, his right hand held up to shush me. "Wait, are you saying you have been here all this time because you thought I was going to come in at the end of the day and let you go? Just because some client bellyached about you? Come now, Melody. If I let employees go every single time a client voiced concerns about them, I would be working here alone. Philip may be a big client and my friend, but he doesn't dictate what I do, how I do it, or who I enlist to help me accomplish my tasks. Besides," he said, leaning back in the chair again, "I don't cave into pressure, not matter where it's from. And I surely don't like being threatened. Philip was just blowing off angry steam, as I'm sure you can imagine. We dropped a big pile of...you know, on his doorstep today. Can't really say I blame him, considering the subject matter."

"Thank you, Roger. That is a huge relief. Yes, I was worried. Terrified, actually. Losing my job would just be the final thin wafer necessary for my brain to explode."

Roger chuckled. "You and Monty Python. Have you ever gone even a week without quoting something from those silly movies?"

I felt the heat rush into my cheeks. "Doubtful. Jack and I both loved the wry British humor."

"Listen, Melody. You tried your best today. I know you are in full press mode to clear Jack's name, and really, I understand your motivations. The evidence you showed us all earlier today does gives rise to his innocence. Hell, if I had a client walk in here with that much information that would easily provide reasonable doubt, I'd never lose a case. But, and please don't take this the wrong way when I say it, I think you need, at least for now, to refocus your sites. Clearing Jack's name is a personal thing for you and it might take a long time to see to fruition. The case I believe should garner your full attention is what happened to him at the jail."

Shocked, I argued, "I am not giving up on my quest, Roger. A lawsuit against the county is not my number one priority at the moment."

"It needs to be. Think about it, Melody. Jack's death at the jail was from negligence on the part of the staff. His guilt or innocence does not play a role in that fact. However, with the documentation you have and the obvious missteps by the staff, you have enough ammunition to aim straight at the coffers of the county. Bertrand is already chomping at the bit to move forward. If you will allow us to take on the case, then I can almost guarantee you the county will cave and throw a load of cash your way to keep it from going to trial. They will have no problem settling to keep things under the rug. Again, not trying to overstep my bounds here, but I imagine finances are dwindling fast for you now that Jack's income has dried up. Filing a suit against the county is the quickest way to replenish your bank account."

I remained silent while I chewed on his words. The one thing I hated about the law was the greediness that seemed to consume it. Money ruled with a green, iron fist. I had wondered several times over the years if that was the first class all aspiring attorneys were forced to take— Greediness 101.

True, my finances were a scary issue I had only touched upon in my head. The numbers all pointed to me being forced to sell my house and move in with either my mother or Regina. Jack's insurance proceeds and small retirement wouldn't begin to pay off our mounds of debt. The funeral, as meager as it was, had wiped out Jack's last paycheck, and my monthly salary didn't come close to covering the minimal monthly expenses.

"The green machine is chugging along, barreling through your thin layer of morals, Melody. Money shouldn't be your god—restoring your husband's good name should be."

A hint of anger at the sound of my Meemaw's cackling voice slithered up my spine. What, had my conscience decided to speak to me in the raspy cadence of my dead grandmother? Oh man, I needed to get some rest and eat because Insanity Island was just around the bend.

Roger watched me with knowing eyes, his lips pursed together as he awaited my response. Suddenly, the light bulb went off inside my head, illuminating the dark halls with a brilliant glow from the epiphany. "If we file a civil suit against the county, well, specifically against the head of the jail, right? For wrongful death—"

"Yes, correct. Then we can introduce all the evidence pointing to Jack's innocence from the get-go. Wait until they get a load of the evidence," Roger finished, smiling from ear to ear when it became clear I understood what he and Bertrand had planned. "The press will have a field day, and Jack's name will be cleared in the court of public opinion once a few *unnamed sources* leak out tidbits of the case to the media. When the news breaks with the truth and the media comes a-callin' on your doorstep, this time, we grant them an interview. Waylay them with all the documentation showing Jack was falsely accused and in-carcerated, which culminated in his life being taken due to neglect. The widow standing up for justice for her husband—people will lap it up. And the county will be falling all over itself to pay for your silence."

Yep, there it was—the greed factor. Roger was lit up like a Christmas tree while he babbled on, no longer directing his words toward me. He was verbalizing his case strategy. I knew he meant well and the plan was a great one in terms of bypassing the red tape of trying to get the police department to reopen Jack's case. I watched Roger as he went into full legal eagle flight and paced around my office, detailing his approach to take on the county and raid the coffers.

This wasn't the first time I had witnessed Roger lose himself inside a case. It wasn't like Roger didn't represent all of his clients with professionalism and his one-hundred percent effort, but a few cases over the years had ignited a deep sense of injustice inside him. The first time I had seen him like this was when a three-year-old girl had been killed in a freak explosion from a faulty generator and he took on the manufacturer. He had turned into a pit bull that latched onto the soft throat of the enemy, not stopping un-til the carcass of the neglectful corporation had its throat ripped out and lay convulsing on the ground.

I tuned Roger out while he jabbered, thanking the Lord for not only placing me in a job that had such a great boss who also happened to be a legal genius, but also for Roger's willingness to help me. If he and Bertrand took from my shoulders the burden of proving Jack's innocence, then that would afford me the opportunity to become an amateur sleuth on my own and start digging around to find the real killer. I bit my lip at the thought, wishing I had the money to hire a private investigator—even one of the guys who did background research for the firm would work. But that wasn't in the financial cards for me, so I would have to learn to be a modern day Nancy Drew on my own.

"Melody, did you hear me?"

"Huh? Oh, sorry, I am just a tad overwhelmed here and a ton of exhausted. Doesn't make for a good combination. What did you say?"

Roger had stopped pacing and stood by the door to my office, his hand on the knob. I knew he hated it when he had to repeat himself and was surprised when he didn't look at me with anger, but sympathy. I'm not sure which was worse.

"I said you need to shut down and go home for the evening. Bertrand and I are meeting first thing in the morning tomorrow to discuss strategy. Right now, there is no need for you to be there. So you need to do three things for me. Are you listening?"

"Yes sir."

"One, go home. Two, eat. Preferably a lot. Three, and this is the most important one, so please pay careful attention—stop worrying and get some rest. Let Bertrand and I take care of this and you concentrate on healing, okay? I...I need you around to keep this place running smoothly."

I felt my throat constrict from the lump of hot tears that appeared. *The rays of the sun always shine brighter after a hard rainstorm.*

Unable to form any words, I nodded in silent agreement. Roger sensed I was on the verge of another crying jag and returned my smile, then left my office in silence. The minute the door was closed, the salty tears sprinted down my cheeks. I wiped them away with shaking fingers, irritated at myself for bawling yet again. I wasn't a crier and this tearing up at the drop of a hat mode I was in needed to hurry up and end. I shut my computer down, gathered up my purse, and called my mom as I headed out to the parking deck.

"Hey, Mom. I've got some good news. I am leaving work now and should be there in about fifteen minutes, after I stop and grab something to eat."

"Well, I can't wait to hear it but I will have no such thing. You make the trip in ten and eat the chicken and dumplings I have warming on the stove. You need some rib-sticking calories, my little sunshine. Be careful driving—keep that lead foot of yours under control."

I couldn't help but smile at how strange life could be sometimes. Truly, the Lord *did* work in mysterious ways. This day started out in the pits and then took a nosedive into the bowels of Hell itself, yet before the day had ended, it had righted itself and turned out better than I thought possible.

CHAPTER 14 – MONDAY EVENING

My EYES BURNED FROM STARING AT THE SAME pieces of paper for the last two hours. A dull ache pulsed behind my sinuses with each breath, and I wished the aspirin I'd taken minutes before would kick in. I rubbed my temples and thought about my earlier visit with Mom.

Although she had been pleased with my report of the events of the day, she couldn't hide her worry from me. I tried my best to put on a happy face, telling her I was fine, physically and emotionally. I even made a big production of eating two bowlfuls of the comfort food she'd fixed for me. She didn't seem to connect the fact the food didn't stay down when I excused myself and went to the bathroom.

With gentle assurances, I told her Bertrand and Roger had everything lined up, and that she need not worry about me. I held her hand in mine at the table and told her my faith was stronger than it had ever been and God would get me through this, and the sadness behind her hazel eyes melted away. When I left her house, my superb acting seemed to have placated her fears and she looked less frail and more in control as I waved goodbye from my car and headed home.

Kendal greeted me at the door when I arrived, his "Watch Melody" shift underway. Regina had gone home to do some much needed household chores and left the duties of keeping me company in the hands of Kendal. The first thirty minutes after my arrival home consisted of re-hashing the day's events to him as I sat and he listened with eager ears. When my story was complete and his questions answered, he headed to the bathroom to work on my leaky toilet.

That had been hours ago and even though I had tried to stretch out on the couch and get some rest, my mind was too keyed up to shut down. Resigning myself to the fact that sleep wasn't a word my body wanted to hear, I had gotten back up and been in the kitchen ever since, pouring over the files pertaining to Jack.

I jumped when Kendal spoke. "I'm finished. The toilet is finally quiet and no longer runnin'. Sorry it took me so long. I hope I didn't wake you up."

Kendal wiped his brow with a dirty hand, then moved over to the sink and stuck his long fingers under the cold water. It was close to midnight and it had taken him almost an hour to fix the guest bathroom toilet. When I had mentioned yesterday the stupid thing wouldn't stop running and asked for the recommendation of a good plumber, Kendal insisted he could fix it. I knew he was just trying to help keep my expenses low, and I did appreciate his kind offer, but I also knew Kendal wasn't the handyman type. Jack used to tease him all the time about being such a dolt when it came to manly mechanical-type things. How many trips had Jack made over to Kendal's to repair something Kendal inevitably broke? Hundreds, it seemed like.

I looked up from the papers spread out all over the kitchen table and smiled. "Oh no. Sleep seems to be my enemy these days. I've just been going over things, writing thoughts and memories down as they come. Thanks, Kendal—you and Regina are Godsends. But, you didn't have to come over so late on a work night. It could have easily waited until the weekend. Here, come sit down and have a glass of tea with me," I said, pouring him one.

He finished wiping his hands on the dishtowel and lumbered across the kitchen floor, his limp more pronounced than normal. It probably hurt his knee to be crouched in the small confines of the front bathroom for so long. He sat down with a loud *plop* in the seat across from me. A twinge of guilt at letting him play plumber hit me as I watched him wince.

"Kendal, I appreciate your help but I really could have called someone to fix it. Your knee's bothering you, isn't it?"

He waved a meaty paw in my direction. "Girl, I won't hear of it. Regina would skin my hide for lettin' you do that, and then cook me up for breakfast. And my knee? Shoot, it hurts all the time no matter what I'm doin'. Otta see me after a huntin' trip! I limp around like a ninety-year-old man then. That's what gettin' long in the tooth does to ya. Body starts failin', hair starts fallin', wrinkles set in and a paunch suddenly appears," he said, patting his belly and then rubbing his knee. "My little trophy from my stupid, younger years wants to make sure I always remember never to race motocross again. Besides," he continued, taking a huge slurp of cold tea, "I won't have you spendin' your money on things Jack woulda normally done. What kind of best friend would I be if I let his widow down? A poor one, that's for sure. And I ain't got no intention of havin' Jack give me a good butt chewin' when we meet again on the other side. Nope, no way. I've already got enough to answer for. Don't need to add to the list."

Oh no, we aren't going there right now. I know this conversation is going to happen, but I need nicotine first. I don't have the mental strength. Change the subject, Mel.

With a tenable grip on my emotions, I replied, "You two have always been thicker than thieves. I don't think he could have loved you more, even if you were truly blood brothers. Now, it's late and I already feel bad enough that you are still here and in pain. Sit a spell and catch your breath, then go home. You don't need to stay here and babysit me, no matter what Regina says. I'm a big girl, I promise." I forced a thousand watt smile to appear, hoping it covered my real thoughts.

Kendal looked down and feigned studying the contents of his glass. He may have been able to hide the feelings raging by looking away, but he couldn't mask the pain in his voice when he spoke. "He loved you so much, Mel. More than I think you really knew."

A wave of mixed emotions hit me all at once. Part of me wanted to cry the tears of mourning for the loss of my husband. Another part wanted to shout *"Oh yeah—then explain why he cheated on me and was going to have a child with another woman!"* And yet another part of me, something locked away so deep its voice was barely audible, whimpered, *"Ah yes, he loved me. And I am just reaping the dark harvest of my wicked seeds, sown in my youth. The sins of the past are interwoven in the tragedies of the present. I killed him, Kendal. I drove him over the jagged edge that is the line between love and hate; devotion and nonchalance. He was a good man and I turned my back on him when he needed me the most. How many times did he reach for me, needing the comfort of his soul mate, only to have me turn away?"*

Instead I said, "I miss him so much, Kendal. I know where he is and that I will see him again, but sometimes, it just doesn't help. There are so many things I need to say to him. Oh God, if I could just hear his voice one more time…"

Sorrow slammed into my chest but I refused to let it overtake me. Thankfully Kendal was still staring at the interior of his glass, which allowed me a moment to compose myself. If he had looked at me with those big, sad puppy dog eyes full of his own grief at losing his best friend, I would have lost it. I took a hefty slurp of tea, stood up, and walked over to the back door. "I wish I could say it's nice outside, but I can't. Join me in the humidity? It's almost midnight, so the mosquitoes should be gone. I need to let Simba out and you and I both look like we could use some nicotine."

Simba bounded out the door and I wasn't far behind her. Kendal rose painfully from his spot at the dining room table and followed me outside. I lit two smokes and handed him one.

"God, standin' out here puffin' away takes me back. Remember how we stood out here and almost froze to death when that big ice storm hit?" Kendal said, seeming as eager to change the subject as I was.

I let out a plume of smoke and it hung in the heavy air around me. "Oh yes! It was so eerie. No noise at all except the sporadic cracking of pine trees. My gosh, I think we were without power for almost two weeks. It was hard to enjoy the beauty of everything covered in ice when the fear of a tree smashing into the house was at the front of our thoughts."

Kendal eased himself into the stand alone swing and smiled at the memories. "I remember Jack givin' me a hard time because I couldn't figure out how to get the generator to work. I felt like a real fool after tryin' for over two hours, only for him to point out it had no gas. Duh. Lost my man card for sure that day."

"Oh now Kendal, don't feel bad. Recall that Jack wrecked the four-wheeler, twice I believe, trying to play the neighborhood big shot by offering to go to the store and fetch supplies for our stranded neighbors. By the time the ice melted, the four-wheeler looked like it had been through a warzone."

Kendal threw his head back and laughed. "I did forget about that! Of course, even the best drivers were crashin' all over the place. How could you not? We had over five inches of ice."

We laughed for a moment at the memories that seemed liked eons ago, but the laughter soon faded and uncomfortable silence ensued. I could tell he had something on his mind that he needed to say and even though I wasn't a betting woman, I would have bet the house I knew what the something was. It had been at the forefront of my own thoughts for quite some time, poking and prodding, like sharp needles underneath a fingernail.

This was the first time that Kendal and I had been alone since this nightmare began. When Regina called me at work and told me she was going to stay at her own house tonight and she had arranged for Kendal to come stay, I had cringed on the inside. I wanted to tell her to call him back, that it wasn't necessary and I would be fine alone. But I knew her well enough to know that arguing with her once a plan was locked in place was pointless. Besides, she would start asking nosey questions if she smelled even the slightest scent of something amiss, and me requesting not to be alone with Kendal would have sent her into sensory overload.

The cicadas, which had been abnormally loud earlier, were oddly silent. It seemed even they knew Kendal and I were about to begin a conversation neither of us wanted to have, and that shameful, hidden secrets were about to be revealed.

I lit another cigarette and listened to the tinkle of the ice in my glass as I summoned up the courage to start the conversation. I was finding it difficult to form words. I knew what Kendal wanted to discuss, but I also knew when I told him the secret I had kept for over twenty-one years, our friendship might not survive the deception. The thought of losing another person I loved in my life made my stomach drop and left me lightheaded.

"Mel, I...I need to talk to you. Need to ask you a few questions. Only ones you can answer. Ain't nobody I've ever known can come close to explainin' God's word in such a way that even an ol' country bumpkin like me can understand."

Thank goodness he spoke first! Okay, so maybe I was wrong. He doesn't want to discuss that night.

I looked across the patio at him as he rocked in the swing. The dim light from inside the kitchen and the faint glow from the moon above us caressed Kendal's features in a way that made it look like a larger version of Jack was sitting across from me. How many times had Jack and I sat in these exact same spots over the years and talked late into the evening? The sting of tears hit my eyes, so I yanked my glasses off and rubbed them away, feigning tiredness.

My eyes still closed, I said, "I don't deserve such praise but, thank you. So, what's on your mind?"

Kendal fidgeted and repositioned his body in the swing. It was obvious he was nervous about whatever he was going to ask me. A full minute passed. "Well, I'm sure I'll screw it up and my question won't make a lick of sense, so bear with me while I try and figure out how to ask it. I think I need to give some back story first, okay?"

"It's okay, Kendal. Just take your time. I'm listening."

"I know me and Jack both have told you some crazy stories about our younger days, like the one I told the other night when I'd had one too many. By the way, sorry about that."

"No need to apologize. We all have dark memories we wouldn't want the world to see and cringe when they appear. Go on."

"Well, I have a story to tell you that even he didn't know about, and pertains directly to my question, which I promise I will get to once I give you some back story here. Of course, you already know Jack and I met in sixth grade, became friends, played every sport our school offered together and pretty much hung out every day, right up until ya'll got married. And I'm pretty sure you know about the day that solidified our friendship."

"Yes, the day you saved him from getting a beating from the local thug after gym class. Guy, wasn't that his name? Guy Powell?"

Kendal's smile was sad, full of wistful memories. "Yep. Guy Powell. I walked in when him and another kid, Tommy Hankins, were harassin' Jack once the locker room was empty. You know, back then, Jack hadn't hit his growth spurt yet. I was almost four inches taller than him, and he was kind of a pale, sickly lookin' kid. Before he met me, he didn't go outside much. You know how he loved to read—that began when he was just a youngin'. So, I walked in and stopped them before they roughed him up over his lunch money and new sneakers. I think Jack may have hung around me back then because he thought I could be his personal brute or somethin'. I don't know. Maybe he thought I was some kind of honorable guy for stickin' up for the wimpy kid. Maybe he admired the fact that I beat the livin' crap out of Guy's face. Maybe he wanted to hang out because he hoped I'd teach him how to fight. Maybe he wanted to hang out with the 'rich' kid from the other side of the tracks. I don't know. We never talked about that day, it just became the startin' point in our journey together."

Kendal took a deep breath. He stood up abruptly from the swing and began to pace around the deck.

"None of those things are why I crushed Guy's nose and bloodied his lip, then kept poundin' on him after he was down until Coach Richards pulled me off. What set me off was somethin' that had nothin' to do with Jack, or could even remotely be considered heroic."

Intrigued, I asked, "Okay, so what was it then?"

Kendal motioned for another cigarette. I handed him one, followed by the lighter, and watched his face light up when the flame sparked to life. He looked so much like Jack that, for a moment, I felt like I was looking at his ghost.

"My home life—it was horrible. We may have lived in an upscale neighborhood in a fine house and materially, I never wanted for a thing. New clothes, new toys, new cars when the time came. But behind the walls of the Rayburn household was a dark prison. A drug addict for a father and a mother who spent her days cleanin' every possible inch of our house, hopin' she'd done it right before Dad came home and covered her in black and blue marks again. When I was still in grade school, Dad left me alone, savin' his rage for my Mom and leavin' me be. I learned to keep as quiet as a church mouse when he was home, hopin' that he wouldn't notice me and hurt me like he did Mom.

"But, when puberty hit and I shot up like a weed, things began to change. Guess he finally noticed me and decided to get his bluff in before I matched him in height and weight. First, it was just yellin', tellin' me what a no good, worthless hunk of flesh I was. That I would never amount to nothin', that I was only alive because my Mom had survived her punishment from him for bein' pregnant. You know, hateful, ugly things to destroy my will to fight back."

"Oh Kendal. I'm...I'm so sorry."

Kendal's pace picked up as his memories took control of his mind. "I never said a word to anyone. Mom and I didn't even talk about it. She'd spent years learnin' to hide the truth from our town. None of the ladies from church or her bridge club knew. She would just cower inside her marble prison until the newest batch of bruises disappeared. Her favorite story to explain away her absence from one event or another was that she was sick. God, everyone in town probably thought she had the worst immune system ever."

"After a few months of his verbal assaults, things became physical with me. A smack upside the head at the dinner table for not finishin' my meal fast enough. A kick in the ribs while I watched television in the livin' room when he passed by, like I was a mongrel in his coked-out-of-his-mind way. He was constantly in my face, warnin' me how tough he was and not to ever attempt to overstep my bounds in the house. Then, when he would start wailin' on Mom, instead of ignorin' me like he'd done before, he'd stare right at me, his face smug, tauntin'. His lips curled back in a sick grin with each blow he landed on my mother's body. Like he was darin' me to step in and rescue her."

"His plan worked and for the first eleven years of my life, I was completely petrified of him. When mom and I would attend church services when she was free from marks, I remember thinkin' each time the pastor mentioned Satan that I already knew what he looked like. I was livin' with him."

My heart ached for my friend. Jack and I had both known Kendal's childhood had been difficult and honestly, we both suspected abuse occurred. Kendal rarely spoke about them and when he did, his upbeat demeanor would change. His voice would become cold, distant and edgy, like he was talking about strangers whom he felt not emotional contact with. I couldn't recall a holiday Kendal ever went to visit them while they were still alive. He preferred to hang out with us. He didn't even attend the funeral of either parent when they passed away, or shed a tear that I could recall, at least not in my presence. But when Jack's parents passed, Kendal wept like he was one of their children.

Now I knew why.

As Kendal relived his violent past, I couldn't help but say a silent prayer of gratitude for the wonderful families both Jack and I had been born into. Neither one of us came from money, but what our households lacked in monetary treasure was more than made up for in the amount of love and support both sets of parents doted on each of us.

I wanted to say something, to offer a word of encouragement, but as I opened my mouth, I closed it again. My gut told me to let him finish. I watched him struggle to rein in his emotions. Men didn't often release such raw, honest thoughts. Most preferred to keep them buried inside until they festered and became septic. Kendal was extracting some of the toxic memories of his past, so I didn't interrupt. Besides, I couldn't help but wonder where he was going with this story.

"But that day in the locker room—something inside me snapped. When I saw the look of fear in Jack's eyes, pinned up against his locker like a wall decoration and then the look on Guy's face—I lost it. It was like instead of seein' the two of them, I saw my dad and me in their places. I was the terrified kid crushed up against the locker by my old man. I...well, I just...oh, you know. Saw red and kinda went nuts. Beat the livin' tar outta that boy tryin' to make my old man pay for all the wrong he'd done to me and my mom."

Kendal's voice was low, barely above a whisper. The pain seeped through his vocal chords and into the quiet, damp night air, hanging over us both like the smoke from our cigarettes. Heavy. Somehow I knew this was the first time that he had shared with anyone the painful journey of his childhood. And I sensed what he was about to share wasn't going to be much better, either.

"Jack and I were like two peas in a pod after that. I stayed over at his house more than I did my own. Now you understand why. I was just as much a fixture at his parents' house as I am here. Deep down inside, I...oh God, I *envied* his life, Mel. I wanted to be him, not hang out with him. Even in my youth, I knew those thoughts were wrong and they made me angry on the inside. Jack's family was poor; we were rich. But Jack had a mom and dad who loved him, supported him and treated him with kindness. I didn't. His mom was warm, welcomin', treated me like I was her own. His dad let me tag along when he and Jack went fishin', or played ball outside or worked on their cars. I mean, I learned how to do things from a man who wasn't my own flesh and blood. Though I enjoyed it, I hated it at the same time." His voice cracked.

Even in the dim light, I could tell Kendal was crying. He composed himself and wiped his nose on his hanky, and my stomach began to churn. I had a feeling I knew what was coming next.

"Sorry 'bout that," Kendal said, using his palm to remove the tears from his cheeks.

"Kendal, you don't have to—" I began, but he stopped me.

"Oh yes, yes I do. Our friendship was based on a lie. Sure, eventually, the envy and jealousy dwindled when I discovered I really *did* like hangin' out with Jack. You know how funny he is...er, was. Always a smile on his face. Always saw the good in others. Ready to lend a hand to anyone in need, no questions asked. What he heard in church, he lived by. Or, at least, he tried to, bein' a preacher's kid and all. I remember thinkin' he was a tad off the times I went with him. He wasn't like the rest of us kids, all fidgety and not payin' attention, too busy lookin' at the clock, waitin' for the borin' sermon to end and Sunday lunch to begin. Not Jack. He listened. Followed along in his Bible, highlightin' passages as the pastor spoke."

I let out a bittersweet laugh. "That was a habit he kept his whole life. I used to tease him about his Bible. Told him it looked like a rainbow had exploded all over it."

Lost in exorcising his thoughts, Kendal didn't respond. I wasn't quite sure he'd even heard me. "By the time our sophomore year rolled around, the moments of wishin' I had his life were few and far between. I think Jack always felt like he owed me for steppin' in and savin' his hide from Guy. Seemed like he was always lookin' for a way to pay me back or somethin'. Just a feelin' I had, you know? Not that anything was ever talked about like that between the two of us. He finally got his chance our last day of school our senior year."

"How?" I asked, trying to recall if Jack ever mentioned anything significant happening during that time. Nothing came to mind.

"By savin' my butt from gettin' locked up," Kendal said, more animated now that the memories he seemed to have buried deep began to flow.

"Guy Powell hated us both ever since I ended his bullyin' days. He dropped out of school our junior year once the drugs got ahold of him. Rumor was that he left our lil' town and was runnin' pot from Dallas to Little Rock on I-30 in his supped up Chevelle. But me and Jack knew he was still sneakin' back to town now and again. I'd wake up to a slashed tire or Jack's house would be sportin' a brick through a window. Another time, I went outside and my brand new red Chevy was yellower than a school bus. Jack's tank had, um, cow poop dumped in it once. We didn't make the connection we might be in danger. I mean, Guy was hittin' our possessions, not us. But, when someone tried to set both of our houses on fire in the space of less than twenty minutes, we knew things had progressed. They went from being irritatin', teenage pranks to somethin' much worse."

Kendal was shaking with anger now. "I went after him that night. Lost all my cool after the fire in our garage was under control and the fireman carried out what was left of my dog, Ranger. I overheard the fire chief tell my dad it looked like he'd been doused with gas, then set on fire. Never said a word to anyone, I just slipped out the back, put my mom's car in neutral, and slid down the back driveway. I stopped at *Whattaburger* and pulled in, lookin' for Guy's drug buddy, Rupert. Asked him real nice if he knew where Guy was. Could tell he was lyin' the minute that mouth of his opened. But, he started singin' real pretty after I yanked him out of his car by the scraggly hair on his head. Told me he'd seen Guy partyin' down in the mud pits off ol' Highway 127 earlier. So, that's where I went."

"I really don't know how Jack found out. Never asked him. That night we didn't talk about. Because when he rounded the bend on that old dirt road, it is the only thing that saved Guy's life. I was so mad, I coulda killed him. But Jack—he still had the cool head. He convinced me to quit beatin' the tar out of Guy, then told Guy if he wanted to continue breathin', he needed to leave town and never come back. And if he ever showed his face again, he wouldn't stop me from finishin' him off. Told him that we'd just bury him and his car in the pits and no one would ever even know he was missin', and sure wouldn't be able to find him, no matter how long they searched. It worked, because Guy limped away and never came back—at least not for several years."

My heart ached. If it had been Simba, I knew I would have gone crazy. "Well, now there is one story that I had not heard before. Oh Kendal, I'm so sorry. What a horrible thing to have happened. Poor Ranger."

"Yeah, it was pretty rough. And I hadn't given much thought to old Guy Powell in years. I mean, after all, it was a long time ago and the last I heard, he was in prison down in Texarkana. But, Jack and I ran into him right before Christmas down in Sheridan. Did he tell you?"

"No." There were many things Jack hadn't told me in the last few months, I was learning.

"Remember when I insisted Jack help me set up my new deer stand?"

"Oh yes, he complained for two weeks. He hated anything that had to do with hunting. He only went because you were driving him crazy."

"Yet another mistake to add to my list of screw-ups. We ran into Guy at the hardware store. He was working there and neither of us recognized him at first. He recognized us though. Followed us out to the parking lot and some choice words were exchanged. Threats made. Apparently, he'd never forgotten that day in the mud pits."

"Threats? Who threatened who? And what kind of threats?"

"Standard posturin' by a one-time bully. He strutted around like an old rooster, cluckin' and a yappin'. Said we would pay for our actions. That he was watchin' us and we would never see it comin'."

I shot up off the chair. "Kendal! Why didn't you tell me this before? We need to call the detective—"

"Mel, I already told the detective the entire story when he interviewed me. He didn't seem to think it was relevant. I tried, I really did. Tried to get him to listen to me, to at least take the time to go and talk to Guy. He never said much, but I could tell by the look in his eyes he didn't believe me."

I couldn't stop my legs from trembling. Yet another new piece to a complicated, convoluted puzzle was now in place. Though a bit farfetched, a real suspect had emerged. Someone with a violent past who held a grudge against Jack. Someone who, according to Kendal, was no stranger to violence. I felt a flash of anger towards Kendal for not telling me earlier. I quashed it with the knowledge he had at least told the police. Plus, I was the one who hid like a child for almost three days and he *had* tried to contact me. The chance to bring it up vanished when Jack died, and things had been so crazy ever since, now was the first opportunity he'd had to talk to me.

I could tell he had more to say and was just waiting for me to give some sort of signal that I was ready to listen. He motioned for another smoke, so I handed him the pack. He lit up, waiting a few seconds to let the nicotine calm his nerves and watching me pace. After a few hefty puffs, he sat down on the swing.

"Continue. I'm still listening. Just trying to absorb everything."

"Once I was bigger than my old man and a star athlete, things got, well, tolerable at home. Lookin' back now, I think the years of drug abuse set in then and the ol' dog lost his bite. When my dad realized I wasn't afraid of him anymore, things quieted down. But the anger inside me, well, it never left. Things went along fine until college. I had the pick of any woman I wanted—until Jack would enter the picture. Women were drawn to him. Did you know that…well, I saw you first?"

Uh oh...this isn't going in the direction I thought it was.
I shook my head no, unable to think of a verbal response.

"I did. God help me, but I was so mad at Jack when he told me the two of you had a class together and were going out on a date. He knew it, too, because he laughed and told me that the 'big jock' just lost out to the bookworm. At first, I laughed it off, but, the first time I saw the two of you together, I got angry. So angry, in fact, I decided to break the two of you up. So, here we are now, and I am finally ready to ask my question. Will God forgive me for my past deeds that ended up leadin' to the death of my best friend?"

My stomach felt like a soccer player had taken up residence and was practicing for the World Cup. I waited for my anxiety level to calm down and chose my words with care. Not just for Kendal's benefit, but mine as well. *Give me the right words, Lord.*

"God forgives all sin, when asked with a humble heart and a willingness to change our ways, Kendal. He knows every mistake we've ever made, or will make. That's all part of being our omniscient Creator. To me, that is the most amazing thing about our Lord. Even though He knew all of our mistakes, He died for us anyway. However, just because He forgives our trespasses doesn't mean we won't reap the harvest of our sinful ways while here on earth. Our forgiveness from Him is for the next life. The one we currently live in still carries the stains of our past."

I saw Kendal's shoulders sag, relief settling over them. I needed to know what he meant by his last statement, though I was terrified of what the answers could be. I sensed this whole thing centered round that fateful night and tied into what I had to confess to him as well. "Kendal, how did you try to break us up, and why do you think that something you did over twenty years ago caused Jack's death?"

Kendal let out a deep sigh. "The girl you saw him kissing in his apartment—the one that led to, um, well, our night together?"

Oh no...

"I am the one who put her up to it. Jack had been tutoring her and I knew from the way she looked at him that she had the hots for him. So, I gave her a hundred bucks and told her to come over at precisely seven-thirty, which is when I knew you two had a date. Jack had no idea she even knew where he lived. He'd been meeting her in the library for sessions. Anyway, I told her that when he opened the door, she was to lay one on him. I...I overheard a conversation the two of you had a few weeks prior about how cheating was a deal breaker, in your opinion...so I set him up."

Dear Lord...this can't be happening.

Kendal was staring at me, waiting for a response. I couldn't seem to remember how to speak. Or breathe. I stared at him in disbelief as tears shimmered down his face, too stunned to even form a tear of my own. He looked terrified as he waited for me to say something about his revelation. Time seemed to stop, almost as if my mind shot out of my body and found itself back inside that night. Memories of that evening flooded my vision as I listened to Jack beg me to believe him when he swore nothing was going on.

Meemaw's voice rang inside my head. *Just like he begged you to believe him that he didn't kill Serena. See, my darlin', all of this started with you. Your sins have come home to roost. If you'd have just listened to me and your Ma's advice and not fornicated, your Jack wouldn't be with me now.*

I had accused Jack of being a liar, given him a loud, tear-filled piece of my mind, and stormed out of his apartment. I screamed at him, saying I could never be with someone who cheated on me. I ran through the streets, tears splashing down my face at my stupidity for losing my virginity to a man who didn't value our love. Hurt, humiliation and shame kept my legs pumping as I ran through the quad.

I found myself sitting alone on a park bench a few blocks from campus, my tears of betrayal piercing the cold night air. Kendal appeared, sitting next to me, trying to comfort my broken heart as he offered me a drink from the bottle hidden inside a brown paper bag. His warm arm encircled my shoulder and he whispered in my ear what a fool Jack was for not seeing what he had in front of him. There was warmth in my belly as the alcohol hit it for the very first time. Our heated lips brushing together, Kendal's words of comfort lulled me into a drunken trance. The evening ended with us both under the warm covers of my bed, the sensation of spinning making me feel like I was dreaming.

The panic and shame slammed into my head the next day when I awoke and looked around with sober eyes.

It took me several minutes to compose myself.

"I...wow. I never knew that. Not exactly sure how to feel about it, either."

Kendal's voice was low and pleading. "Oh Mel, please forgive me. I was young, stupid and vain. Hated myself ever since. It got worse a few weeks later, after you got so sick and were in the hospital. I...I never realized how much Jack really loved you until then. At the time, I sort of thought the relationship was another short-lived college romance. He didn't know it, but I heard him prayin' in the chapel, beggin' God to heal you and spare your life, and thanking Him for you decidin' to stay with him. Never seen a man so broken nor watched one cry like that before. But I did that day, and the shame I felt for what we done has stayed with me ever since."

The hospital. Oh God, I have to tell him. Everything ties back to that one horrid night. A moment of weakness snowballed and created this avalanche.

For a split second, the thought hit me square in the face—and if Kendal wasn't so much taller and broader than Jack—I would have given serious consideration that Kendal was the man in the video. He just proved he was capable of meddling in our lives, and he had wanted me. I dismissed the thought as soon as it crossed my mind. Though their features were near identical, Jack and Kendal looked nothing alike in the body structure department.

I was bombarded with mixed emotions. Fury at Kendal's actions pulsed in my temples, yet shame at my own slammed inside my chest. Just because Kendal made some stupid play for me over twenty years ago using a twisted game he concocted didn't negate my own responses. Had I been a stronger in my faith, I wouldn't have wandered down the path that destroyed my world. And Jack's. And Serena's.

And soon, Kendal's.

"Sin's ripples spread across the pond, my dear. Nothing is left untouched."

I ignored the warped voice of my Meemaw inside my head, though her words were dead on. I couldn't hold it in any longer. It was time to exorcise the cancer.

Holding back my tears, I kept my voice steady as I revealed the secret that no one knew except me, God, and my attending doctor. The secret, it seemed, had twisted around inside of us all, intertwining our lives without mercy. Like barb wire wound tight around an ancient fence post, time had embedded the barbs deep.

"Kendal, we all make choices in life. Sometimes they are the right ones, sometimes they aren't. Interfering in mine and Jack's relationship—wrong one. Our um, night together, oh so wrong. I assumed Jack was guilty, not only that night so long ago but when he was arrested, and those two decisions were definitely wrong. Jack's choice to have an affair wasn't the greatest decision he ever made. That choice, and mine to freak out and not believe him and do everything in my power to get him out on bond, resulted in Jack's death," I said, my voice wavering. I took a fresh swig of cold tea before I continued.

"It's called being an imperfect human being. Let me share with you a piece of wisdom that my mother told me a long time ago. If you believe that God has the ability to forgive us for our mistakes, yet you don't forgive yourself, then you are putting yourself higher than the Almighty. That's called pride, plain and simple. Just as we are to forgive those who sin against us, we are to forgive ourselves as well. If you don't, as you well know, the seeds of guilt and regret take up residence inside us, sometimes growing to monstrous proportions. And believe me, you aren't the only person who holds secrets in their hearts. I...I have one too that I need to confess to you right now. You know, the Bible says to 'confess your sins one to another' and now, I really understand why. Keeping them just tacks on extra guilt that compounds over the years, and in this case, resulted in tragedy."

Confused, Kendal stared at me, his lips crushed together in concentration while he contemplated my words. I let out a heavy sigh and felt the weight of my words bog my tongue down. I motioned for a smoke from Kendal and waited until the tip of it glowed red before I began.

"The reason I was in the hospital and almost died from massive blood loss was not because of a stomach ailment. I had a miscarriage. I didn't know it at the time, but I was pregnant with twins—what the doctor called 'ectopic' pregnancies—one in each tube. They ruptured while I was in class and I almost didn't make it to the hospital in time. I was in a lot of pain but just assumed it was a really painful case of cramps. But, when I saw how much blood I was losing, I realized it wasn't just a rough period. How I remained conscious while I drove myself to the emergency room can only be attributed to the Lord. My tubes were shredded. The doctor told me I would never be able to have children after the damage was assessed. And he was right."

I paused and watched as Kendal digested what I'd just said. It took a few minutes but at last, the entire picture became clear for him.

"Pregnant? With twins? That was about a month after—"

"Six weeks to be exact. I didn't know I was pregnant until I went to the hospital. But when I awoke in the bed after surgery and the doctor told me he was sorry, but I'd lost the babies, I sort of flipped out. A hysterical crying jag is a better description. I only calmed down when the doctor assured me that he was bound by my wishes, since I was an adult, not to say anything about the situation to anyone who asked. Since I didn't have insurance, there would be no probing questions asked. So, he kept his promise and played along with my story about a bleeding ulcer when my family and Jack came to visit. I couldn't tell anyone because I didn't know which one of you might be the father. Considering I was pregnant with two babies, it could have been you both."

I felt it coming and knew I was helpless to stop it. A tidal wave of emotions, bottled up right next to the secret in the farthest recesses of my soul, overcame me. It was like I poked a hole in a pent-up dam.

"My fault...all of it...my fault Jack's dead...should've told the truth...might have lost him but he'd still be alive...spent all our money on fertility treatments...knew I couldn't conceive...pushed him away...into the arms of another...abandoned him...left him in jail...now, he's gone. Oh God..."

No more words erupted as great sobs heaved out of my chest.

CHAPTER 15 – MONDAY EVENING

CRAIG KNOWLES COULDN'T SLEEP. AGAIN. HE wondered how many hours of life he'd given up by denying his body rest. He slammed the case file shut and cursed inside his empty kitchen. A glance at his watch caused him to close his burning eyes. Two forty-five in the morning. Six plus hours he'd spent sorting through the stacks of evidence for the umpteenth time.

Every case he'd been lead on during the last five years would overtake his world until concluded. All the late nights, days away from home and no sleep would turn Craig into a short-tempered bear. His compulsion to solve mysteries had ruined his last two marriages. At forty, Craig realized he'd made his choice in life. His sense of justice, his never-ending quest to solve the seemingly insolvable, would be his mate for life.

Craig's hand grazed over the stubble on his chin. He wondered if this case would be the one that pushed him over the edge. The Delilah to his Samson.

The murder of Serena Rowland wasn't just any case. It had all the elements that screamed *headliner*. A beautiful, high society victim. The daughter of one of the richest men, if not *the* richest man, in Arkansas. The *only* child of a man whose personality was gruff on a good day, detestable on the bad ones. An illicit affair with a married, much older man. A pregnancy the result and the catalyst that ended her life. The man accused and arrested for her murder dead as well, a victim of ironic fate.

When Craig was first assigned the case, he attacked it as he had every other one he'd ever worked—with tenacity. Like a pit bull, he sunk his teeth into the meaty flesh of the mystery and didn't let go. When the captain of his division yanked him behind a closed door and insisted that the case be given top priority, it didn't matter. The captain's relentless hounding didn't add much to Craig's determination to find the killer. There wasn't much room for more pressure from others.

The mounds of evidence pointed to Jack Dickinson. In the hotel room, Craig had scrolled through the text messages in Serena's smartphone first. There were numerous messages that included racy pictures between her and a number she had labeled "Jackie-Boy". The most recent had been sent right before her death. Craig hit the jackpot when he checked her emails next. Hundreds of emails between her and Jack's work email address, most of them pathetic, lovey-dovey mush from Serena. A ten-year-old would have been able to deduce that Jack and Serena were involved in an affair, and that Serena had very strong feelings for Jack. Craig also noted that Jack's responses were less affection-laden than Serena's. He sensed that Jack wasn't looking for love, only a fun diversion from the boring life of a college history professor.

In other words, solving the case had been as simple as connecting the virtual dots. And it happened in less than twenty-four hours. When Craig showed up on Jack Dickinson's doorstep early Monday morning, the man caved, admitting to the affair in the space of mere minutes. Craig recalled feeling a sense of satisfaction when he cuffed the man, his anticipation of marking the case closed in such a short time almost making him smile.

When the news broke about Jack Dickinson's death, Craig found himself a tad disappointed. Not that he wasn't glad the murdering jerk was dead, but now he wouldn't be able to watch him squirm in court. Craig knew he was hated by almost every defense attorney in the state. He had impeccable case files and on-target investigation techniques to thank for that. However, the universe had taken the matter up and dealt out swift justice, so he closed the case and began working on the others that had piled up.

That all changed after the meeting at Roger Stanek's office earlier. Craig felt his blood pressure rise at the memory. He went to the fridge and refilled his water, his gut in knots. He was angry at himself for bending under the pressure to solve the case, moving faster through the evidence than normal. Had he taken more time, been more precise, he would have noticed the inconsistency of the pictures, or had a chance to interview the neighbor—the one who, if she was telling the truth, blew a huge hole in his case.

Craig was also irritated that his obvious mistake was caught by the perp's wife and lawyer. When they presented their findings, he'd felt like someone had just punched him in the solar plexus. Craig was used to having his work dissected by defense attorneys while he sat by smiling, knowing his case was impenetrable. This one was different. He felt it. That small voice in his mind told him they were right.

Craig hated that voice. Because it meant that he'd arrested an innocent man. One who was now dead, which meant Jack Dickinson's blood was on Craig's hands.

His cell buzzed with an incoming text. Maybe it was Liz, the sexy blonde from *Grains & Beans* who seemed to be content with "booty calls", as she liked to call them, about twice a month. He hoped so, because a romp with her would ease his tensions for sure.

Craig felt a twinge of disappointment when he saw the message was from Lee German, his buddy who worked at the medical examiner's office. Like Craig, Lee worked odd hours and once immersed inside a case, lost track of all time.

Lee: You around?

Craig: Yep. What's up?

Lee: Hittin gym. Need a sparring partner

Craig's fingers tightened around the phone. The text was a secret code they'd worked out years ago when one of them had something of great importance to tell the other. Lee and Craig had been friends since their Marine Corps days and worked the same odd hours, so no one would think it out of the ordinary. Just two friends catching up while they worked to retain their youth and sanity with exercise.

The truth was that the gym late at night was the perfect place to discuss cases without worrying about anyone overhearing their conversations. The tension in Craig's shoulders increased and the hair stood up on his arms. He knew the only time a visit to the gym was requested by either of them was when something major was going on. The last time Lee requested one, the information he provided ended up costing a seasoned detective his job for tampering with evidence.

Craig: On my way

He moved into action, the adrenaline overriding his fatigue. He gulped down a protein shake, hoping it would not only give him some much needed energy, but also help quell the burning in his gut. He slung his sports bag over his shoulder and secured his copy of the Rowland case file he kept in his small safe. Another habit he'd developed years ago, after seeing other, more seasoned detectives, misplace files and crucial evidence. His way of circumventing that was to always keep a full copy at home. During his brief second marriage, he'd thought that if he was home more often, the boat wouldn't rock so hard. He'd later discovered that his wife wanted his body *and* mind at home, which wasn't an option when his nose was buried in piles of evidence.

Craig navigated the quiet streets of Little Rock, his Jeep the lone vehicle on the road for most of his drive. The air conditioner was on full blast, yet didn't seem to make a dent in the heat. Craig felt the sweat pool under his arms and soak the back of his shirt. He couldn't recall a hotter summer. The weather was always strange in Arkansas. Extreme highs and frigid lows. Normally, by this time of year, everything would turn ugly yellow from lack of rain. Not this year. The amount of torrential rain had kept the foliage green and the humidity so dense it was hard to catch his breath.

He couldn't wait to unleash his frustration with this case on the bag. By the time he was finished, the gym would probably need a new one. It had taken all of his intestinal fortitude to not smash his fist in his captain's face earlier. Craig felt his blood pressure soar as he recalled the unpleasant conversation.

****

"Knowles, the case is closed. Jack Dickinson is dead. You did a fine job on the evidence, which all points back to him. Doesn't matter what his wife, his lawyer, his preacher or God himself says. You've got plenty others that need your attention."

"Sir, I realize this is a very sensitive case—"

"You bet your ass it is. Philip Rowland and his wife have gone through enough. I should be dressing you down for even considering attending such a farce of a meeting, and for not alerting me ahead of time about it. I thought I made myself crystal clear from the beginning that this case was to be handled with the utmost delicacy. I'll give you the benefit of the doubt, though. I will assume that you were unaware of the intentions of that slime ball LaFont when you decided to show up at Stanek's office."

"Reasons aside for my attendance, it doesn't negate the information presented—"

"Doesn't negate? Knowles, are you outta your mind? I'm surprised I have anything left to sit on after the ass-chewing Philip Rowland gave me today. So, before I lose any more flesh on my rump, let me make things perfectly clear to you. Are you listening?"

"Yes sir."

"The Serena Rowland case is solved. Jack Dickinson killed her. And since Jack is now also dead, there is nothing left for you to work on. No getting ready for trial, nothing. Over. Put. To. Bed. Do you understand the words that are coming out of my mouth, Knowles?"

"Yes sir."

"I'm not sure you do. You look tired, worn out. Obviously, this case got to you. So, consider yourself on paid vacation for the next week."

"But sir—"

"Knowles, if you want your vacation to be *unpaid*, then by all means, say another word."

****

Craig felt his grip tighten around the steering wheel. He nudged his tongue around the sore spot inside his cheek. A dime-sized chunk was missing from after he'd clamped his jaws down to keep his mouth shut. He'd left the captain's office in silence, never even stopping by his desk. He went straight home and pulled out his copy of the case file, then began comparing the evidence he collected with the new information provided by Mrs. Dickinson.

Two hours in, his stomach began to burn. Now, as he pulled in to the parking lot of the gym and saw Lee's Dodge was there, the fire in his gut erupted. The sensation he used to get when on point, like he was walking into a trap or something, bore down on him.

Lee was waiting inside. "About time, PB. What did you do, keep it under twenty-five?"

"Says the guy who lives and works three blocks away. Recall, I had to drive over ten. Unlike you, I obey traffic laws—even when the streets are empty."

"What good is it to be a cop when you can't bend the rules? I mean, come on...who's going to give you a ticket? The bad Detective Pit Bull is feared by all. Notice I didn't say big. Just bad."

Craig threw his bag on the floor and rummaged around for the tape, a hint of a smile on his lips. Pit Bull is what everyone in his platoon called him. At five foot nine, Craig had worked hard on building his physique's bulk, since he could do nothing about his stature. He shot a glance at Lee, who towered over him at six foot two. His nickname was a perfect fit as well—Giraffe. Lee even sported bright red hair and pale skin so covered in freckles that their sergeant had often ribbed him about covering up while in the hot desert sun. Lee's long, gangly arms and legs didn't help matters.

"I know you didn't call me down here just to listen to your sparkling wit. Here," he said, handing the tape to Lee, "wrap yourself up. I think I'd rather hit you instead of the bag. You're getting on my nerves already, Giraffe."

"Wait until I tell you what I found out. Then you will really want to hit someone. And it won't be me. Not that I'm worried. You hit like a girl."

"Drop it on me. I'm already angry. And you run like one."

"Jack Dickinson didn't kill that girl."

Craig's heart began to pound. "Come again?"

"Listen," Lee said, lowering his voice. He scanned the weight room once before he plopped down on the bench next to Craig. "Thurman has been acting weirder than normal ever since that Rowland girl hit the table. Antsy. Edgy. He's always been diligent about checking and re-checking findings before signing off on them, but not this time. He went beyond diligent. Obsessed is a better word. He literally stood behind me and watched while I performed the test on Jack's clothes. I mean, come on. It's not like I just started working there or something."

"Get to the part about why Jack didn't do it."

"I'm trying. Stop interrupting me. Well, I finished the analysis on the clothes you brought in last week—"

"And I'm just now hearing about the results?"

"Do you want me to finish this or not?"

"Sorry."

"Anyway, there wasn't a trace of blood on the shirt or pants. Not even a dribble. There were a few strands of Serena's hair on his shirt, but that's it. This, of course, shocked me. If those are truly the clothes he had on that day, then even if he'd washed them, they would still have traces. I mean, the girl was pretty beat up. Her blood would have been splattered all over him.

"I noted my findings, signed off on the electronic report and, as standard protocol, submitted a hard copy to Thurman. In person and not just on his desk. I told him my findings and he tried to play it off, like it was no big deal. The look on his face told me a different story. He freaked. Less than a minute later, he was out the door."

"Could you please make this story shorter than your neck? I'm wasting precious time that I could be pounding your face in right now."

"You'll want to go have a drink when I finish, I promise. So, yesterday afternoon, I overheard part of his phone conversation with a guy he kept calling Philip. Dude was seriously getting his ass ripped off. I was out back sneaking a smoke when Thurman came out, I think to do the same thing. He's a closet smoker, you know. Anyway, I couldn't hear everything, but this Philip guy was screaming about new evidence, pictures and a new witness or something. Thurman was pacing like a cat in front of a kennel full of starving dogs. I distinctly heard the voice say 'make it go away' and Thurman kept nodding his head yes. A few minutes later, Thurman went back inside."

"What time was this?"

"Around five. Thurman locked himself in his office and I went back to mine. But about two minutes later, something told me to go look in the Rowland electronic case file. I mean, Philip's the name of the vic's father, so I kind of put two and two together."

"You should have been a cop."

"I am in more ways sometimes than you are, smart ass. I find what *you* can't. Anyway, sure enough, my document was open. I tried telling myself that Thurman was just late in signing off on my findings. My gut told me otherwise. I watched and waited until the document was closed then went in and tried to open it, but I couldn't. It was locked with a new password. About three minutes later, Thurman stormed out of his office like his ass was on fire. I've never seen him move so fast. He was in such a big hurry, he left his door unlocked. I, of course, didn't want him to get in trouble for breaking SOP, so I decided to go shut it. After I looked around his office, of course."

"Please tell me that you decided to wander over to his computer and check it. For security reasons, you know, in case he forgot to shut it down?" Craig implored.

"He left it on, alright. I had to sit down when I realized I was looking at my, well, not my *original* report anymore. It had been altered. He changed it, stating I *had* found blood on Jack's clothes and that it was a match to Serena's. Why would he do that? I mean, he's risking his job and even arrest for tampering with evidence if it ever got out. I don't know for sure, but I am willing to bet that he was talking to Philip Rowland, and for some reason, they want to make sure that it looks like Jack Dickinson killed Serena."

"It could be construed that way…"

"I'm not through sharing all the good news, PB."

"There's more? Wonderful."

"Yeah, and this is the really interesting part. After I realized Thurman changed my report, I remembered that the news reported that Jack Dickinson died from an allergic reaction to penicillin. When I heard that on the radio last week, I attributed the mistake to the media. You know, they never seem to get all their facts straight before they start yammering about something. Always in a hurry to 'break' a news story before the competition does. Anyway, since I was sitting at Thurman's desk..."

"Let me guess—the report states otherwise?"

"No! That's just it. The autopsy report on Dickinson was the exact same as what was reported on the news."

"And this is odd, why? Other than the fact that for once, the media got their facts straight."

"I assisted Thurman with that autopsy. Jack Dickinson died from an allergic reaction alright, but not to penicillin. From peanut oil. His stomach contained two undigested Oreo cookies. When I ran the sample, I noted the high amount of peanut oil in his system and on the cookies. Thurman and I specifically talked about it as the obvious cause of death. But, there is no mention of that *anywhere* in the report I was looking at."

"What the hell?"

"My thoughts exactly."

Craig verbalized his internal thoughts, "If that was Philip Rowland on the other line with Thurman, why in the world is he calling Thurman about a closed case? Why is Thurman jumping like a trained monkey under Philip's command? As the vic's father, doesn't it stand to reason he would want the killer brought to justice? If there was any doubt as to the identity of who killed his daughter..."

"Then it makes no sense that he isn't standing on the rooftops or in front of every available camera, demanding the police figure out *who* killed his little precious. Not insisting that it remained closed."

"Exactly."

"Oh, two more items I believe you will find interesting. I've saved the biggest two for last. One is that after discovering the omission of the tainted cookies, I spent the next few hours digging. Look what I came up with." Lee scrambled through his bag and produced a legal size manila folder.

With a sense of reluctance, Craig opened it, peeked inside and scanned the pages. His heart pounded. "This certainly rules out coincidence or blind luck. Jesus, if this don't beat all. How did you...?"

"I continued to rifle through Thurman's computer. I know, I know. Low-life hacker moves, but I couldn't help it. Anyway, I found an email from the head of the detention center dated two days ago. It contained their findings on the internal investigation into the death of inmate Dickinson. The name of the jailer who escorted him to the infirmary rang a bell. Took me an hour to figure out why.

"When I did, I called Janine. My sweet baby sis still works at Harrison High School and she remembered Bill Withem. He was the basketball star whose budding career ended after a horrific car accident. Get this—he dated Serena Rowland all through their senior year. Not many people knew, I guess they tried to keep it under wraps or something. Janine said she thought it was because the Rowland wealth train didn't veer off into poor-mans-land."

"How in the hell has this other piece of news been kept silent? This, oh shit, it changes everything."

"Beats me. The report was generated three days ago by Thurman himself. He should have noted it in the file, but he didn't. Nor did he contact your office with this new little revelation, at least that's how I'm reading your shock. He's doing his best to hide it. Lucky for you I am a pretty good detective. I looked at the autopsy report for Serena, and it still shows that the DNA of her fetus matched Jack's. As you can see from what I found here, that's not the case. Not even one allele matched up."

"If Jack Dickinson isn't the father, then who the hell is?" Craig wondered, his stomach in his throat.

"That's for you, oh great detective, to figure out. I leave the mystery now in your capable hands. You get to finish putting all the clues together and figure out just what in the hell is going on. It seems that when you figure out who the father of Serena's baby was, you will find the guy who killed her. Then again, maybe I'm the only one who thinks this whole thing reeks worse than a bloated body."

Craig set the file down on the bench and rubbed his gloved hand across his neck. Anger danced inside him and threatened to take over his body. The sense that his life was about to experience a dramatic change made him feel ill. The evidence Lee had formed certainly wasn't anything Craig wanted to look at. It seemed that everyone wanted Jack Dickinson to be known as Serena Rowland's killer and the father of her unborn child, whether he was or not.

Craig didn't have a smart comeback for his friend. At the moment, all he saw was red. He needed to hurt something. Now. Fortunately, Lee recognized the wild look on Craig's face as he stood up and remained silent, watching Craig attack the bag with ferocious intensity.

The bag never stood a chance. In less than two minutes, Craig had busted a hole through the side.

****

Philip Rowland sat on his back deck and smoked another stogie. His wife slept in blissful ignorance upstairs. Philip hadn't told her about his meeting at the lawyer's office yesterday afternoon. The thought of sharing the news made his skin crawl. Miriam's state of mind already teetered on the edge. Philip feared the latest twist would send her into a complete mental breakdown. He'd lost his daughter and a grandbaby. No way in hell would he lose his wife, too.

Not as long as he had breath in his lungs and money in his pocket.

He'd thought he solved the problem by snuffing out a trial, but Philip couldn't shake the sensation that he'd been wrong.

Dead wrong.

The scent of sweet cherry floated around his head in the darkness, hanging in the humid air like a shimmering ghost. Philip knew the smell would adhere to every part of him and that Miriam would scold him for smoking. Then again, maybe not. She hadn't paid much attention to him during the last two weeks. Miriam hadn't cooked, cleaned or even shopped since the detective rang their doorbell and destroyed her world. Her fragile mind spent most of its time reliving life with their daughter. Tonight was the first time she hadn't slept in Serena's old room since they found out about her murder.

Murder. The word tumbled over and over in Philip's mind, in sync with the cigar he spun through his chubby fingers. His only child ripped away from him. Philip was no stranger to the word, for his hands were stained with the blood of others. However, when the act affected your own life, it was another story.

Another story indeed.

The pain of losing Serena lifted briefly when the news reported the death of her killer, that monster, Jack Dickinson. He hadn't spoken with the Witham boy since the funeral. Not for lack of trying on Bill's part, though. Philip cringed every time he recognized the boy's number and sent the call to voicemail. It was too much of a risk to talk to him, at least for a while. He had been relieved, the heavy tension that gripped his heart lessened. For a few days, the satisfaction of knowing the bastard was rotting away in his grave let Philip release some of his pent-up rage.

The pressure release was short-lived though.

Philip had thought everything was sewn up tight. He'd called in the mountain-high pile of favors that the state medical examiner, Thurman Turner, owed him. One short phone call containing a veiled threat of exposure of Turner's hidden secrets. Turner's proclivity for gambling and drug abuse were great tools that Philip had used in the past as insurance to get what he wanted. This time, the phone call ensured that the autopsy on Jack Dickinson would reveal a simple, accidental death. Philip knew an official inquiry would follow Jack's demise and he didn't want any hint of a planned killing to be the final outcome. It had to be concluded that the death wasn't from foul play so Philip's name wouldn't somehow get tied to the hit.

Philip stared out into the expanse of his manicured back yard. The lights surrounding the pool cast eerie shadows across the light blue water. His throat tightened at the memories of all the times he caught Serena swimming in the dark late at night. How many times had he warned her of the dangers of being in the water alone? He'd chide her with empty threats of punishment, and her response would be a big smile. They both knew Philip was wrapped around her finger and that he would never follow through with his threats, for he never had. How could he? Her sweet face and tender heart would render him into a big old teddy bear.

Philip fought for control over his emotions. He hated getting older—it somehow weakened him. Even before Serena's death, Philip found himself giving people second chances and the benefit of the doubt, when his usual response had always been swift and angry. It wasn't like him. Philip heard the voice of his father, long since buried in Wrightsville's Eternal Slumber cemetery, growl from within him. The voice mocked his emotions, teasing his sensitivity.

What happened to your balls, lil' Phil? Did that old battle ax you married make them shrivel up and fall off? Did you lose them the day you fainted when you daughter was born? Maybe while you were passed smooth out on the floor the doc cut them off. All that blood made you woozy, weak. Candy ass. You ain't the boy I raised. No siree. My boy was a fighter—a winner. Took nothin' from no one and gave the same back. If you'd done a better job raisin' that lil' slut, bustin' that backside when she misbehaved, she wouldn't be here with me. Spare the rod, spoil the child. Don't ya know that's what the Book says?

It took three huge puffs of the pungent cigar to chase the words of his father out of Philip's head. His stomach lurched in protest, his head tingling. He pondered how it was possible to feel so much love and grief, yet so much hatred at the same time. Philip wanted the nightmare to be over. He wanted a scab to start hardening on the wound and stop the pain. That couldn't happen if people kept ripping it off, like the scumbag LaFont and his sniveling client, Melody Dickinson. Philip puffed away like a freight train, his anger skyrocketing. He'd exchanged some rather harsh words with Roger yesterday. Philip still couldn't fathom why the one person who knew him better than his own wife had blindsided him like he did.

Roger knew both sides of Philip. Most people only saw the powerful entrepreneur who amassed one of the largest fortunes in the state. Philip knew his reputation as a ruthless, cutthroat businessman cloaked him like a second suit. He didn't care, in fact, that was exactly how he wanted people to feel about him—to be intimidated by him and fearful when he spoke or entered a room. Kindness and civility were not part of Philip's repertoire. They sounded nice to the ears, but in reality, hostile takeovers and blackmail had made Philip filthy rich.

Most of the land owned by generations of his family was located further down south. The farms of cotton, wheat, soybean and corn generated hefty profits each year. The Rowland clan never wanted for money, but when Philip came along, he discovered a hidden treasure in the vacant acres owned up north. The natural gas and shale that sat underneath the empty land made him damn near a billionaire when he leased out the mineral rights.

It also made him some powerful enemies. Land that had been leased to hunters and a very large section courted by housing developers was now producing truckloads of cash for Philip. When leases were terminated and offers ignored, the anger and resentment felt by others boiled over into a war. Philip had procured the services of Roger to help keep the peace when the legal battles began. When throwing cash into the hands of those who screamed the loudest didn't work, Philip discovered the best leverage of all: blackmail.

For a few years, Philip devoted his time to hunting out and dredging up any piece of dirt on those who stood in his way. And oh what dirt he found. The sheriff of one county was ousted when it leaked about his preferences in sexual partners—courtesy of some of Philip's best snooping. The one who replaced him was handpicked, his campaign funded by Philip. The few stragglers who wouldn't bow down to Philip's threats or succumb to the lure of cash met untimely and painful deaths. Philip made sure all his bases were covered in that area as well when he saw that Thurman Turner was appointed Chief Medical Examiner with the state.

Yet Roger also knew the side that only Miriam and Serena knew, when the gruffness and sharp edges disappeared. There was nothing Philip wouldn't do for the two most important women in his life. Nothing. God Almighty couldn't stand in his way if Philip caught a whiff of unhappiness. Roger knew that, yet had the audacity to side with his secretary and not Philip.

Philip meant every word said when he had grabbed Roger by his collar and shoved him up against the walls at his office yesterday. He smiled a tad at the memory of the fear in Roger's eyes, for Roger knew all too well the ugly side of Philip. He'd growled in his face like a rabid dog, calling Roger everything but a white boy, and threatened to destroy his practice if Roger didn't drop not only his whiney assistant, but the ridiculous notion of someone else having killed Serena.

Though he never mentioned it and never would, Philip could tell by the look on Roger's face that he knew. He saw the look of clarity sink in when Philip threatened to castrate him and give his family jewels to his dog if the case was reopened. Roger had started to protest, trying to seek out and connect with the Philip's paternal side. He had asked why Philip didn't want to leave any stone unturned that pertained to Serena's killer. Philip's reply was a tighter grip around Roger's throat and a slow, methodical movement of his head, indicating no.

After he left Roger's office, he made a beeline for Captain Hogue's office. He didn't stop and speak to anyone when he walked in, wearing the mask of grieving father. A hushed conversation inside the captain's office did the trick. The captain was well aware of the debts he owed Philip and offered a nod of his bald head. Philip walked out of his office, confident the case would remain closed.

The phone call to Thurman had been a bit different. By then, Philip was driving aimlessly around Little Rock, unwilling to go home until he knew his business was handled. He'd unleashed his rage on Thurman, the images of the photos flashing through his head, intensifying his anger.

Just like they were doing now.

Philip lit another cigar and poured a full glass of whiskey. He wasn't going to let this get under his skin. He wouldn't dwell on the fact that maybe Jack Dickinson hadn't killed Serena, and that he'd orchestrated the death of an innocent man.

No. He would drown out the small voice whispering inside his head with booze. He'd covered all the bases. No further investigation would happen. The autopsy report was sealed tight. No holes. No worries.

Philip threw back a hefty swig of the booze. He wished he believed that.

****

The sheets were stuck to Bill Witham like a second skin. Even though he was born and raised in Arkansas, his bulky frame never could stand the heavy humidity. All three of the other seasons were fantastic, but the price he paid each summer for staying was buckets of sweat.

Bill reached up with shaking fingers and ran his hand through his damp hair. He muttered to himself, cursing his decision to stay in this hot hellhole. It was the third night in a row that the disturbing nightmares jerked him awake, leaving him lying in a bed soaked in his sweat. The urge to vomit made Bill lurch from under the covers and run to the bathroom, but he produced only dry heaves.

Bill leaned back against the wall, the cool tile in his small bathroom a welcome relief. He wondered when, if ever, the nightmare that had become his life would end. Not that he had walked into his decision blindly. He knew the risks, the questions that would be asked and the intense scrutiny. None of that bothered him. Bill had glided through the investigation like butter over a hot biscuit. No one saw or heard anything. No odd moments had been caught on camera. Nothing suspicious had been seen by anyone. Even Sergeant Collins had backed him up, stating he was the one who requested Bill take Dickinson to the infirmary to get fixed up. Not to be outdone, Bill held up his end of the badge and said he had no idea how Inmate Dickinson had received the wound to his eye.

The plan went off without a hitch, followed by the absurd ruling of the coroner's office. That was an added bonus that Bill never saw coming. Bill had not mentioned anything during the internal investigation about the Oreos. His plan all along had been to admit that they must have fallen out of his pocket when he was helping Jack back into his cell—if it ever came up. Stupidity for leaving leftover dinner in his pocket and ashamed to admit he violated policy by having food on his person.

For three days Bill had waited, his nerves on edge and ready to snap, for the report to be concluded. To his surprise, the death was ruled accidental from an allergic reaction alright—but not to peanut oil. When Bill's supervisor called and told him the good news, he'd almost fainted from shock. It wasn't a stroke of luck or incompetence from the staff at the coroner's office, that's for sure.

Bill knew *exactly* where his saving grace came from. He may not be the brightest bulb in the room, but Bill knew that Philip Rowland had friends in high places. If he'd ever had any doubts about that, he didn't after the false ruling was made. There was no other explanation; the man he wished he could call father had stepped in and saved Bill's neck. To Bill, it seemed it was Philip's way of thanking him for avenging Serena's death.

What Bill didn't understand was why Philip Rowland wouldn't return any of his phone calls or why he couldn't sleep for more than two hours without suffering horrible nightmares. He'd done what he set out to do, which was kill the bastard who strangled the life out of his lovely Serena. Bill had made sure that the grieving Rowlands wouldn't have to go through a long, drawn out trial. Serena's name would vanish from the tabloids and someday only be remembered by those who'd loved her.

Bill's chest tightened. Memories of the best years of his life, his time with Serena, flew by, intertwining with his glory days from high school. All the hard work he'd put in to pulling himself out of the drug haze he'd been in, cleaning up his life and making something of himself, and all the efforts to win back the one woman that had made his heart twitch, had been done for nothing. Serena was gone. Her beautiful smile would never look his way again. Her sweet voice would never speak his name. He would never get the chance to tell her how sorry he was, how he'd changed. Never get to feel her warm skin, kiss her sweet lips.

Bill pulled his legs to his chest and lowered his head. The sadness inside his mind made it heavy, unstable. He didn't understand why the killing of Jack Dickinson hadn't made his load a bit lighter, why his pain of losing Serena wasn't soothed. How come he didn't feel a sense of satisfaction?

And why, every time he closed his eyes and tried to sleep, did strange images of his blood-covered hands haunt him?

Bill Witham didn't know. All he knew for sure was that the best years of his life were over, and the one person who'd kept him going was buried in a pink casket less than twenty minutes from his apartment. In the darkness of his cramped bathroom, Bill fought the urge to join her.

CHAPTER 16– TUESDAY MORNING

"How did Roger take it when you called in?" Regina asked me as she puttered around the kitchen. She was concocting some delicious looking casserole for dinner with swift, practiced moves.

"Relieved and a tad smug. I think he's just been waiting for me to admit I am not ready to come back to work. Guess he was right all along. I should have listened." I watched with mild awe while she wielded the sleek, long silver blade and chopped vegetables. If I were to attempt what she was doing, I would be missing a few fingers.

When I woke up earlier, my head pounding and throat hoarse from a long night of tears, Kendal was nowhere in sight. I tried to remember when he left, but couldn't. I must have really sunk into a heavy sleep after my tears spilled out. I'd stumbled into the kitchen to make some coffee and been surprised to see Regina. Not only had I missed Kendal leaving, but never heard her arrival. *Good thing neither of them are killers or I'd be dead.*

Once I'd fixed coffee and begun the process of getting around for the day, I knew there was no way I'd make it to work. It was already well past eight and I couldn't form a cohesive thought, so working would have been a waste of time. My heart was heavy, my mind stuck wandering the gray sadness that permeated every inch of me. My body felt like I'd slept on a pile of rocks. Every inch of me hurt. Today, I felt every bit over forty.

"So, what happened? Did Kendal talk some sense into you last night? That was my hope, at least. You weren't listening to the rest of us, including your mother," Regina reprimanded, popping her dish into the oven.

"Regina…"

"Don't 'Regina' me. You have been pushing yourself way too hard. I can't say I understand everything you are going through, because that would be a lie. I can say, however, that the human mind and body can only withstand abuse for so long without shutting down. Judging by the dark circles around your eyes," she said, grabbing her tea and sitting down next to me, "you are very close to the off switch getting flipped. What time did you go to bed? Did Kendal make you eat?"

"I don't remember and yes."

Regina's eyes locked with mine, searching for a lie. I tried my best to keep my face neutral but knew it was a losing battle. The bags under my eyes and the deep lines of worry I saw when I had put in my contacts earlier told the truth. My inability to hide my emotions on my face was a running joke in my small circle of family and friends. My mother liked to say that my forehead was one of those blinking signs set out in front of businesses, constantly blaring for the world to see what was on my mind. Roger had mentioned several times that although I had the mind for it, I would flop as a lawyer because I couldn't hide my thoughts from my face.

"Honey, I'm worried about you. We all are. Maybe it's time you go see a doctor. I don't recommend medication, especially after what Xanax did to me after my divorce. Put me right smack dab in the middle of la-la land, but maybe it wouldn't affect you that way. Or maybe the doctor could recommend a top notch therapist to work with you while you sort all this mess out. Who knows? Maybe there is a new, homeopathic version of Xanax out there that works but isn't habit forming. Those are things you should discuss with your doctor. You need to give your body and mind a chance to cope with all of this. Leave the sleuthing and searching to others. At least until you get some of your strength back."

"No, I am already drinking too much. Adding drugs would just make things worse because I might never stop. My mind would enjoy being numbed too much."

"I wouldn't let you become a pill head or an alcoholic. There's only room for one friend with those problems," she said, her smile warm and tender. The reference to Kendal's battle with the bottle and her bout with prescription meds left a sour taste in my mouth. "But, I do have some news that might perk you up without the aid of chemicals. Wanna hear it?"

Oh yes, anything to get my mind off of last night.

"Sure thing. Hit me."

"Last night after I finished cleaning, I uploaded a few pics of my new paintings on my blog and then cruised through the virtual highways of social media. I had an invitation to an event by some kid I didn't know and almost deleted it, until I saw the event name."

I tried not to smirk or roll my eyes. I hated social media. With a passion. Jack and I both did—or had. Neither of us ever succumbed to the constant pleadings of our friends and family to join. Why bother? If we wanted to talk, we called. If we wanted to share a gift, family photo or note, we mailed it or delivered it in person. It seemed silly and frivolous to us both. Too cold and impersonal, virtual reality left no room for true human interaction anymore. Since I wasn't a member I had no idea what Regina was talking about.

"Event? Invitation? Speak English for those of us who are still old school."

"Okay. A few of Jack's current and former college students have banded together and started a 'Justice for Jack' campaign online. They invited me to view their blog and to help spread the word. Right now, over five thousand people have joined and the blog is growing fast. And not just here in Arkansas. I noticed some of the bloggers were from other states. These kids not only are touting Jack's innocence but also asking everyone to sign an online petition to convince the police department to reopen the case. They are planning a rally on the steps of the capitol on Friday morning. They even have all the pictures up, showing the differences in the evidence that you noted. There, how's that?"

"Are…are you serious?"

"Sweetie, we aren't the only ones who not only loved Jack, but believe he didn't kill that tramp. Mrs. Preston's affidavit is even on there. There were over four hundred comments on the blog last time I checked. The majority of them were in full agreement that Jack was railroaded."

"All of the pictures *and* the affidavit? How in the world…?"

"My guess would be LaFont, or at least someone from his firm. I noticed one blogger was particularly eloquent in the comments they made, so I checked the IP address. Guess where it came from?"

"If I knew what that meant, I would venture a guess."

"Internet Protocol. Every computer has an address, sort of like a VIN number on a vehicle. It identifies them. Anyway, the post was made by someone with the same address as LaFont's law firm. So, it seems that he's on the ball, or one of his staff, starting a grassroots campaign. And, it's working."

Stunned by this newest revelation, I leaned back in the chair and stared out the window. I couldn't fathom, couldn't process, what this meant. Tears welled up in my throat at the thought of complete strangers, at least to me, supporting Jack. Taking time from their busy schedules to rally together in hopes of clearing my husband's name.

And all I'm doing is reopening old wounds and sulking.

I didn't want to cry, for Heaven knows I shed enough tears. Unleashing my deepest, darkest secret and watching Kendal's face last night when the truth came out had broken what was left of my spirit. My reserves were depleted, dried up. The pressure valve of guilt may have been opened and the full well of guilt drained, yet I still felt empty.

"Oh God...I don't know what to say. It's kind of them all, but..."

Unable to finish, the sobs broke free. In the comfort of the walls inside my home, the place I was entombed to walk alone as a widow, I wept. Regina crouched down next to me, her embrace gentle. I buried my face in her shoulder and sobbed.

The next two hours we spent on the couch as I retold her between crying spurts the conversation that had transpired between me and Kendal. She never asked a question or interrupted while I rambled on, sometimes choking out my words. At last the tears stopped and I sat scrunched up against the end of the couch, spent. If I kept crying like this, I would shrivel away to nothing. Regina waited with the patience of a saint and made sure I was finished blubbering before she spoke.

"Are you finished?"

I nodded.

"Good. Now, you listen up, girl. I may not be a rocket scientist or a psychologist or even a pastor, but that doesn't change what I'm about to say. You all made some bad choices, true. Everyone does. There isn't a soul that's ever walked this earth that hasn't. And maybe, just for the sake of covering all bases, those decisions influenced the way things turned out in all of your lives. But only to a degree because decisions made by others are involved as well.

"Some are strangers, some are not. Yes, Kendal shouldn't have meddled in your relationship with Jack. No, you shouldn't have slept with Kendal to spite Jack or ease your pain, even if you were deceived into doing so. Yes, you should have told them *both* about the babies. No, Jack shouldn't have cheated on you and yes, you should have come clean about the past a long time ago.

"All of that doesn't change the fact that Jack didn't deserve to die in jail for a crime he didn't commit. You know that. I know that. A *lot* of people know that. So please, please Mel, stop beating yourself up over things you can't change and start focusing on the ones you *can*. Because the Melody I know is a tough chick. One who doesn't crack under pressure. In fact, the hotter the oven the better the cookies, so to speak. The Melody I have always looked up to, the one I counted on for moral and spiritual support who had such strong faith you could practically see it oozing out of her—where did she go? You can save your guilt trips for when you are old and in a home. By then, you will have dementia and won't remember any of this anyway."

I tried to raise a smile but couldn't seem to make my facial muscles respond. "Everyone has a breaking point, Regina. I reached mine. Simple as that. We tried to get the case reopened and failed. Miserably. And I thought coming clean about my past would help, but it only made things worse. And I can't shake the images of the baby. A baby fathered by Jack who wasn't ours. God, it's tearing me apart. Truth is supposed to set you free, but I still feel trapped. No, I feel—broken."

"Who wouldn't feel that way? You have lost a lot, plus you've been holding this ton of guilt, this painful secret, back for so long. You just need to remember broken things can be repaired. That's what I'm here for—what we're all here for. Consider your family and friends your superglue."

"If only it were that easy. I have to live with the fact that my actions and inactions led Jack down his final path on this earth. And I don't know how to do that. I don't. And I think my broken heart is way past glue."

"Forgive the cliché, but you tackle each day and don't fret over tomorrow. Get through the now. Besides, God provides the spiritual glue, or did you forget that too? What was it you told me when I was wallowing in my pity-pond? 'God won't put on us more than we can carry?' Right?"

"Yeah, that's what I said," I admitted with reluctance.

Regina reached across the couch and pulled my face toward hers. "Not so easy when you are the one with the blisters and aching back, is it?"

I wiped a stray tear from my face and felt the flush in my cheeks. "No, it isn't. I mean, Jack broke the vows of our love, but so did I. And I held a dark secret from him for much longer than he did from me. Now, he's gone. I can't look him in the eye and confess my sins to him. I can't tell him how sorry I am for what happened. He isn't here for me to tell him that not only do I forgive him but, most importantly, I hope he forgives me. My words, my choices, my decisions. They ruined so much. And I can't tell the man God gave to me how ashamed I am for every-thing. How pathetic and weak I feel for letting him hold on to the false hope of children and all the money we wasted trying to get pregnant. For nothing. I can't throw myself at the mercy of his love and hope he grants forgiveness, be-cause he isn't here to give it."

Regina looked at me for a full minute before she re-sponded. "Could you please tell me what happened to my best friend Melody?"

"What?"

"The Melody I know wouldn't be spouting that bogus crap. She would know, right away, that all this negativity is coming straight from the bowels of Hell itself. She would also know that it isn't her Meemaw's voice she's hearing inside her head, filling her up with lies. That's coming out of the mouth of Satan himself. She would understand that her weaknesses are being exploited, her sadness trumping and blocking out God's love. She would believe that her husband is in Heaven and can see and hear everything that is going on down here, and that he forgives her. And she would also believe that the ultimate forgiveness we humans can obtain is from God, not man."

Taken aback, I felt a twinge of anger seep through my sadness. "Are you mocking my pain?"

"Of course I'm not. I'm commenting on the fact that the Melody I leaned on during my emotional breakdown didn't let me stay in my guilt and sadness. She told me to give my pain over to the Lord and let Him handle it. And I distinctly remember her telling me that, as a believer, we are to rejoice when the sun shines on us and when it rains. Both are necessary for life."

"I know that here," I said, pointing to my head, "but my heart doesn't. At least not yet. The eighteen inches between the two seems like light years."

"You are being way too hard on yourself. And you are letting your sorrow cloud your vision. You aren't just Jack's wife. Or my best friend. Or the only child of your mom and dad. Or the woman who keeps the offices of Stanek, Overton & Smith running smoothly. Remember who you told *me* I was when I was full of doubt and pain?"

"Yes," I sniffled.

"A child of the King, that's what you told me. That I was a child of the King. And I know you weren't lying to me or blowing smoke in my face, which means *you* are a child of the King, Melody. And so was Jack. Regardless of the mistakes made here on earth by the two of you, or anyone who believes for that matter, the debt was paid over two thousand years ago, remember? Nothing, not even death, can take that away from either of you."

"I know. I just, oh I miss him so much. And I can't spend the rest of my life being coddled by my friends and family. I mean, I can't even go into our bedroom without falling apart. I can't sleep unless I am holding something that still smells like him. And I can't shake the voices in my head that keep telling me I failed him. That it's my fault he's gone. My fault he strayed. I know I need to be strong and lean on the Lord, but sometimes, it just seems easier to give up."

"Give up? Again, I ask you, where is my friend Melody? You don't give up. Never have. Why, Simba is living proof of that! Anyone else would have put the poor thing down, but not you. You wouldn't give up hope that she still had a fighting chance. And me? Well, my sobriety is proof of your tenacity, too. How many trips to rehab did you encourage me to make before I kicked my little addiction? Everyone, including my doctors, told you to stop trying, that I was a lost cause. That I was nothing more than a hopeless addict who would never make it and someday die from an overdose. Yet, you didn't. You stood by me and showed me the way, Melody. When no one else cared and the world was ready to toss me aside, you stood firm. How many nights did you pray with me? Read me scripture? Share your love of Jesus with me, and His love for us?"

She squeezed my hands. "You are the strongest person I know my friend. Even your own mother leaned on you when your dad was in the hospital. Why, she had *you* be the one to stay in the room with him after he was taken off life support because *she* couldn't do it! Even your boss leaned on you when his wife was sick and dying. And, he trusted you enough to leave the day to day operations of his law practice in your hands while he took a sabbatical—after you'd been there less than a year. The Melody we all know and lean on may bend, but she doesn't break. Just like your mom said, our Melody is kind of like a willow branch in the storm. That Melody is our earthly version of the Lord's strength. A messenger of forgiveness and love, but also a warrior full of strength."

I smiled at my best friend as fresh tears sprinted down my cheeks. "You know something? You are the most wonderful friend ever put on this earth. I love you."

"Hey, I'm just passing along the advice that a friend gave me once. A really smart friend who never backed down from a challenge. A friend who was the champion for the underdogs of the world who wouldn't turn tail and hide just because someone told her no or didn't agree with her. You are the sort of friend who everyone, including yours truly, always came to when life's problems seemed overwhelming and the advice given was full of hope and love. So, ready for my tip of the day?"

Smiling now, I said, "Hit me."

"Buck up, suck it up, wipe those tears away, and let's find Jack's killer."

We both laughed and I thought about all she had said. Her words made sense. If the situation had been reversed, they were almost verbatim what I would have said to comfort her. But my smile disappeared when the entire crux of the conversation seeped into my head. Her obvious slip made my stomach drop. "You mean *Serena's* killer."

"No, I mean *Jack's*. If you are finished feeling sorry for yourself and listening to me pour out all that mushy goop, I have some more news to share from the 'Justice for Jack' site. I planned on telling you earlier but you wigged out on me and then sunk into a deep well of guilt. I'm hoping my little pep talk helped you climb out. If not, this little tidbit certainly will."

My emotional state did a one-eighty, from abject sorrow to overwhelming dread. "Killer? What are you saying, Regina? Jack died from an allergic reaction to medication. How can that be construed as murder?"

"Let me show you." Regina hopped off the couch and was across the floor in a flash, grabbing her laptop out of her bag and firing it up.

My heart felt like it was going to explode out of my chest. *Murdered? Jack? In jail? How could that have happened?*

My conversation with Kendal about Guy Powell drifted to mind. The crazed, drugged out ex-con with his long-seated grudge against Jack. Maybe he wasn't an "ex-con" any longer. Was it possible that he had been inside the very same jail that Jack had been in? Did he orchestrate it that way? No, that wasn't possible. Jack died from a shot of penicillin. That had nothing to do with Guy Powell, or anyone else for that matter. It was an accident. Even Jack didn't know he was allergic to penicillin, so how would anyone else?

But was it possible that Guy had been following Jack and knew about his affair with Serena? Did he kill her and frame Jack and the reaction to the medication was just an added bonus, not part of his original plan? My mind spun as numerous, farfetched possibilities raced by.

Simba whined by the door. Funny, her bathroom breaks seemed to coincide with my need for nicotine. On shaking legs, I stood up and grabbed Regina by her elbow while she fiddled with her computer and ushered her, and Simba, out the patio door. I snatched a smoke and the lighter off the table and sat down on the swing. Regina did the same while she waited for the page she was looking for to load.

"Look, see? This entry right here. No way is it a 'coincidence.' No way in hell."

I blew out a plume of smoke and squinted at the screen. The words sent a chill of fear through me.

"Anyone remember Bill Witham? You know, the basketball player? My cousin knows him. Played on the same team. And he said Bill used to date Serena Rowland back in high school. Said Bill was tore up when she dumped him after his accident. He sort of fell off the radar for a few years, but my cousin ran into him a few months ago at a gas station in Markham.

Guess where he was going all dressed up in his uniform? He was headed to work and get this: As a jailer at

Pulaski County Detention Center. Doesn't anyone think that's an odd coincidence? The murder victim's ex happens to work where the accused killer is locked up at? Something stinks in Denmark. Stinks bad. I know that was months ago and he may not work there anymore, so does anyone here know someone who works at the jail? Maybe find out if he is still employed there? If he is, then that's where the investigation needs to start."

I took another swig and breathed out unsteadily, my hands shaking as I tried to make sense of this newest addition to my living nightmare. "I'm not sure there's enough brain matter left in my head to grasp all this. I mean, I know someone else killed Serena. The question as to who that might be was possibly answered by Kendal last night. Makes sense. An old enemy from long ago comes back to seek revenge and make Jack pay. Maybe this Guy Powell character had been following Jack and discovered he was having an affair with Serena and decided to frame Jack. Okay, I can see that. And, if that's way off base and it's someone else with a grudge against Jack or maybe even Serena, I get that too. Now, we are going to throw in that Jack didn't die from accidental allergic reaction and that someone killed *him*? Oh dear Lord. I don't know if I can handle anymore."

"Mel, like I said earlier, the actions of others we can't control. Someone decided to frame Jack for murder. And it looks like someone decided to end his life to keep him quiet. Silence his yelps of innocence. Or maybe he didn't really die from an allergic reaction. If this post is right and this Bill Witham dude still works there, maybe he killed him some other way and the jail is covering it up? You know, to keep their image from being tarnished? Heaven knows the Pulaski County jail has suffered from major bad press for years now. Not only from overcrowding, shady employees, and staff and budget issues, either. Remember the uproar years ago when the jail wouldn't accept any more inmates, so the cops just started chaining people to each other outside? That freak show made the national news! So, it seems much better to say 'oops, an accident' rather than 'oh crap, we have a killer on staff'. I don't know. Hell, maybe this Bill guy killed Serena? Maybe the torch for her never fully burned out and he was stalking her. It's possible he found out about the affair and her pregnancy and then decided to kill her and make it look like Jack did. What I do know is I feel right here," she said, pointing to her chest, "that something is very wrong with the entire picture."

I felt it too. For the first time since Jack's death, I felt the sensation of hope pound through my heart. Hope that his name would be cleared. Hope that the guilty stains of the past would be washed away. Hope that my last act of love for my husband would not just be to clear his name, but bring peace to us both for our mutual mistakes.

The sadness and despair vanished. I could almost feel my broken spirit mend back together. What replaced it now was raw determination to solve this convoluted puzzle. "Regina, when did you say this group is meeting at the capitol?"

"Friday at ten in the morning. Why...oh wait, are you...?" Regina's eyes grew wide with excitement.

"Oh, you betcha I am. Do whatever voodoo you do on that thing and let the organizers know I plan on attending. If the police and Philip Rowland won't listen to my lone voice, maybe a multitude will get their attention. I'm going to call Channel Eight and let Ms. Erin Corpian know I'm ready to talk to her. Wonder how long it will take to change that detective's mind when the news airs a report on this?"

"Now *that's* my girl!" Regina said, her fingers flying across the keyboard. "Justice for Jack!"

I closed my eyes and prayed, *Yes, justice for Jack. Please, Lord. Grant justice for Jack.*

CHAPTER 17 - TUESDAY AFTERNOON

CRAIG KNOWLES TRIED TO HIDE HIS IMPA-
TIENCE. He hated waiting. His ex-wives both told him on
numerous occasions that he had the patience of a small
child. He used to argue with his first wife, telling her he
wasn't impatient, just demanding. After their divorce and
his remarriage to number two, he heard the same lectures
almost verbatim and accepted the fact that it was just part
of his personality. Unfortunately, wife number two did not
accept it. The laundry list of reasons for filing for divorce
was long, and one of the top five "flaws" she mentioned
was his impatience.

In fact, Craig thought his childlike patience should be
considered a good day. On one like today, when Craig
hadn't slept in over twenty-four hours, the patience of a
small child would have been an improvement.

For the last twenty minutes, Craig had forced his temper back and kept his mouth closed, except for an occasional slurp of water. He wanted to scream at the inept day

manager but refrained from releasing his pent-up anger and giving him a piece of his mind. Since he wasn't supposed to be working on the Rowland-Dickinson case, or any case for that matter, he decided not bring any more attention to himself than necessary.

He sat inside a quaint booth inside *The Duchess* and played around with the few remaining ice cubes in his glass. It wasn't even noon yet and the temperature outside was pushing one hundred, so he was glad that he was at least indoors while he waited. The place was empty at eleven in the morning; the rich young crowd that frequented the place wouldn't start arriving until after five. By five thirty, *The Duchess'* parking lot would be full of high-priced luxury cars driven by the young bucks in their three piece suits. Their quarry: the hot young females dressed to impress, looking for their next hook up with money.

Arriving at *The Duchess* earlier, Craig had maintained a low profile until the day manager poked his head out from his office. The last thing Craig needed would be to run into Philip Rowland, which was a distinct possibility since he owned the place. None of the other employees recognized Craig, which is exactly what he'd been hoping for. Craig had found a semi-comfortable booth in the bar and then called the main number, asking to speak to the manager on duty.

In hushed tones, Craig stressed the need for secrecy and the item he was requesting. He asked the manager to hurry and threw in the old "life or death" situation, hoping to speed things up. Craig grimaced at the realization that the ploy had not worked. The guy was as slow as molasses on a frozen morning.

Craig tried to ignore the questioning stare of the bartender from across the room. If the guy gave Craig one more odd look, he feared what he might do. He could see himself snapping and saying something that would give away the fact that he wasn't just a patron. One quick flash of his badge and a few words to the nosey tool that he was an agent for the Alcohol Bureau Control, sent in to watch the place for underage alcohol sales, or planting his face on the bar if he didn't plant his eyes elsewhere, would guarantee Craig better treatment—or at least stop him from being stared at like he was from another planet.

Distracting himself, he fiddled with his straw and thought about Jack's widow. It took him a second to recall her first name was Melody, but he sure remembered everything else about her. She was a tall glass of water, probably about five foot ten without heels on. Curvy in all the right places like a woman should be. She had long copper hair and the greenest eyes Craig had ever seen. When he first met her, he was so mesmerized by their bright color that he guessed they had to be contacts. They had peered at him during the meeting—waiting, watching. He recalled he had felt almost like a mouse caught in a trap as the green-eyed hunter studied her prey. Craig had felt the emotional weight behind them as she laid out the reasons why her husband wasn't guilty of murder.

His pulse quickened at the memory. Even though Craig had been drawn to her that day, it wasn't only because of her looks. Yes, her features were pretty, but there was something else that made her irresistible, like a magnetic pull on his soul. Something Craig had never experienced before. He couldn't put his finger on it. He was attracted to her, but not only in a sexual way. Craig didn't know what to make of the strange connection. Was it the undertone of strength and humility, mingled with intelligence and determination that drew Craig to her?

Craig had pushed those sensations aside when she hit his ego hard as she presented her facts. Facts that he should have caught from the beginning when he was assigned the case, but didn't. For a split second, Craig had felt like he was a cadet at the academy and the instructor ripped his final to shreds in front of the entire class.

Craig had been proven wrong not only by Melody's gut instincts and undeniable love for her husband, but science as well. He couldn't ignore the hard gut kicks any longer or deny that truth. He'd arrested an innocent man and set in motion a chain of events that would leave Melody a widow.

And a killer still on the loose in Little Rock.

Craig planned on contacting Melody later in the evening. He wanted to get the information he was impatiently waiting for first. He didn't want to show up on her doorstep without a peace offering, preferably in the form of solid proof that not only was she right, but he was working on solving the case that had destroyed her life and ended Jack's.

He owed her that.

His patience long gone, Craig felt some tension in his neck release when he saw the manager walk through the glass doors, his nametag announcing he was "Dejawn Jones – Asst. Manager".

"Here it is! Sorry, someone filed it under Rosala instead of Gonzales. I printed out her address and phone number, but I doubt you will have any luck."

"Why is that?" Craig questioned. He motioned for the manager to lower his voice before the bartender caught wind of their conversation.

The manager huffed and slid the piece of paper across the tabletop, hissing under his breath, "Ms. Gonzales has not reported to work since the day of the murder. Hasn't answered her phone either when we called her several times. Quite shocking, actually. She was one of the few employees we had who we could always count on. Never late. Always on time. Only missed work twice in the last three years to take her kid to the doctor. We need more like her. Lots have left after Serena's murder. Guess they figure if the boss's daughter isn't safe here, no one is."

Craig kept his words short, clipped and emotion-free. "Anyone gone to check on her?"

"No. We've been too busy to run around chasing employees who don't show up. Between you cops, the media, trying to hire new employees and fixing the security cameras in various areas, things have been insane."

"I see."

Mr. Jones bristled. "I don't think you do. You have no idea the kind of heat that came down from on our former manager, Andrew, when Mr. Rowland found out half our security system was dead. He spent a fortune on the system and because of lack of care, it ended up near worthless."

"Former? When did that happen?"

"Mr. Rowland fired Andrew less than twenty-four hours after you guys left the hotel. When he got wind that the security cameras out front and in the parking lot weren't functioning, he blew a gasket. Andrew's just lucky Mr. Rowland didn't beat him to a pulp. Sure looked like he was going to. I've never seen him so angry."

"It's understandable why he was so upset. After all, his only child had been murdered under his roof, so to speak. And this hotel is the most expensive around and likes to promote itself as exclusive and very safe. What a way to find out it actually isn't."

"No kidding. It's been awful for all of us, but I can't begin to imagine how hard it's been for the Rowlands."

Craig decided he'd been polite and patient long enough. He pushed his empty glass aside and stood to leave, reaching his hand out to shake the man's hand, stopping short when Mr. Jones asked, "What I don't understand is why you didn't check up on Ms. Gonzales yourself, or someone from your department? I mean, it's been over a week since I called."

"Called?" Craig felt the hairs on the back of his neck rise. He hoped his pupils didn't reflect his surprise. He eased back into the booth.

"I called last Sunday and left a message about Ms. Gonzales. You asked me to follow up with all employees who were here that day that hadn't been interviewed yet, remember? She was the last straggler. Since we hadn't heard from her, I left her information with your boss, Captain, oh I forget his last name."

"Captain Hogue?"

Mr. Jones scrunched his face in confusion. "Yes. I gave him the contact information already. Didn't he pass it along?"

Craig held his tongue and didn't respond. He waited to let Mr. Jones form his own conclusions.

"Why are you here asking for information you already have? How is secondhand news about a housekeeper a life or death situation? What's really going on here, Detective?"

"Listen. This investigation is over. The killer met cosmic justice already. It's not the murder of Philip Rowland's daughter I'm here about."

"Then why are you here? I don't understand."

"I am not really at liberty to divulge that information, Mr. Jones. Let's just say that I am working the angle not at the instructions of the Little Rock Police Department. Bigger dogs with larger bites and territories are interested in a case of, hmmm, shall we say, the origins and ties of certain workers of Hispanic descent."

"Is *The Duchess* under federal investigation? Ms. Gonzales—was she not legal? Oh shit, Mr. Rowland will flip out," Mr. Jones whispered, his eyes the size of quarters and his face the color of blanched rice.

"I'm sure it's all just a misunderstanding. That's why I need to talk to Ms. Gonzales. Believe me, I understand the stress and strain Mr. Rowland has been through the last two weeks. I plan on doing everything in my power to make this investigation go away without a peep. It's just fortunate that the, um, big dogs came sniffing over to my side of the fence before barking at Mr. Rowland's door. It gave me the chance to clear the doubt without Mr. Rowland ever being bothered about it. Understand what I'm saying?"

Mr. Jones nodded in agreement, the look of concern creased on his forehead. "Ya, you bet I do. Okay, not a word. You were never here."

Craig smiled and stood up to leave. "Right. I knew I could count on you. The rest of the staff—not so much."

"That you can for sure. What's that old expression? Mom's the word?"

"Mum's the word. And if him, or anyone else asks," Craig said as he cut his eyes over toward the bartender, "I was here about a job as the new head of security. Right?"

"You got it. Anything for Mr. Rowland."

"He's lucky to have such a devoted employee. Have a good day, Mr. Jones."

****

Craig slipped out the side door, climbed into his Jeep and cranked the air to full blast. The cold air sprayed across his sweaty brow, cooling his damp skin. He hoped that Mr. Jones bought his bogus story and would keep quiet, at least long enough for Craig to dig further into this nightmare case.

He wished it would calm his thoughts, but he knew it wouldn't. His stomach juices were on full burn. The knowledge that Melody had been right and that her husband was innocent tore at his insides. Craig had come face to face with his mistakes last night when Lee shared the news. Craig felt just as responsible for making her a widow as if he'd pulled the trigger himself.

His gut instincts were working overtime with all the new information spinning through his mind. He forced his thoughts to the task at hand. He'd only had this feeling of dread dance a jig in his innards twice before. Both times occurred in the dry, parched deserts of Afghanistan and both times had been dead on. He chuckled in the quiet confines of his Jeep, realizing the irony that each time a sense of dread overtook him, Lee had been involved. The first two instances, Craig had saved Lee's life. On this occasion, he wondered if the opposite would be true, because Craig knew himself well enough to realize that his gargantuan mistake would drive him over sanity's edge if he couldn't, somehow, make it right.

He punched in the address of Ms. Gonzales' home and waited for his GPS to pick the best route, hoping he wasn't too late.

While he followed the android voice giving him directions through his speakers, the knot in his gut grew bigger. If his captain had been given the information and didn't pass it along, that spelled more trouble for him. Craig had never been fond of his captain and felt that he was a whipped puppet for those who held the real power. He'd seen it before during his years on the force. Cases that were solid, evidence tight and strong, vanished under piles of red tape, or charges were dropped to insignificant misdemeanors when the guilty should have had the proverbial "book" thrown at them. Backroom deals and courtroom trickery happened every day.

Craig knew it was like that in every police department around the country. Money bought things, including not guilty verdicts or leniency for those who could afford it and paid off the right people. He'd seen it too many times. It made Craig furious. All the hard work cops on the front lines put in by risking their lives to perform their duties, only to see their investigation flushed down the crapper when some slick tongued legal-eagle swooped in. Keeping the scum off the streets was a never ending battle, and one that the good guys like Craig seemed to lose more than win.

Craig thought about last night as he drove. After his meeting with Lee, he'd stayed up all night reading through his notes again. His bloodshot eyes and overtaxed brain sought out the pieces he missed the first time. He honed in on the interview with Jack Dickinson's best friend Kendal. He re-read the brief notation he'd made about a childhood enemy named Guy Powell.

Craig recalled cringing inside when he read the short entry he'd made about Guy and the fact that he hadn't followed up on the lead. During the interview, when Kendal mentioned he and Jack had a run in several months ago with Guy in Sheridan, Craig questioned him about any other threats or trouble over the last few years from Guy.

After Kendal told him no, Craig dismissed the idea that a bully from countless years ago would pop up and start stalking Jack out of the blue, much less orchestrate a murder and frame Jack. When Kendal mentioned Guy's criminal history of drug running and abuse, Craig had completely tossed out the idea of Guy being involved. Drug runners and dealers didn't work that way. If they wanted someone out of the picture, they killed them. A drive-by shooting, a staged break-in and robbery that ended with the victim's brains splattered all over the floor and walls. Bing, bang, boom. Over. Done.

Those types of criminals killed for two reasons: to rid themselves of an enemy and to send a message to other enemies not to cross them. They didn't go to elaborate extremes of digging through someone's personal life, discovering the dirty deeds they may or may not be involved in, buying clothes that resembled ones the victim wore, then following them to a hotel to kill a lover and pin the murder on their target. Nope. Not only did most common street thugs not have the time to plan something like that, but most of them had ruined so many of their brain cells by some means that plotting something out to that detail would require more brain matter than what was available to them. Besides, it made a bigger statement to the other thugs when the life of someone ended with a bullet to the head and blood in every direction.

Craig concluded that it would take someone with intimate knowledge of Jack, his lifestyle and the fact that Jack was doing the booty-bongo with Serena to pull off what Kendal had suggested.

However, after going over his interview notes like a hawk, Craig decided he needed to exhaust every possible suspect, since the guy he arrested sure didn't seem to be the right one. It took was less than a half hour of points and clicks on the Internet to discover that Guy Powell wasn't the killer, either. Though they did have almost identical body structure, Guy had been a guest at Pulaski County Detention Center, awaiting someone to bail him out when Serena was strangled.

Craig had felt dejected and elated at the same time, for Guy could be scratched off the list as being Serena's killer, but couldn't from Jack's. Craig wondered if Guy's presence in the same jail as Jack tied in somehow with the fact that Serena's ex-boyfriend, Bill Witham, worked there as well. Was it possible that Guy and Bill were working in cahoots together? Did Bill Witham, the jealous ex, kill Serena when he discovered she was seeing someone else and pin it on Jack?

Craig shook his head at that thought. He'd looked up Bill Witham online and found several articles from years ago when he was a basketball star, listed at six foot five, which was two full inches taller than Jack. The person who exited the elevator the second time was close to an inch shorter than Jack. Was it possible that Bill hired someone to kill Serena and frame Jack? God knows Bill was surrounded on a daily basis with the dredges of society and could have easily found a willing assassin. Craig wondered if Bill had somehow found out about Serena's pregnancy and snapped, realizing that any hope of resurrecting a relationship with her was over.

It was possible. Craig had worked other cases over the years with lesser reasons for people committing murder. Sometimes a motive wasn't even necessary. But there was the odd twist with Guy Powell. If what Kendal had related to him about Guy's hatred toward Jack were true, it was within the realm of possibilities that Guy was connected, at least on the outer fringes. Had Guy stalked Jack and found out about his affair with Serena? Could he somehow have managed to find out about Bill Witham's ties to

Serena, and maybe the two of them concocted a scheme to kill Jack once he became an inmate at the jail? Or was it just some weird, cosmic accident that brought Bill and Guy together and culminated with the deaths of Serena and Jack?

The annoying voice of the GPS pulled Craig's attention back to the present. *"You have arrived at your destination."*

Rather than stopping, he continued to drive past the small, dilapidated house on the left. He noticed no cars were in driveway and the curtains were pulled shut behind the black bars over the windows. Craig felt a bit of anger rise up. All the places on the street were shanties—an embarrassment to the city. If it were up to Craig, he'd raze the entire area and build a park, anything to rid the area of the drugs and violence that infested it.

He wasn't quite ready to stop. The area of town he was in was rough. The year wasn't even half over yet and ten murders, mostly drug related, had already occurred in the three block radius of Ms. Gonzales' house. Had he been in his unit, he wouldn't have batted an eye because he knew the hood rats would scurry off to hide from the police. Since he was driving his Jeep, he figured he would be accosted by the local thugs who trolled the streets, thinking he was trouble. Craig knew from years of experience that those who called the squalid area home remembered every vehicle that came through, for their survival depended upon it.

On his second circle of the block, Craig eased his Jeep to the curb in front of the short driveway. He slid his Glock in the side holster mounted on the driver's door. He knew it was a risky move, but if he showed up unannounced with his gun on his hip, he stood no chance of anyone opening the door to him. He scanned the area and made sure no one was around, then stepped out into the heat. He locked his Jeep and strode up to the door, his eyes hidden behind dark sunglasses. The weird sensation of being watched pricked at his sticky skin and Craig grinned a bit, enjoying the thrill of the game. He'd been addicted to the adrenaline surge ever since he was old enough to grasp the concept of the sensation, which is why Craig had joined the military and then become a cop.

If anyone was inside the house, they had no intention of answering the door. He called Ms. Gonzales' cell phone with the hopes that it would ring inside. When it didn't, Craig debated for only a split second and opted not to leave his card. He didn't want to scare her off when she did arrive home, nor give his boss any hint of what he was doing.

Right now, Craig was working for himself.

Irritated, he walked back to his vehicle, clicking the key fob to start his Jeep when he was a mere ten steps away. The hackles rose on the back of his neck, his senses aware that he was not only being watched, but stalked. Two hooded figures flanked him on the left and two on the right, all moving in fast. Craig knew that if he bolted to his Jeep, the predators would jump to action and give chase. He surmised he could outrun the ones on his right, but the ones on his left were closer. Instead of running, Craig lengthened his strides. When his feet hit the black pavement, he hit the alarm button on the fob. He knew the shrill sound wouldn't stop the men from following him, but it did surprise them enough to slow their gait down. It was just enough time for Craig to reach the driver's door and yank it open.

In one swift movement, Craig was on even ground. He pulled his gun and braced his back against the doorframe. The incoming gang froze in their tracks. "Not here to cause any trouble, gentlemen. Just wanted to talk to Ms. Gonzales is all. She hasn't shown up for work in over two weeks and her boss is worried."

"Ain't nobody care about us. Whatcha comin' up in here for, lyin' like that for? Cops don't go checkin' on people, makin' sure they's a'ight. Ya'll only come here to pick up bodies," the closest man argued.

"Any other day, I would agree with you. Today, that isn't the case. The folks over at *The Duchess* are concerned about Ms. Gonzales. Said she's one of their best employees and since I'm still working a homicide case that happened there not too long ago, they asked me to stop by to check on her."

"Yo, I know you. You worked on Jamal's murder case, right?"

Craig cut his seasoned eyes over to the voice on his right, giving the kid a quick once-over. To his relief, Craig recognized him as well. Jalel's older brother, Jamal, had been gunned down last year less than a block from here. Jamal had been seventeen and Jalel around thirteen. Smart kid with inquisitive eyes, ones that had yet to be tainted and turn dark from the drugs his older brother had been dealing. The boy holding a gun at him now had the same features, but the look of innocence was long gone.

"Yes Jalel. It's me, Detective Knowles."

"I *told* you he was a cop!" the one closest to Craig crowed.

"He's lyin'. He's just here to harass us! I say let's send him home in a body bag. Send a message that we aren't to be messed with. Don't come snoopin' 'round our hood. We take care of our own."

"Shut up! I got this. Ya'll leave us be. It's cool. It's cool. Me and the Detective are just gonna chat a bit, then he'll be on his way, won't you?" Jalel barked.

"Sure thing, Jalel. Just as soon as I confirm that Ms. Gonzales is okay."

Jalel motioned for the others to leave with a curt nod of his head. They followed his instructions, muttering as they walked away, their posture and attitude leaving a trail of anger lingering in the air. It was obvious to Craig that Jalel had taken his brother's place in the neighborhood. The kid wasn't even old enough to vote or drive, yet he commanded respect from the others, who were at least five years older than Jalel. Craig wondered how long it would be before he was working Jalel's homicide, after one of Jamal's underlings went rogue and killed him over a drug deal gone bad.

When the three other bangers disappeared around the corner, Craig eased himself into the leather front seat and pulled in a heavy gulp of cold air from the vents. He motioned for Jalel to join him on the passenger side. With the grace of a jungle cat, Jalel moved around the vehicle and was in the seat next to Craig.

"Nice ride. Why'd you come here in this?"

"Because I'm here on my own time, not in my official capacity."

"Uh huh. Why you really here?"

"I believe Ms. Gonzales is afraid to come back to work because she might have seen something. Something she doesn't want others to know she witnessed. I wasn't lying when I said she hasn't been to work in two weeks. I just spoke with her boss less than an hour ago."

Craig watched the façade of tough street urchin drop for a few seconds. Although he had never lived the kind of life Jalel had, he had watched the interaction between the impoverished neighbors. Most of the time, they stuck together. Even the ones who didn't join the banger lifestyle were still watched over because somewhere down the line, they were related to one another. Poverty bred more poverty, and once in the cycle, it was near impossible to break out. Since Jalel's house was less than a block away, Craig assumed that Jalel knew Ms. Gonzales, and his assumption was verified by the look of sadness on Jalel's face.

"For real? You ain't here to hassle?"

"Jalel, I need to talk to her. I just want to ask her if she saw something that might be of help to me. I am working a case—"

"Yeah, I know which one you's workin', too. That rich bitch that got snuffed at the hotel. It's where Ms. Gonzales worked at. That don't make sense to me, though. Your guy—he's already been iced for that. What good will it do to talk to anyone else?"

"Because the man I arrested didn't do it. Now I'm trying to find out who did. And Ms. Gonzales is my last hope to finding out who killed that girl and framed someone else."

"You mean she's your last hope to ease your soul, right?"

"Look Jalel. I'm no different than anyone else. I'm human. I make mistakes. Sometimes those mistakes are as simple as putting diesel in my tank rather than gas when I'm in a hurry. Other times, the mistakes are huge and innocent people get hurt. And if I've learned anything in my forty-plus years on this earth, it's that it takes a real man to admit his faults and make things right. It's much easier to pretend they don't exist, but only in the beginning. Eventually, your faults invade your dreams and make your life a living hell."

Craig watched Jalel sort through what he said. He knew he was taking a gamble by revealing all his cards, but he was following his gut. Craig sensed that Jalel knew where Ms. Gonzales was, or at least how to get in touch with her. He also hoped that his little impromptu speech would sink in through the hard living Jalel had experienced during the past year. Maybe give him hope that he could change his circumstances before he became yet another sad statistic.

"Tell you what. Give me your digits and if Ms. Gonzales wants to talk to you, I'll hook the two of you up. Cool?"

Craig smiled at the face of the man-child next to him. "Cool."

Jalel nodded, took the phone number, and slipped out of the Jeep without another word. Craig eased his way through the tight streets of Little Rock's rendition of the ghetto, hoping that his next stop proved to be more informative and less intense.

But somehow, he knew his surprise visit to Bill Witham's house would be anything but simple.

CHAPTER 18 – TUESDAY EVENING

I CLICKED MY PHONE SHUT AND SET IT BACK IN my lap, then closed my eyes before the first burst of hairspray shot out. "Well, everything is all set. Erin Corpian will be here tomorrow afternoon for an interview, and so will Roger and Bertrand. Please, please tell me you will be here? I don't want to ask my mother but I think I'm going to need a friendly face to look at," I pleaded.

"Like I would miss it! Now, you just quit worrying about tomorrow. You have a whole bunch of supporters behind you, plus you have me. This is the right step, I just know it. Someone is going to see the report and realize they have information that might be useful. And even if that doesn't happen, the police will be under so much pressure from us that they will have no choice but to reopen the case. Now, hold still while I finish your hair! This one spot back here isn't playing right. The color looks fantastic though. All your grays are gone! Forgive me for preening you like a pageant contestant, but there was no way I was going to let you be on camera with dull hair." Regina's sweet laughter and gentle brush strokes reminded me of the way my mother used to work through the knots in the back when I was too young to do it myself.

"I'm hoping that's why Detective Knowles called, too. Not my hair, I mean reopening the case," I clarified. "He was sort of vague on the phone earlier, but did insist upon meeting in person."

"Hey, maybe he's been thinking about the evidence you showed him. Or someone pointed him to the *Justice for Jack* site. I can't imagine that he would contact you for any other reason other than admitting you were right. What time is he coming again?" Regina asked as she handed me the small makeup mirror. She spun my chair around so I could see her masterpiece.

I admired my reflection for my best friend's sake. "He wanted to come tonight, but we already had plans with Mom. I told him to stop by tomorrow morning around nine."

"Oh goodie. He's a cutie. Morning coffee with a hunk who carries a gun and handcuffs," Regina teased. "Good way to start the day."

"Regina!" I couldn't hold in my own laughter. The woman always said whatever was on her mind, even more so when it came to men.

"I'm just playing, girl. I like making you smile."

"You are so sweet. Okay, listen, thanks for everything. I...I couldn't have come this far without you." I smiled, then stood up and hugged her neck.

"Oh, don't go getting all emotional on or I'll have to re-touch my makeup! Besides, aren't we going to be late for dinner with your mom?" Regina asked, shooing me out of the bathroom and into the kitchen.

"No, we still have...oh gosh! Why didn't you tell me it was eight o'clock? We should already be there. You know how I hate being late!" I cried, hopping around on one foot as I tried to get my shoes on.

"I think I did just tell you. Come on, I'll drive. You're kinda scatterbrained."

"I've got to let Simba out first."

Regina put her hand on my arm. "Honey, you just let her in less than ten minutes ago. She's fine. Come on, you need to get out of this house and go hug your momma. Now, before the rest of your brain cells evaporate."

"Well, I'd say I'm losing it but apparently, I'm way beyond that. It's gone. No brain cells left to evaporate."

"That's why you have me. I do still have a few. Another reason why you keep me around. Well that, and this," Regina said, holding up the umbrella in her hands, "since it's supposed to storm tonight. It hasn't even been three hours since I washed your grays away. Someone has to keep your hair safe from the coming downpour, right?"

I stopped in the middle of walking down the stairs and looked at my outfit.

"What are you doing?" Regina asked.

"Making sure I'm fully clothed and that I have my purse and keys. At the rate I'm going, I'm bound to leave the house in my bra and panties."

"Now that I might let you do. It would be rather hysterical."

The heavy summer air slapped us in the face as we walked out to Regina's car. Gun metal gray clouds spun over our heads, the smell of rain thick in the air. At least the sky hadn't turned the sickening shade of green that signaled the likelihood of a wicked tornado.

Regina was backing out of the driveway when I remembered I hadn't checked my mailbox in days. "Oh, hey, would you stop and let me check the mail? I forgot."

"You best hurry before the bottom drops out."

I jumped out, trotted over to the mailbox and retrieved the stack of mail. I hurried back inside the car and thumbed through the pile. Bills, bills, more bills. A few straggler sympathy cards from distant relatives and old friends were there, but not the one letter I was looking for from Jack's employer. Regina heard my disgusted sigh.

"Nothing?"

"Nope. Not a thing. I mean, I don't have to have a letter. Why can't they just call me? Send me an email? Something to let me know they received the forms and are at least working on it. I don't know how much longer I can hold the creditors at bay."

"Have you called them?"

I dropped the mail in my purse and fumbled with my seatbelt. "Three times. Their system seems to be set up in such a way that you just end up punching buttons and going in circles, never getting to the point of actually speaking with a human being. It's ridiculous. I need to know something soon. Funds are running out fast."

Regina reached over and patted my hand. "Doll, you don't need to worry about that, remember? I have already started mentally planning out your move. Whenever you are ready, *mi casa es su casa*."

"I still plan on moving in regardless of whether Jack's life insurance pays out. Even if, as Bertrand and Roger are sure is going to happen, a settlement from the County lands in my lap. It would have to be close to a million for me to be able to keep the house and live without having to eat only ramen noodles the rest of my life. Besides, I—"

"Honey, if the real reason for your move is to run from the memories of Jack around every corner, then don't do it. You'd have to leave the state and move to some gawd-awful place you two never visited. And you both pretty much hit all the states except a few stragglers back east. You could move to the middle-of-nowhere-Alaska and Jack's memories would still be in your mind. Move because you *want* to, not because you think you *need* to. And if the thought of moving in with your crazy best friend makes you cringe, the other option is to let me—"

"Oh no," I interrupted. "I already told you I am not going to take any money from you. Though I appreciate the love and sentiment behind the gesture, I just can't. My reason for leaving is a healthy combination of both, I guess.

True, eventually I will be able to get past the pain and be able to walk into a room without falling to pieces. Maybe even sleep in our bed. But it's just too big, too much for me to handle financially and physically. The cleaning, the yard, the upkeep—it was hard when we both did it together, and it will be impossible for me to do alone."

Regina smiled but I could tell she wasn't buying my story. The words were an obvious lie and we both knew it. The truth was, I couldn't wait to escape the walls and never look back. That part of my life was over—gone. If I stayed, confronted on a daily basis of what once was and now never would be again, I would never heal. Every inch of the house would be a reminder of our life together. The ache in my heart would never mend, even to a level of being able to function like a normal person again.

I knew the loss of my Jack would never quite go away. My mother had moved when Dad died into a smaller place for the exact same reasons. I remembered helping her move. It had been hard on us both. Since she had bought a smaller home, we had to go through tons of stuff and make hard decisions on what to keep and what to give to Goodwill. Years and years of memories had to be sorted through. In the end, Mom opted to donate the majority of her furniture, claiming to want a more modern look. I knew that was a load of hogwash. She didn't want the constant reminders of Dad. At the time, I struggled with my own irritation at her decision to rid herself of a lifetime of memories.

Now, I understood why she made the painful choice. Surrounding herself with objects that reminded her of what her life had been would be too painful.

Even when Mom spoke of Dad nowadays, her face would remain stoic, but her words and voice betrayed her pain. I knew she missed him terribly. How could she not? Their thirty-five-year union had made them twain, one flesh. No two people ever loved each other more, at least not in my opinion.

I didn't wish to talk about the subject anymore, so I changed the conversation to the weather and how crazy the abrupt changes in the seasons had been. "Remember last Christmas when we had all that snow?"

"Do I! The entire state shut down for over a week. Oh, and remember how beautiful the lights looked against the snow at the Garden in Hot Springs? We left just in time before the roads became a sheet of ice! Ugh, I couldn't count the times I trudged out to my car just to charge my phone. At least last year it was snow rather than all that ice. How long ago was it we got all the ice? Like ten years?"

"Eleven, I think. It was beautiful for sure, like living inside a snow globe. Too bad the beauty was marred by the freezing cold and the fact that if you tried to get out and enjoy the beauty, you ended up on your butt. Or in a ditch. I felt so sorry for people who didn't have a generator or a fireplace. But last year, it was like Snowmageddon. At least we could go out and play in the snow without slipping and busting our butts on the ice. I hope we don't see either of those kinds of winter again for a hundred years. That is, after all, why we live in the south, right? Mild winters. It surely isn't for the summers."

"No kidding. Oh, and this spring, all those parts of the state that got all that rain? It's mid-summer, everything is supposed to be ugly brown by now. All this water has made for lovely green foliage, but it was so sad to watch the news reports from the flooding. And I can't remember a summer when we've had so many thunderstorms. Thank goodness we haven't had any tornadoes. I hope we make it to your mom's before the downpour hits. Looks like those clouds are full of lots of water."

Sure enough, before she pulled into the carport at my mom's, lightening skittered across the darkened sky, followed by a crack of thunder that made Regina's car vibrate. In the blink of an eye, rain began pouring from the sky. The storm was coming in fast and expected to drop over two inches of rain during the night, with warnings that wind gusts of sixty miles an hour were possible. I knew I wouldn't have to do too much convincing to have mom come back and stay with me and Regina tonight. I couldn't wait to share the *Justice for Jack* site. She would be just as stunned as I still was when she realized how many people supported him.

Regina shut the car off and reached behind her seat, producing another umbrella. We bailed at the same time from the car, our feet splashing through the water that had already pooled in Mom's driveway. We shook off the water from the umbrellas and burst through the carport door into the kitchen.

"I am so glad that your mom's famous spaghetti is on the menu for tonight! That marinara that she makes is magical, and just what we need to forget about the storm. And the pasta will help put some more weight back on you. You realize you look sort of like a scarecrow, right?"

"Well, it isn't going to be very good if Mom overcooks it!" I said, noticing the pots on the stove were overflowing. The water had boiled over and the red marinara sauce seeped out from under the lid, covering the countertop and splashing the vent.

I moved to turn everything off. "Mom? We're here. Are you still in the shower?" I called out inside the quiet house.

No answer.

"Mom? Mom, are you okay?" I shouted as walked into the living room, then down the hallway toward the bedrooms. "Okay Mom, I'm officially freaking out here. Where are you?"

I checked all the rooms as I passed them, leaving Mom's for the last. The door to her bedroom was ajar so I walked in, hoping I wouldn't find her dressing. The last time I walked in on her changing clothes, I got an earful about manners and etiquette. I scolded myself for worrying. She probably just had her hearing aid out while she was in the shower and didn't hear us. The light from her bathroom peeked from under the closed door. I thought my heart was going to explode from relief when I heard the water from the shower.

Thank God! Get a hold of yourself girl!

I knocked on the door. "Hey Mom, Regina and I are here. We'll finish up dinner, so just come on out when you're ready, okay? Oh, and the storm is getting pretty nasty, so how about we just pack it up and take it back to my house and eat?"

No answer.

I knocked again, this time harder. "Mom?"

I tried the door handle but it wouldn't move. I leaned over and turned on the lamp on her dressing table so I could see. Stepping back over to the door, I saw water streaming out from underneath it.

"Mom!" I screamed. I backed up a few steps and threw my body into the door. "Regina! Hurry! Call 9-1-1!"

The door didn't budge so I backed up and slammed into it again. I heard the wood crack but it still held. As tears ran down my eyes, I screamed, "Jesus, help me!"

The last impact splintered the door frame and I burst through the doorway. My heart froze when I saw her lying on the floor in her bathrobe. In a second I was next to her, searching for a pulse. "Mom? Can you hear me? Mom?"

Sobs erupted out of me when her eyes fluttered open. I could hear Regina in the background on the phone and prayed help was coming.

"Going to get my wings," Mom whispered, and closed her eyes as her chest quit moving.

"No!" I screamed. *"Fight!* I can't lose you! Fight, Mom!"

As I performed frantic compressions on my mother's frail chest, I became aware that Regina was doing her breathing. Time stood still for me as we worked in tandem on keeping my mother's blood and oxygen flowing through her.

When the paramedics arrived, Regina dragged me away with promises that I could ride with Mom to the hospital. We watched from the bedroom as they assessed my mother, hooked an I.V. up and then loaded her into the ambulance. I climbed in last and held her cold hand as the sirens screamed through the streets of Little Rock to the hospital.

****

"Come, unto me. I will give you rest. Take my yoke upon you. Hear me and be blessed."
The voice croaking out the ancient hymn was full of sorrow, the notes off-key and the pacing all wrong. No lyrical organ or piano accompanied the horrid sounds. It was nothing like the beautiful song I recalled from my youth, sitting in church with my parents. The pain-filled voice kept repeating the same verse, the halting words echoing inside my brain. Somewhere in the dark recesses of my numbed mind, I heard myself scream for the singer to stop.

That thought left when I realized the pathetic garbles were produced from my own vocal chords. I clamped my dried lips shut and stared down at the worn out hymnal I held in my lap. Even though I couldn't see, I knew it was opened to *Come Unto Me*, my mother's favorite hymn.

No tears were left to cry. I'd shed so many during the last four hours that my tear ducts were empty. Earlier, when the floodgates opened and the wetness left my eyes, my contacts had been displaced under the deluge of salty liquid. It didn't matter that I couldn't see. I wasn't looking at anything anyway. Life had lost all its color. Everything was drab and lifeless, no vibrancy left in my shattered world. I was numb now, unable to focus visually or mentally.

Everything was gone. In less than three weeks, my life had undergone a paradigm shift. Nothing was the same. I had been stripped of all the titles that I used to hold—the ones that molded and shaped me into the woman I once was. Melody Marie Basset Dickinson—wife of Jack Dickinson and daughter of the late Jerome Basset—and now, the late Lucinda Basset. Wife and daughter had been replaced with *widow* and *orphan.*

Another funeral to plan. Another round of familiar faces stained with tears would walk by while they whispered their words of condolences to my deaf ears. Their hushed words spoken to each other as they thanked their lucky stars that their own lives weren't as screwed up as mine. Once the service was over, they would all leave and return to their normal lives and I would be left alone to navigate a whole new existence.

Alone.

The hospital chapel was quiet. I tried to recall when I arrived, but couldn't. Time had lost all meaning to me the second Dr. Hertzog informed me of Mom's passing from a massive heart attack. He mumbled his condolences, but the words weren't comprehended by my ringing ears. A fleeting memory of Regina's soft sobs and warm hands passed by, followed by a burst of color as I fled the waiting room and ran through endless corridors of the hospital.

Mom and Dad were gone. My husband was gone. My two babies were gone. All that remained for me now was to continue to be Melody Dickinson, paralegal. That's it. A life filled with billing, typing, pleadings and filings. I wouldn't go home to a husband and be his wife any longer, for my house was empty. Couldn't pick up the phone and talk to my mother about my day or share precious mother-daughter moments ever again. When was the last time I told her I loved her? Or how much I adored the fact that she had been my mother? Did I tell her what an incredible woman I thought she was and what an honor it had been to be her daughter?

Oh God, who will I be now?

My brain and heart seemed disconnected, like the lines had been severed. I felt no anger, no pain, no guilt, no remorse, no sadness or regrets. I couldn't feel anything inside the black void that I was trapped in. I felt my fingers and my limbs, but couldn't seem to control them.

I just continued to sit, locked away inside my mental tomb.

There was no need to ask God why this had happened. I already knew the answer. Mom hadn't been in the best of health and the events of the last two weeks pushed her fragile body over the edge. I thought that I'd been doing her a kindness by keeping her shielded from my pain and not falling apart every time I saw her, or leaning on her for strength like I did Regina and Kendal. I'd put on a brave face, smiled, laughed and reassured her I would be okay, that Jack and I would weather our marital hurricane.

When Jack died, all the bravado disappeared. Everything changed—for all of us. I tried to put on the mask of control around Mom, but how insensitive and stupid was that decision? She had loved Jack from the first moment I brought him home to meet her and Dad. His tragic passing, compounded with the circumstances that surrounded it, had just been too much for her aging body to withstand.

Had I made the right decision to shelter her? Should I have let my true thoughts and emotions out so she would feel more comfortable releasing her own in front of me? If I'd given her the chance to extract some of her own pain, shouldering some of it myself, would this have happened?

I would never know—and that was the hardest pill to swallow.

Choices. Decisions. Thousands made each day. What to wear. When to get up. What to eat. Friends to make. Projects to be completed. Who we talked to and what we said. What we shared with others and what we kept to ourselves. Who we decided to love and who we chose to hate. Whether we served God and listened to His words, His warnings, heeded His wisdom. Whether we stayed on the moral pathway of life or strayed. Each choice, each *temptation,* affected not only our own lives, but those around us. Sometimes, the effects weren't seen for years; other times, they were immediate.

My choices in life ignited a long fuse that reached out and wrapped itself around the people I loved the most. Its slow burn ignited stragglers from the lives of others around me and now we were all burned. No one was left but Regina. If anything happened to her, I would collapse from the inside and wither away to nothing.

Death always comes in threes, my dear. My child is now with me, and so is Jack and your daddy. It's quiet here—peaceful. You should see Jack. He loves the babies. Holds them all the time. We are just one big, happy family. We only need one thing to complete our happiness. You. Come, join us. Don't be shy. We always have room, even for the most grievous of sinners like you.

"Melody?"

Kendal's voice was a welcomed reprieve from the dismaying voice of my Meemaw in my head. Insanity was around the next bend in the road, but for now I was hearing the voice of the man whose life I'd ruined less than three days ago inside my mind. Satan does enjoy his petty torments, I decided.

"Melody? I'm sorry I just now arrived. I hope it's okay, but Regina called me and told me what happened. Please, don't be upset with me for comin', but I just couldn't stay away."

I heard the creak of the pew and felt Kendal ease his body down next to mine. In my mind, I acknowledged his presence, yet I couldn't seem to make my body physically respond.

"Honey, Regina and I are here for you, ready to take you home. Come on, it's late. You need to get some rest."

It took a few minutes, but I found enough coordination to make my lips move. In a raspy voice, I began to sing again, *"I am meek and lowly, come, and trust my might."*

Kendal's warm arms encircled me from my left and Regina murmured from my right, her fingers stroking my hair. Both joined me for the next chorus, their voices just as choked up and out of tune as my own. As we started to sing it the third time, I lost track of the words. My tongue seemed too large for my parched mouth. My vision spun and the grays surrounding me started to turn black. I tried to pull myself out of the vortex, but it was too late.

****

The smell of fresh summer rain, gardenias and apple pie settled over me, covering my yellow sundress and exposed skin with their sweet aromas. The late afternoon sun caused the humidity-laden air to exude languid balls of steam across our front yard. Miniature rainbows danced across the damp grass, sending multi-colored prisms bouncing off the tender blades in all directions.

I heard the gentle creak of the aged rocking chair and turned my head in the direction of the sound. My mother's eyes stared out across the beautiful display of nature while she shelled the big bowl of black-eyed peas in her lap. Her thick, auburn hair was loose for a change, and cascading in waves around her shoulders, the ends beginning to curl from the humidity. She was still wearing her black dress from Meemaw's funeral and sweat had formed around her temples and neck from the heavy frock.

Momma's face looked tired. I didn't know how to react to the sadness that had replaced her usual smiling face. I had never seen her cry until three days ago and it seemed like once she started, she couldn't stop. The more people came, the more she cried. Now that the visitors were gone, her sobs had left as well, replaced with a few stray tears trickling down her face.

Once all the people at the house had left, Daddy had made me change. He then sent me outside with instructions to start shelling peas and enjoy the cooling rain that he sensed approaching. My six-year-old mind, focused on trying to comprehend what it had witnessed, didn't think to ask questions.

All I knew for sure was that Momma and most every other female member of my small family had cried today and the men, including my father, hadn't said many words. Everyone had been dressed in their best Sunday clothes and it wasn't near Sunday. Instead of the pastor standing alone at the front of the church to deliver his sermon, he stood to the side and spoke in a low voice, pointing several times to the shiny box that my Meemaw slept in. The only familiar thing that had occurred was when a few of the ladies I recognized from church stood up and sang *Amazing Grace.*

Three days ago, when the pastor came to the house, it was the first time in my life I had been truly scared. Because when he finished talking to Momma on the porch, she began to scream, *"No! No, she can't be gone! I need her. Oh Lord! Why?"* Doc Robinson came to see Momma, and Daddy told me to go outside and find our dog Crackers and give him a good brushing. I may have been young, but I knew something was wrong, so Daddy didn't have to ask me twice. I had stayed outside until Cracker's coat was as shiny as a new penny and Momma's crying had stopped.

I had overheard enough whispered words during the next two days to understand that my Meemaw had died, but I didn't know what that meant and was too afraid to ask anyone. People were always coming and going now, bringing enough food to last us a year. I didn't understand what "paying respects" meant, but since there was so much food, I figured it must have something to do with eating. Funny thing was, no one ate any food but me.

For the first time in days, the house was quiet. Daddy had left to take my cousins from El Dorado to the train station, so it was just me and Momma. I stole a peek at her while she shelled her peas and noticed her face was dry, and decided it was safe to ask her a question. "Momma, what does 'paying my respects' mean?"

"Child, come here and sit with me a spell. I've got some explainin' to do and I'm sorry I didn't do it before." Momma set her bowl of peas on the floor next to her and motioned for me to come over and sit with her. She wiped her purple-stained fingers across her damp face, leaving a small trail of violet on her forehead.

Eager to be close to her again, I hopped from my perch on the swing, trotted across the front porch and nestled into her soft lap. She produced a small brush from the folds of her dress and began to comb my unruly hair, something she hadn't done for days. I had done the best I could while getting ready for church earlier, but I couldn't reach the back very well. Her warm, patient fingers worked through the knots.

"Well, honey, when someone passes away, friends and family stop by to tell those left behind they are sorry for the loss of their loved one. Like your Aunt Junie and Uncle Bert. They came all the way from Dallas to say goodbye to Meemaw and tell us how sorry they were for our loss."

"Passes away?"

"It's a kind way of saying that someone has died, honey."

"Oh, like the time when Daddy told Aunt Junie that her new dress made her look 'as fine as frog hair' when he really meant it was ugly?"

Momma's gentle laugh made my heart sing. I was proud that I'd made her smile and laugh for the first time in three days. "Sort of. We've talked about usin' our manners before and how sayin' ugly things about others will hurt them. It's sort of like that, honey. Passin' away from this life on to the next is much more pleasin' to the ears and easier on the heart than sayin' someone died."

I thought about that for a minute. "Is Meemaw in Heaven with Jesus, like what Pastor Otts talks about in church?"

"Yes dear. Meemaw has passed on and is with Jesus now."

"When is she coming back? And how will Jesus know who she is? She left her body here."

Momma stopped brushing my hair. I heard her clear her throat and worried that she was going to start crying again. I wanted to kick myself for making her upset.

"Baby, come on. Let's go take a walk. I think I can explain this better if I show you."

I slid off her lap and slipped my hand inside hers, happy that she was smiling instead of frowning. Her hair looked like it was on fire when the sunbeams hit it and I wondered why she never wore it down. She looked like an angel.

We walked through the front yard to her flower garden. She stopped in front of the plant closest to us and pointed at the grayish-brown mound on the branch to her right. "Do you remember what I told you this is?"

"Umm, it's a bug crisa, right?"

"Close. A chrysalis."

"Nasty worms live in it, right? Daddy said they made the chrys...chrysalis from worm spit. Gross."

"Well, do you see any worms in there now?"

I bent down and looked closer. "No, it's empty. Where did the worm go?"

Mom stood up and looked around the garden until she spotted what she was looking for on the bush to her right. She pointed to a delicate yellow butterfly with black dots on its wings that perched on an open gardenia bud. "Right there."

"Momma, that's a butterfly, not a worm!"

"Yes, it is a beautiful butterfly and true, it looks nothin' at all like the funny little worms we seen out here a few weeks ago. But they are one in the same, I promise. You see, the worm lives its short life here in the garden, and when its time is over, it builds the chrysalis and goes to sleep inside. Once it goes to sleep, it passes on to its next life. What emerges out from the little nest here is a butterfly."

Stunned, I looked at my momma with doubt. "You're just joshin' me, momma! Those ol' slimy worms don't have wings!"

"Oh, Melody, look! Right there—one is about to pop out! You'll get to see the change for yourself!" Momma said, hoisting me up on her hip so I could see.

Sure enough, she was right. For the next few minutes, we watched in silent awe as the butterfly emerged from inside the dark chrysalis. It struggled to free itself from the confines of the hardened worm spit, and once freed, sat still as it's curled up wings began to dry. I was still in doubt about Momma's claim that it was the same creature as the worm, but I trusted my Momma's words.

"Melody, do you think that the dainty, delicate butterfly would want to go back to bein' a worm?"

"On no! It is too pretty now, plus, butterflies can fly!"

"I agree, my child. Now, think of your Meemaw's passin' the same way, honey. She passed on to Heaven. The body we knew her here on earth has changed, and now in Heaven…"

"She has wings! Meemaw has angel wings and can fly around in Heaven with Jesus!" I exclaimed.

"Yes, honey. Meemaw has wings now. And she is watchin' over us from above."

"But, she won't come back because she likes her new wings better than walking?"

"Something like that, yes."

"Won't she miss us? I know I miss her already. And if Meemaw has a new body and is flying around in Heaven, then why were you crying? Aren't you happy for Meemaw?"

"Of course I'm happy for her, baby. And I know she is happy and that I will get to fly away with her one day as well. We all will, when it's our time. I cried because I miss her and wasn't quite ready to let her go. But my tears are gone now because I have faith in that."

"Faith in what, Momma?"

"That I will see her again. In Heaven someday, when it is my time to sprout wings and fly. And when we are reunited, it will be forever. Just two happy butterflies flitterin' around in the skies above. It will be that way for all of us—one day. Even you. So, don't fret for what was inside the empty shell, darlin' Melody. Rejoice in the glory of new life and new beginnings that emerged from it."

Momma put me down and we walked back to the front porch to resume shelling the peas. I was still a bit confused about everything, but certain about one thing: Momma wasn't crying anymore after she explained to me where Meemaw was, and seeing her smile was all that mattered to me.

****

My heart fought my body's urging to wake up. I yearned to remain in the warm, sweet spot between consciousness and sleep, basking in the comforting recollections of my childhood. My reality was too painful, and my dreams had been full of treasured memories with my Mom and Dad. The one about the day of Meemaw's funeral was so real that I could still smell the wet rain, the gardenias and her favorite perfume—Night Jasmine.

I shifted on the couch and pulled the afghan over my head, unwilling to acknowledge the morning sun streaming through the windows downstairs. Though my heart still ached for the loss of my mother, I knew where she was and that she was happy—she had her butterfly wings at last. The journey without her and Jack would be bone-crushing lonely. I clung to the hope that the peaceful images of my youth surrounding me would carry me through the dark ones popping up. My thoughts were no longer numbed by grief or shock. The next step in the process of dealing with death wound through me: anger. I could feel the sharp vines of fury fill my veins, ensnaring me as it crawled around inside like poison. And that scared the living daylights out of me, because I didn't want to be consumed by hatred for the person or persons responsible for destroying my world.

Thank you, Lord, for reminding me of that day. I feel You here with me. I feel Your strength float down on me, like a silken gown of love just embraced my soul in my dreams. Through the fire and through the flames, I will walk beside You—as long as in the end, I can fly with my loved ones. Please, help me overcome the fury pounding in my head. Let Your healing waters of forgiveness wash over me and snuff out the flames of wrath.

I knew I wouldn't be able to sleep again, so I stayed still and listened the familiar voices of Regina and Kendal and breathed in the delicious smells coming from the kitchen. Part of me wanted to get up and join the living, but my body held me hostage, unwilling to move, so I remained in my warm cocoon.

At first they spoke in hushed tones, their quiet bantering unintelligible while they rattled the pots and pans upstairs and cooked breakfast. But when they finished and moved to the living room, I could make out their conversation. Even though I didn't enjoy the subject matter of their dialogue, the fact that they loved me enough to still be here made the crushing pain in my heart lessen a fraction.

CHAPTER 19 – WEDNESDAY MORNING

"Ms. CORPIAN, THIS IS REGINA PEARSON. I'M calling about Melody Dickinson and your scheduled interview today. She won't be able to make it and asked me to contact you to set another time. Yes, that would be great. Thank you so much for understanding. No, I'm not sure when that will be yet. The arrangements are still pending. I will have her call you to reschedule the interview when she is ready to talk. Now, if you'll excuse me, I have other calls to make. Yes, thank you too Ms. Corpian, I will pass along your condolences. Goodbye."

"From what I heard on this end, sounds like that news lady still wants to interview Mel. Am I right?"

"Wow Kendal, that woman can gab! Yes, I believe so. At least she *seemed* to understand. I mean, how could she not after all that's happened? Oh, I still can't believe all this. It's breaking my heart to watch Melody suffer so much. I'm really worried about her—and so is Roger. He was so kind on the phone last night when I called him. I thanked the Lord after I hung up. At least he is a lawyer with a heart. If she were still working at her old teaching job, she'd have been fired by now. I can't help but wonder when God is going to give her a break and throw some happiness her way?"

"I'm worried too, Regina," Kendal admitted. "When I picked her up last night and carried her to the truck, it was like picking up a body pillow. She's light as a feather. She needs to eat. How much weight you reckon she's lost?"

"I'm afraid to think about that. Too much, that's for sure. She's a ghost of her former self. At least breakfast is ready. I'm going to go wake her up. Getting food in her belly is more important than sleeping at this point."

"Oh Regina, give her a while longer. At least while she's asleep, her mind has a chance to rest. Maybe just an hour more?"

"Half, Kendal. Then I'm going to wake her up and force feed her biscuits and gravy. If she won't eat them, I'll threaten to put an I.V. in and feed her through a tube. I can still remember how to start one."

"That pile of food smells too good not to eat. You are such a wonderful cook! Dontcha worry none. She'll eat. Maybe not a plateful, but some. Now, you said to that reporter gal that you had more calls to make. Anythin' I can help with?"

"Actually, yes. If you don't mind, please call Brunie Funeral Home in Benton and let them know about Ms. Lucinda's passing and what hospital she's at and that her final resting place will be next to Mr. Jerome at Ten Mile Cemetery. If they ask when the service should be, just tell them that someone will get back in touch with them about that. Here's the number."

"You think they'll take instructions from me, Regina? I'm not family."

"Kendal. Honey. This is Benton we're talking about. Not Little Rock. News travels faster than a bolt of lightning down there in that tiny berg. Everyone in that town knows Mel's family and probably already knows of Ms. Lucinda's passing. I'm sure they are wondering why no one has called yet. They won't bat an eye. Promise. If they do, you just tell them you are Mel's cousin."

"If you say so."

"Now, that's how I like to hear a man respond to my instructions! Kendal, you are one in a million. A great friend to all of us, even with everything that's happened."

"She...oh boy, she told you, didn't she?"

"Yes, she did. She was really worried that after she told you and your less than thrilled response, the friendship was destroyed. She couldn't hold it all inside anymore—and it seems you couldn't hold your secret any longer, either. She needed to release her pain and ease yours at the same time."

"Yeah, I was shocked. Still am, sort of. Here we both carried this big secret around inside us for so many years and we both felt so much guilt. And, we both assumed our sins are what caused Jack to die. I pulled the guy card and left. Not because I was upset with her but because...well, I couldn't face her anymore. She started cryin', sayin' everythin' was her fault, but it's not. It all falls back on my shoulders. And they just don't seem big enough to carry all this."

"Kendal, what has happened isn't your fault. Or Melody's. You both need to stop this crazy line of thinking. It's not healthy and it isn't helping anything. Mistakes of the past will not tarnish the happiness of the future. I simply will not let them. You are a good person, Kendal. A kind heart and a warm spirit. So was Jack. So is Melody. Heck, so am I, for that matter. We can discuss the ramifications of past misdeeds sometime *way* off in the future. But right now, we must concentrate our efforts on helping our friend get through this pile of mud she's walking through. So, put on your waders and join me in the muck, son."

"Okay, okay. You're right. What else can I do to help?"

"Stop yappin' and get on that phone and call the funeral home. I need to call the Detective and let him know what's going on and tell him not to stop by today. Oh crap! Look at the time! I should have called him sooner! He'll be here any—"

****

The sound of the doorbell and Simba's barking from the back yard forced my swollen eyelids open. I heard Regina tromp down the stairs and open the front door, then realized she was talking to Detective Knowles. I debated only a split second as to whether I would remain in the warm folds of the couch and continue to hide my pain under the comforter that still faintly smelled like Jack, or get up and go talk to the Detective.

Please, God. You know my heart's desire. I pray that his eyes have been opened to the truth. As heartbroken as I am, You haven't let me come this far and experience all this for nothing. Is the lesson I am to learn from all of this to stay faithful through the triumphs and the trials? Is it to not succumb to the pull to seek revenge on the person who started all this by killing Serena, then Jack, and now—by osmosis—Mom? Somehow, I feel that it is. No, I know it is. And I praise You, Lord. For the sun and the rain. But please, Lord. Let him be bringing some sunshine. I'm drowning from all the water and terrified of the coming hurricane of fury.

"I'll have her call you later this afternoon, Detective."

Something whispered inside me to get up and talk to him, and I listened. "Regina—it's okay. I'm awake. If Detective Knowles can wait just a few minutes, I'll meet you upstairs," I called.

There was a brief silence, followed by the door closing and two sets of footsteps going up the stairs. I unwound myself from under the warm cotton cocoon, feeling every bit of my age, and headed to the small downstairs bathroom to freshen up. I washed away the last remnants of sleep from my face and mind, wondering if I would ever be able to sleep in my room again. I had tried last night, but couldn't bring myself to climb beneath the sheets. I sensed that until I found justice for my Jack, I would remain unable to rest my head in the same spot.

Drying my face, I made a mental note to tell the Detective about the *Justice for Jack* site before he left. If he had come here for any other reason than to throw his support in our direction, I would point him to the site and tell him to investigate the jailer and Jack's old nemesis, Guy. My gut wound tight at the thought, and the acidic rumblings told me I was on target with that line of thinking.

Semi-presentable and with a fresh pair of contacts in place, I trudged up the stairs and into the bright living room. The sun blared through the windows, casting brilliant yellow rays off the shiny hardwood floors. From the sheen and the smell of lemon, it seemed Regina had spent some time cleaning, as she tended to do when she was upset. *God love her.*

"Good morning. Sorry to keep you waiting, Detective." Three sets of eyes trained on me. I felt like a fish in a bowl as I walked across the living room floor and toward the kitchen. "Give me just a moment to get some coffee."

"Already poured you a fresh cup, sweetie," Regina said, lifting the steaming mug toward me. "Black as coal, of course, along with an extra shot of espresso. How you drink that motor oil I'll never know, but it's guaranteed to start your engine."

"My rock. Thank you." I took a sip of the stout brew and forced myself not to look down to check if I was fully dressed. The way the three pairs of eyes watched me made me wonder if I had missed a button or something, but I guessed the reasons were much more dramatic than me being half-clothed. Once seated on the couch, I looked over at the detective, sort of expecting to see the same arrogance and irritation that he had exuded during our first, unsuccessful, meeting. I was shocked to see the opposite.

The hard edges around his eyes and lips were gone. The brusque demeanor and rigid posture had been replaced with an air of something else that I was having trouble placing. Sadness? Regret? Embarrassment? Awkwardness? No, it wasn't any of those, because there was also an undercurrent of excitement—a faint sparkle in his brown eyes.

He cleared his throat before speaking. "Mrs. Dickinson, I…I can come back and speak to you another time if that's more convenient. I didn't…I'm sorry. I didn't know about your mother's passing until I arrived. I'm truly sorry for your loss."

Judging by the look on his face, I sensed his words were sincere. "Thank you, Detective. I appreciate your offer, but the next few days aren't going to be any better, so now is as good a time as any."

"Are you sure? I don't want to intrude."

"Please, Detective. If you have bad news to drop on me, may as well go ahead. The pile is already sky high, so one more wafer won't hurt. And if what you have to say is good news, then Heaven knows we could all stand to hear it."

Detective Knowles nodded and cut his glance over to Kendal and Regina. I sensed he didn't wish to discuss what he had come to say in front of them. The coffee was working and it registered in my brain that he was wearing jeans, a plain white t-shirt, and no badge around his neck or on his hip.

No gun, either.

He's off duty, which means whatever he has to say is mighty important if he decided to waste time on his day off here. Or he isn't here in his official capacity at all.

Regina must have picked up on his vibe too because she rose gracefully from her chair and put her hand on Kendal's shoulder. "Kendal, I believe you have a call to make and I have a huge mess in the kitchen to clean. Melody, I'll make a plate for you and be right back. Detective, would you like some biscuits and gravy? I made plenty."

A reluctant Kendal pulled his frame up from the end of the couch and followed Regina's lead, shooting one last worried glance back at me. I nodded to reassure him.

Detective Knowles gave me a good once over, then replied to Regina, "My mouth's been watering ever since you opened the front door and the smell of homemade gravy hit me. Thank you for the kind offer. Haven't had time to eat since, oh, sometime early yesterday."

I was about to protest and tell Regina to forgo bringing me a plate, but then I looked down at the coffee mug in my hands and saw my lap. My clothes were hanging off of me, my legs lost inside my jeans. The skin on my arms and fingers was drawn tight over protruding bones. It was like it was the first time I had looked at myself and witnessed what I had been doing to my body. I was slowly starving myself while I moped inside my grief. Once I recognized the fact that I looked like a walking skeleton, my appetite roared back. My stomach growled in agreement.

Regina was back in a flash with two plates covered in biscuits and gravy. She gave me a stern look as I reached for mine, her eyes ordering me to eat. She handed Detective Knowles the second plate with a big grin, then turned back to me to watch me take the first mouthful. A triumphant smile spread from ear to ear when I did.

"Now, you two eat and chat. Let me know when you want refills."

"Thank you, Ms....Ms. Pearson, right?"

"How kind of you to remember my last name, Detective. Please, call me Regina. Enjoy." Regina gave me a coy wink and floated out of the living room and out the back door, Kendal on her heels. The two things Regina loved more than anything in this world were cooking and the attention of a good looking man—and not always in that order.

A few more small bites down and a tad more energized, I asked, "So, you haven't eaten since yesterday? Why is that, Detective?"

He swallowed his mouthful of biscuit as color rose in his cheeks. "I was a tad busy chasing leads, Mrs. Dickinson."

"Did you catch any?"

He wiped a dribble of gravy from his chin, the stain on his cheeks darkening. "Actually, yes. That's why I am here. Well, that and a few other things," he said, lowering his voice. He glanced around to make sure that Regina and Kendal were out of earshot before he continued, "I have several things I'd like to discuss with you, again, if you feel up to it."

"I do. Continue."

"First, I owe you an apology."

"For?"

"Arresting your husband for a crime he didn't commit is the first one."

I was thankful I hadn't put another bite of food in my mouth because I would have choked. My throat locked at his words and my heart pounded in my head. Did I hear him right or was that just what I *wanted* to hear? To ensure that I wasn't still dreaming, I bit the inside of my lip. Sure enough, the pain, followed by the taste of rust, was there. The detective took my silence as a sign to continue.

"The second is that I'm sorry I didn't pay more attention to the evidence and caved under pressure from my superiors to close the case fast. And three, for letting my pride get in the way the day you tried to show all of us the reasons why you felt your husband didn't kill Ms. Rowland. Because, well, because now I believe it, too. And lastly, certain things have come to light in the last forty-eight hours that have led me to believe that your husband's death wasn't an accident. I believe, wholeheartedly, that it was planned. In other words, he was murdered."

No tears, Melody. Stay strong. Don't let your emotions run free. Find out whether he is really telling you the truth. Use Roger's techniques—ask questions that require more than a yes or no response. Listen. Think rationally and not emotionally.

I set my coffee mug and plate down on the end table beside me before my shaking hands dropped them or gave away the fact that I was a jumbled mess on the inside. With every ounce of composure I could muster, I levelled my gaze at the detective, unwilling to show my true thoughts. "Tell me, Detective, what made you change your mind?"

"The look on your face gives away your real feelings, Mrs. Dickinson. I see the doubt there—the disbelief in regards to my sincerity. I understand completely and don't blame you one bit. If the tables were turned, I am certain I would be thinking the same thing. No, wait, that's not true. I wouldn't be thinking the same thing because I wouldn't be kind enough to even allow you inside my home, much less hear what you had to say. That is one reason why I am here today on my own time, not the department's, because, well, this is personal for me now."

"What you really mean is that the department isn't willing to reopen this investigation, are they?" A twitch of his jaw and the flash of anger in his eyes told me I hit the mark. "I see. So, is this your scheduled day off or a forced one?"

"I'm officially on vacation."

"Hmmm, an unplanned one would be my guess. Unpaid?"

"No, paid. But only because I didn't protest when informed the case will remain closed."

"Informed by?"

"My captain. He was, um, rather adamant the Rowland case was over."

"Did you tell him about all the new evidence?"

"I tried. He wouldn't listen. That's when my vacation began."

I mulled this latest piece of news around. He wasn't saying much but didn't need to expound; I could read between the lines. The police department didn't want to risk the chance of exposing their mistakes to the public by investigating and discovering that the man they arrested had been wrongfully accused. "You said one reason. What are the others? You still haven't told me what made you change your stance."

"There are some things I simply can't share with you just yet, ma'am. At least not until they are fully investigated. I can, however, hit the highlights. I made a huge mistake once and I don't plan on doing that again. And, it may take a while to unsort this mess since I am working this case without the consent or knowledge of the department. But I came here today to make a promise to you, face to face. Didn't seem right to say it over the phone—you needed to hear it in real time, not over the airwaves."

"Alright—I'm listening."

"I won't rest until I figure out exactly who killed Serena Rowland, framed your husband for her murder and then silenced him in jail. Because I have no doubt now that is *exactly* what happened."

Thank you, Jesus. He has seen the light!

Instead of feeling the urge to cry, I felt like jumping up and running in circles round the living room. Kind of like what Simba did during her morning food ritual, minus the wagging tail. If my mind kept shifting from one emotion to the other like this, my brain cells would burst and leak out of my ears and nose. Grief, then joy. Anger, then giddiness. I wondered for a moment if this is what insanity felt like.

I had been waiting for this moment—this spark of hope to clear Jack's name. The small flame had been snuffed out that day in the conference room and then stomped into the ground when Mom passed away. I had too many things to think about and no mental control to focus on one particular thing at a time.

An odd memory from my childhood took center stage in my thoughts. I had been in third grade, the lanky tall girl in my elementary school and the only kid left standing in a vicious game of dodgeball. Surrounded by kids who had seemed to be my friends, all screaming and yelling, "Peg her! Peg her!" as everyone threw the hard rubber balls full speed at me from all directions. There had been too much visual stimulation coming at me, too much to try and focus on, so in the end, I just covered my head with my arms and sank to the ground.

I'd given up then—but I knew I wouldn't this time. The Devil may have had his minions chunking painful obstacles at me, but I wouldn't cower this time. *"No I won't...back...down...hey, baby. There ain't no easy way out..."*

The rush of excitement made my entire body quake with joy. I didn't say anything while I replayed his words over and over in my mind. Detective Knowles was not the type of man who admitted fault easily, nor did he take well to having his mistakes pointed out. My guess was that he had never, even to solve a difficult case, exposed his soft underbelly like he had just done.

No sleep. Not on duty. Apologetic. No doubts. I mulled those phrases over. Whatever evidence he uncovered, whether by contemplating what he'd been shown last week or finding new information out on his own, had caused him do a one-eighty from his previous perceptions about Jack.

Blinking back my manic thoughts, I found my voice. "Please, tell me why. You don't have to go into detail, just the surface is fine. But I need to know what changed your mind. Somehow, I don't think it was just what I showed you, since you seemed to have brushed it off that day. Did you finally check out Guy Powell and Bill Witham? Was it the *Justice for Jack* website?"

Even though I wasn't a cop and had no professional training in reading facial expressions, I saw a fleeting glimpse of shock on the detective's face, followed by conflict. He clenched his jaw so tight that the small vein running from his jawbone up to his temple throbbed with each thump of his heart. He looked away from me and back down at his half-eaten plate full of breakfast, unwilling to meet my inquisitive and pleading stare. His tension and unease filled the living room as he struggled with his thoughts.

After several long minutes he cleared his throat, took a sip of coffee and looked over at me, his dark brown eyes betraying his inner turmoil.

"Mrs. Dickinson—what I'm about to tell you can go no further than this room. I am already jeopardizing not only my job but the livelihood of others by even being here. This bomb will come out eventually, but it can't right now. Not until this case is solved. However, I can't *not* tell you because if it weren't for...my errors in judgment...you wouldn't be hearing this from me. You'd be hearing it from your husband. You need to know—but you also must know that someone is trying very hard to keep what I'm about to say hidden—and as of yet, I haven't figured out who or why. So, I need you to trust me and not ask me any questions after I tell you the bare minimum—because I won't answer them. Too much is at risk right now."

I swallowed hard, my chest tightening in response to not only his words, but mannerisms. He seemed nervous—edgy. He was doing his best not to fidget in the chair across from me, like a little kid forced to sit still during church. No wonder. If what he said was true, and I sensed it was, mine wasn't the only life altered by this tragedy.

"Detective, I understand how investigations work and keeping the confidentiality of your sources. I really do. So, I won't ask you to divulge anything that might jeopardize what you are doing. But, again, I will ask you: are you looking into the possible involvement of Guy Powell and Bill Witham? A simple yes or no response is sufficient."

"Yes."

I clapped my hands and had to force myself to remain seated. "That is great news! Regina, Kendal and I all believe those two are somehow tied together in this mess. Have you talked to either of them yet?"

"I spoke with Mr. Witham yesterday but have not had a chance to meet with Mr. Powell."

"The look on your face now betrays your thoughts, Detective. You think—oh my God—you think that Bill is involved, don't you?"

"Yes."

"What about Guy? Have you made any contact with him? If you can't find him, Kendal might be able to help. He ran into him at Christmas in Sheridan."

"Not necessary. I know where he is, but I haven't figured out how to see him just yet."

I pondered his statement and then it hit me. "He's in jail, isn't he?" The detective nodded in agreement. "In jail...at Pulaski?"

"Yes."

I let that heavy brick he just tossed me sink in. Bill Witham—the ex-boyfriend of Serena—now a jailer for Pulaski County. Guy Powell—enemy of Jack with a score to settle—an inmate at the same place. Though crazy and improbable, it couldn't be sheer coincidence. It made sense to me now why the police department didn't want to re-open the investigation. Not only would it tarnish their image, but the reputation of the jail as well, and had the potential to end up costing the county millions—just like Roger said. It was damage control with a heavy dose of the "good ol' boy" system in place to cover each other's asses and bury the truth so deep under the jail it would never be uncovered.

At the expense of my husband's name. No way was that going to happen. No way in Hell. "I'm guessing that these little revelations aren't the thing you previously referred to that Jack himself should be telling me."

"No, they aren't. None of that information can be shared to anyone, and this last bit certainly cannot. Under any circumstances. If it gets out, then it will come back to me as the one who leaked it, and I doubt I will be able to continue my investigation, much less be employed in law enforcement. This is just between the two of us, agreed?"

"Agreed. What is it?"

He paused, pain and excitement vying for control over his face. There was a look of pity, followed by angst, then an overshadowing of guilt. I couldn't imagine what he was being so cryptic for and why in the world he thought it was something that Jack should have been telling…

All of a sudden it was like the Mack truck that had been sitting on my chest for over two weeks, slowly crushing the life out of me, was roaring to life and speeding off. The haze of the last three gut-wrenching weeks lifted off of my broken heart. I could breathe. Jack had already bemoaned his innocence in Serena's death, admitted to their affair and the fact that he would soon be a father. There was only one thing that I could think of that Jack would need to say to me face-to-face that he hadn't already. One hand flew to my mouth and the other hand to my stomach as the truth slammed home.

"Jack…wasn't the father, was he?" I whispered through my tears of joy.

Detective Knowles' smile was a strange mixture of happiness at telling me the news and fear of the repercussions of spilling the beans. He nodded his agreement.

Thank you, Lord. Thank you. He did bring sunshine. Oh God! Warm, beautiful sun.

I closed my eyes and shut out everything else, basking in the happiness of the newfound knowledge that Jack hadn't fathered a child with another woman. Questions bubbled below the surface of my thoughts but I pushed them away. I wanted to savor this news. This revelation came from left field and was not something I had even been praying for.

Jack and Serena had an affair. He admitted to it and told me the reason that he fled the hotel was the announcement from Serena that he was going to be a father. The baby was the catalyst that spurred the detective to arrest Jack. Poor Jack spent his last few days here on earth thinking he was the father. And my mother! Oh, I couldn't wait to tell her…

In an instant the warm glow from the detective's words turned into a red, throbbing haze. It burned a hole inside of my heart and sparked the flames of fury. The man sitting across from me was the one who had arrested Jack for a crime he not only didn't do, but had no motive in committing. Had he been more diligent, lined his ducks up in a row before he condemned Jack, I wouldn't be a widow. My two closest friends wouldn't be stuck doing their best to help me plan my mother's funeral because I was screwed up from all of this and couldn't think straight.

Why didn't he wait for the DNA results to come back before he arrested Jack? If he had, Jack would be by my side, right now. Along with my mother. All of us would be rejoicing at the news of viable suspects and that fatherhood had not been in the cards for Jack.

I tried to control my anger, but it was a lost cause. The poison of hatred seeped into every crevice in my mind. Rage clouded my vision and filled my head with its orange flames. I'd wandered through the valley of life and fallen so many times I couldn't stand it any longer. I felt my soul falter on the dark, slippery road and skitter off into the dark abyss. The bread crumbs of the light of God's love were gone from my heart, covered by a throbbing mass of blood red. Hatred toward the man sitting in front of me— *in Jack's chair*—for putting me inside this living nightmare slithered through me. The heat intensified and pushed all reasoning out of me in one low, dark hiss as the emotional volcano erupted, "Get out."

"Mrs. Dickinson, please."

"I said get out. I mean it. Get out of my house and don't even *think* about contacting me until you have the *real* killer behind bars."

"If I could just—"

I stood up from the couch and in three quick strides crossed the room, my finger in his face, my voice low so Kendal and Regina wouldn't hear. Had I been a man, I would have punched his lights out. Even though I wasn't, I still had to fight the urge to hurt him.

"If you think you can ease your conscious by coming over here and telling me all this, you're wrong. Dead wrong. Your *errors in judgment* cost me my entire existence, *Detective*. Jack's dead because you arrested an innocent man way before you completed your investigation. And now, my mother has died from a massive heart attack because she couldn't handle all the stress. Stress brought on by your shoddy investigation. Do you realize what you've done? You destroyed my family's world because you kowtowed to pressure by others to hurry up and box the lid on the embarrassing end to Ritchie Rich's daughter."

"That's not tru—"

"I'm not finished, *Detective,*" I shot back, my finger still millimeters from his nose. I took a deep breath to refresh my lungs so I could unload some more righteous indignation in his face, courtesy of my sharp tongue. Before I could unleash my wrath, he grabbed my finger with both hands and pushed it out of his face. I started to jerk away, but something stopped me.

There were tears glinting in his eyes. Real, fresh tears. They weren't enough to spill down his face and had I not been inches from them, I would never have noticed. Nonetheless, they were there and their presence knocked me for a loop.

"You're right. You have every reason to hate my guts and want to stomp and spit all over me for what has happened. I don't blame you one bit, in fact, I feel the exact same way," he choked, his words full of pain. "I didn't come here to upset you any further, Mrs. Dickinson. I came here because I felt you needed to know, needed to hear it from me, the man who put your husband behind bars. And what you need to know is that I believe with all my heart he was innocent. I also wanted to let you know that I won't stop investigating this case until I get to the very bottom of it and figure out why Mr. Dickinson was the target of a large, and quite vast, conspiracy. Because I believe that's what's going on here—and the players involved don't play nice, Mrs. Dickinson."

"Let go of me," I said with more gusto than I felt. True, genuine remorse shone like a beacon on his face. His words sent shockwaves through my heart. A conspiracy? I couldn't fathom what he meant by that.

He stood up and pulled me closer, his words faint and full of despair. "Please, Mrs. Dickinson. You need to trust me on this. I can't say much more, but I can tell you this— until I unravel this mess, you are in danger. From what I've been able to uncover so far, this goes much deeper than either of us can really imagine. Not even behind walls of reinforced concrete and bars was safe. So please, lay low and keep your phone with you at all times and for God sake, don't go anywhere alone. And don't say a word about what I just revealed to anyone, including Roger, Bertrand, and especially not your friends or family. Understand?"

I wanted to protest. I wanted to tell him I had no family to tell, to go straight to hell and offer explicit directions on exactly how to get there and what to do upon his arrival. But I couldn't. My brain was telling my body to lose all control and grab the closest instrument to me and bash him over the head—to make him pay for what he'd done to me. To Jack. To my mom. Images of me landing a solid kick to his groin flashed into my mind. My limbs shook as I tried to override my wicked thoughts of vengeance with what my heart was telling me, which was to keep my temper in check and heed his advice.

Though improbable, it made sense. I already knew Jack didn't kill Serena. It had been just an added bonus to hear that the child in her belly hadn't been his. But that knowledge brought us back to square one, which was who *did* kill her and decide to frame Jack? Other than the man Kendal mentioned, Guy Powell, who seemed to have a morbid fascination with making Kendal and Jack pay for some teenage grudge, who else would go to such lengths to ruin Jack's life? What did Bill Witham have to do with all this? Was it simply an ironic twist of fate? Was it rational thought overridden by the knowledge of Serena's death, and the inability to control his own need for revenge that ended Jack's life?

As I grappled with everything the detective said, the last piece slammed into the forefront of my thoughts. My heart skipped two beats as I ingested his words. "You said Jack and Serena weren't the only targets—so who else is on the hit list?"

The detective released his tight grip on my hands, his eyes clouded with worry. "I don't know for sure."

"Don't lie to me again, Detective. I'm learning how to read you. Who is it?"

He didn't answer, but his eyes betrayed his thoughts.

I'm the target.

Oh God.

CHAPTER 20 – WEDNESDAY AFTERNOON

THE HOUSE WAS QUIET. KENDAL HAD LEFT FOR work and Regina for a doctor appointment and trip to the grocery store. Simba slept at my feet, her tail and feet twitching every now and then, probably from chasing squirrels or cats in her dreams. For a moment, I envied her blissful serenity and wished that I could crawl inside her dream-state and get lost frolicking around in the confines of sleep-induced reality.

The afternoon sun had burned the puffy clouds away with its intense heat and warmed the water molecules in the air. The combination made it feel like I was sitting in a steam bath at the gym. I ignored the sweat that clung to me and continued slowly pushing my bare feet against the concrete of my deck. The slight movements rocked the swing back in forth in gentle waves.

I had begged off going to the store with Regina, feigning a sinus headache and ignoring the warning of Detective Knowles not to be alone. At this point, if I was really a target, then whoever was behind it all just needed to get on with their plans. Quit being a coward and come face me. If

I was lucky, I'd put up a helluva fight, win and smile while I watched them pay for their actions. If I was luckier, they would best me and I would begin my next journey in eternity, flying around with my butterfly wings alongside my loved ones in Heaven.

Mom's funeral was all set for Friday afternoon at two o'clock. Regina had given me a funny look, but thankfully said nothing in front of Kendal when I told them to change the funeral from Saturday to Friday. I saw the questions looming behind her eyes. She wondered why I changed the date to the day that I was to go to the *Justice for Jack* rally at the capitol. My eyes must have conveyed my determination because she kept these thoughts to herself.

Kendal seemed oblivious to the dramatic shift in my demeanor when the detective left. But after our conversation a few nights ago, things had become strained between the two of us, and we were both keeping our distance from each other. Our dirty little secrets were free, but I sure didn't feel cleansed. I doubted Kendal did, either.

When the detective left, I said very little other than the fact he was now on our side and working the case. I made sure to hammer home that this was all very hush-hush and to not say a word about his visit. That seemed to quell Kendal's concerns, but my hasty departure to take a shower and unwillingness to expound on anything else only piqued Regina's.

One good thing about having a close friend is that they learn to read your face. They understand your expressions, the nuances in your voice, and your body movements. I could tell that Regina read mine like an open book. She knew within seconds of looking at me that something was very, very wrong. I could read hers, too, and recognized the look of deferring to my wishes. She knew better than to ask and would wait until I let down the wall I'd just erected around myself.

For the past hour, I had accomplished only three things: smoked an entire pack of cigarettes, thanked God countless times for the news I heard earlier, and contemplated whether I should or shouldn't call Roger and Bertrand. They needed to know the news dumped on me by Detective Knowles. Conflict raged inside me. On the one hand, I'd promised the detective I would not tell anyone. While he continued to work on the case in stealth mode, sharing obvious confidential information might jeopardize things. The flip side was my promise to Jack at his funeral; a promise whispered to the silent grave to do whatever necessary to clear his name.

I realized that promise won the battle when I snatched my phone off the swing next to me and dialed Roger's number. I didn't really know Bertrand and had no real reason to trust him. Roger, on the other hand, I did and knew I could. Besides, I knew if I kept this bottled up any longer I would explode. What I really wanted to do was call Erin Corpian and tell her to come over for an earful. That would surely get the ball rolling for a full review of Jack's case when she revealed on primetime that Jack Dickinson wasn't the father of Serena Rowland's love child.

"I wasn't expecting to hear from you today, Melody. Regina said you were knocked out."

"I was, earlier," I admitted. "I've been up for a while now. Had things to do today. Couldn't hide under the covers all day long."

"Melody, I'm so sorry about your mom. She was a good woman."

"Thank you. I still can't believe she's gone."

"Have you, I mean, did you, uh, is the funeral set yet?"

"Yes. Just a graveside service at Ten Mile in Benton on Friday at two o'clock. I hope you don't have court that day. I could use another friendly face."

"No, I'm free that day, but isn't that the day of the rally at the capitol? I thought you were attending."

"Great, thanks. And yes, it is the same day. I just, oh I just can't muster the strength to show up right now. From what I can tell, the site and the supporters are all raring to go whether I'm there or not. I need to say goodbye to my mom first, then maybe I will find the inner courage to shout from the rooftops that I wasn't married to a killer."

"I think that is a good idea. Give yourself time to heal from these wounds, Melody. You've sustained some traumatic injuries to your psyche these last few weeks."

The lump in my throat pushed against my vocal chords. I took a swallow of tea and pushed it back down, then changed the subject. "Listen, I called you because I have some things I need to tell you that I just can't over the phone. How's your schedule this afternoon?"

"I have a new client coming in at three, but I can always reschedule. Why, what's up?"

"Some new breaks in the case. Ones I won't discuss except in person. They are very significant, mind you, so do you mind stopping by?"

"Of course not, Melody. Should I bring Bertrand as well?"

"No, please don't. I'm...I'm not comfortable sharing what I found out with anyone right now, except you. I haven't even told Regina or Kendal yet. Kendal is at work and Regina went to the doctor and out shopping, and knowing her, that could take all day. Shiny things distract her, even when buying food. I'm going to be out for a while myself, so any time after three would be a good time to come over since neither of them will be here."

"If there is something you need, I can pick it up on my way over," Roger offered.

"No, it's nothing like that. I have to stop by my mom's and pick out an outfit, then take it to the funeral home. It's something I want to do by myself, you know?"

"Oh yes, how well I do. Let me finish up a few motions and shut down for the afternoon, then I'll be there. Three did you say?"

"Yes, that's perfect. Listen, thanks, Roger. For everything. I...I don't know how I could have gotten through this without all your support and understanding. Means a lot."

"No need for thanks. Consider it done. See you soon."

The call disconnected. I turned my face to the west and watched storm clouds form in the distance. The air was heavy and thick with humidity and a slight haze of gun metal gray and olive green shimmered in the sky. The barometric pressure had shifted and my fake sinus headache was now real. It pounded in my temples as the pressure mounted behind my eyes. I rubbed my head to alleviate some of the pain, and hoped that the winds shifted and took the storm in another direction. If it stayed on its current trajectory, the wicked looking clouds would pass right over the house and deposit gallons of rain, or worse, judging by the colors in the sky.

I didn't want to be stuck inside when I unloaded the news to Roger later. I wouldn't be able to unleash my inner turmoil unless I puffed away like a freight train. God, I really needed to give the habit up again, but right now, I couldn't.

Maybe once the detective solved this case and cleared Jack's name, I could.

With one last puff, I stood up, gathered my phone and drink and went inside. Simba popped up and was right behind me. She looked wounded when I made her stay outside. I stood in the kitchen for a few seconds and fought the urge to scream. The silence was worse than a houseful of people. The room seemed to get smaller, the walls crushing in around me. My heart pounded in my ears as the unnerving sensation of being smothered pushed the air out of my lungs.

I grabbed my purse off the table, ran down the stairs two at a time and out to my car. Although I dreaded the task of picking out my mother's final outfit, I couldn't spend another second alone in the house. The place I used to call home was now just walls that housed ghosts of my past in every room. Somehow, I knew that until Jack's killer was caught, I would never be able to come to terms with my life and learn to move on.

But as I drove down the streets toward my mom's place, I knew that wasn't the only reason I ran like a crazy woman from my kitchen. It was time. Time to stop waiting around for others to make things right in my world. It was time to seize the reins and lead my own way; time to stop playing by the rules and take back my life. I'd felt the shift inside of me when I blew up earlier. A seismic shift that rattled my core and altered my perception, brought upon by the knowledge that the detective felt that somehow the nightmare wasn't over yet. That now I was in danger and maybe a target as well. A small part of me, barely a whisper, was trying to hang on to my sanity, to keep myself from diving headfirst into the murky waters of rage.

My new purpose seemed crystal clear and shouted like a tornado siren in my head. I wasn't going to let Detective Knowles screw up again. No way. It was time to start my own investigation—and my first stop was going to be to find and talk to Guy Powell.

My foot tromped on the accelerator as my anger rose. I barreled through the streets, trying to outrun my fury at myself for not fighting sooner. Had I done so, I wouldn't be forced to pick out another outfit to bury a loved one in.

****

Craig Knowles had never felt like such a worthless piece of trash. He had hoped to provide good news to help ease the loss, and ended up producing a torrent of anger from Mrs. Dickinson. He couldn't blame her and agreed with everything she said to him in her fit of rage; he'd tossed another spoonful of salt on her open wounds. It was his fault that her life would never be the same.

It had taken everything in him not to reveal the entire truth of the situation to her when he saw the tears form in her eyes. Craig had wanted to tell her about his visit with Bill Witham yesterday, too. The look of confusion on Bill's face when he opened his front door and found Craig standing there had morphed quickly to terror when Craig informed him who he was. He'd watched Bill squirm and sweat under Craig's pressing questions about Jack Dickinson. The man almost fainted when a nonchalant Craig mentioned how hard Serena's death must have been on Bill, with him being her ex and working in such close proximity to her alleged killer. The real kicker had been the look on his face when Craig mentioned divine justice had been doled out without the assistance of the legal system. Respiratory failure from an allergic reaction to peanut oil—and how fitting it was that the man accused of strangling the air out of Serena's lungs died a similar death.

Though Bill Witham made no confession, Craig had recognized the nonverbal cues: sweat pouring off his milky white face as the blood drained from it, constantly shifting eyes and fidgeting hands. When Craig left Bill's house yesterday evening, he was more than convinced Bill Witham had played a pivotal role in the death of Jack Dickinson.

Melody had seen through his attempt to mask his true thoughts. Craig wanted to kick himself for going over to her house in the first place. Had he just finished his investigation and solved the case, Melody would be unaware of the dangers that Craig felt lurked around her.

He felt ashamed for hiding the entire truth from her but knew that until he uncovered everything and sorted out the convoluted, intricate mess, he couldn't. Heat flushed his cheeks at the memory of grabbing Melody's hand. He was a professional and knew better than to get emotionally involved, but he couldn't seem to ignore the feelings that rolled around inside of him.

Craig knew he needed to refocus. He needed to stop thinking about Melody Dickinson that way. She'd just lost her husband for God's sake, and now her mother! Still, Craig felt drawn to her deep devotion, her unwillingness to give up, and her feisty spirit.

Pulling into the parking lot of the grocery store, Craig collected his thoughts and began to work a plan up for the day. He had screwed up this case before. He'd cracked under the pressure from his superiors to solve it in record time, to put a shiny star in the eyes of not only the public, but the mighty Phil Rowland. Craig swore under his breath. He never should have been assigned the case to begin with. He hadn't had a day off in over a month and had been running on fumes as it was.

For a moment, Craig wished he'd never met Lee at the gym the other night, for ignorance really was bliss. He couldn't shake the feeling that this case would be his last one. Craig knew he would never be able to take lead again without second guessing every move, each piece of evidence. His trust in his own instincts had been blown to hell, replaced with the heaviness of remorse and guilt over the death of Jack Dickinson.

Craig settled his own mental torture by making a promise to himself. Once he'd unraveled the tangled knots and solved this one, it would be time to retire from law enforcement. Between his military service and fifteen plus years on the force, he'd seen enough bloodshed to last three lifetimes. If he didn't get out now, Craig feared his perception on mankind would be so tainted that he would never recover and become like so many other cops who turned into raging addicts to dull the horrific images seared into their brains. Or even worse—become so jaded and traumatized that the only way to stop the pain was to eat your gun.

He'd sidestepped several offers from his Uncle Rex over the years to partner up and help him run his sporting goods stores, thinking the boredom of a repetitive job and the same scenery behind a desk each day would drive him bat-shit crazy. Craig winced at the thought now, wishing he was locked inside the mundane rather than stuck in the well of guilt he currently resided in. Maybe it was just because he wasn't looking at life through the eyes of a mus-cled-up youngster any longer. Maybe age did truly bring a bit of wisdom.

Craig pushed all that mental crap aside, along with the sense of intensity he felt churning inside of him. He needed to leave the angst that crawled around inside his head out of the picture and methodically focus on his agenda for the day.

Priority number one was figuring out a way to visit Guy Powell in jail without arousing suspicion or his visit being reported to his captain. Priority number two was to find Ms. Gonzales and talk to her, because his instincts told him she knew something. Craig opened his eyes and grabbed his cell phone, hoping that he'd missed a call while the phone had been on silent at Melody's house. He felt a surge of irritation when he saw none.

Craig glanced at his watch. It was almost ten. Shift changed at the jail at eleven a.m., which would be the perfect time to go in. But if just one person slipped up and mentioned his impromptu visit to his captain, he would be toast. He needed a plausible reason to be there. Craig dug deeper back into his memory and recalled the name of the narcotics officer on Powell's arrest warrant. Craig didn't know the guy very well, but from what little he'd heard about him, he seemed to be a stand-up cop. Craig fumbled around in his console and looked for the list of department numbers. Once in hand, he snatched his phone off the seat to make the call. Before he could finish tapping in the numbers, it began to vibrate with an incoming call from a blocked number.

It took three full rings before Craig followed his gut and answered an unknown number, something he rarely did. "Knowles."

"Took ya long enough."

Craig's heart rate spiked when he recognized the voice on the other end. "Hey Jalel. Sorry, my phone was on silent. Do you—"

"Ain't got time for a convo. Where ya at?"

"West Little Rock. Where do I need to be?"

"Boyle Park in twenty minutes. If ya late, we ain't waitin'. Go to the swings at the back next to the last ball field on the right."

"We? You and Ms. Gonzales? Is she willing—?"

The line went dead and Craig didn't waste any time. He tore out of the parking lot and headed to the freeway. Jalel had said "we" and that could only mean one thing—he'd found Ms. Gonzales and somehow convinced her to agree to meet him. And they'd picked Boyle Park—one of the most crime ridden places in the county. A once beautiful public park with several baseball fields was now a haven for drugs, illicit sex trade operations and gang violence. Kids didn't go there to play—they went to be played, get laid, get high or die.

The location told Craig that Jalel and Ms. Gonzales wanted no part of being on Craig's turf. Whatever Ms. Gonzales knew must be substantial, or she wouldn't risk stepping foot into Boyle Park, even escorted by a banger.

****

Craig stepped out of his Jeep into the bright afternoon sun, his boot-clad feet crunching the gravel underneath him. He'd made the drive across town in record time and still had three minutes to spare. Though no cars were present, Craig saw Jalel and a woman he assumed was Ms. Gonzales sitting on a dilapidated picnic table next to the broken swings. Neither of them moved as Craig walked over.

Through his sunglasses, Craig took the few seconds he had to scan the perimeter. His nerves were on edge, his senses on heightened alert. The sensation of walking into a trap hit him again, just as it had at the gym the other night. He hoped this time he would hear something that would help his case.

A quick perusal of the area verified that he wasn't about to be ambushed, and Craig turned his gaze to Ms. Gonzales. Even from a distance, Craig sensed her fear. He adjusted his stiff stance and gait and tried to appear less gruff as he crossed the last twenty feet separating them.

Jalel motioned for Craig to sit at the other end of the small table. Without a word, Craig eased his body down and removed his glasses. Rather than making the poor woman anymore uncomfortable, Craig focused his attention to Jalel and addressed him while watching Ms. Gonzales through his peripheral vision. "Thank you for waiting."

"No need. You was on time," Jalel said, and Craig noticed a change in the kid's inflection. Behind the dark eyes that had probably seen just as much screwed up crap as Craig's, there was softness. A glow of compassion for the woman seated next to him passed across Jalel's face as he motioned for Ms. Gonzales to speak.

Craig surmised that Ms. Gonzales was in her early forties and around five foot three. Her dark brown eyes bounced back and forth between Jalel and Craig, and she muttered a few words under her breath that sounded like a Spanish prayer. Craig watched Jalel reach over and pat her quaking hand. Craig didn't understand or speak Spanish, but he picked out enough to comprehend that Jalel was telling Ms. Gonzales to not be afraid.

"She don't speak much English, so I'm gonna tell you what she says, okay?"

"Okay."

"Make your questions short. Translatin' ain't easy."

"I will."

"Before she says a thing, she has a few conditions. Wants your word on all of it or she walks."

Craig held in his irritation. "Such as?"

"First that you don't ever bring her in for questioning. What she says you heard from a lil birdie, got it?"

"Go on."

"Second, she don't want her name or what she's about to tell you brought up. Ever. You try and use in it an arrest warrant, she'll deny it. Try to make her testify, she'll run.

All you're gettin' today is a onetime tale. I tried tellin' her she was crazy. Told her to just move away and never come back. Dude will never know where she went. But she says she can't. Says the Devil himself is hauntin' her at night. Won't let her sleep. Says if she tells the truth, she can pass the curse on to you and that you will be responsible for protecting her from him. What you do with what she tells you is your problem, not hers. Agreed?"

Craig nodded and reached into his pocket, pulling out his note pad. The minute he set it on the table and flipped it open, Ms. Gonzales spewed out words so fast even Jalel couldn't make them out. Craig watched her eyes on his hands and realized the problem. "Okay, Jalel? Tell her I'm sorry and that I won't take notes." He slid the notepad back into his pocket.

"Él lo siente. No va a tomar notas."

"Tell her she isn't in any trouble."

"Usted no está en problemas."

"I just need her help. That's all. I just need to know why she didn't go back to work at the hotel."

"Él necesita su ayuda."

Ms. Gonzales's eyes were still wide, fearful, and fixed on Craig, but she was listening to what Jalel was saying. Craig noticed droplets of sweat running down her face and chest, and it dawned on him another reason she was so petrified.

"Tell her I don't care about her papers. I'm only here to talk about *The Duchess*."

"Uh, not sure I know how to say that."

"No INS?" Ms. Gonzales asked, her voice quiet, breathy.

Craig shook his head. "No INS. I am a detective with the police. I am working on a case…a woman was killed at the hotel you work at. *The Duchess?*" He could sense her fear. She may have been afraid of being deported, but she was absolutely terrified of whatever it was she knew about Serena Rowland's murder.

"Si, *The Duchess*. No more work there. No go back."

"Ms. Gonzales, tell me why. What did you see that makes you not want to go back?"

Jalel and Ms. Gonzales exchanged knowing glances. She pulled out a slim cigar from her pocket and fiddled with her lighter. Her hand shook as she took a few puffs.

"It's okay, ma'am. You have my word. I'm just trying to solve this murder. The man who was arrested—he didn't do it. He didn't kill that girl. And now he's dead and his wife is alone. Please, if you know something, tell me. I swear to the Heavens above that what you say stays between the two of us. You will never hear from me again."

She nodded at Jalel and as if pre-practiced, he turned and walked twenty yards away, then sat down on the edge of a broken piece of wood that had been part of a sandbox at one time. Ms. Gonzales waited until he was out of earshot before she continued. Craig realized then that not only did she have evidence, but she knew who the murderer was. She didn't want to vocalize her memories to anyone other than him.

"You know who it is, don't you?" Craig confirmed, managing to control the excitement in his voice.

"Sí."

"Tell me what happened."

"I was late to work Saturday. Missed the bus. I run down the street and go to back. No want to be seen in front. Cameras in back no work. Went to closet on my floor to get cart. We leave them there for that."

"You mean there is a cleaning cart left in the storage closets on each floor?"

"Sí."

"You said 'we'. I assume that means that the entire staff knows they are there and use them instead of going down and signing in, so your boss won't know you're late?"

"Sí."

Craig marveled at her sudden command of the English language. The little dance with Jalel earlier must have been a test to see if he would agree to her terms. He nodded for her to continue.

"I listen to music," she said, motioning to her ears, indicating ear buds. "I no hear anything. I moved cart and was in closet getting mop. Then door shut. I open and see him on floor. He fell over cart."

"What did he look like?" Craig prodded, fighting the urge to take notes.

"He wear jeans, shirt and hat. Uh and, oh, no word. Um, peluca." Ms. Gonzales raised her hands over her head and grabbed a handful of her hair. "Peluca."

"Wig? He was wearing a wig under the hat?" Craig's mouth was dry.

"Sí…wig. No his hair. He on top of cart and hat and uh, wig, fell off. Blood on shirt and jeans. I stay inside closet when I see blood."

"Did you see his face?" Craig queried, forcing his voice to remain calm.

"He get up and put hat on with wig. He in big hurry but I see his face. I not know what he doing, but I no ask. I wait until he leave."

"So you saw him and recognized him. Didn't you think it was odd that a man, covered in blood, was running down the stairwell? And once you realized you knew who he was, why didn't you tell the police when we arrived?"

"I not know about girl! I no think about man in stairs, I just go to work. See lots of things at hotel. Not my business. I hear before I leave to go home. When I hear, I run home. No police."

Craig tried to keep the frustration out of his voice. If he said what he was really thinking it would scare the timid woman away before he got the name. He wanted to let the story flow from her, but at the same time, he was chomping at the bit for her to spit out the name. "You were afraid to go to the police since you aren't legal, correct?"

"Sí."

"As I said earlier, Ms. Gonzales, I don't care about your legal status. Please, continue."

"I cry on way home. She a nice girl. I watch her grow up. Señor Rowland love her. I remember man on stairs. All the blood. I know he kill her. I told my husband what I saw and who killed her. We not know if he saw me and I not go back to work. We left house and stay in motel. Manny go work in Texas to send me money so I can go, too. No work at hotel, no clean houses. Just hide—with this."

Craig watched as Ms. Gonzales reached inside her purse and produced a small package wrapped in a brown paper sack. Her hands shook as she unfolded the paper and exposed a toothbrush inside a clear, plastic baggie. She slid the bag across the wooden table to Craig. "Manny made me go get the next day. I clean his house on Sunday mornings. He not there—he always at gym. I not want to go inside. Manny yelled at me, said one last time. He wait in car and I went inside. Told me to get it. Said it would keep me safe from man. Make him afraid of me if he found me. I not understand why, but Manny told me to trust him."

Craig felt like he'd just won the lottery. The DNA of the man Ms. Gonzales saw with blood on him was now in his hands. He moved with calculated ease and made sure not to touch the baggie as he wrapped the paper back around it, struggling to maintain his composure. Between the intense afternoon heat and his nerves on edge while he waited for Ms. Gonzales to finish her story, he was about to explode. He needed to get Lee the toothbrush as quickly as possible. He also needed a name, and it was time to stop pussyfooting around with Ms. Gonzales.

"You recognized the man in the stairwell as the one who's house you clean, right?"

Ms. Gonzales lit up another cigar and nodded in agreement. Her fear from earlier had diminished a little. Craig sensed she felt relieved to get this off her chest. "I need his name, Ms. Gonzales."

She hesitated, holding on to the last edges of her safety net. She blew out a huge plume of smoke and spoke the name.

Craig couldn't stop the string of expletives that rolled off his tongue when she did. His worst fears in this case were confirmed: Melody was in danger.

Craig didn't waste time with idle chitchat. He thanked Ms. Gonzales and Jalel, then ran across the baseball field to his Jeep. Grit and gravel spewed from behind his tires when he gunned the engine. Hitting the freeway, he floored it, his anger level off the charts. He tried telling himself to calm down and not jump to conclusions until Lee confirmed the DNA, but the acidic burn in his stomach told Craig he had the father of Serena's child and her killer. He'd been right under their noses the entire time, watching and listening, playing the part of concerned friend with enough gusto to win an Oscar.

Craig knew he was breaking every single piece of evidence collection and protocol standards possible, and he didn't care. He was also well aware that he was risking not only his career, but Lee's as well, and again, he didn't care. He pushed away the thought, replacing it with concerns for Melody's safety.

Thankful that the traffic was sparse, Craig sent a text to Lee:

Gym. Now. Got some new moves to show you

Craig drummed his fingers on the steering wheel while he sped toward downtown and waited for a response. In less than two minutes, he was rewarded.

On my way. Good moves?

Craig's cynical laughter filled the inside of his Jeep as he typed:

Unbelievable

CHAPTER 21 – WEDNESDAY, LATE AFTER-NOON

I FOUND IT ODD THAT WHEN I HAD BEEN IN-SIDE my mom's quiet house, scrounging through closets and drawers to find the proper attire for her to be clothed in forever, I hadn't shed a tear. Nor did I cry when I dropped off the yellow sundress with her favorite white, floppy, wide-brimmed hat and matching shoes at the funeral parlor. I also grabbed the picture from her dresser of the two of us on my wedding day. The funeral director looked at me with pity when I handed him the items. Though he didn't say anything, I'm sure he understood the sentiment. I doubted I was the first person who'd brought in treasured trinkets to put in the casket that no one else, except me, would see or know were inside. At her house, I felt her presence. Her smell—her warmth—enveloped me. It brought me comfort and made me smile. And I somehow felt proud that I picked out the perfect outfit for my southern belle mother to rest in.

Leaving the parking lot of the funeral home, I expected the tears to race down my face, but they didn't come then, either. I wasn't exactly numb, but I felt a part of my mind overtake my pain, squashing it down into a tiny little box to be opened another day. Sheer anger controlled me now.

I cranked up the music and clenched the steering wheel as I handled the Camaro through the curvy roads of Highway 35 toward Sheridan. The trees whizzed by in a blur of green. The tires hugged the road and the engine roared beneath me. I pushed the car and my driving skills to the limit as I careened down the empty, two-lane highway. As the car ate the pavement in front of me, I let my senses control my thoughts and embraced the sheer enjoyment of the moment.

Twenty minutes later, my fingers cramped and knuckles bone white, I pulled over at Gas-n-Go to fill up the tank. The drive helped me clear my head and forced me to concentrate on nothing but the road. I'd discovered in my youth there was freedom behind the wheel, and never strayed from that mentality as I grew up. Every vehicle I'd ever owned had been a sports car of some sort. When the road and I became one, I was no longer the broken woman mourning the loss of her loved ones. I hadn't thought about all the things the detective told me or felt that strong sense of foreboding that I had inside my kitchen earlier.

Now, all I felt was bubbling anger. Raw, red anger. No more waiting around like a little mouse, timidly peeking out from its little hole to see if it was safe to scurry across the floor. A sense of duty and power raced through me. It was time to find Guy Powell. I didn't have a plan of action other than surprise. He wouldn't be expecting to come face to face with me or answer my blunt questions. My haphazard plan was to catch him off guard and get him to slip up and say something incriminating in front of me. If that didn't work, at least he would be on edge, knowing I was on to him. One thing I had learned from working in a legal office is that criminals, no matter how smart they were, always screwed up somewhere. Especially if they knew they were under scrutiny.

I pushed the gentle voice begging me to turn around and go home from my mind. No longer would I listen to the side of me who always followed the rules. That boring individual who planned ahead for months for everything from birthday celebrations to Christmas—all for what? For this? Doomed to spend the remainder of her years wandering through the valley of life alone? No way. The woman who wore practical clothes to work and thick, cotton sweats to bed had died in the hospital along with her mother yesterday.

Time for the side I previously only let out behind the wheel to emerge. To hell with tact or grace, it was time for the dark, dangerous thrill seeker who didn't take no for an answer—or shit from anyone—to take control. Meemaw wasn't whispering in my head anymore because she didn't need to. I clung to the anger and wielded it like a club. While I drove, the fight inside my mind became epic. Ultimately, I decided that God gave me both sides—the dark and the light—and sometimes to defeat evil, you must embrace it.

I paid for my gas and hit the road again. I was less than two miles from Tray's Trinkets, which was the only hardware store in Sheridan. I debated calling my friend Carol at the county clerk's office and asking her to look Guy up and see if he was still in jail, but changed my mind before I dialed. I didn't want to involve anyone else nor risk the chance of anyone blabbing that I'd been inquiring about him. The less others knew about what I was doing, the better.

Since I had no idea what Guy looked like nor whether he was even at work, I decided to do a bit of snooping. I reached behind my front seat and grabbed my old baseball cap, yanked my hair through the back, kept my sunglasses on and stepped out into the heat. Sweat pooled fast under the brim of my hat as I walked, possibly due to the relentless sunshine. Or the fact that I was riding a high from adrenaline and fear. Maybe all of it.

The small store looked like it had been there since the Civil War. The wood, décor, and smells all combined to make my stomach do a flip when I opened the door and stepped inside. It took a few seconds for my eyes to recover from the blazing sun. Thankfully, no one seemed to notice a customer had walked in and I stood at the front en-entrance undisturbed, scoping the place out.

The inside of the building was dark enough that I removed my sunglasses to see. I scanned the aisles, all six of them, for an employee. At the end of the fifth aisle, I saw an older man with snow white hair and a slight build mopping the floor. I approached slowly, not sure if it was Guy or not. Kendal had said he was a heavy drug user and I'd seen what years of drug abuse did to the human body. Some of Roger's clients had been heavy abusers. A forty-year-old woman came to mind, who had looked all of seventy when she attempted to hire Roger to represent her after her mobile meth lab blew up and caused a five car pileup on the freeway. She'd left in a huff after hearing his fees.

My pace was slow, my tennis shoes silent on the ancient linoleum floor. I studied the build of the man, my heart pounding faster as I got closer. He wasn't much taller than I was and had a slender yet muscular build, but his movements were slow, halting. He didn't have the fluidity of movement of a younger man. I didn't realize how intently I'd been studying him until I felt my stomach drop when he yelled, "You done stackin' those drill bits, boy?"

"Hold on to your horses, old man. I'll be done in a sec."

"Don't you back talk me, boy! You get out here and finish this here moppin'. I'm goin' for a smoke."

"Oh sure, leave all the work to me now. If you think just 'cause you bailed me outta jail means I'm now ya—"

"One more word outta that nasty mouth of yours, Guy, and I'm gonna fire ya. Sure 'nough as a tick sucks blood on a deer. Don't care none if you's kin or not."

Before the old man turned around and saw me, I shifted directions and darted over to the empty aisle next to him. I grabbed the closest thing in front of me—two rolls of duct tape—then followed the narrow aisle toward the back of the store. I stopped in front of the thick curtain separating the front and back. It took a few seconds to spot him in the storage area piled from floor to ceiling with junk.

"Can I heep ya?"

I spun around and found myself face to face with the old man. He smiled, gracing me with his toothless mouth and rank breath. Out of the corner of my eye, I watched for signs that Guy heard us and was relieved to see that he hadn't moved from his task of stacking boxes.

"Oh, uh, yes. I was wondering. Do you have any more of this?" I asked, holding up the tape. "I didn't see any more on the shelf and uh, well, I'm painting and..."

His crooked grin expanded as he yelled over my shoulder, "Guy? We got any more of this here tape?"

Guy turned around and walked toward us and my heart and breathing stopped as my mouth went dry. Curly, dark brown hair peppered with flecks of gray poked out from under his dirty baseball cap. A Chicago Cubs baseball cap. Though his face was full of more wrinkles than Jack's, Guy had the same chiseled cheeks, a similar profile. The same slight swagger to his gait.

A thousand thoughts raced through me all at once. It was one thing to plan scenarios out in your mind, but quite another when you faced them in reality. My body began to shake as the enormity of being within inches of the monster who ruined my life took over. Images rushed through my mind. Jack sitting in jail. His casket and gravestone. Serena's destroyed face. My mother on the bathroom floor. All rational thought disappeared from my head. The sounds and smells around me vanished, and like a horse with blinders, all I saw and felt was him.

There was a blank stare on his face as he stood in front of me and looked at the tape in my hands, pointing with his dirty fingers to the aisle I'd just come from. His mouth moved but I didn't hear any sounds. My eyes were frozen on his as I watched his nonchalant stare turn to recognition and a wry smile tug at his cracked lips. I saw his lips mouth my name, but the only sound in my head was the rush of blood as fury overtook me.

My limbs were on autopilot and I watched in slight awe as my right arm shot out, the heavy roll of tape firmly clenched in my fingers, and connected with the ugly, bulbous nose on Guy's face. Though I didn't hear the impact of my fist and the tape as they smashed into his head, I felt the shockwave of the bones in my fingers break, yet felt no pain. The sensation of glee at watching Guy's nose explode raced up my arm and through my chest. Spittle and blood spewed from Guy's mouth and nose as he staggered backward and lost his footing on the slippery floor.

The old man next to me stood rooted to his spot, his thin mouth hanging open as he stared from Guy's body on the floor back to me. My chest heaved from the adrenaline rush and finally, the sound of the blood in my ears was gone, replaced by the string of curse words that Guy shouted from the floor. He was trying to stand up but his equilibrium was skewed. I took a step closer to him, then turned my attention back to the old man.

"That was for my mother and trust me, he has this coming."

Before he could respond or Guy could move out of the way, I raised my foot and brought it down with every ounce of strength in me right between Guy's legs. His bloodied hands left his crushed nose and cupped his family jewels when I drew my foot back.

"That one was for my husband. The final blow will be for me, and will be delivered by the police when they arrest your sorry ass for killing Serena."

Guy couldn't utter a word and I wondered, as I threw the duct tape down beside him and turned to walk out of the store, if he'd even heard me. He was rolling around on the filthy floor, his mouth frozen in the silent scream of agony at his balls being busted. The old man didn't offer any comfort. He didn't come after me, either. His eyes betrayed his amusement at seeing his kin in such agony. I graced him with a wicked wink and walked out of the store.

By the time I made it to my car and clambered inside, my legs were shaking so much that to an onlooker I probably seemed drunk. I started the engine and held my sweaty face in front of the cold air streaming out of the vents, never taking my eyes off the front door. I wanted to see if Guy was going to come after me, which I fully expected to happen once he caught his breath. There were only two vehicles in the parking lot, both of them beat up trucks that looked like they were held together with rust and spit. If he wanted to chase me, I'd blow his doors off.

At last my legs stopped quaking and my heart rate returned to normal. I felt a strange mixture of emotions. Exuberance at releasing my pent up anger on the man who ruined my life, and disgust at my enjoyment of causing another person pain. The high had been intense as I stood over his body and unleashed my rage. But now that the intoxication was wearing off, the crash was overwhelming. My hand was throbbing and already swelling. I realized that for a few seconds, had I had the means to it, I could have killed him. The thought made me dizzy and I barely had time to jerk the door open before my disgust spewed out of me and all over the hot pavement.

I reached inside the console and grabbed a few tissues, wiping away the remnants on my chin. I fumbled to get the key into the ignition and glanced up to make sure that Guy or his kinfolk weren't on their way to my car. My chest tightened when Guy limped out the front door. Thankfully, he never even looked my way as he ambled over to the rust bucket closest to the door and tried to climb in. I felt a surge of pride as I watched him struggle into the front seat and relived the moment my foot stomped on him. It wasn't until I heard the sound of a door closing that I realized a vehicle had pulled up next to Guy's truck.

For a split second, I hoped that what I was about to witness was another beat down of Guy, this time not by the hands of Jack's widow, but his best friend. The huge grin on my face at seeing Kendal stride over to Guy disappeared as, instead of rendering him to a bloody pulp, Kendal began to talk.

Guy reached into his truck and produced a manila folder and handed it to Kendal, who palmed an envelope into Guy's hand, and the exchange was sealed with a handshake. The unthinkable betrayal hit me almost as hard as Jack's. Suddenly, what had happened to me, Jack, and by extension, my mother, came in to clear view.

Kendal and Guy had orchestrated the whole thing. They were in cahoots together—it all made sense now. Kendal's late night confession on how he tried to sabotage mine and Jack's relationship so many years ago. His slow burn of jealousy over the years, the flame ignited by the run in with Guy back at Christmas, and an unholy alliance started.

I was beyond livid. Rational thought escaped me. Disconnected from reality, I saw a lightning bolt skitter across the sky and pulled my attention away for a brief second from the scene in front of me. The pull to go home was overwhelming. I ignored the shooting pain in my right hand as I slammed the car into gear and my tires barked, sending plumes of rank black smoke in the air behind me. I had to get to Detective Knowles and tell him what I just witnessed.

I didn't bother to look back to see if Guy or Kendal were following me. Hell, I didn't care. I hoped they were, because if they could keep up with me, then they would end up following me to my house, which is where Roger would be in less than an hour. And Detective Knowles, as soon as I called him.

Then I remembered Regina could return from shopping at any moment and wind up alone in the house with Kendal, if somehow he beat me home.

I reached over to the passenger seat and grabbed my cell phone, almost hitting the car coming at me in the opposite direction head on. I swerved and ignored the honk of the irritated driver. After six attempts to connect with Regina and Detective Knowles, I threw my phone on the floorboard and cursed the small, piss ant town of Sheridan for their lack of cell phone towers.

Once I crossed over into Pulaski County, I knew service would be up and running again. I pushed my foot to the floor and glanced once in my review mirror. I wasn't surprised to see Kendal's truck half a mile behind me. I made a hard right and zoomed on to the freeway, the back end of my Camaro fishtailing. Back on the main highway, I turned on my flashers and let the horses run free. I quit looking at the speedometer when it rose past one hundred miles per hour.

All I could think of was the faster I got home, the faster Kendal and Guy would be arrested and this nightmare my life had become would at last be over.

Bastards.

CHAPTER 22 – WEDNESDAY, LATE AFTER-NOON

AFTER GIVING THE TOOTHBRUSH TO LEE, CRAIG opted to wait in the gym for the results. He had a lot of pent up anger that needed to be released. Since he'd ruined the punching bag earlier in the week, he ran laps on the inside track, but collapsed on the floor after the sixth mile.

He glanced at his watch, noting it had been a little over an hour since Lee left for the lab. The wait was driving him insane. He wanted nothing more than to go and pick up the bastard and have a few private moments alone with the guy before he officially arrested him.

Craig jerked when his cell phone rang. The casing was all sweaty and he fumbled to keep it in his hands. His heart sunk when he realized the number wasn't Lee's.

"Knowles."

"You sure are a difficult man to get in touch with, Detective."

"Excuse me?"

"This is Detective Craig Knowles of the Little Rock Police Department, isn't it?"

"Who's asking?"

"Alex Renfro."

Craig felt a bit lightheaded, and not just from his run. He wondered why in the world the lead Pulaski County Prosecuting Attorney was calling him. It surely couldn't be for anything good. He did a quick mental rundown of all his other open cases to confirm none of them were being handled by the man.

"Sorry, sir. Didn't recognize your number. Yes, you have the right number. What can I do for you?"

"Your Captain informed me you were on vacation. You are still in the area, correct?"

"Yes sir," Craig said as he stood up and walked back to the locker room. "Why?"

"Because I need you down here in my office right now. We…have a situation. A very *volatile* situation."

"I'll be there in five," Craig said, ignoring his sweat-stained clothes and body. He slid on his ball cap, grabbed his bag, and raced out to the parking lot.

The acid in his stomach and the rank taste in his mouth told him things just went from bad to worse.

****

It took Craig less than three minutes to navigate the one-way streets of downtown Little Rock and pull up in front of the prosecutor's office. He ignored the *No Parking* sign, drove onto the sidewalk and threw his Jeep into park. He forced his feet to walk at an acceptable pace as he opened the glass doors and entered the foyer.

He didn't even have to walk up to the receptionist. Alex Renfro was waiting in the lobby on one of the gaudy, overstuffed couches and rose to meet him. He didn't offer his hand or even a smile as he asked, "Detective Knowles?"

Craig nodded. With a curt nod of his balding head, Alex Renfro turned on his heels and motioned for Craig to follow. He led Craig down a series of endless halls until they reached Renfro's private office. Renfro unlocked the door and held it open for Craig, then locked it behind him after they both were inside.

"Sit, please," Renfro grunted, his voice taut.

Craig sensed the tension in the air. "You said on the phone that you have a volatile situation that you needed my help with?"

Craig had never seen the calm and collected Alex Renfro anywhere close to being rattled. He'd only met him before once, right after Alex was elected, but had seen him numerous times on the local news during the last two years. Always poised and in control, Alex Renfro was impeccably dressed and never showed a hint of stress. Today, as he wiped his hands over his bald head to wipe the sheen of sweat away, Craig noticed a slight tremble in his hand.

"Are you still working the Rowland-Dickinson case?"

Momentarily taken aback, Craig cleared his throat before responding. "As you mentioned earlier, I'm on vacation."

"A vacation suggested by Captain Hogue I assume?"

Craig offered a slight nod of agreement.

"I see. With strict instructions not to work that, or any other case, correct?"

"Yes."

"He didn't seem too interested in talking to me earlier. Actually, he blew me off, which was rather surprising. Not the typical response I'm used to receiving from your department." Alex Renfro leaned back in his seat and gave a heavy sigh. He rubbed his eyes for a moment before he continued, "I need to ask you some things and I want honest answers. Just between the two of us."

"Okay."

"Do you believe you made the right choice in arresting Jack Dickinson for the murder of Serena Rowland?"

Craig felt his stomach drop to the floor. "No, I don't."

"Would trying to rectify that decision be the reason you are on vacation?"

"Yes."

"Well, let me congratulate you, Detective. Your instincts might just be correct. I have serious doubts now myself that Mr. Dickinson killed that girl. I will admit, your original case file delivered to me seemed to nail Mr. Dickinson's coffin shut. However, after a new development was brought to my attention today, I'm beginning to think we are on the brink of a disaster, one that will affect both of our careers negatively." Alex Renfro nodded his head to the manila envelope on his desk.

Craig reached across the desk, picked it up and scanned the contents. Several photographs cataloged the relationship between Jack Dickinson and Serena Rowland. He continued to flip through the images, his blood running cold when he realized not all of the pictures were of Jack and Serena. The ones at the end were between her and another man. The same one whose DNA Lee was testing at the lab.

"Those were brought in earlier today by some lowlife thug named Guy Powell. He came to see LeAnn Balatnick, the deputy P.A. handling his drug case. He wanted to use the pictures as some sort of bargaining chip to get her to drop the charges against him."

Craig stared at the images in front of him, willing his vision to clear. Ms. Gonzales had been one hundred percent on target. "How did he come by these?"

"Oh, quite an interesting story he shared with LeAnn. You see, he hated Jack Dickinson so much that he decided to have him followed—to see what kind of dirt he could dig up on him to use to ruin his life. He hit the jackpot when the private investigator discovered the affair. Said he sent the first round of pictures of Jack and Serena to Jack's house, then a week later to Jack's office, and finally, Mrs. Dickinson's office. His little plan of revenge was interrupted when he was arrested on drug charges. Said he was surprised to find some new pictures from the private investigator in his mailbox when he was released yesterday. Knew right away he had a gold mine when he recognized Serena's *other* lover. Thought that he might have stumbled upon some sort of conspiracy to frame his arch enemy. LeAnn said the little bastard was actually giddy."

Craig let out a long sigh. "Oh, it's a goldmine all right, but it doesn't even begin to trump mine."

For the first time during their hushed conversation, Alex Renfro's eyes showed a spark of hope. "Which is?"

For the next twenty minutes, Craig went over all the information he'd obtained during the last three days, including his conversation with Bill Witham and his suspicions about Bill and Guy's involvement in the death of Jack Dickinson. Craig almost laughed at the expression on the D.A.'s face when he got to the part about Thurman Turner, the possible conversation with Philip Rowland, and the fake reports and testing at the State Crime Lab. When Craig finished his story about the earlier meeting with Ms. Gonzales and the fact that he was waiting for the DNA results to be confirmed, the color began to appear in Alex's cheeks again.

"You realize that if that test result comes back positive..."

"All hell will break lose? Oh, you bet I do. The only good thing about this latest twist is that Mrs. Dickinson will finally be able to say her husband's name is cleared."

"When the press gets wind of this, the shit-storm will cover us all. It's going to be an uphill climb to prove to the public that we weren't involved or trying to keep this covered up."

"True. But to be honest with you, I don't give a shit anymore what the public thinks. Or my Captain, or even you for that matter. What I do care about is making this right, for all the parties involved. If the corruption extends so far that I have to arrest the Governor himself, I will. Whatever it takes to right the wrong."

Before Renfro could respond, Craig's cell phone rang. They exchanged glances, each realizing that the call would confirm their worst fears and probably end both of their careers in the matter of a few seconds. He put the phone on the desk and clicked the speaker button. "Knowles."

"Uh, am I on speaker?" Lee asked with a hint of concern.

"Yes. I'm at Alex Renfro's office. He brought me here to show me some more evidence in this case."

"So, well, um, yeah, Mr. Renfro? You aren't going…"

"It's okay, son. I'm on your side, though God knows I don't want to be. What's the verdict?"

"We have ourselves a winner, gentlemen."

"Thanks, Lee. We'll be in touch."

"Never had a doubt that you would. Just one favor?"

"Of course," Craig replied, his focus elsewhere as he wondered how in the hell he was going to tell Melody. The truth was going to crush what little spirit she had left.

"When you come to arrest Thurman, give me a heads up so I can have my camera ready. That's a photo op I don't want to miss."

Craig, Alex and Lee wrapped up their conversation and Craig ended the call, feeling his pulse quicken. He could barely contain the raging anger swirling through him. He waited to hear the words from Alex.

"I'll handle the medical examiner and your boss. You go find the daddy and tell him the happy news. After you cuff him and Mirandize him, of course."

Craig didn't wait for another word to fall. He burst out of the D.A.'s office and sprinted down the hall and stairs. Once inside his truck, he tried calling Melody as he pulled into the afternoon traffic. He needed to warn her, and swore like a sailor when she didn't answer. He left a voicemail instructing her to call him as soon as she got the message.

At a red light he made one more phone call before pulling into the gas station less than three blocks from his next stop, planning to change into his street clothes and vest before he made the arrest. His heart pounded as he waited for the phone to be answered, anger causing it to soar into the stratosphere when the receptionist informed him her boss had left for the day and she didn't know where he was.

Craig forced his voice to remain steady when he replied, "Patch me through to his cell phone, please."

"Oh, I don't know sir. I'm not supposed to…"

"Tell him it's Detective Knowles and it's an emergency."

"Yes sir, right away sir."

Craig's heart rate sped up when, a few seconds later, the call was connected but went to voicemail. "Listen, we've got a big problem. Melody is in real danger. I need you to go to her house and stay with her. Do not let anyone else inside. Call me back as soon as you get this message."

To save time, Craig decided to just change clothes inside his Jeep. Securing his Kevlar and zipping up his jeans, he wondered if this arrest would be the last one he ever made.

CHAPTER 23 –
WEDNESDAY, EARLY EVENING

THE STORM I HAD BEEN RUNNING FROM CAUGHT up with me about ten miles from my house. The only good thing about the pouring rain, intense lightning and black clouds was that I shook Kendal from my tail. Once I hit the gas pedal with my lead foot, I put enough distance between the two of us that he'd never catch up. I took the next exit and drove the back roads home.

I had to slow down when the rains came. I'd tried my phone two more times earlier and the call still hadn't connected. Now that I had crossed over into Pulaski County, I prayed it would work. The battery blinked red but I had two bars of service. Hallelujah!

I hit redial and tried Detective Knowles one more time. My heart jumped in my throat when he answered. "Oh, thank God! Hey, it's Melody. Listen, I need you to meet me at my house. Kendal and Guy are behind all of this. Kendal was following me but I lost him. He will probably beat me home."

"Mel is that you where you danger Kendal stay put my way…"

The garbled noise in my ear ended when my phone died. I was screwed; I had no car charger with me. In a fit of anger, I threw the useless thing to the floorboard of my car and refocused my concentration on the road. The wind was picking up and the pine trees lining the highway were bending to the will of the storm. It was three in the after-noon and dark outside. The ominous tint of dark green that permeated the entire area was a sure sign of approaching severe weather.

Though I didn't have many more miles to go, I thought about what little I could understand from my short conver-sation with the detective. He mentioned danger and Kendal and to stay put—he was on his way. I wanted to give the car some more gas to get home sooner, but the rain was coming down so hard I could barely see thirty feet in front of me. My hope was that during his investigation, Detec-tive Knowles had figured out that Kendal was involved. And it sounded like he was on his way to my house, so that was a good thing.

Because if Kendal was there and the detective wasn't, I was afraid of what I might do left alone with Kendal. Nev-er, in my entire life, had I been so angry—and so ready to inflict physical damage to another human being. The last tendril of sanity that kept my mind grounded had been cut off. I had let the flood of fury wash over me when I tore out of the parking lot. Kendal's betrayal burned through me and seared away everything else. How could he? After all the years he'd been friends with Jack? I fumed when I thought about the amazing job of acting he'd done all these years as the doting best friend. How could he have destroyed the lives of people he claimed to love? I had wanted to hurt Guy, and did to a point. But Kendal? Ken-dal I wanted to destroy. No jail time for him. He needed to be dispatched immediately—and I was just the gal to pull the trigger.

My entire body was one giant knot by the time I pulled up in my driveway. I let out a sigh of relief when I realized neither Kendal nor Regina were there, but Roger's car was, parked next to the mailbox. He got out and opened his umbrella as I pulled up. Thank goodness! At least Roger could keep me from ripping Kendal apart until the detective arrived and arrested his sorry ass.

I retrieved my cell and shoved it deep inside my purse, then opened the door. Thoughts of my painful limbs were wiped away as I stepped out of my car and was drenched in seconds. I winced as I used my swollen right hand to shut the car door. The thunder was so loud my car shook from the concussion. I felt awful for leaving Simba outside, and motioned for Roger to follow as I took off for the front door. Inside I ran upstairs and straight to the sliding glass doors. Simba was cowering under the swing on the deck. She whimpered as a crack of lightning slammed so close that I felt the electrical surge.

The minute I opened the door she shot in and barreled down the stairs to the basement, almost knocking Roger off his feet as he came up the steps. He stopped awkwardly inside the kitchen and leaned against the door frame, staring at my disheveled appearance while he shook the water from his umbrella. I ignored him for a second and plugged in my cell, then moved over to the drawer and pulled out several hand towels to dry myself off with. "Hmmm. Seems fitting I am soaked since I'm mad as a wet hen. Say, did you bring your cell? I need to make a few calls. Mine is dead." *It's not the only thing that's about to die.*

"No, I left it at work. You sounded distraught earlier and I just assumed our conversation would be a difficult one, so I opted to leave it there. Figured we didn't need any interruptions. So tell me, what did you want to share with me earlier that you felt you couldn't on the phone?" He looked hopeful.

I waved the soaked towel in his direction. "Shoot! I've got to call Detective Knowles. And Regina. It...oh, that doesn't matter now. My phone will charge in just a second—at least long enough to make a call or two. Anyway, this morning when I called you, what I had to tell you was all questions, possibilities. After my visit to Sheridan, it's all out. I know the truth. Say, did you lock the front door when you came in?"

"No, but I will if you'd like. And could you calm down just a bit? You're kind of running in all directions here. I'm having trouble keeping up."

"Please. I don't want Kendal coming in here before Detective Knowles arrives. And I'm sorry, just a lot going on right now inside my head. I'm surprised I'm not in a corner drooling."

While I finished drying off, Roger ambled down the stairs. I let my breath out and tried to relax. I rolled my knotted shoulders a few times, trying to loosen them up. I needed to calm down now that I was home and the cavalry would be here soon. Roger was back in a flash, his face unreadable as he set his briefcase on the counter. He walked over and sat down in the kitchen chair closest to him. "You said the truth is out and you don't want Kendal coming in here. What did you mean by those statements?"

Another bright bolt of lightning was followed by an ear-splitting crack of thunder and then darkness as the lights flickered once and went out. So much for charging my phone so I could call Regina. Hopefully she was still inside a store somewhere, waiting out the storm. I glanced out the window and winced when I realized the storm was right on top of us and the entire neighborhood seemed to be without power. The eerie green haze had followed me from Sheridan. I bent down to wipe up the water that had puddled underneath me while I answered, "You aren't going to believe this, but Kendal and Guy are behind all this. Though I'm not exactly sure of all the details yet."

"What makes you say that? Is that what Detective Knowles told you earlier today? Did he find some evidence linking the two of them together? Is that what you wanted to discuss with me?"

I finished wiping the floor and stood up, tossed the wet towel to the sink, then pulled out a chair and sat down at the table with Roger. At least the kitchen had a lot of windows to provide some light, although the funky green color that streamed through the windows made Roger look ill. I glanced down at my hands and noticed my own skin reflected the same ghastly pallor. The tint made my hand look even worse, so I went to the fridge, grabbed some ice, rolled it into a dishtowel and sat back down. Roger watched my movements but didn't say a word, waiting for me to answer him.

"Well, yes and no. Detective Knowles wasn't exactly forthcoming with information this morning, but he did allude to the fact that he was on to something, and that it somehow all tied back to me. I sort of lost it then and told him to leave until he figured out *exactly* what was going on. But after my little trip to Sheridan and what I witnessed while I was there, I understand now why he didn't tell me. Sort of."

Roger's brow furrowed with questions. I didn't seem to be doing a very good job explaining the events of the last few hours. Then again, my mind was so screwed up at the moment it was a wonder I could even form a complete sentence.

"Tell me, what did you witness in Sheridan, Melody?" Roger prompted.

"For starters, I made a trip to the store where Guy Powell works at. Decided I was going to start my own investigation since relying on the police to handle things seemed like a sick, cosmic joke. When I walked in and saw him, realized how much his body structure looked like Jack's, I, um, sort of lost it and hit him."

"You did *what?*" Roger sputtered.

"Yup, popped him right in his nose and knocked him on his ass. Then, I planted my foot in his...uh, his crotch. Told him who I was and that I was on to him. You know, to shake him up and hope that he'd say or do something to incriminate himself."

"And did he?"

"No. It seemed all he could do was writhe around on the floor and groan. So I left."

"Did I miss something here? The part that connects Kendal to all of this?" Roger asked, confused.

I took a deep breath before I continued. "When I walked out to my car, I was a mess. Realized how close I came to seriously hurting another person—and how much I enjoyed watching him suffer. I looked at the blood on my hands and it made me nauseous and I got sick. But, when I cleaned up and started the car, I thought I was about to see more violence because Kendal drove up. Parked right next to Guy's truck and got out, just as Guy limped out the front door. I kind of got excited, thinking Kendal had come down to whip the fire out of Guy, too. But I was wrong. Dead wrong."

"Go on," Roger urged.

"I could tell they were talking, but I couldn't hear what they were saying. What I could tell was that no fists were going to be flying. They seemed, I don't know, civil to-ward each other. Kendal just calmly walked over to Guy's truck and waited for Guy to hand him a big envelope. When he did, Kendal passed a smaller envelope to Guy and then went back to his truck. Like I said, I don't know what was inside those envelopes, but there cannot be any plausible explanation why Kendal would be even *talking* to Guy, much less exchanging documents of some sort with him, unless they are working together."

Roger gazed out the window as the storm raged out-side. I could tell that his legal mind was processing what I'd just said, trying to make sense of it all. His thoughts seemed a million miles away and he mumbled something under his breath just as another loud clap of thunder shook the kitchen.

"I'm sorry, what did you say? Sounded like pictures."

Roger ignored my question and responded with one of his own, his voice distant and heavy. "Melody, do you remember our conversation not long ago about Corinne?"

"Yes, however, I fail to see…"

He held up his hand for me to stop and continued. "When she died, my entire life changed. All our hopes, dreams and plans together ended with her final, painful breath. I never told a soul this, but after she passed, I climbed into the bed next to her and held her until her body turned cold. I don't know why. It was like I was trying to hold on to her life force, her essence, hoping that somehow, it could pass over to me to help ease the pain of losing her. But it didn't work. I was destroyed and beyond devastated once the last bit of her warmth was gone."

Despite everything that was going on, I held my tongue and let him finish. It seemed wrong to stop him now, since obviously being inside this situation with me had brought a lot of painful memories back for him. Rather than respond, I moved my hand across the table and held his while he continued. Though sort of odd, it felt right—fitting. No one can understand the grief of a widower except for another widower or widow.

"I thought maybe after I took her ashes and scattered them, the dead part of my soul would come to life again. It didn't happen. If anything, I felt even worse, since I was in the place she wanted to visit more than anything in the world. How many times had I promised to take her, then changed plans at the last minute because I let my job get in the way? 'Oh, let's go next Spring, baby. I've got to finish this case first. Can't leave in the middle of it.' That's what I'd tell her. The problem was that there was *always* a case waiting in the wings. In other words, I gave higher priority to my job and my ego than the desires and needs of my wife."

"The pain never lessens, does it? Is that what you are trying to tell me?"

Roger chewed on the inside of his cheek, his eyes full of tears. He moved his hand from mine and stood up, then walked over to the sliding glass door. Though I almost fell out of my chair, he didn't even flinch when a tree limb snapped in the back yard and crashed to the ground. The wind howled outside and the weeping willows in the back-yard bent so far over that the tops almost touched the soaked ground.

"No, it did finally ease up, but not from time, therapy or some mystic religious experience. You see, I thought I'd lost my one shot of being with a truly remarkable woman. Corinne was so loving, so animated and so kind to others. She never met a stranger, never turned her back on a lost cause. Not only was she generous, kind and beauti-ful, but she had this wicked sense of humor. And a laugh that was so contagious, when you heard it, you couldn't help but laugh, too. When all that mixed together with her intelligence, it made for a combination of my dream mate. No, it was finding love again that brought me out of my mourning. It was almost like I've been living an epic Shakespearean drama or something. True love lost, true love found. Only the second time around, the object of the affection was with another, unaware of my deep love for her."

It took a few seconds for his words to sink in, but when they did, what he mumbled earlier became clear in an in-stant. It took several tries to get my lips to move as I stared at his rigid back in sheer disbelief, noticing for the first time the similarities between his physique and Jack's. "Pictures. You said pictures earlier, didn't you?"

No response other than a slight nod of his head.

"Pictures of what, Roger?"

Like watching a movie in slow motion, Roger turned and faced me. His eyes were red rimmed, his cheeks flushed and wet with tears. A slight tremble shook his body as he reached over and flicked the latch open on his briefcase. When he pulled it back and held out his hand, I gasped at what he held.

"A package containing these photographs was sent to the office a week before Serena was killed. They were addressed to you, but since she opened the mail, you can understand why Serena brought them to me instead. Mr. Powell paid an impromptu visit to the office this morning as well, right after you and I spoke. Seems he thought that he could procure some cash to help in his defense by blackmailing me. So, your assumption about Mr. Powell was semi-correct. He did, for lack of a better term, start the ball rolling when he sent these."

I fought to control the tears that sprung forth when I saw the photos of Jack and Serena. My vision swam as I peered through the moisture at the other pictures. I barely heard the booming thunder or the wail of the tornado siren over the pounding of my heart in my ears.

I was staring at pictures of Serena and Roger as they embraced in various stages of undress, in what I could only assume was her apartment.

"I...you...I don't understand. You were in love with Serena, too? Oh my God...you were, weren't you? You found out about her and Jack when Guy sent these pictures and decided to make her and Jack pay, didn't you? Holy fucking shit! You son of a bitch!"

The violent storm raging outside reflected the one inside of me. Consumed by numbing fury, I dropped the photos and lunged headfirst toward Roger's chest. My head made contact with his stomach just as his hands wound around my waist. We toppled over and rolled across the kitchen floor. I was blind with fury as my hands, feet, fingers and teeth sought out anything to connect with. I punched, clawed, screamed and kicked until Roger gained the upper hand.

In one swift movement, he wrapped both his arms around my chest, pinning my own at my sides. Before I could blink, he immobilized my legs and we were now frozen in battle in the middle of the kitchen floor. Lying on top of him with my back crushed against his torso, I couldn't see his face, but I could tell from his labored breathing that he was just as exhausted as I was.

My lungs struggled for air as his grip on me tightened. I tried to move, but it was no use. It was like being held by a vice. *Where is the detective? Oh God, please forgive me for thinking it was Kendal! Please, please help me now, Lord. Give me the words to say to keep him talking until help arrives. Better yet, just let the storm take us both now. I'm ready to come home. I won't be able to live with all this. This just isn't real, it isn't happening.*

"Why, Roger? Why did you have to frame Jack? And how could you have been so cruel, so vicious, to the woman you supposedly loved? You beat her to a pulp."

Though his grip was still rock solid, I felt Roger press his nose into my hair. His hot breath grazed my ear and neck, his voice raised as he spoke over the sounds of the storm outside, "Melody, you still don't see, do you? Serena wasn't my second shot at true love. You were. I did this for you. For us."

I struggled to move my ear from his vile words but his grip intensified. "For us? What us, Roger? I'm just your secretary for God's sake! There is no us! What the hell are you talking about?"

"Ah, but there could have been. Believe me, I was more than content loving you from a distance. Even though we didn't have a chance to connect physically, I was able to satisfy that side of myself by basking in working alongside you each day. I cherished every smile, each laugh, all your smart retorts and wry sense of humor. I watched you struggle with your inability to have a baby, heard you cry in the restroom at night when you thought everyone had already left. My heart broke to see you so sad. So many times, I fought the urge to hold you, to gather you into my arms and tell you it would be okay. And, believe it or not, I actually hoped that Jack was providing for all your needs as a husband, since I knew I never could. That's how much I love you, Melody. For your happiness, I stood back and let another take care of you when I craved for it to be me."

I couldn't handle this. I had to be having a nightmare, because if this was real, my mind and heart wouldn't be able to live with it all. "So what, Serena was just a hot little morsel to sink your teeth into once the cravings for me became unbearable?"

"I'm a man, Melody. She was young, sexy, and most importantly, willing. She was just a moment of weakness though. Until she started working for us, I remained faithful to you. Hadn't been with another since Corinne passed away. Serena provided me with a minor distraction that only happened a few times. When I was with her, I closed my eyes and pictured you, even called out your name during, well, you know."

"Yet, in the end, you decided to ruin my life by killing her and framing Jack. Yeah, that's true love, Roger," I spat.

"I was *trying* to do the right thing, Melody!" Roger yelled. "When Serena stormed into my office with the pictures, she was in a panic. She had just found out she was pregnant the day before, and thought the pictures were a sign that she and Jack needed to just go ahead and come clean. She wanted to tell you about the baby, about her love for Jack. She wanted the end result to be that Jack divorced you and married her so they could raise their baby together. I tried to convince her otherwise. That too many people would be hurt by her actions. I even offered to marry her. Told her I could provide the kind of life she was used to for her and the baby. She…she just laughed at me. Sat in the chair across from me and laughed. Said I sounded like a crazy, desperate old man. Said the only reason she ever slept with me was because she'd been hot and horny for Jack and he hadn't given in to her advances."

"Roger, didn't it ever occur to you that the baby might be yours?"

"Of course not, my love. Oh, it sounds so good to finally say that to you! My love," he repeated. "No, when

Corinne first became ill, I had a vasectomy. I didn't want to take the chance of getting her pregnant when she was so sick. And I knew how much you wanted a baby. How it would devastate you when you found out Serena was pregnant with Jack's. So that's when I decided to kill Serena and let Jack take the fall. I knew it would be painful for you at first, especially the trial, but once Jack was convicted and gone, I'd be there to pick up the pieces and we could finally be together."

Horrified, I tried to keep my brain from shutting down. "Are you saying your little deceitful drama didn't include having Jack killed in jail?"

"Absolutely not! If he were dead, the memory of his betrayal would fade away with time. Soften your heart toward him. If he were still alive and in prison, your anger toward him would always be at the surface, keeping the two of us glued together. Believe it or not, I was upset when he died. I knew how much it hurt you. That's why, even though it went against everything in me and opened the possibility up of the truth coming out, I didn't stop you from trying to reopen the case to clear his name. I...I just hoped you'd run into a brick wall and eventually give up."

Keep him talking. Find out all the information you can to nail his sorry ass to the wall! Don't give up. Oh, please Lord, don't let me give up! "How in the world did you pull all this off, Roger? I mean, you even had on the same outfit and ball cap like Jack's. You even had the foresight to buy pink underwear."

"It was rather easy, my love. Once I formed my plan, I just followed Jack for a few days on my own. Watched what he wore to school. He didn't stray much from one day to the next. Jeans, t-shirts and loafers. The panties were a no-brainer. I knew from experience Serena only wore pink undergarments."

"You sent the text, didn't you? The one of Serena at the hotel in her underwear?"

"She already had typed it out and just failed to hit send. I guess I interrupted her when I arrived. I just punched a few buttons and delayed the time it was to go out. It was the final nail, so to speak."

Hot tears cascaded down my face, my heart beyond broken. I was shattered on the inside. Detective Knowles had been right: all of this tied back to me in ways that I doubted I would ever truly fathom. I felt my mind and body begin to shut down from the overload of events.

I heard what sounded like another crack of thunder and realized the walls and floor were vibrating. Roger must have felt it as well because his grip loosened and he rolled on top of me. His eyes were wild with fear, anger, love and sadness all mixed together.

"Best laid plans, right? I'm sorry, Melody. I never meant to hurt you. I truly didn't. My love for you is what kept me going after I lost Corinne. But, I realize now that all I've managed to do was destroy your world. The only good thing that came from this is that at least you won't have to spend the remainder of your life living in a world where Serena Rowland was the mother to Jack's child and not you."

"That would be a really nice sentiment if it weren't for the fact that you were the father, not Jack," boomed the voice of Detective Knowles over the siren and wind.

Roger didn't flinch and never took his eyes off mine. I saw the shock of the detective's words burn behind his eyes, his face contorting in agony. For a split second, I felt his pain. Pain from the knowledge that none of this should have ever happened and that he had killed his unborn child.

"Roger, it's over now. Let go of her and get up."

Tears flowed down Roger's face and dripped off his chin onto mine. Roger closed his eyes, bent his head down and planted a delicate, light kiss on my cheek. I felt his body shift and he whispered in my ear, "I love you, Melody. Forever."

Just as Roger began to push himself off of me, I felt the floor shift. Detective Knowles was yelling something at Roger, but I couldn't hear anything over the deafening roar that filled the house. In one swift motion, Roger grabbed me by my shirt, heaved me off the floor, and shoved me into the arms of Detective Knowles, who stood less than five feet from us, his gun trained on Roger. His body moved with lightning speed as he tried to lower his gun from my trajectory but lost his footing on the wet floor. Between the house shaking, the wet surface and the force of my body crashing into his, we fell to the floor at the top of the stairs.

Strong arms grabbed my shoulders and pushed me as I heard the detective yell, "Get downstairs now! It's coming!"

I turned my head back to the kitchen for a split second. The last thing I saw was Roger standing in front of the sliding glass doors, his arms lifted to Heaven as the ceiling was ripped away. A last push sent me tumbling down the stairs, and I saw
nothing more.

CHAPTER 24 – SATURDAY MORNING

I WOKE UP IN A FOG, STILL GROGGY FROM THE pain medication. The bright sunlight streaming in from the window hurt my eyes. I blinked and tried to focus, then remembered that I wasn't wearing contacts. I reached under the stiff pillow to retrieve my glasses, stopping short as I realized I wasn't at home. A bitter, cynical laugh caught in my throat. I didn't have a home to go to anymore. The twister had destroyed it. A rather fitting end since everything else in my life lay in ruinous heap as well.

"Good morning, sunshine. Look, I brought you a present."

Though I couldn't make out her face, I recognized the voice of Regina. Her fuzzy shape walked toward me and she leaned over and kissed my forehead. I felt her place something in my hand. Immediately recognizing the shape, I smiled and put them on.

"How did you find them?"

"Oh, I didn't. I just went to your eye doctor and had him make you a new pair. Got you some contacts, too," she smiled, patting her purse. "Because you know how much I love to shop! After all, it saved me from occupying the bed next to you."

I snorted at the irony. "Indeed it did. Not many people can say shopping saved their life!"

"So true! Hmm, there was something else the eye doc wanted me to tell you. What was it? Ah yes, he said not to wear the contacts until you are off the pain meds. Something about dry eyes and corneal abrasions."

"Okay, I won't. And listen, thank you. For everything."

"Um, we've already had that talk once before, I believe. Remember? Anyway, I have a few other things to share. I've contacted everyone that I can think of and told them the new time for your Mom's funeral is Monday at two. Oh, and get this—Brunie Funeral Home is doing the service for free."

I struggled to sit up in the hospital bed. Every movement was a new experience in pain. Regina set her purse down on the small table beside the bed and had my arm in a flash. Her strong hands helped me situate my torso so my broken leg was still propped up but my back wasn't in such a bind. "For free? Why?"

"Mr. Brunie didn't say. He was just adamant. Tore the bill up right in front of me."

"Hmmm. Interesting. Guess Mom was right."

"Right about what?"

"She always felt Mr. Brunie had a crush on her ever since high school. Maybe this is his way of showing it."

"That's sweet," Regina said as she busied herself with checking my myriad of bruises and cuts. "Some more money came in today. The total now is over fifteen thousand dollars."

I gritted my teeth. "I don't want charity from people who don't even know me! I'm just some sad story they heard about on the news."

"Mel, I realize you are still in a lot of physical pain and doped up, so I will ignore that drug-induced ugly remark. People are trying to help you and not just ones from the *Justice for Jack* site, but from all over. Most of the money is for all of you who lost your homes in the storm. Twenty three in all were destroyed in the path, though yours was the only one in your neighborhood. Thankfully, no lives were lost, just property damage."

I appreciated Regina's tact in overlooking the demise of my former boss. "I'm sorry. I didn't mean to sound so mean. I'm just, oh boy, I don't even know what I am anymore. It's not that I don't appreciate what others are doing, I just wish it wasn't necessary. You know me—I am sort of a loner."

"No you aren't. You are the giver. Always have been. Now you get to experience what being the recipient feels like. Sometimes, it's nice. Other times, you sort of feel embarrassed."

"That's an understatement. Mortified beyond belief is more like it," I grumbled as heat flushed my cheeks.

"Well, that's why you have me around. To point out your flaws and steer you in the right direction. So, new subject: has your doc been by today?"

"Yes, early this morning. Why do they insist on making rounds at the crack of dawn?" I whined.

"Beats me. So, what did he say? Any idea when you'll be released? I'm ready to practice my rusty nursing skills on you. I've even set up my bedroom for you since it's on the first floor. See, I think of everything."

I smiled at her and reached out my left hand to grab hers. Though I didn't say it because I knew I'd start crying, I let my eyes express how much I appreciated and loved her. She and Kendal were all I had left now. "He said I could leave tomorrow as long as I take it easy. Like I can do anything but take it easy. I can't even hobble around on crutches because of this stupid cast," I said, holding my broken right hand up off the bed. "At least this injury I enjoyed getting."

"Oh Mel, I still can't believe you and Detective Knowles survived. When I saw the damage, well, it's a God thing all right. A true miracle. Your house is in pieces."

I was glad I was on pain medication because it helped block out the heartbreaking pangs of sorrow in my chest. It also gave me the ability to change the subject on a dime. "Listen, talk to the guy over at the *Justice for Jack* site. Tell him to please put something on the page asking people to send their donations to a different cause, because I don't need it."

"Mel, you have big expenses—"

"I spoke to the insurance adjuster earlier," I interrupted. "Seems he is on the same time schedule as the doctor, since he called me so early. He said the house sustained enough damage that rebuilding will cost more than it's worth, so I'm taking the money and paying the mortgage off, then listing the land for sale. Besides, you knew already that I had decided to move because I couldn't stand being surrounded by all the memories. I didn't want to struggle to scrape together enough cash each month to pay the bills, either."

"Well, that's good news, but you will need a vehicle. And an entire wardrobe, though you are welcome to share mine until you are able to go shopping. Oh, and you will need furniture. I mean, you are basically starting all over again."

"The other joyful tidbit of news the adjustor told me is that when they removed the trees and assessed our vehicles that were under them, they are both totaled as well. So, it seems the tornado was sort of a good thing, since it pretty much wiped out most of my debt. Still have a few maxed out credit cards and it looks like some new medical bills coming after this lovely stay here, but I'll make it. Mom's house is paid for and fully stocked with furniture, so that only leaves buying a car. Plus, Jack's retirement and pension should kick in soon, so I'll be fine," I reassured her.

"Are you sure you don't want to change your mind and come live with me? At least for a while until you find a job? I mean, you aren't planning on going back to..." Regina seemed to know better than to finish her sentence.

"Maybe for a few weeks, if that's okay. And not just no but *Hell no*. I won't ever step foot back inside that place again. In fact, I will never, ever work in the legal field again. Rick Overton called yesterday and said the firm was disbanding and all the lawyers were venturing out on their own. He actually had the gall to ask if I wanted to work for him and offered almost double my previous salary."

The disbelief on Regina's face was comical. "After everything that's happened, I can't believe he would even ask! What a jerk. So, if you aren't going to be a paralegal anymore, what are you going to do?"

"You know, I could kick myself for leaving teaching to begin with and going for the money rather than what I loved doing. Before I landed in here, I had been rolling around the idea of teaching again. Believe it or not, I already have a job waiting for me," I informed her.

Regina blinked twice in shock. "You what? How did you manage that? And where?"

"I called Everett Wilkins—Jack's boss at UALR—this morning. Told him I wanted to get back to teaching and before I could say anything else, he...oh...he offered me Jack's old job teaching history," I said, the last part causing a heavy hitch in my throat. I still hadn't processed the news myself.

"Mel! That's great! You'll be out of that cast and all healed up before the fall semester starts in September. Perfect timing! Of course, every gift from above is given at the perfect time. No doubt about it."

I felt the tears lock in my throat and decided to change the subject again before they burst out of me. I hadn't cried since arriving at the hospital. I knew it was because I was still in shock from not only my physical injuries, but the ones to my soul. And after everything that happened, all the betrayal, the loss, the death, the gut wrenching sorrow and heartache, I doubted I would ever share my real pain with anyone. The quiet whisper of my mother's sweet words had replaced, thankfully, the demonic drone of my Meemaw in my head, gently urging me to bring all my baggage to the Lord for healing. I cleared my throat. "How's Simba?"

"Don't you worry about that hairy beast. Kendal's been taking care of her. Never seen a man so devoted to an animal before. The vet fixed her right up and she's been the queen of Kendal's bed ever since. I mean, he dotes on her. Kind of a turn on, if you ask me."

"I'm glad she's better. Oh, I miss her so much. But one question—how do you know she's sleeping on Kendal's bed?"

Regina's cheeks turned bright pink. "Uh, well, that was the last bit of information I was going to share with you. You see, it's like this—"

I held up my hand to silence her. "I'm just yanking your chain, Regina. I saw the sparks between you two during the last few weeks, so I'm not surprised. I'm happy for you both. Guess I should have played matchmaker between the two of you long ago."

Regina let out a huge huff of air. "Oh, thank goodness. I wasn't sure how to tell you or how you would react. I mean, after all that has happened…"

"If there is anything I've learned from this nightmare, it's that life can be over in the blink of an eye, so cherish and embrace the love of others before it's too late and they're gone. And don't you worry about me, Regina. As my Daddy used to say, I'm fine as frog hair. The willow tree may be bent but it didn't break."

The voice of Bertrand LaFont intruded into our conversation. "Well said, Mrs. Dickinson. And you're right—

you'll be more than fine once the County settles the law-suit."

Regina and I shared a look of disgust. My lawyer stood in the doorway, holding an enormous bouquet made from just about every flower imaginable. I felt Regina tense up and knew she was about to unleash a verbal assault on him, so I gave her hand a gentle squeeze, followed by a slight nod of my head. Without a word, she rose off the bed and left the room, eyeing Mr. LaFont as she shut the door behind her.

"Thank you for the flowers," I said with civility.

"They aren't the only gifts I brought, Mrs. Dickinson. Do you feel up to a few minutes of chatting with me?"

I noticed he was wearing casual clothes and had no gel in his hair. The normal arrogance he wore like an accessory was missing as well. His voice was quiet, almost pleasant. Even in my foggy haze, I realized I was looking at the real LaFont. This time, he was the one who was raw and exposed rather than me. Hell, my life was public fodder now—nothing was hidden. "Sure, though I can't say how long that will last. The medication sort of makes me hyper one minute and a drooling zombie the next. What brings you by?"

His stride was slow and methodical as he moved across the floor and set the flowers down on the bedside table. He eyed the chair next to it. "May I?"

"Of course."

He settled into the seat and looked about as comforta-ble as I felt. "Well, before we discuss what I came here for, I just wanted to say how sorry I am. I...I promise you, I didn't know about Roger. In all my years of practicing law, I've never been so shocked."

I bit my lip and responded to his statement with a nod.

"There is no easy way to approach all this, so I'll not dance around it. Thurman Thomas, you know who he is, right?"

"Yes. He is the state medical examiner."

"'Was' would be the appropriate word. He was arrested yesterday. One of the deputy examiners, Lee German, is functioning as interim chief examiner in his place. And apparently, Thurman's arrest and Roger's death triggered an interesting domino effect in others."

"What do you mean?" I asked.

"First of all, Roger sent a letter confessing everything, his involvement, the pictures, all of it, to Alex Renfro. He mailed it the day he died. Not only did he mail a copy to Alex, but to the newspaper as well. My guess is that he knew the truth was about to come out, so he wanted to tell you first and then clear Jack's name in the public's eye."

Dumbstruck, I shot back, "But why would he do that? If he wanted to confess, why didn't he just tell Detective Knowles in the very beginning? Or Alex Renfro? Once he did, it would have come out anyway when he was arrested for Serena's murder."

"He never intended to be arrested, Mrs. Dickinson. After he told you, he planned on killing himself."

"What? How do you know that?"

"Several reasons. His gun was found under the front seat of his car—loaded. Also, he mailed something to me as well. Two letters—one for me and one for you. The letter to me contained his last wishes in the form of a make-shift suicide note. It outlined his plan to come clean to you, then go to the place he proposed to Corinne at Mount Harbor and shoot himself. He said he knew the truth was about to blow wide open after his visit from Guy Powell. The letter also included his last Will and Testament. He...he left you everything, Mrs. Dickinson, and named me as Executor."

I wanted to throw up. If my body wasn't semi-numbed from the medication in my I.V., I probably would have. "I don't want anything from him. Won't accept it. If you're the Executor, then give it all to charity or something. I don't care what you do with it, just don't try to give me one red cent. That bastard ruined my life and his offering of blood money to ease his conscious can't make it right. "

"I thought that might be your reaction, so I prepared a list of charities I thought you could peruse later, maybe once you leave the hospital and are feeling better. There is no hurry. Since he had no children or heirs, his estate can just sit tight."

I gritted my teeth and asked, "You said a domino effect? What else happened?"

"Bill Witham killed himself yesterday morning. Went to Serena's grave and shot himself in the head. Though he didn't leave a suicide note, he did write some of his thoughts down on a notepad. It was like a rambling love letter to Serena, explaining how he avenged her death by poisoning her killer with peanut oil and how he hoped she was proud of him. How much he missed her and couldn't sleep because when he did, all he could do was dream about holding her again because living here without her was destroying him. He also mentioned how upset he was over the fact that Serena's father hadn't spoken to him since he accomplished what Mr. Rowland asked him to. The preliminary investigation has concluded that when the news broke about Jack's innocence, he couldn't live with the fact that he killed the wrong man—and at the behest of Mr. Rowland. I imagine that broke the last bit of sanity he had and pushed him over the edge."

The pangs of grief at the tragic news throbbed inside my chest. "Dear God. Please, tell me there isn't any more."

"I wish that I could, but I cannot. Philip Rowland was the last domino to fall. He died just a few hours ago from massive head trauma after he wrecked his car last night."

"How awful! Oh, his poor wife. She must be in agony. But, I don't understand. Why do you think his death is tied to the others?"

"For one, his blood alcohol content was over two point zero and Philip never drove while intoxicated, much less when sober. He had a driver, but he sent him home for the day, telling him he wanted to be alone to go visit Serena's grave. Two, he left his will and all his legal papers out on his desk, which, according to his secretary, were always kept under lock and key. And three, he withdrew all of his money in the form of cashier's checks from all of his accounts and had a courier pick them up right before he left work to deliver to his wife. Then he got in his Porsche and thankfully made it out of the city limits before he smashed into a tree. Police report estimates he was travelling over eighty miles an hour—and there were no skid marks."

"Oh dear Lord. How many lives will be ruined before this is truly over? Do you think he did that because he couldn't handle the fact that Roger killed his daughter? I mean, they were very close."

"I wish I could say that was the reason, but I don't believe it is."

"If not that, then what?"

"Mind you, this is still all being investigated, but it seems that Mr. Rowland had something to do with the false reports issued by Thurman Thomas. The prosecutor subpoenaed his phone records the day Philip crashed. So, it appears that rather than dealing with the fallout, combined with the loss of his daughter, Roger's involvement and the possibility of conspiracy to commit murder, he opted to not face it. All the particulars are still sketchy but that's the way things are pointing. Now that Detective Knowles is awake and able to talk, I'm sure all the missing pieces will be forthcoming."

I felt the medicine begin to take control of my mind. I knew I wasn't going to last much longer, so I said, "You said something about the County when you walked in. Please, tell me and make it quick. I don't know how much longer I can keep my eyes open."

To my surprise, Mr. LaFont smiled. "This news I don't mind sharing. After all that has happened, the County wants to settle as soon as possible, before the egg dries on their faces. The offer on the table is five million. Do you want me to counteroffer?"

I wasn't sure if my head was spinning now from the medication or the news. Though it was more blood money that would never bring my Jack or mother back to me, my share would be enough that I could breathe without concern again. I tried to figure out what Bertrand's percentage would be, but my fuzzy brain couldn't concentrate on the numbers. "Help me out here. What would that be after your thirty-three percent?"

"Finally! The question I've been waiting to answer. Mrs. Dickinson, I know it won't change what has happened, but hopefully, it will give you some stable ground to stand on. I decided to forego my percentage, so you will get it all. Now, other than healing, you just need to figure out what you would like to spend it on, once you sign the papers of course."

I felt the tears leak out of my eyes and their wetness form on the pillow, but I couldn't get my mouth to speak the words from my heart. I drifted off into peaceful sleep, thanking the Lord in my mind as I marveled over the gems of love He always left behind, even in the wickedest of storms.

He had just granted me the biggest, most precious stone—justice for Jack.

CHAPTER 25 –SIX MONTHS LATER

THE NIGHT SKY WAS CLEAR, FOR THE BRISK
breezes earlier had blown all the clouds away and exposed
a sky full of vibrant, twinkling stars. I felt the frigid air in
my leg and fingers. Though the broken bones had healed at
last, the remnants of the injuries lingered with the changing temperature.

I glanced at my watch and smiled. In less than ten
minutes, the lights would be turned on and the newest addition to the millions of other lights would be revealed. I'd
waited five long months for this day, my final act of love
for Jack and my mother.

For a few quiet moments, I stared into the moonlight
sky and embraced the peacefulness my heart felt. Though
my steps had been slow, I was making progress down the
pathway to healing. Once I left Regina's and settled in to
my new home at Mom's house and started my job, I found
myself taking another step each day. Though many nights
had been spent crying myself to sleep, I found solace during the day in all the blessings I still had in my life. Now,

almost six months later, I was able to close my eyes at night and rest without staining my pillow with the saltiness of my tears.

My job at the university was more than fulfilling. The students were a joy to teach and I found myself looking forward to seeing them each morning. Something about their youthful vigor brought a smile to my face. For the first time in a very long time, I felt useful and knew what I was doing was making a real difference to others.

I had watched Regina and Kendal's relationship blossom over the summer and fall and was thankful that at least some happiness had come from all the sorrow. At first it was rather odd, considering everything, especially the awkward conversation that Kendal and I had once I left the hospital. I had still been a tad wary about what I witnessed that day in Sheridan between him and Guy. He explained that he had been doing a bit of reconnaissance of his own. When he reconnected with old ties in Sheridan and discovered Guy had hired a private investigator to take incriminating pictures, Kendal contacted him and offered the one thing an addict wants besides drugs: money.

His plan had been to fool Guy into thinking he wanted the pictures so he could keep them from me and destroy them, then actually take them to Detective Knowles. At the time, Kendal hadn't been aware of the other set with Roger and Serena. It wasn't until he sat in the waiting room of the hospital with Regina that he even remembered the envelope. When he opened it, he told me he'd almost fainted. The tension between the two of us was washed away with our tears as we cried together. He forgave me for thinking the worst of him and we both agreed that it was high time to put the past behind us and bury the mistakes we both had made.

My counseling sessions with Pastor Trent helped as well. He listened and didn't judge or admonish my thoughts and feelings, even when, during the first few, I was so full of anger that my words would have been continuously bleeped had they been on television. The majority of my anger was at Jack for cheating on me, but a good portion was also directed internally for my own mistakes. After months of soul searching, I came to realize that none of us could shoulder all of the blame for what had happened. We were imperfect human beings that had each made mistakes that simply compounded and created a voracious monster which, once unleashed, destroyed us all.

Pastor Trent concurred with my mother's wedding day advice—communication was the key. He also added that wisdom, patience, honesty and forgiveness, together with communicating with others, were what held relationships together. And he was right. Had secrets not been kept between me and Jack, I wouldn't have pulled away from him and he wouldn't have strayed. If the detective wouldn't have succumbed to the pressure to solve the case quickly, Jack would have never been behind bars. If Philip Rowland and Bill Witham had practiced a bit more patience, they wouldn't have jumped to the conclusion that Jack was Serena's murderer and conspired to kill him. If Thurman Thomas didn't have a closet full of his own secrets that he wished to be kept hidden, he wouldn't have been so easily molded by Philip's heavy hand. Each transgression piled upon the one before it and the monster grew to epic proportions.

But the biggest catalyst of all was grief. It changed people. The overwhelming loss of a loved one caused all of us to do things completely against our personalities. Our internal moral compasses had been skewed by a heavy cloud of sorrow. Consumed by our losses, none of us had clean hands in our responses to death. We all were guilty of reacting emotionally, assuming things before the truth was known.

At the end of each visit, Pastor Trent would slide over a handwritten note with a listing of particular scriptures he wanted me to read before our next meeting. I would go home and read them, feeling the Lord speak to my heart, and as time passed, my anger eased and finally ceased.

When Pastor Trent noticed the change in me, he asked if I would like to help out in the nursery. At first, I balked at the idea, afraid that being around the sweet babies would rip my old wounds open again. But one day while at the grocery store, I watched a young mother dote and coo to her little bundle as she shopped, and realized I didn't feel the lump in my throat like I used to, so I gave the nursery a shot the next Sunday. Though they weren't mine, I bonded with each snuggly baby and showered them with hugs and kisses for an hour and a half each week. Soon, I realized the longing for one of my own had lessened as I came to grips with my new life.

Mrs. Preston and I had grown very close during the last few months. It was like the Lord placed her in my life as a surrogate mother. Her outrageous stories of her younger days always brought a smile to my face, though I didn't believe half of them. As with any true southern woman, she enjoyed embellishing her tales, but I didn't care. We spent a lot of time together discussing what I should do with the money, and when I told her my idea, she loved it and helped me with the preliminary drawings.

There was only one thing in my life that I hadn't settled yet and that was how I should go about thanking Detective Knowles for saving my life. Even though I had known he was in the same hospital as me, I refused to go see him once I was released. I was still too angry at that point. When Regina suggested that I at least call him, I declined. My thought process at the time was that if it weren't for his original mistake, neither of us would be in the situation we were in. While I spouted these angry words to Regina, I knew they were horrible things to say and think, but I couldn't help it. I knew seeing his face would keep the wound fresh and I needed to heal.

I had burned the letter that Roger left me without ever reading it. Nothing he could have said would lessen the painful outcome of his misplaced, so-called "love" for me. Though I did understand the pain of losing your spouse and could sympathize with his sorrow, the path he chose after his wife's death I couldn't fathom. While awake, I refused to think about him or speak his name. Even during my counseling sessions, I steered clear of talking about him. I figured if I didn't think about him, eventually memories of my former boss and what he did would cease to exist. It worked, to a point. Rarely during waking moments did I think of Roger—but the day on my kitchen floor still haunted my dreams, though the nightmares were decreasing as I learned to let go of the hate inside my heart.

I took a deep breath and watched the hot steam leave my mouth and disappear into the air. It was time to stop wandering down memory lane and get going. I straightened my hat and slid on my gloves, forcing myself not to limp as I made my way out to the main courtyard. This would be my tenth year as a volunteer at the Garden and it would have been Mom's fifteenth. It was a holiday tradition that we both had enjoyed doing together. Although the place was spectacular during the other three seasons with all the beautiful arrangements of flowers, shrubs and trees, it became a magical fairyland during the winter. It was the perfect place to have a memorial for Jack and Mom and the decision as to what to do with the money from the County had been an easy one to make.

The owner of the Garden, Mollie Gateway, had asked me to do the honors of turning on the switch. Though the light show started on December first, I had requested the newest addition not be turned on until Christmas Eve. I had thanked Mollie for not only granting my request, but understanding when I rejected her offer. I told her I preferred to be with friends and family only when they came on, because I didn't want to cry in front of all the onlookers. She caved with a hint of sadness and offered the duty to another staffer.

"There you are! We've been looking all over for you. It's almost time!"

Regina and Kendal were sitting on the small bench closest to the front gates, bundled from head to toe. They rose in unison, holding hands as they walked over to me. I hugged them both and smiled, pointing to the small golf cart about ten feet away. "Hey, not to worry. I'm driving us over there. Come on."

"Oh Lord, please tell me that thing doesn't go over ten miles an hour? With you behind the wheel, I'll be scared," Kendal teased.

"Gee, Kendal. Love hasn't changed that sharp wit of yours, has it?" I replied as I scooted around and climbed in to the driver's seat. "Say, where's Mrs. Preston? I thought she was riding with you?"

"Aww, I'm just joshin' ya girl. Don't worry, she's on her way. She's ridin' with a friend. They're gonna meet us at the display. But, before we head over there, let me snap a picture of my two favorite gals."

Regina's warm face pressed against my cheek in a na-nosecond, followed by her hand in front of my face. "So, you already know I can't keep a secret for more than a second, but you will be happy to know you are the first person we've told. Look what I got for Christmas!"

Kendal snapped the shot just as my mouth fell open from shock at the enormous diamond sparkling on her ring finger. My two rocks would soon become one unit.

I beamed. "Awww, congratulations! What wonderful news, though can't say that I'm shocked. When's the big day?"

"Decided it was high time to make an honest woman outta her," Kendal said, easing his bulky frame into the cart, "and that decision I am stayin' out of. I ain't no dummy. I already know my part will only be to show up. I'll leave the plannin' to the two of you."

"It's going to take a lot more than a shiny bauble and your last name to do that," Regina spouted back. "Now, see there? That's why I'm marrying him. He knows I'm the boss already!" We all laughed as I drove along the winding, paved trails of the Garden to the designated spot while Regina talked a hundred miles an hour about her wedding plans. When I pulled up and parked, she reached over and hugged me.

"Oh Mel, what a wonderful idea. I still can't believe you did this. What an awesome tribute to Jack and your mom. I just know they are smiling down on you right now, pleased as punch."

I shrugged off her compliment. "It's my way of making sure the world never forgets them, that's all. Besides, I had no desire to keep the County's money. I wouldn't have it if it weren't for…"

"Let's not talk about that tonight, okay? Tonight is the time for celebrating. God's love for mankind and ours for Jack and Ms. Lucinda. Oh, and look! The plaque is stunning! *'In Memory of Jackson Tyler Dickinson and Lucinda Barrett—may you both soar on your wings until we meet again and fly together.'* How beautiful."

Before I could respond, the hum of electricity surrounded us, followed by the lights. We all stood in awe, taking in the amazing display in front of us.

I had donated almost the entire amount I received from the County to the Garden, in exchange for the services of Ralph Jenkins, the light designer of the Garden. The money bought an additional two acres of empty land adjacent to the already thirty acres owned by the Garden. The wooded land was full of pine and oak trees around the edges and a perfect, open glen in the middle. Though Mrs. Preston and I had given the rough idea of what I wanted and had seen Mr. Jenkins' sketches on paper, seeing it completed was astounding.

The trees were decorated in solid purple, each strand wrapped by hand from the roots to the very tops, and down the expanse of each branch. The glen had been transformed into a sea of pink flowers, varying in size from two feet to eight feet. The stems were trimmed in bright green and a brilliant yellow center graced each open flower.

But the effect that left us all speechless was the butterflies. The first set on our left started out small, maybe a foot across, and sat on top of an empty chrysalis rimmed in dark blue lights. Orange and black lights created the wings of the butterfly and the lights moved in perfect unison, giving the illusion of flight to the next flower. With each short stop, the butterfly grew in size, and once it landed on the last large flower, the wings shimmered as it rose up gracefully through the tops of the trees and disappeared. The process started all over again, repeating every minute.

"Oh darlin'! That's simply breathtakin'. Better than this old mind could have ever imagined."

We all turned around to the sound of Mrs. Preston's voice, her excitement contagious. My smile and response were cut short when I recognized her escort. I shot a look at Regina and she gave me a sheepish grin and shrugged, but the twinkle behind her eyes was a dead giveaway. She knew. I could tell Kendal did as well due to the smirk on his face and the fact that he wouldn't look me in the eye.

It took me a few seconds to find my voice and manners. I moved over and hugged Mrs. Preston's neck. "Isn't it just wonderful? Thank you so much for helping me do this." I let go and cleared my throat, then turned my attention to her guest and acknowledged him. "Detective Knowles. How nice of you to bring Mrs. Preston here. I wasn't aware the two of you were acquainted."

Mrs. Preston waved off my comment with her gloved hand. "I need to get a bit closer to see all the details." She shooed me away and walked over to where Regina and Kendal stood, leaving me and the detective stranded.

"Mrs. Dickinson. Good to see you again."

I eyed him with suspicion, fully aware that this was all planned. If my friends weren't within earshot, I would have let my thoughts erupt. Instead, I lowered my head and turned my body to face his, my voice quiet. "I'm afraid I can't say the same thing, Detective. Why are you here?"

"It's just Craig now."

"What?"

"I'm no longer at the police department. Haven't been for a few months now, so it's just Craig."

I studied his face and noted the thick, dark scar that started in his hairline and disappeared under his shirt. Regina had told me his injuries had been extensive and that he would have died from the massive amount of blood he lost if Kendal hadn't arrived and pulled us free from the rubble when he did. Kendal's tire had blown the day he was chasing me, leaving him stuck out in the raging storm as he changed it. We marveled later at how something that seemed a stumbling block at the time turned out to be a saving grace, for if he'd have been at the house any sooner, Kendal would have been in the debris along with us.

"You didn't answer my original question—why are you here?"

"I was offered a chance to escort a sweet lady on Christmas Eve to go look at the beautiful lights in Hot Springs. How could I refuse?"

"Easy. You just say 'no thank you'."

"I tried. But they are very persuasive," he replied, glancing past me at the group of traitors.

I could feel the electricity of their stares. Boy, would I let them have an earful when we left. "Yes, they can be. I'll deal with them later, but for now, answer one question for me."

"Okay."

"Why are you *really* here?"

His eyes reflected much deeper thoughts than what his words conveyed. "I feel we have some unfinished business. I've been waiting to hear from you, but it appears I will be a shriveled up old man who can't hear a thing by the time you get around to calling me."

Ouch. Guess I deserved that. Okay, you're right. I should have contacted you sooner and expressed my thanks for everything. For that, I'm sorry. But surely you can understand why I haven't?"

"It's cold and that makes my brain run slow, so no, I don't understand. Care to explain it to me over a cup of hot chocolate? I saw a stand about a hundred yards back there," he said, pointing behind him.

I recognized the look behind his deep set eyes and it confirmed my suspicions—he had feelings for me. They held a silent desperation, a quiet plea for acceptance of what he wanted to offer me. Seeing his face made me realize the real reason I had stayed away from him and shunned him like he had the plague.

It wasn't just because looking at him brought to the forefront of my thoughts all the painful memories I had been trying to work through. It was because I felt the spark, too. We had a connection—a bond forged from the tragic events that brought us together. No matter how hard I tried, how much I wished it weren't true, Detective Craig Knowles would be a part of my life story.

In the full two minutes we stood there under the cold, star-filled sky, the rainbow of colors glimmering behind us, I finally closed the door inside my heart to the life I had once led with Jack, and decided to open up the new one without him. Glancing behind me, I saw Kendal put one arm around Regina and pull her tight to his side as he hugged Mrs. Preston with the other. Even from this distance, I could feel their love while they gazed upon the newest addition to the Garden. I let my gaze settle on the light show as the butterfly started from its empty shell and touched upon all the flowers before ascending toward the Heavens to begin its new life. It was time for me to do the same, and it would start with a cup of hot chocolate.

Let go, and let God. "You realize I have nothing to offer other than friendship. I'm still kind of a mess on the inside."

"I'm not asking for anything. I'm simply here. Shall we?"

I nodded in response and we started our walk toward the hot chocolate stand. I didn't know how this would end. Didn't know what tomorrow would bring. What I did know was that I still had friends, some old and some new, who loved me unconditionally. I had been blessed with support and love in ways I still couldn't fathom, a lot from complete strangers. And I knew every single act of kindness was God's way of comforting my soul as I stumbled through the path of life. Maybe the jagged road had finally turned to a straight path—at least for now.

One thing I knew for certain that I would never stray from again was my faith. Even if this part of the journey wasn't an uphill battle and lasted only briefly, I would be ready when the path became covered in painful rocks again. Because next time, I would cling to my faith and never let go.

I smiled at Craig, then decided to ask him a question that had been bothering me for some time, even though it would take my mind back to that horrible day. "How did you get inside my house? The front door was locked."

A large puff of steam lingered over his head when he let out a heavy sigh. "Believe me, I was shocked when I arrived and discovered it wasn't. I had been pounding on the door, but guess you didn't hear me over the storm. I was about to kick it down when something told me to try the knob."

I didn't say anything for a few minutes while we continued to walk. I let my mind wander back to that day. I had told Roger at the beginning of our conversation that the detective was on his way, so why didn't he lock the door to keep him out? *No, don't go there. It doesn't matter now. It's over. Time to switch topics.* "So, what are you doing with yourself now that you aren't a cop anymore?"

"Decided to join my uncle's business. I am now head of security and marketing at Rex's Outdoor Oasis. What about you? Are you enjoying your new job?"

"Very much. My students are great. And, I get a chance to teach the next generation that old adage about history."

"Which one is that?"

"You know, those who don't learn from history are doomed to repeat it? It certainly is true in my life."

"Wise words, indeed," Craig said as he handed me a steaming cup of chocolate. He brought the rim of his up and gently touched mine. "Here's to the future—a new one formed by not repeating the past."

"Amen to that, Craig. Amen to that."

THE END

To learn more about Ashley, please
visit her website
http://www.ashleyfontainne.com

www.ingramcontent.com/pod-product-compliance
Lightning Source LLC
Chambersburg PA
CBHW020819180626

46814CB00001B/21